The Noble Rogue

Baroness Emmuska Orczy

The Noble Rogue

The present edition is a reproduction of previous publication of this classic work. Minor typographical errors may have been corrected without note, however, for an authentic reading experience the spelling, punctuation, and capitalization have been retained from the original text.

ISBN: 978-1-64799-131-9

PART I

CHAPTER I

This act is an ancient tale new told.

—*Shakespeare*

M. Legros, tailor-in-chief to His Majesty Louis XIV and to the Court of Paris and Versailles, bowed himself out of the room; with back bent nearly double, and knees trembling in the effort, he receded towards the door even whilst Monseigneur the Archbishop spoke a final and encouraging benediction.

"Have no fear, my good Monsieur Legros," pronounced Monseigneur with urbane kindness; "your affairs shall come under the special notice of the Holy Father. Be of good cheer, right and justice are on your side. Solemn vows cannot be flouted even in these days of godlessness. Go in peace, my son; you are dismissed."

"And if the Holy Father—hem—I mean if Monseigneur would take cognizance of the fact—hem—that I will place—" stammered M. Legros with some confusion. "I mean, Monseigneur—that is—I am a man of substance—and if the sum of fifty thousand francs—or—or a hundred thousand—"

"Nay, my son, what would you suggest?" quoth Monseigneur with a slight lifting of elegantly-arched brows. "The thought of money doth not enter into the decrees of the Holy Father."

"I know—I know, Monseigneur," said M. Legros with ever-growing confusion. "I only thought—"

"An you thought, my son, of pleasing God by the bestowal of alms in these days of licentiousness and of evil luxury, then by all means do so in accordance with your substance—I will see to the proper distribution of those alms, good Master Legros—the two hundred thousand francs you speak of shall be worthily bestowed, our promise thereon."

M. Legros did not think of protesting. The sum mentioned by Monseigneur was a heavy one in these days, when the working and trading classes had but little left for their own pleasures once the tax collector had passed their way. But the worthy tailor had made no idle boast when he said that he was a man of substance; he was well able to pay a goodly sum for the gratification of his most cherished desire.

He received his final congé almost on his knees, then he disappeared through the doorway. Lacqueys to the right of him,

1

lacqueys to the left of him, lacqueys all the way along the carpeted stairs down to the massive front door, formed a living avenue through which M. Legros now passed with his back not yet fully straightened out after its many humble curvatures.

Soon he reached the narrow, ill-ventilated street on which gave the great gates of Monseigneur the Archbishop's palace. Instinctively M. Legros gave a deep sigh of content and relief, inhaling the fresh autumnal air which could not altogether be excluded even from these close purlieus where roof almost met roof overhead, and evil-smelling gutters overflowed along the roughly-constructed pavements.

The good master tailor had succeeded passing well in his momentous errand. Monseigneur had been overgracious, and two hundred thousand francs was after all only a small sum to come out of Rose Marie's ample marriage portion. M. Legros now walked with a brisk step along the right bank of the Seine, then crossing the Pont Neuf he found himself near the Châtelet prison, and thence by narrow by-paths at his own front door in the Rue de l'Ancienne Comédie.

Here he gave a sharp rap with the polished brass knocker, and within a very few seconds the door was opened and an anxious feminine voice hailed him from out the darkness of the narrow passage.

"Eh bien?—Monseigneur?—What did he say?"

M. Legros closed the door behind him with great deliberation, then he turned, stretched out both arms and, catching the speaker round the shoulders, imprinted two well-sounding kisses on a pair of fresh young cheeks.

"He says," said the worthy bonhomme gaily, "that Rose Marie, the fairest maid in France, shall be called Countess of Stowmaries before the year is out, for right and justice and indissoluble marriage vows are all on her side."

A little gasp—which sounded almost like a hysterical sob—broke from the woman's throat. It seemed as if the news—evidently very anxiously expected—was overwhelmingly good. There was silence in the little passage for a moment, then the fresh voice, now quite cheerful and steady, said lightly:

"Let us go and tell maman!"

Together father and daughter went up the steep, slightly-winding stair which led to an upper story. Rose Marie, silent once more, felt as if her young heart would presently burst through her corselet, so rapidly did it beat with excitement and anticipation.

She followed her father into the large, cheerful-looking room which gave on the first landing. Here a bright fire blazed in an open hearth; blue cotton curtains hung on each side of the single, narrow window, through which the last rays of this October day struggled faintly.

A large iron stewpot, from which escaped a jet of savoury-smelling steam, stood invitingly upon the hob, and beside the hearth, wooden spoon in hand, her ample proportions carefully draped in a thick brown linen apron, stood Mme. Legros herself, the wife of one of the wealthiest men in the whole of Paris.

"Eh bien! Legros, 'tis good news then?" she asked with cheerful optimism, whilst a benevolent smile shone all over her round face, red as an Eydam cheese and quite as shiny and greasy, for Madame had been cooking and she was mightily hot.

"The best, Maman," came in hilarious accents from her husband; "our daughter shall be installed in her English castle before many moons are over. The Holy Father himself will interfere, and this—this—milor Stowmaries will have to obey at once—failing which 'twill be excommunication and nothing less than that."

M. Legros had thrown himself into the tall-backed chair, black with age and the smoke from many a previous stewpot, and had stretched out his legs before him, in order that his dutiful daughter Rose Marie might the more easily divest him of his high out-door boots.

Kneeling before her father, she performed this little service for him with all the grace of loving girlhood, and he cocked his cropped head on one side and looked down at her with eyes in which merriment struggled with happy tears.

She was so good to look at as she knelt thus on one knee, her fair hair—touched with the gold of the sun of her native Provence—falling in thick ringlets round her young face. She was so girlish and so pure, fresh as the hawthorn in May, and withal luscious to behold like a ripening fruit in June.

"Nay! nay!" said M. Legros with mock gravity, as he put his now stockinged feet to the ground and rose with a great show of ceremony; "this is no place for Madame la Comtesse of Stowmaries. She must not kneel at any man's feet, not even at those of her fond old father. Come to my arms, my girl," he added, once more resuming his seat, his voice breaking in the vain endeavour to seem flippant; "sit here on my knee. Maman, for the Lord's sake put down that spoon, and sit down like a Christian and I'll tell you both all that Monseigneur said to me."

With a happy little sigh Rose Marie jumped to her feet. Obviously her young heart was still too full for speech. She had said nothing, practically, since her first greeting to her father, since she had heard from him the good news—the confirmation of her hopes.

Her cheeks were glowing until they quite ached with the throbbing of the veins beneath the delicate skin, and the palms of her hands felt cold and damp with suppressed nervousness and excitement.

Obedient to her father's call, she came close to him and perched herself on his knee, whilst his arm sought her slender waist and clung to it with all the gentle firmness born of his fond paternal love, of his pride in the beauty and grace of his child.

3

Mme. Legros—somewhat reluctantly—had pulled the stewpot further away from the fire, and put her wooden spoon aside. Then she sat down opposite her lord and her daughter and said blandly:

"I am listening."

"Monseigneur was most affable," now began M. Legros, speaking with some pride at the recollection of his late reception in the Archbishop's palace, "but from the first he bade me to be brief, so as I had rehearsed the whole scene in my mind over and over again, and knew exactly what I wished to say to His Greatness, I was able to put our case before him in the most direct, most straightforward way possible. Now if you will listen very attentively and not interrupt me I will tell you word for word just what passed between Monseigneur and myself."

"Go on, Armand," said Madame; "I am burning with impatience and I'll promise not to interrupt."

As for Rose Marie, she said nothing, but from the expression in her eyes, it was obvious that she would listen attentively.

"Monseigneur sat at his desk and he was pleased to tell me to be seated. Then he said: 'Commence, my son; I am all attention.' He fixed his eyes upon me and I then began my narrative. 'My wife had a distant relative,' I said, 'married to an officer in the army of the English king. At a time of great pecuniary distress this fashionable lady bethought herself of her connection with the humble tailor of Paris and wrote to him an amiable letter suggesting a visit to his modest home.' That was so, was it not, Maman?" he asked, turning for confirmation to his buxom wife.

"Exactly so, Armand," she replied in assent; "except that the fashionable lady was at pains not to tell us that her husband was in prison for debt over in England and that she herself was almost destitute—and to think that I was such a simpleton as not to guess at the truth when she arrived with her little boy, and he with his shoes all in holes and—"

"Easy—easy, Mélanie," rejoined M. Legros tartly. "Am I telling you my adventures of this afternoon, or am I not?"

"But of a truth thou art telling us, Armand," replied fat Mme. Legros blandly.

"Then I pray you to remember that I said I would not be interrupted, else I shall lose the thread of my narration."

"But thou didst ask me a question, Armand, and I did answer."

"Then do not answer at such lengths, Mélanie," quoth the tailor sententiously, "or I shall be an hour getting through my tale, and that savoury stew yonder will be completely spoilt."

Harmony being thus restored under threat of so terrible a contingency, M. Legros now resumed his narrative.

"I did tell Monseigneur," he said with reproachful emphasis, "that at the time that Mistress Angélique Kestyon came on a visit to us in company with her small son, then aged six and a half years, but without nurse, serving or tiring woman of any kind, we were quite unaware of the distressful position in which she was, and in which she had left her lord and master over in England. I then explained to Monseigneur how Mistress Kestyon seemed over-pleased with the grace and beauty of our own child Rose Marie, who had just passed through her first birthday. She would insist on calling the wench Rosemary, pronouncing the name in an outlandish fashion, and saying that in England it stood for remembrance. A pretty conceit enough, seeing that our Rose Marie once seen would surely never be forgotten."

And a vigorous pressure on Rose Marie's waist brought an additional glow to the girl's bright eyes.

"At this point," continued M. Legros, "it pleased Monseigneur to show such marked interest in my story, that he appeared quite impatient and said with a show of irritation—which could but be flattering to me:—'Yes! yes! my son, but there is no need to give me all these trifling details. I understand that you are rich, are of somewhat humble calling, and have a daughter, and that the English lady was poor, if high-born, and had a son. Ergo! the children were betrothed.' Which, methinks showed vast penetration on the part of Monseigneur," added the worthy bonhomme naïvely, "and gracious interest in my affairs. Whereupon, warming to my narrative, I exclaimed: 'Not only betrothed, Monseigneur, but married with the full rites and ceremonials of our Holy Church as by law prescribed. My wife and I— so please Your Greatness—thought of the child's future. It has pleased God to bless my work and to endow me with vast wealth which in the course of time will all pass to our Rose Marie. But here in France, the great gentlemen would always look askance at the daughter of the man who made their coats and breeches; not so in England where trade, they say, is held in high esteem, and in order that our child should one day be as great a lady as any one in the land and as noble as she is beautiful, we wedded her to a high and mighty well-born English gentleman, who was own great nephew to one of the most illustrious noblemen in that fog-ridden country—the Earl of Stowmaries, so he is called over there, Monseigneur!' and you may be sure," continued M. Legros, "that I mentioned this fact with no small measure of pride."

"Well, and what did His Greatness say to that?" queried Mme. Legros, who would not curb her impatience, even for those few seconds whilst her man paused in order to take breath.

"Monseigneur did not seem over-pleased at seeing me display quite so much pride in empty titles and meaningless earthly dignities," rejoined M. Legros lightly. "His Greatness was pleased to rebuke me and to inform me that he himself was well acquainted with the distinguished English family who bears the name of Kestyon of Stowmaries. The Kestyons are all good Catholics and Monseigneur thought that this fact was of far greater importance than their worldly

5

honours and their ancient lineage, and should have weighed much more heavily with us, Maman, when we chose a husband for our daughter."

"We should not have given Rose Marie to a Protestant, Armand; you should have told that to Monseigneur. No, not if he had been the King of England himself," retorted Mme. Legros indignantly.

"The King of England is as good a Catholic as any of us, so 'tis said," commented M. Legros, "but this is a digression, and I pray you, Mélanie, not to interrupt me again. I felt that His Greatness had lapsed into a somewhat irritable mood against me, which no doubt I fully deserved, more especially as Monseigneur did not then know—but 'tis I am digressing now," resumed the good man after a slight hesitation. "In less time than I can repeat it all, I had told Monseigneur how directly after the marriage ceremony had been performed, we found out how grossly we had been deceived, that le Capitaine Kestyon, the husband of Mistress Angélique, had been in a debtor's prison in London all the time that his wife was bragging to us about his high position and his aristocratic connections; we heard that the great Earl of Stowmaries not only refused to have anything to do with his nephew, who was a noted rogue and evil-doer, but that he had a son and three grandsons of his own, so that there were a goodly number of direct inheritors to his great title and vast estates. All this and more we heard after our darling child had been indissolubly tied to the son of the best-known scoundrel in the whole of England, and who moreover was penniless, deeply in debt, and spent the next ten years in extracting our hard-earned money from out our pockets."

The recollection of those same ten years seemed to have even now a terrible effect on the temper of M. Legros. Indignation at the memories his own last words evoked seemed momentarily to choke him. He pulled a voluminous and highly-coloured handkerchief from the pocket of his surcoat and moped his perspiring forehead, for choler had made him warm.

Mme. Legros—equally indignant in retrospect but impatient to hear Monseigneur's final pronouncement on the great subject—was nervously rapping a devil's tattoo on the table. Rose Marie's fair head had fallen forward on her breast. She had said nothing all along, but sat on her father's knee, listening with all her ears, for was not he talking about the people who would be her people henceforth, the land which would be her land, the man who of a truth was her lord and husband? But when Legros, with just indignation, recalled the deceits, the shifts, the mean, mercenary actions of those whose name she would bear through life, then the blush of excitement seemed to turn into one of shame, and two heavy tears fell from her eyes onto her tightly clasped hands.

"Father, Father!" cried fat Mme. Legros in horror, "cannot you see that you have made the child cry?"

6

"Then heaven punish me for a blundering ass," exclaimed Legros, with renewed cheerfulness. "Nay! nay! my little cabbage, there's naught to cry for now; have I not said that all is well? Those ten years are past and done with and eight more lie on the top of them— and if Monseigneur showed some impatience both at my pride and at my subsequent indignation, he was vastly interested, I can tell you that, when he heard that the son and three grandsons of the great English nobleman were by the will of God wrecked while pleasure-cruising together off the coast of Spain and all four of them drowned, and that the old lord himself did not long survive the terrible catastrophe, which had swept four direct inheritors of his vast wealth and ancient name off the face of the earth and into the sea. His Greatness became quite excited—and vastly amiable to me: 'Ah!' he said, 'then surely—you cannot mean—?' You see Monseigneur was so interested he scarce could find his words. 'Yes, so please Your Greatness,' quoth I with becoming dignity, 'the husband of our Rose Marie, the son of the capitaine who in life had been nought but a rogue, has inherited the title and the wealth of his great-uncle. He is now styled by the English the Earl of Stowmaries and Rivaulx, Baron of Edbrooke and of Saumaresque, and he has many other titles besides, and one of the richest men in the whole of England!' 'Mais, comment donc!' exclaims Monseigneur, most affably, and you'll both believe me, an you will, but I give you my word that His Greatness took my hand and shook it, so pleased did he seem with what I had told him. 'We must see the lovely Comtesse of Stowmaries!—Eighteen years ago, did you say, my son? and she was a baby then! The decrees of God are marvellous, of a truth!—And your Rose Marie a great English lady now, eh?—with a quantity of money and a great love for the Church!—By the Mass, my son, we must arrange for a solemn Te Deum to be sung at St. Etienne, before the beautiful comtesse leaves the sunny shores of France for her fog-wrapped home across the sea!' Nay! but His Greatness said much more than that. He spoke of the various forms which our thank-offering might take, the donations which would be most acceptable to God on this occasion; he mentioned the amount of money which would most adequately express the full meed of our gratitude to Providence, by being given to the Church, and I most solemnly assure you that he simply laughed at the very thought of the Earl of Stowmaries contemplating the non-fulfilment of his marriage vows. I pointed out to His Greatness that the young man seemed inclined to repudiate the sacred bond. We had not seen him since the ceremony eighteen years ago, and after our final refusal to further help his parents with money or substance, we had even ceased to correspond. His parents had gone to live in some far, very far-off land across the ocean, where I believe cannibals and such like folk do dwell. They had taken the boy with them, of course. We thought the young man dead, or if alive then as great a rogue as his father, and mourned that our only child was either

7

a girl-widow, or the wife of a reprobate. "Tis eighteen years,' I said, 'since those marriage vows were spoken.' 'Were they fifty,' retorted His Greatness, 'they would still be sacred. The Catholic Church would scorn to tie a tie which caprice of man could tear asunder. Nay! nay!' he added with sublime eloquence, 'have no fear on this matter, my son. Unless the Earl of Stowmaries chooses to abjure the faith of his fathers, and thereby cause his own eternal damnation, he cannot undo the knot which by the will of his parents—he being a minor at the time—tied him indissolubly to your daughter.' Thus spoke His Greatness, Monseigneur the Archbishop of Paris," concluded M. Legros, with becoming solemnity, "and in such words will the message be conveyed to the man who by all laws human and divine is the husband of Rose Marie Dieudonnée Legros, our only and dearly loved child."

There was silence in the small room now. The fast-gathering twilight had gradually softened all sharp outlines, covering every nook and cranny with a mantle of gloom and leaving the dying embers of the fire to throw a warm glow over the group of these homely folk: fat Mme. Legros in cooking apron of coarse linen, her round, moist face pale with excitement, the sleeves of her worsted gown rolled back over her shapely arms; the kindly tailor with rubicund face gleaming with pride and paternal love, one arm still encircling the cherished daughter whose future had been mapped out by him on such glorious lines, and she, the girl—a mere child, fair and slender, with great, innocent eyes which mirrored the pure, naïve soul within, eyes which still looked the outer world boldly in the face, which had learned neither to shrink in terror, nor yet to waver in deceit, a child with rosy, moist lips which had not yet tasted the sweet and bitter savour of a passionate kiss.

The silence became almost oppressive, for Mme. Legros dared not speak again, lest she irritate the mightily clever man whom God had pleased to give her as husband, and Rose Marie was silent because, unknown even to herself, in the far-off land of Shadows, the Fates who sit and spin the threads of life had taken in their grim and relentless hands the first ravellings of her own.

Vaguely now, for her ears were buzzing, she heard her father speak again, talking of Monseigneur's graciousness, of the intervention of the French ambassador at the Court of the King of England, of an appeal to the Holy Father who would command that the great English milor shall acknowledge as his sole and lawful wife, Rose Marie Legros, the daughter of the Court tailor of Paris.

It was so strange—almost uncanny, this intervention of great and clever gentlemen, of Monseigneur the Archbishop of Paris, whom hitherto she had only seen at a great distance passing through the streets in his glass coach or celebrating High Mass at the great altar in Notre Dame, of the King of England, whom she had once seen at a pageant in Versailles, actually talking to young King Louis himself, the

8

greatest man in the whole world and most wonderful of all, of the Holy Father, second only on earth to le bon Dieu Himself—all, all of these great and marvellous people troubling about her, Rose Marie.

For the moment she could not bear to think of it all, and she supposed that she must outwardly have looked as strange as she felt herself to be from within, for maman suggested that the child was overwrought and must go to her room, where presently she should partake of fricassée of chicken and a glass of good red wine with a little clove and cinnamon in it, the panacea, in good Mme. Legros' estimation, for every ailment of body, mind or heart.

CHAPTER II

True hope is swift, and flies with swallows' wings;
Kings it makes gods, and meaner creatures kings.

—*Richard III. V. 2*

Rose Marie hardly knew how she reached the tiny room up under the sloping roof, which room was her very own.

She only realised that she longed to be alone to think matters out all by herself, and then to indulge in a long and happy cry.

Oh, yes! she was quite, quite sure that she was very happy, and that it was because of this great happiness which filled her heart to bursting, that she felt so very much inclined to cry.

Presently maman came in with the red wine and the fricassée and was horrified to find the child in tears.

"My pigeon, my little cabbage, but what ails thee, my jewel?" ejaculated the good old soul, as she hastily put down the platter and bottle which she was carrying and went to kneel beside the narrow bed in the wall, from the depths of which came ominous sounds of a girl sobbing.

"Nothing, Maman, nothing!" said Rose Marie, smiling at her mother's anxiety and hastily endeavouring to dry her tears.

"Nothing—nothing—" grumbled Mme. Legros, "one does not cry for nothing, my child—"

"And I am vastly silly, Maman, for doing it—but I assure you that it is nothing—and—and—"

The young voice broke in renewed sobs, and two arms were stretched forth from out the bed and sought the mother's kindly

9

shoulder, whereon a strangely overburdened childish heart could sob itself out in perfect peace.

"There! there! my little cabbage," said Mme. Legros, trying with tender pattings of the soft fair hair to soothe this well-nigh hysterical outburst, "of a truth, thou hast been overwrought, and it was not right for father to speak of all this before thee. Thou didst not know that the young English lord had endeavoured to break his marriage vows, and that thy father and I have been working hard in order to bring influence to bear upon the rogue. Fortunately now we have succeeded, with the help of Monseigneur, so there is no need to cry, my cabbage, is there?"

"No, no, Maman, it is not that," said the girl more quietly; "I cannot quite explain to you what it is that made me cry—for I have known all along that milor—now that he is a milor and passing rich—was anxious to forget us humble folk, who helped his parents in their need—I have felt the shame of that before now, and it never made me cry. But to-day—somehow—Maman, darling," she added, sitting up quite straight in bed and looking at her mother with enquiring eyes, whilst her fine brow was puckered in a deep frown of thought, "somehow I feel—I cannot quite explain how it is—I feel as if my old life was finished—quite, quite finished—as if nothing would ever be quite the same again—my little room here, the pink curtains, that chair over there—they do not seem the same—not quite, quite the same—Maman, cherie, I suppose you don't understand?"

And the great childish eyes sought anxiously the mother's face, longing for comprehension, for the explanation of an unaccountable mystery.

"No, my pigeon, I confess I do not understand," quoth worthy Mme. Legros drily, "for I do not see—nor would any sensible person admit—that a great English milor just because he is thy husband—can from all that distance, from the other side of the sea, change thy room and thy chair, nor yet thy curtains, though the latter, I will say, sorely need washing at the present moment," she added with sublime irrelevance.

The girl sighed. Maman for once did not understand. Nor of a truth did she understand herself. She had tried to explain it all but had signally failed—had only succeeded in suggesting something which of course was supremely silly.

"I'll tell thee how it is, Rose Marie," resumed Mme. Legros with firm decision, "thy stomach is in a disturbed condition, and a cup of cold camomile tea thou shalt drink to-morrow before rising. I'll see to the making of it at once,—for it must be brewed over-night to be truly efficacious,—and come back and give thee thy supper a little later on."

Mme. Legros struggled back to her feet, happy to have found in a prospective cup of camomile tea a happy solution for Rose Marie's curious mood. She took up the platter again, for the fricassée must be kept hot, and the child must eat some supper a little later on. The good

10

woman's heart was filled with that cheerful optimism which persistently seeks the good side of every eventuality and nearly always finds it. In this case Mme. Legros failed to see that anything but good could come out of the present position. That same wonderful optimism of hers had not been altogether proof against the events of the past years, when she first began to realise that the marriage which she—more so than her husband—had planned in conjunction with Mistress Angélique Kestyon, was destined to prove a bar to her daughter's happiness.

In those far-off days eighteen years ago, Mme. Legros had still fostered in her homely bosom the—since then—aborted seeds of social ambition. Well-connected on her mother's side, with a good English family, she had wedded the Paris tailor for pecuniary rather than for sentimental reasons, and she had a sufficiency of sound common sense to understand that as a tradesman's wife she could not in these days of arbitrary class distinction aspire to remain within that same social circle to which her connections and parentage would otherwise have entitled her. But though the seeds of ambition lay dormant in the homely soil of her husband's back shop, they were not then altogether destroyed.

Mélanie de Boutillier had been well past her youth when she married Armand Legros; when her baby girl was born, and the mother with justifiable pride realised that the child was passing fair, those same seeds once more began to germinate. The visit of the English relative—high-born, well-connected and accompanied by a boy not yet seven years of age, brought them to final perfection. What Mélanie de Boutillier had failed to obtain, Rose Marie Legros should possess in measureless plenty, and little Rupert Kestyon, great nephew of an English milor, should be the one to shower the golden gifts on her.

All these schemes seemed at first so easy of accomplishment. It had been useless afterwards to cry over undue haste; at the time it seemed right, fitting and proper. Times then were troublous in England; Mistress Angélique Kestyon feared the democratic spirit there. It seems that the English were actually fighting against their king, and that the fate of the great noblemen in the country was in consequence somewhat uncertain; but only temporarily, of course, for King Charles Stuart would soon overcome his enemies and duly crush the rebellious traitors who had taken up arms against him. In the meanwhile the children would grow up, and anon when the Court of England had resumed its former splendour, Rupert Kestyon, the dearly-loved relative of the powerful Earl of Stowmaries, would introduce his beautiful bride to the charmed inner circle of English aristocracy.

It all seemed so clear—so simple—as if, of a truth, the match and its glorious consequences had been specially designed by Providence for the glorification and social exaltation of Rose Marie Legros. Surely

11

no one in those days would have thought that any blame could be attached to the parents for hurrying on the marriage ceremony between the two children, whose united ages fell short of a decade.

The catastrophe came afterwards when the tale of deceit and of fraud was gradually unfolded. Then came the requests for money, the long voyage to America, the knowledge that milor Stowmaries not only had no love for these relatives of his, but had finally and irrevocably refused to help them in their distress, unless they took ship for a far distant colony and never troubled him with sight of their faces again.

Good Armand Legros, who adored his daughter, was quite broken-hearted. Madame tried to remain hopeful against these overwhelming odds—always thinking that—though it had certainly pleased God to try the Legros family very severely for the moment—something would inevitably turn up which would be for the best.

The immediate result of that unvarying optimism was that she continued Rose Marie's education on the same lines as she had originally intended, as if the girl-wife was indeed destined anon to grace the Court of the King of England. The child was taught the English language by one of the many impoverished English gentlemen who had settled in France after the murder of their king. She learned to write and to read, to spell and to dance. She was taught to play on the virginals and to sing whilst playing a thorough-bass on the harpsichord. Nay! her knowledge, so 'twas said, extended even as far as geography and the Copernican system.

Her mother kept her apart from girls of her own age, unless these belonged to one of those few families where learning was esteemed. She was never allowed to forget that some day she would leave her father's shop and be a great lady in England.

Whilst Mme. Legros and the kindly bonhomme Armand gradually drifted in their middle age to the bourgeois manners and customs of their time and station, they jealously fostered in their only child that sense of elegance and refinement which mayhap she had inherited from one of her remote ancestors, or mayhap had received as a special gift from the fairy godmother who presided at her birth.

Mme. Legros cooked and scoured, Master Armand made surcoats and breeches, but Rose Marie was never allowed to spoil her hands with scrubbing, or to waste her time presiding over the stewpot. Her father had bought her a pair of gloves; these she always wore when she went out, and she always had stockings and leather shoes on her feet. As the girl grew up, she gradually assimilated to herself more and more this idea that she was to be a great lady. She never doubted her future for a moment. Her father from sheer fondness, her mother from positive conviction, kept the certitude alive within her.

But it became quite impossible to keep from the girl's growing intelligence all knowledge of the Kestyon's misdeeds. The worthy tailor who was passing rich kept but a very small house, in which the one

12

living room, situate just above the shop, was the family meeting ground. Rose Marie could not be kept out of the room every time her father and mother talked over the freshly-discovered deceits and frauds practised by their new relations.

We must suppose that the subject thus became such a familiar one with the child-wife from the moment when she first began to comprehend it, that it never acquired any horror or even shame for her. Mistress Angélique Kestyon had grossly deceived papa and maman; they were not so rich or so grand just now as they had represented themselves to be, but it would all come right in the end—maman at least was quite sure of that.

If—as time went on and Rose Marie from a child became a girl— that pleasing optimism somewhat gave way, this was no doubt due to too much book learning. Rose Marie was very fond of books, and books we all know have a tendency to destroy the innocent belief in the goodness of this world. This at least was Papa Legros' opinion.

Mme. Legros spoke less and less on the subject. She hoped.

She hoped resolutely and persistently, whilst the Kestyons from distant Virginia begged repeatedly for money. She went on hoping even whilst urging her husband to cut off further supplies, after ten years of this perpetual sponging. She still hoped whilst no news whatever came from the emigrants and when the rumour reached her that young Rupert Kestyon had died out there.

At this point, however, her optimism took a fresh turn. She hoped that the rumour was true, and that Rose Marie was now free to wed some other equally high-born but more reliable gentleman. She continued to hope despite the difficulty of proving that the young man had really died, and Monseigneur the Archbishop's refusal to grant permission for a second marriage.

Then when the news filtered through from England as far as the back shop in the Rue de l'Ancienne Comédie that Rupert Kestyon was not only alive but had—by a wonderful, almost miraculous series of events—inherited the title and estates of his deceased kinsman and was now of a truth by the will of God and the law of his country milor of Stowmaries, and one of the greatest gentleman in the whole of England, Mme. Legros' optimism found its crowning glory in its justification.

That the young milor seemed disinclined to acknowledge the daughter of the Paris tailor as his wife and that he seemed to be taking serious steps to have the marriage annulled, were but trifling matters which never upset Mme. Legros' equanimity.

She was quite sure that the marriage could not be annulled without special dispensation from the Holy Father himself, and equally sure that that dispensation would never be granted. She had perfect faith not only in the sacred indissolubility of the marriage tie, but in the happy future of Rose Marie.

13

When Monseigneur the Archbishop of Paris granted her Armand a special audience, whereat the tailor had begged permission to lay the family case before His Greatness, Mme. Legros never for a moment doubted the happy issue of that interview: and when her man came home and told his satisfactory tale, maman was in no way astonished.

Her optimism had been justified: that was all.

But what did astonish the good soul was the fact that the child— Rose Marie—sat crying in her bed, whereas she should have been singing and laughing all about the place.

Therefore, maman, with commendable forethought, prescribed cold camomile tea as a remedy against what was obviously but a sharp attack of megrims.

CHAPTER III

*Come Care and Pleasure, Hope and Pain
And bring the fated Fairy Prince.*

—Tennyson

And in the narrow bed built within the wall in the tiny room, wherein a tallow candle placed on a central table threw only very feeble rays, the girl Rose Marie lay dreaming.

She—Rose Marie—the daughter of Papa Legros—as he was uniformly called in the neighbourhood—she was now a great lady, by the will of God and the decree of the Holy Father himself. She would have a glass coach like the ladies whom she had so often seen driving about in Versailles, and sit in it, dressed in the latest fashion and holding a fan in her hand, which would be encased in a lace mitten.

At this point in her dreams Rose Marie sat up in bed, very straight and dignified, with her little hands folded over the cotton coverlet, and she bent her young head to right and to left, like one saluting a number of passers-by. A nod accompanied by an encouraging smile indicated the greeting to a supposed friend, whilst a condescending nod and a haughty stare suggested the presence of an acquaintance of somewhat low degree.

Thus Rose Marie had seen the ladies behave in their coaches in Versailles. She had seen Maria Mancini bow serenely to her admirers, and the Queen Mother bestow the stony stare on her detractors. She had watched, wondered and admired, but never had she tried to

14

imitate until now—now that her smile would be appreciated by many, her frown be of consequence to others.

Up to now it had not mattered. Though her father was reputed to be wealthy, he was only a tailor, who had to bow and scrape and wallow before the great gentlemen of the Court. Aye! and had more than once been soundly thrashed because of the misfit of a pair of Court breeches.

And Rose Marie had oft sighed for greatness, for the gilded coach and a seat at the opera, for silken dresses, flowers, patches and rouge. She was only a child with an acutely developed sense of sympathy for everything that was dainty and refined, everything that smelt sweetly and was soft and tender to the touch.

Thus she went on dreaming her dream in content, never doubting for a moment that happiness lay closely linked with this sudden accession to grandeur. The fact that her lawful lord and husband had shown a desire to break his marriage vows, and to take unto himself some other wife more equal to him in rank and breeding than the humble tailor's daughter, troubled Rose Marie not at all. With sublime faith in the workings of Providence, she put her husband's reluctance to acknowledge her down to his ignorance of herself.

He had never seen her since the day of the ceremony, eighteen years ago. She was a baby in arms then, whilst now—

Rose Marie drew in her breath and listened. Maman was evidently not yet coming up. All was still on this upper floor of the house. Rose Marie put her feet to the ground and rose from her bed. She picked up the candle from the table and tripped across the room to where—on the whitewashed wall opposite—there hung a small gilt-framed mirror.

Into this she peeped, holding the candle well above her head. Her face wore neither the look of vanity, nor even that of satisfaction: rather was it a look of the closest possible scrutiny. Rose Marie turned her head to right and left again, but not—this time—in order to enact a private comedy, but in order to convince herself in her own mind that her cheeks had indeed that peach-like bloom, which her overfond father had so oft proclaimed, and that her hair was sufficiently brilliant in colour to be called golden, and yet not too vivid to be called "roux."

We may take it that this scrutiny, which lasted nearly twenty minutes, was of a satisfactory character, for presently, with a happy little sigh, and heaving breast, Rose Marie tripped lightly back to her narrow bed in the wall, and squeezed herself well within the further dark angle, to which the flickering light of the tallow candle had no access.

This she did because she had heard maman's step on the stairs, and because her own cheeks now were of a flaming red.

15

PART II

CHAPTER IV

For what is wedlock forced but a hell.

—1 Henry VI. V. 5

"My Lord is sad."

"Oh!—"

"My Lord is weary!"

"!!—"

A pause. Mistress Julia Peyton, you understand, was waxing impatient. Can you wonder? She was not accustomed to moodiness on the part of her courtiers; to a certain becoming diffidence mayhap, to tongue-tiedness—if we may be allowed so to call it—on the part of her young adorers fresh from their country homes, fledglings scarce free from the gentle trammels of their mother's apron strings, to humility in the presence of so much beauty, grace and wit as she was wont to display when taken with the desire to please, to all that yes, yes and a thousand times yes, the adorable Julia was fully accustomed. But to silence on the part of the wittiest gentleman about town, to moodiness akin to ill-humour on the part of the most gallant young rake this side of Westminster—no! no! and a thousand times no! Mistress Julia would have none of it.

Her daintily-shod foot beat a quick measure against the carpets, her fingers delicately tipped with rouge played a devil's tattoo on the polished top of the tiny marqueterie table beside her, and her small teeth, white and even as those of a kitten, tore impatiently at her under lip.

Still Lord Stowmaries paid no heed to these obvious signs of a coming storm. He lolled in an armchair opposite the imperious beauty, his chin was resting in his hand, his brow was puckered, and oh! most portentous outward indication of troubles within! his cravat looked soiled and crumpled, as if an angry hand had fidgeted its immaculate whiteness away.

At last Mistress Julia found herself quite unable to control her annoyance any longer. Granted that Lord Stowmaries was the richest, most promising "parti" that had ever come her way; that he was young, good-looking, owned half the county of Hertford, and one of the oldest names in England, and that, moreover, he was of sufficiently amiable disposition to be fashioned into a model husband by and by! granted all that, say I! Had not all these advantages, I pray you to admit, caused the fair Julia to hide her ill-humour for close on half an hour, whilst the young man frowned and sighed, gave curt answers to her most charming sallies, and had failed to notice that a filmy handkerchief, lace-edged and delicately perfumed, had been dropped on that veriest exact spot of the carpet which was most conveniently situated for sinking on one knee within a few inches of the most adorable foot in London?

But now the irascible beauty was at the end of her tether. She rose—wrathfully kicking aside that same handkerchief which her surly visitor had failed to notice—and took three quick steps in the direction of the bell-pull.

"And now, my lord," she said, "I pray you to excuse me."

And she stretched out her hand in a gesture intended to express the full measure of her wrath.

Lord Stowmaries roused himself from his unpleasant torpor.

"To excuse you, fair one?" he murmured in the tone of a man who has just wakened from slumber, and is still unaware of what has been going on around him whilst he slept.

"Ay, my good lord," she replied with a shrill note of sarcasm very apparent in the voice which so many men had compared to that of a nightingale. "I fain must tear myself away from the delights of your delectable company—though I confess 'twere passing easy to find more entertaining talk than yours has been this last half-hour."

"Would you be cruel to me now, Mistress?" he said with a deep and mournful sigh, "now, when—"

"Now, when what?" she retorted still pettishly, though a little mollified by his obvious distress.

She turned back towards him, and presently placed a hand on his shoulder.

"My lord," she said resolutely, "either you tell me now and at once what ails you this afternoon, or I pray you leave me, for in your present mood, by my faith, your room were more enjoyable than your company."

He took that pretty hand which still lingered on his shoulder, and pressing it for a few lingering seconds between both his, he finally conveyed its perfumed whiteness to his lips.

"Don't send me away," he pleaded pathetically; "I am the most miserable of mortals, and if you closed your doors against me now, you would be sending your most faithful adorer straight to perdition."

"Tut, man!" she rejoined impatiently, "you talk like a gaby. In the name of Heaven, tell me what ails you, or I vow you'll send me into my grave with choler."

"I have been trying to tell you, Mistress, this past half-hour."

"Well?"

"But Lud help me, I cannot."

17

"Then it's about a woman," she concluded with firm decision.

He gave no reply. The conclusion was obvious.

The fair Julia frowned. This was threatening to become serious. It was no mere question of moodiness then, of ill-humour anon to be forgiven and dissipated with a smile.

There was a woman at the bottom of my lord Stowmaries' ill-humour. A woman who had the power to obtrude her personality between his mental vision and the daintiest apparition that had ever turned a man's brain dizzy with delight. A woman in fact who might prove to be an obstacle to the realisation of Mistress Julia Peyton's most cherished dreams.

All thoughts of anger, of petulance, of bell-pulls and peremptory congés fled from the beauty's mind. She sat down again opposite the young man; she rested her elbows on her knees, her chin in her hands; she looked serious, sympathetic, interested, anything you like. A sufficiency of moisture rose to her eyes to render them soft and lustrous, appealing and irresistible. Her lips parted and quivered just sufficiently to express deep emotion held courageously in check, whilst from beneath the little lace cap one or two rebellious curls free from powder, golden in colour, and silky in texture, were unaccountably allowed to escape.

Thus equipped for the coming struggle, she repeated her question, not peremptorily this time, but gently and in a voice that trembled slightly with the intensity of sympathy.

"What ails my lord?"

"Nothing short of despair," he replied, whilst his eyes rested with a kind of mournful abnegation on the enchanting picture so tantalisingly near to him.

"Is it quite hopeless, then?" she asked.

"Quite."

"An entanglement?"

"No. A marriage."

Outwardly she made no sign. Mistress Julia was not one of those simpering women who faint, or scream, or gasp at moments of mental or moral crises. I will grant you that the colour left her cheek, and that her fingers for one brief instant were tightly clutched—no longer gracefully interlaced—under her chin. But this was in order to suppress emotion, not to make a show of it.

There was only a very momentary pause, the while she now, with deliberate carelessness, brushed a rebellious curl back into its place.

"A marriage, my good lord," she said lightly; "nay! you must be jesting—or else mayhap I have misunderstood.—A marriage to render you moody?—Whose marriage could that be?—"

"Mine, Mistress—my marriage," exclaimed Lord Stowmaries, now in tones of truly tragical despair; "curse the fate that brought it

18

about, the parents who willed it, the necessity which forced them to it, and which hath wrecked my life."

Mistress Julia now made no further attempt to hide her fears. Obviously the young man was not jesting. The tone of true misery in his voice was quite unmistakable. It was the suddenness of the blow which hurt her so. This fall from the pinnacle of her golden dreams. For weeks and months now she had never thought of herself in the future as other than the Countess of Stowmaries, chatelaine of Maries Castle, the leader of society both in London and in Newmarket, by virtue of her husband's wealth and position, of her own beauty, tact and grace.

She had even with meticulous care so reorganised her mind and memory, that she could now eliminate from them all recollections of the more humble past—the home at Norwich, the yeoman father, kindly but absorbed in the daily struggle for existence, the busy, somewhat vulgar mother, the sordid existence peculiar to impoverished smaller gentry; then the early marriage with Squire Peyton. It had seemed brilliant then, for the Squire, though past his youth, had a fine house, and quite a few serving men—but no position—he never came to London and Mistress Julia's knowledge of Court and society was akin to that which children possess of fairies or of sprites.

But Squire Peyton it appears had more money than he had owned to in his lifetime. He had been something of a miser apparently, for even his young widow was surprised when at his death—which occurred if you remember some twenty-four months ago—she found herself possessed of quite a pleasing fortune.

This was the beginning of Mistress Julia's golden dreams, of her longings towards a more brilliant future, which a lucky second marriage could easily now secure for her. The thousand pounds a year which she possessed enabled her to take a small house in Holborn Row, and to lay herself out to cut a passable figure in London society. Not among the Court set, of course, but there were all the young idlers about town, glad enough to be presented to a young and attractive widow, endowed with some wealth of her own, and an inordinate desire to please.

The first few idlers soon attracted others, and gradually the pretty widow's circle of acquaintances widened. If that circle was chiefly composed of men, who shall blame the pretty widow?

It was a husband she wanted, and not female companionship. Lord Swannes, if you remember, paid her his court, also Sir Jeremiah Harfleet, and it was well known that my lord of Craye—like the true poet that he was—was consumed with love of her. But as soon as Mistress Julia realised that richly-feathered birds were only too willing to fly into her snares, she aimed for higher game. A golden eagle was what she wanted to bring down.

And was not the young Earl of Stowmaries the veritable prince of golden eagles?

19

He came and saw and she conquered in a trice. Her beauty, which was unquestionable, and an inexhaustible fund of verve and high-spirited chatter which easily passed for wit were attractive to most men, and Lord Stowmaries, somewhat blasé already by the more simpering advances of the Court damsels, found a certain freshness in this young widow who had not yet shaken off the breezy vulgarity of her East Anglian home, and whose artless conversation, wholly innocent of elegance, was more amusing than the stilted "Ohs!" and "Luds!" of the high-born ladies of his own rank.

The golden eagle seemed overwilling to allow the matrimonial snare set by the fair Julia to close in around him: she was already over-sure of him, and though she did not frequent the assemblies and salons where congregated his lordship's many friends, she was fully aware that her name was being constantly coupled with that of the Earl of Stowmaries.

But now she saw that she had missed her aim, that the glorious bird no longer flew within her reach, but was a prisoner in some one else's cage, fettered beyond her powers of liberation.

But still Mistress Julia with persistence worthy a better cause refused to give up all hope.

"Tell me all about it, my lord," she said as quietly as she could. "It had been better had you spoken before."

"I have been a fool, Mistress," he replied dully, "yet more sinned against than sinning."

"You'll not tell me that you are actually married?" she insisted.

"Alas!"

"And did not tell me so," she retorted hotly, "but came here, courting me, speaking of love to me—of marriage—God help you! when the very word was a sacrilege since you were not free—Oh! the perfidy of it all!—and you speak of being more sinned against than sinning. 'Tis the pillory you deserve, my lord, for thus shaming a woman first and then breaking her heart."

She was quite sincere in her vehemence, for self-control had now quite deserted her, and the wrong and humiliation which she had been made to endure, rose up before her like cruel monsters that mocked and jeered at her annihilated hopes and her vanished dreams. Her voice rose in a crescendo of shrill tones, only to sink again under the strength of choking sobs. Despair, shame and bitter reproach rang through every word which she uttered.

"As you rightly say, Mistress," murmured the young man, "God help me!"

"But the details, man—the details—" she rejoined impatiently; "cannot you see that I am consumed with anxiety—the woman?—who is she?—"

"Her name is Rose Marie," he replied in the same dull, even tones, like a schoolboy reciting a lesson which he hath learned, but

20

does not understand; "she is the daughter of a certain M. Legros, who is tailor to His Majesty the King of France."

"A tailor!" she gasped, incredulous now, hopeful once more that the young man was mayhap suffering from megrims and had seen unpleasant visions, which had no life or reality in them.

"A tailor's daughter?" she repeated. "Impossible!"

"Only too true," he rejoined. "I had no choice in the matter."

"Who had?"

"My parents."

"Tush!" she retorted scornfully, "and you a man!"

"Nay! I was not a man then."

"Evidently."

"I was in my seventh year!" he exclaimed pathetically.

There was a slight pause, during which the swiftly-risen hope a few moments ago once more died away. Then she said drily:

"And she?—this—this Rose or Mary—daughter of a tailor—how old was she when you married her?"

"In her second year, I think," he replied meekly. "I just remember quite vaguely that after the ceremony she was carried screaming and kicking out of the church. That was the last I saw of my wife from that day to this—"

"Bah!"

"My great-uncle, the late Lord Stowmaries, shipped my father, mother and myself off to Virginia soon after that. My father had been something of a wastrel all his life and a thorn in the flesh of the old miser. The second time that he was locked up in a debtor's prison, Lord Stowmaries paid up for him on the condition that he went off to Virginia at once with my mother and myself, and never showed his face in England again."

"Hm! I remember hearing something of this when you, my lord, came into your title. But these—these—tailor people—who were they?"

"Madame Legros was a distant connection of my mother's who, I suppose, married the tailor for the same reason that I—an unfortunate lad without a will of my own—was made to marry the tailor's daughter."

"She is rich—of course?"

"Legros, the tailor, owns millions, I believe, and Rose Marie is his only child. It was the first time that my poor father, Captain Kestyon, found himself actually in prison and unable to pay his debts. The Earl of Stowmaries—a wicked old miser, if ever there was one—refused to come to his rescue. My mother was practically penniless then; she had no one to whom she could turn for succour except the cousin over in Paris, who had always been kind to her, who was passing rich, burning with social ambition, and glad enough to have the high-born English lady beneath her bourgeois roof."

"And that same burning social ambition caused the worthy tailor to consent to a marriage between his baby daughter and the scion of

21

one of the grandest families in England," commented Mistress Julia calmly. "It were all so simple—if only you had had the manhood to tell me all this ere now."

"I thought that miserable marriage forever forgotten."

"Pshaw!" she retorted, "was it likely?"

"I had heard nothing of the Legros for many years," he said dejectedly. "My father had died out in the Colony: my mother and I continued to live there on a meagre pittance which that miserly old reprobate—my great-uncle—grudgingly bestowed upon us. This was scarce sufficient for our wants, let alone for enabling us to save enough money to pay our passage home. At first my mother was in the habit of asking for and obtaining help from the Legros!—you understand? she never would have consented to the connection," added the young man with naïve cynicism, "had she not intended to derive profit therefrom, so whenever an English or a French ship touched the coast my poor mother would contrive to send a pathetic letter to be delivered in Paris, at the house of the king's tailor. But after a while answers to these missives became more and more rare, soon they ceased altogether, and it is now eight years since the last remittance came—"

"The worthy tailor and his wife were getting tired of the aristocratic connection," commented Mistress Julia drily; "no doubt they too had intended to derive profit therefrom and none came."

"Was I not right, Mistress, in thinking that ill-considered marriage forgotten?" quoth Lord Stowmaries with more vehemence than he had displayed in the actual recital of the sordid tale; "was I not justified in thinking that the Legros had by now bitterly regretted the union of their only child to the penniless son of a spendthrift father? Tell me," he reiterated hotly, "was I not justified?—I thought that they had forgotten—that they had regretted—that Rose Marie had found a husband more fitted to her lowly station and to her upbringing—and that her parents would only be too glad to think that I too had forgotten—or that I was dead."

There was a slight pause. Mistress Julia's white brow was puckered into a deep frown of thought.

"Well, my lord," she said at last, "ye've told me the past—and though the history be not pretty, it is past and done with, and I take it that your concern now is rather with the present."

"Alas!"

"Nay! sigh me not such doleful sighs, man!" she exclaimed with angry impatience, "but in the name of all the saints get on with your tale. What has happened? The Legros have found out that little Rupert Kestyon hath now become Earl of Stowmaries and one of the richest peers in the kingdom—that's it—is it not?"

"Briefly, that is it, Mistress. They demand that their daughter be instated in her position and the full dignities and rights to which her marriage entitle her."

"Failing which?" she asked curtly.

"Oh! scandal! disgrace! they will apply to the Holy Father—the orders would then come direct from Rome—I could not disobey under pain of excommunication—"

"Such tyranny!"

"The Kestyons have been Catholics for five hundred years," said the young man simply, whilst a touch of dignity—the first since he began to relate his miserable tale—now crept into his attitude. "We do not call the dictates of the Holy Father in question, nor do we name them tyranny. They are irrevocable in matters such as these—"

"Surely—a sum of money—" she hazarded.

"The Legros have more of that commodity than I have. But it is not a question of money. Believe me, fair Mistress," he said in tones which once more revealed the sorrow of his heart, "I have thought on the matter in all its bearings—I have even broached the subject to the Duke of York," he added after an imperceptible moment of hesitation.

"Ah? and what said His Highness?" asked Mistress Julia with that quick inward catching of her breath which the mentioning of exalted personages was ever wont to call forth in her.

"Oh! His Highness only spoke of the sanctity of the marriage tie—"

"'Twas not likely he would talk otherwise. 'Tis said that his bigotry grows daily upon him—and that he only awaits a favourable moment to embrace openly the Catholic Faith—"

"His Majesty was of the same opinion, too."

"Ah? You spoke to His Majesty?"

"Was it not my duty?"

"Mayhap—mayhap—and what did His Majesty say?"

"Oh! he was pleased to take the matter more lightly—but then there is the Queen Mother—and—"

"Who else? I pray you, who else?" said Mistress Julia now with renewed acerbity. "His Majesty, His Royal Highness, the Queen—half London, to boot—to know of my discomfiture and shame—"

Her voice again broke in a sob, she buried her face in her hands, and tears which mayhap had more affinity to anger than to sorrow escaped freely from between her fingers. In a moment the young man was at her feet. Gone was his apathy, his sullenness now. He was on one knee and his two arms encircled the quivering shoulders of the fair, enraged one.

"Mistress, Mistress," he entreated, whilst his eager lips sought the close proximity of her shell-like ear; "Julia, my beloved, in the name of the Holy Virgin, I pray you dry your tears. You break my heart, fair one. You—O God!" he added vehemently, "am I not the most miserable of men? What sin have I committed that such a wretched fate should overwhelm me? I love you and I have made you cry—"

23

"Nay, my lord," whispered Julia through her tears, "an you loved me—"

She paused with well-calculated artfulness, whilst he murmured with pathetic and tender reproach:

"An I loved you! Is not my heart bound to your dainty feet? my soul fettered by the glance of your eyes? Do you think, Mistress, that I can ever bear to contemplate the future now, when for days, nay! weeks and months, ever since I first beheld your exquisite loveliness, I have ever pictured myself only as your slave, ever thought of you only as my wife? That old castle over in Hertfordshire, once so inimical to me, I have learnt to love it of late because I thought you would be its mistress; I treasured every tree because your eyes would behold their beauty; I guarded with jealous care every footpath in the park because I hoped that some day soon your fairy feet would wander there."

Mistress Julia seemed inclined to weep yet more copiously. No doubt the ardently-whispered words of my lord Stowmaries caused her to realise more vividly all that she had hoped for, all that was lost to her now.

Oh! was it not maddening? Had ever woman been called upon to endure quite so bitter a disappointment?

"It's the shame of it all, my lord," she said brokenly, "and—" she whispered with tenderness, "I too had thought of a future beside a man whom I had learned to—to love. I suffer as you do, my lord—and— besides that, the awful shame. Your favours to me, my lord, have caused much bitter gall in the hearts of the envious—my humiliation will enable them to exult—to jeer at my discomfiture—to throw scandalous aspersions at my conduct—I shall of a truth be disgraced, sneered at—ruined—"

"Let any one dare—" muttered the young man fiercely.

"Nay! how will you stop them? 'Tis the women who will dare the most. Oh! if you loved me, my lord, as you say you do, if your protestations are not mere empty words, you would not allow this unmerited disgrace to fall upon me thus."

Who shall say what tortuous thoughts rose in Mistress Peyton's mind at this moment? Is there aught in the world quite so cruel as a woman baffled? Think on it, how she had been fooled. The very intensity of the young man's passion, which had been revealed to her in its fulness now that he knew that an insuperable barrier stood between him and the fulfilment of his desires, showed her but too plainly how near she had been to her goal.

At times—ere this—she had dreaded and doubted. The brilliancy of his position, his wealth and high dignity had caused her sometimes a pang of fear lest he did not think her sufficiently his equal to raise her to his own high rank. At such moments she had redoubled her efforts, had schemed and had striven, despite the fact that her efforts in that direction had—as she well knew—not escaped the prying eyes of the

24

malevolent. What cared she then for their sneers so long as she succeeded?

And now with success fully in sight, she had failed—hopelessly, ridiculously—ignominiously failed.

Oh! how she hated that unknown woman, that low-born bourgeoise, who had robbed her of her prize! She hated the woman, she hated the family, the Parisian tailor and his scheming wife. God help her, she even hated the unfortunate young deceiver who was clinging passionately to her knees.

She pushed him roughly aside, springing to her feet, unable to sit still, and began pacing up and down the small room, the tiny dainty cage wherein she had hoped to complete the work of ensnaring the golden bird.

"Julia!"

He too jumped to his feet. Once more he tried to embrace the quivering shoulders, to imprison the nervous, restless fingers, to capture the trembling lips. But she would no longer yield. Of what use were yielding now?

"Nay! nay! I pray you, leave me," she said petulantly. "Of what purpose are your protestations, my lord—they are but a further outrage. Indeed, I pray you, go."

Once more she turned to the bell-pull, and took the heavy silken cord in her hand, the outward sign of his dismissal. Some chivalrous instinct in him made him loth to force his company on her any longer. But his glowering eyes, fierce and sullen, sought to read her face.

"When may I come back?" he asked.

"Never," she replied.

But we may be allowed to suppose that something in her accent, in her attitude of hesitancy, gave the lie to the cruel word, for he rejoined immediately:

"To-morrow?"

"Never," she repeated.

"To-morrow?" he insisted.

"What were the use?"

"I vow," he said with grim earnestness, "that if you dismiss me now, without the hope of seeing you again, I'll straight to the river, and seek oblivion in death."

"'Twere the act of a coward!" she retorted.

"Mayhap. But Fate has dealt overharshly with me. I cannot face life if you turn in bitterness from me. Heaven only knows how I can face it at all without you—but your forgiveness may help me to live; it would keep me back from the lasting disgrace of a suicide's grave, from eternal damnation. Will you let me come to-morrow? Will you give me your forgiveness then?"

He tried to draw near her again, but she put out her hand and drew resolutely back.

25

"Mayhap—mayhap," she said hurriedly. "I know not—but not now, my lord—I entreat you to go."

She rang the bell quickly, as if half afraid of herself, lest she might yield, after all. Mistress Julia knew but little of love—perhaps until this moment she had never realised that she cared for this young man, quite apart from the position and wealth which he would be able to give her. But now, somehow, she felt intensely sorry for him, and there was quite a small measure of unselfishness in her grief at this irrevocable turn of events. The glance which she finally turned upon him softened the cruelty of his dismissal.

"Come and say good-bye to-morrow," she murmured. Then she raised a finger to her lips. "Sh!—sh!—sh!" she whispered scarce above her breath; "say nothing more now—I could not bear it. But come and say good-bye to-morrow."

The serving man's steps were heard the other side of the door. He was coming in answer to the bell.

Lord Stowmaries dropped on one knee. He contrived to capture a feebly-resisting little hand and to impress a kiss upon the rouge-tipped fingers.

Then after a final low bow, he turned and walked out of the room.

CHAPTER V

There is nothing but roguery to be found in villainous man.

—I Henry IV. II. 4

Mistress Julia Peyton waited for a few moments until the opening and shutting of the outer door proclaimed the fact that young Lord Stowmaries had really and definitely gone.

Then she went to the little secrétaire which stood in an angle of the room, drew forth a sheet of paper, took a heavy quill pen in her hand, and feverishly—though very laboriously—began to write.

It was a difficult task which the fair lady had set herself to do, for neither writing nor spelling were among her accomplishments, being deemed unnecessary and not pertaining to the arts of pleasing. But still she worked away, with hand cramped round the rebellious quill, dainty fingers stained with the evil-smelling black liquid, and her brow

26

puckered with the intensity of mental effort, until she had succeeded in putting on paper just what she wished to say:

"To siR john Ayloff at His resedence in lincoln's inn Filds.
"Honord Sir cosin: This to Tell yo That i wish to speke with yo This da and At ons opon a Matter of life and Deth.
"yr obedt Servt

"Julia Peyton."

A goodly number of blots appeared upon this missive as well as upon Mistress Julia's brocaded kirtle, before she had finished. But once the letter duly signed, she folded and sealed it, then once more rang the bell.

"Take this to the house of Sir John Ayloffe at once," she said peremptorily to her serving man who appeared at the door, "and if he be within bring him hither without delay. If he be from home, seek him at the Coffee Tavern in Holborn Bars, or at the sign of the Three Bears in the Strand. But do not come back until you've found Sir John."

She gave the letter to the man, and, as the latter with a brief word indicative of obedience and understanding prepared to go, she added curtly:

"And if you do not find Sir John and bring him hither within half an hour, you may leave my service without notice or character, but with twenty blows of the stick across your back. You understand? Now you may go."

Then—as the man finally retired—Mistress Julia was left alone to face the problem as to how best she could curb her impatience until the arrival of Sir John.

Her threat would lend wings to her messenger's feet, for her service was reckoned a good one, owing to the many lavish gifts and unconsidered trifles which fell from the liberal hands of Mistress Julia's courtiers, whilst her old henchman—a burly East Anglian relict of former days in Norfolk—loved to wield a heavy stick over the backs of his younger subordinates.

If Sir John Ayloffe was at home, he could be here in ten minutes; if he had gone to the Coffee Tavern in Holborn Bars, then in twenty; but if the messenger had to push on as far as the Strand, then the full half-hour must elapse ere the arrival of Sir John.

And if he came, what should she say to him? Of all her many adorers, Sir John was the only one who had never spoken of matrimony. A distant connection of the late Squire Peyton's, he it was who had launched the young widow on her social career in London and thus enabled her to enter on her great matrimonial venture.

Sir John Ayloffe, who in his early youth had been vastly busy in dissipating the fortune left to him by a thrifty father, was chiefly occupied now that he had reached middle age in finding the means to live with outward decency, if not always with strict honesty. Among

27

these means gambling and betting were of course in the forefront. These vices were not only avowable, they were thought gentlemanly and altogether elegant.

But how to gamble and bet without cheating is a difficult problem which Sir John Ayloffe never really succeeded in solving. So far chance had favoured him. His various little transactions at the hazard tables or betting rings had gone off with a certain amount of luck and not too much publicity.

He had managed to keep up his membership at Culpeper's and other fashionable clubs, and had not up to the present been threatened with expulsion from Newmarket. He was still a welcome guest at the Coffee Taverns where the young bloods congregated, and at the Three Bears in the Strand, the resort of the most fashionable young rakes of the day.

But one or two dark, ugly-looking clouds began to hover on his financial horizon, and there was a time—some eighteen months ago— when Sir John Ayloffe had serious thoughts of a long voyage abroad for the benefit of his health.

This was just before he received the intimation that his cousin— old Squire Peyton—had left a young and pretty widow, who was burning with the desire not to allow her many charms to be buried in oblivion in a tumble-down Norfolk manor.

Although Mistress Julia Peyton knew little if anything of spelling and other book lore, her knowledge of human—or rather masculine— nature was vast and accurate. After half an hour's conversation with her newly-found kinsman, she had gauged the use which she could make of him and of his impecuniousness to a nicety.

He was over-ready, on the other hand, to respond to her wishes. The bargain was quickly struck, with cards on the table, and the calling of a spade by its own proper appellation.

Mistress Julia Peyton was calculated to do credit to any London kinsman who chose to introduce his most aristocratic friends into her house. And remember, Sir John Ayloffe had plenty of these, and was to receive a goodly sum from the young widow for every such introduction. Such matters were not difficult to arrange at a time when money was scarce and love of display great. The fair Julia lost nothing by the business. Her house, thanks to Sir John, was well frequented by the pleasure-loving set of London.

Then there loomed ahead the final and great project: the marriage of Mistress Julia! and herein Sir John's cooperation was indeed to be well paid. From one thousand pounds, up to five, was to be his guerdon, according as his fair kinswoman's second husband was a wealthy baronet, a newly-created peer, or the bearer of one of those ancient names and high dignities or titles which gave him entrées at Court, privileges of every sort and kind, which his wife would naturally share with him.

When the brigantine Speedwell went down off the Spanish coast with all on board, the late Earl of Stowmaries lost at one fell swoop his only son and heir, and the latter's three young boys, who were all on a pleasure cruise on the ill-fated vessel. The old man did not survive the terrible shock of that appalling catastrophe. He died within six months of the memorable tragedy, and Rupert Kestyon—the son of the impecunious spendthrift who was lying forgotten in a far-off grave in a distant colony—became Earl of Stowmaries, one of the wealthiest peers in England.

In a moment he became the most noted young buck of the Court of the Restoration, the cynosure of every feminine eye. He was young, well looking, and his romantic upbringing in the far-off colony founded by his co-religionists, made him a vastly interesting personality.

Mistress Julia, as soon as she heard his name, his prestige, and his history, began to dream of him—and of herself as Countess of Stowmaries. Once more Cousin John was appealed to.

"Six thousand pounds for you, Cousin, the day on which I become Countess of Stowmaries."

Only the introduction was needed. Mistress Julia, past-mistress by now in the art of pleasing, would undertake to do the rest.

Young Lord Stowmaries was a member of Culpeper's. Sir John Ayloffe contrived to attract his attention, and one day to bring him to the house of the fascinating widow.

Sir John had done his work. So had the beautiful Julia. It was Chance who had played an uneven game, wherein the two gamblers, handicapped by their ignorance of past events, had lost the winning hand.

And it was because she felt that Cousin John had almost as much at stake in the game as she had, that Mistress Julia Peyton sent for her partner, when Chance dealt what seemed a mortal blow to her dearest hope and scheme.

CHAPTER VI

'Tis dangerous when the baser nature comes
Between the pass and fell incenséd points of mighty opposites.

—Hamlet V. 2

Less than twenty minutes after the despatch of her missive—

29

twenty minutes which seemed to Julia more like twenty cycles of immeasurable time—Sir John Ayloffe was announced.

He entered very composedly. Having been formally announced by the servant, he waited with easy patience that the man should close the doors and leave him alone with his fair cousin.

He scarcely touched her fingers with his lips and she said quickly:

"'Twas kind to come at once. You were at home?"

"Waiting for this summons," he replied.

"Then you knew?" she asked.

"Since last evening!" he said simply.

He was of a tall, somewhat fleshy build, the face—good-looking enough—rendered heavy by many dissipations and nights of vigil and pleasure. His eyes were very prominent, surrounded by thick lids, furtive and quick in expression like those of a fox on the alert. The heavy features—nose, chin and lips—were, so 'twas said, an inheritance from a Jewish ancestress, the daughter of a rich Levantine merchant, brought into England by one of the Ayloffes who graced this country in the days of Richard III.

It was the money of this same ancestress which had enriched the impoverished family, and had at the same time sown the seeds of that love of luxury and display which had ruined the present bearer of the ancient name. From that same Oriental ancestress Sir John Ayloffe had no doubt inherited his cleverness at striking a bargain as well as his taste for showy apparel. He was always dressed in the latest fashion, and had already adopted the new modes lately imported from France, the long vest tied in with a gaily coloured sash, the shorter surcoat with its rows of gilded buttons, and oh! wonder of wonders, the huge French periwig, with its many curls which none knew better than did Sir John how to toss and to wallow when he bowed.

His fat fingers were covered with rings, and the buckles on his shoes glittered with shiny stones.

Julia, quivering with eagerness and excitement which she took no pains to conceal, now dragged Sir John down to a settee beside her.

"You knew that my lord of Stowmaries was a married man, and that I have been fooled beyond the powers of belief!" she ejaculated, whilst her angry eyes searched his furtive ones, in a vain endeavour to read his thoughts.

"I heard my lord's miserable story from his own lips last night," reiterated Sir John.

"Ah! He told it then over the supper table, between two bumpers of wine, to a set of boon companions as drunken, as dissolute as himself? Man! man! why don't you speak?" she cried almost hysterically, for she had suffered a great deal to-day, her nerves were overwrought and threatening to give way in the face of this new and horrible vision conjured up by her own excited imagination. "Why don't you describe the whole scene to me—the laughter which the tale evoked, the sneers directed against the unfortunate woman who has been so hideously fooled?"

Ayloffe listened to the tirade with the patience of a man who has had many dealings with the gentle if somewhat highly-strung sex. He patted her twitching fingers with his own soft, pulpy palm, and waited until her paroxysm of weeping had calmed down, then he said quietly:

"Nay, dear coz, the scene as it occurred round the most exclusive table at the Three Bears, in no way bears resemblance to the horrible picture which your fevered fancy has conjured up. My lord of Stowmaries told his pitiable tale in the midst of awed and sympathetic silence, broken only by brief exclamations of friendship and pity."

"And my name was not mentioned?" she asked, mollified but still incredulous.

"Not save in the deepest respect," he replied, whilst a line of sarcasm quickly repressed rose to his fleshy lips. "How could you suppose the reverse?"

"Ah, well, mayhap, since women were not present. But they will hear of it, too, to-day or to-morrow. The story is bound to leak out. My lord of Stowmaries' attentions to me were known all over the town—and to-day or to-morrow people will talk, will laugh and jeer. Oh! I cannot bear it," she added with renewed vehemence; "I cannot—I cannot—I verily believe 'twill drive me mad."

She rose and resumed her agitated walk up and down the small room, her clenched fists beating one against the other, her trembling lips murmuring with irritating persistency.

"I cannot bear it—I cannot bear it. The ridicule—the ridicule will kill me—"

Suddenly she paused in her restlessness, stood in front of Sir John and let her tear-dimmed eyes rest on his thick-set face.

"Cousin," she said deliberately, "you must find a way out of this impasse."

"You must find a way out of it," she reiterated firmly.

He shrugged his shoulders, and said drily:

"Fair Mistress, you may as well ask me to reconcile the Pope of Rome and all the hierarchy of the Catholic Church to the idea of flouting the sacrament of marriage, by declaring that its bonds are no longer indissoluble. The past few centuries have taught us that in Rome they are none too ready to do that."

"I was not thinking of such vast schemes," said Julia in tones as dry as his had been. "I was not thinking either of corrupting the Roman Church, or of persuading one of her adherents to rebel against her. My lord of Stowmaries has already explained to me," she continued with bitter sarcasm, "that against the Pope's decision there would be no appeal—he himself would not wish to appeal against it. His love for me is apparently not so boundless as I had fondly imagined, its limits meseems are traced in Rome. He has given me to understand that his wife's people—those—those tailors of Paris—actually hold a promise from the Pope that a command will be issued ordering that their daughter be installed and acknowledged as Countess of Stowmaries and that without any undue delay. Failing which, excommunication for my lord, scandal, disgrace. Bah! I know not!—these Romanists are servile under such tyranny—and we know that not only the Duke of York, but the king himself is at one with the Catholics just now. No—no—no—that sort of thing is not to be thought on, Cousin, but there are other ways—"

Her eyes, restless, searching, half-fearful, tried to fix the glance of his own. But his shifted uneasily, now responding to her questioning look, anon trying to avoid it, as if dreading to comprehend.

"Other ways, other ways!" he muttered; "of a truth there are many such—but none of which you, fair Cousin, would care to take the risk."

"How do you know that?" she retorted. "There are no risks which I would not run, in order to free the man I love from the trammels of an undesired marriage."

Cousin John said nothing in reply. His eyes, still furtive in expression, were no longer restless. They were fixed upon the beautiful face before him, the luminous eyes, the daintily-curved mouth, the rounded chin—a transparent and exquisite mask which scarcely concealed now the strange and tortuous thoughts which chased one another behind that white brow, smooth as that of a child.

She held his gaze, willing that he should read those thoughts, wishing him to divine them; in fact, to save her the humiliation of framing them into words. But as he seemed disinclined to speak, she reiterated with slow and deliberate emphasis:

"There are no risks, Cousin, which I would not run."

"'Tis nobly said," he remarked, without attempting this time to conceal the sarcastic smile which played round his sensuous lips. "Odd's fish! the man whom you have honoured with such sublime devotion is lucky beyond compare."

"A truce on your sneers, Sir John," she retorted imperiously; "you said that there were several ways whereby that hateful marriage could be annulled. What are they?"

Sir John Ayloffe glanced down the length of his elegant surcoat; with careful hand he smoothed out a wrinkle which had appeared in the well-fitting breeches just above his knee, he readjusted the set of his fringed scarf, and of his lace-edged cravat. All this took time and kept Mistress Julia on tenter hooks, the while she felt as if her temples would burst from their throbbing.

Then, at last, Cousin John looked up at her again.

"Poison," he said drily; "an Italian stiletto an you prefer that method. An hired assassin in any event—"

A shudder ran down her spine. Had she really harboured these thoughts herself, and had Cousin John merely put her wild imaginings into words? Thus crudely put they horrified her—for the moment—and she looked down almost with loathing on the man who accompanied each grim suggestion with a leer, which caused his thick lips to part and to disclose a row of large, uneven teeth stained with tobacco juice and giving his face a cruel expression like that of a hyena.

"You see, there are always means, fair Cousin," continued Sir John with pleasing urbanity; "it is only a question of money—and of the risks which one is prepared to run. Beyond that, I believe, that the task, though difficult, can be accomplished in Paris. There are some amiable gentry there ever ready to do your bidding, whatever it may be, provided you are generous—"

She passed the gossamer handkerchief over her dry lips.

"I had not thought of crime," she murmured.

"Had you not?" he said blandly. "Yet 'tis the most easy solution of the difficulty."

"But there are others," she insisted.

"I fear not."

Again she paused, then continued, speaking very low, scarce above a whisper.

"You would help me, of course?"

"I could certainly go over to Paris," he said with marked hesitation, "always providing I were plentifully supplied with money—a voyage of reconnaissance, you understand—nothing more—"

"Which means that you will not help me."

"The risks are too great, Cousin—I—"

"You would not care to run them, in order to be of service to me?"

"Frankly—no!"

"And suppose, Cousin John," she now said more quietly, once more sitting down beside him, "supposing, I say for the sake of argument, that I were to come to you and tell you that I will give half of my fortune to the man who will at this juncture so ordinate matters that my marriage with the Earl of Stowmaries once more becomes not only feasible, but inevitable. What then?"

"Then—also for the sake of argument," he rejoined blandly, "I would ask you, fair Cousin, of what your fortune consists."

"Squire Peyton left me £20,000 and the principal is still intact."

"Deposited—where?"

"The bulk of it with Mr. Brooke the goldsmith. He pays me six per cent. per year thereon. It hath sufficed for my needs. No one—except you, Cousin, now—knows the extent of this fortune. Half of it will suffice me for pin money, once I am Countess of Stowmaries. My lord would marry me—if he were free—an I had not a groat to my

33

name, nor more than one gown to my back. Ten thousand pounds shall be yours, Cousin, if you can bring this about."

"Call it £12,000, Mistress, and it shall be done," he said cynically.

"How will you do it?"

"Let that be my secret for the nonce."

"I'll give you no advance, remember," she said quickly, for she had seen the swift glitter of joy in his eyes, at the first mention of money, and she knew full well that she could not count on the most elementary feelings of honesty on the part of this unscrupulous gambler.

"Then I can do nothing," he concluded decisively.

"What do you mean?"

"Only this, fair Cousin, that putting aside the question—a somewhat humiliating one for me, you must admit—that your refusal to place certain funds in advance in my hands, implies a singular and—if I may say so—an ill-considered want of trust on your part; putting this question aside, I say, you must understand that nothing in this present world can be accomplished without money, and I am reduced to my last shilling."

"Have I not said that £10,000 shall be yours the day that my marriage with Lord Stowmaries is irrevocably settled?"

"£12,000," he corrected suavely.

"Very well, then, £12,000. We'll have the bond duly writ out and signed."

"And you, fair Cousin, will immediately place in my hands a first instalment of £2,000."

"Failing which?"

"As I have had the honour to tell you, I can do nothing. This is my last word, fair Cousin," he added, seeing that Mistress Julia still seemed inclined to hesitate.

There was silence in the little room for a few seconds, a silence all complete save for the solemn ticking of a little French clock over the hearth. Sir John Ayloffe lounging on the settee with one firm leg clad in the new-fashioned tight breeches stretched out at full length, the other doubled inwards, so that the satin shimmered and crackled over his knee, his jewelled hands toying with the lace cravat, or with the dark curls of his periwig, looked now the picture of supreme indifference.

It almost seemed as if £12,000 more or less in his vest pocket would affect him not at all. But the fleshy lids had half-closed over the prominent eyes, and from beneath their folds he was watching the fair young widow, who made no attempt to hide her hesitancy and her perturbation.

He knew quite well that his personality, the weight of his whole individuality, would win against her prudence in the end. He was fully aware that among the crowd of her several adorers, she had no one to whom she could confide her present troubles, no one whose aid she could with so much surety invoke. Few were so resourceful, none quite so unscrupulous, as Sir John Ayloffe where his own interests were at stake.

That £12,000 which was to be his price would mean the final ending of his shiftless career. He felt himself getting older every day, and the thought of what the morrow might bring—a morrow when he would no longer be active and alert, neither amusing nor interesting to those whose company was a necessity to his livelihood—that thought was embittering his present life, until at times he wondered whether a self-inflicted sword thrust to end a miserable existence were not the most desirable contingency after all.

How he would earn that £12,000 he did not know as yet. His secret was that he did not know. But he had lived for the past twenty years in sublime ignorance of the various shifts which he might be put to from day to day, and he knew that he could trust to his imagination to find a means now, when the result would mean security in old age, peace from that eternal war against chance—almost a fortune in these days when money was scarce after the great turmoil of civil war.

Therefore, though he said no more, though he assumed an indifference which he was very far from feeling, he not only watched Mistress Julia, but with every nerve within him, with all the magnetism of his powerful personality, he willed her to accede to his wishes.

She, feeling this subtle influence in the same manner as in ages to come mediums were destined to feel the influence of hypnotic power, she gradually yielded to his unspoken desire—yielded to him whilst believing that she held the threads of her own destiny, and that the final decision only rested with her.

Then she rose and went to that same little bureau in the angle of the room, at which just an hour ago she had penned so laboriously the missive which had summoned Sir John Ayloffe hither. This time, as she sat down to it, she took from beneath her kerchief a small key which was fastened round her neck by a silk ribbon. With this she opened one of the drawers of the bureau, and after another moment of final hesitation she deliberately took a packet from the drawer.

The packet was tied up with green cord; this she untied with a hand that trembled somewhat with feverish excitement. Having selected a paper from among a number of others, she once more fastened the green cord, replaced the packet in the drawer, locked the latter and replaced the key in the folds of her gown.

Then paper in hand she turned back to the settee whereon lolled Sir John Ayloffe, and holding the paper out to him, she said:

"This is an order requesting Master Brooke, goldsmith, of Minchin Lane, to hand over to you on my behalf the sum of £2,000."

Sir John roused himself from his well-studied apathy. He took the paper from Mistress Julia's hand, looked at it very carefully, then folded it and prepared to slip it in his breast pocket.

35

"Remember, Cousin," she said calmly, "that if I find that you have deceived me in this, that you have deliberately robbed me of this £2,000 without having any intention or power to help me in my need, that, in such a case you will lose the only friend you have in the world. I will turn my back on you for ever; you shall never darken the threshold of my door, and if I saw you in want or in a debtor's prison, I would not pay one farthing to help you in your need. You believe that, do you not?"

"I believe that a woman thwarted is capable of anything," he retorted with a sneer.

"There I think you are right, Cousin," she assented, whilst a look of determination which assorted strangely with her otherwise impulsive ways marred for a moment the childlike prettiness of her face. "You would find me very hard and unforgiving, if you cheated me of my hopes."

"Very hard, I doubt not," he said blandly. "Did I not see a while ago, fair Cousin, your gentle soul taking in with scarce a thought of horror my first suggestion of poison or hired assassin?"

"Tush, man! prate not so lightly of these things. Bah!" she added with some of her former vehemence, "there are other things that kill besides poison or stilettos—things that hurt worse than death—things that no Countess of Stowmaries could endure and live. You have your £2,000, man—go—go and think—a fortune an you succeed."

Sir John Ayloffe smiled. The lady had at last shown to him—mayhap without meaning to do so—the real desire of her heart. She had also set his active brain athinking. As she said, it would be a fortune if he succeeded.

He had placed the valuable paper carefully away in his breast pocket; he tapped this pocket gently to feel that it was secure. Then—as obviously the interview must now come to an end—he rose to go.

Vague thoughts were already floating in his mind, and when she too rose to bid him farewell, and her fevered eyes found his and held them, he responded with a look of distinct encouragement.

Long after Cousin John's footsteps had ceased to echo along the short flagged corridor, Mistress Julia Peyton sat musing, whilst a sigh of content and of hope ever and anon escaped her lips. Her face was quite serene, her expression one of anticipation rather than of trouble. Never for a moment did a pang of conscience trouble her. Remember, that the unknown Countess of Stowmaries—the daughter of the Paris tailor—was but a shadowy personality to her. Less than two hours ago, Mistress Julia was not aware of her existence.

Was it wrong then to wish her out of the way? With commendable satisfaction, the outraged beauty realised that she felt no direct wish for any bodily harm to come to her successful rival. And pray, how many women would have had such scruples? A certain feeling of self-righteousness eased Mistress Julia's soul at the thought.

36

No. She wished the real and only Countess of Stowmaries no bodily harm. She had made Cousin John understand that, she hoped. Crime might mean remorse, which would be unpleasant, also fear of discovery. Mistress Julia hoped now that she had made Cousin John understand quite clearly that she wanted neither poison nor hired assassin for the end which she had in view—not at first at any rate—later on, mayhap—if other schemes had failed—

There are things which hurt worse than death—and Mistress Julia had placed in the hands of an unscrupulous gambler the means whereby such things could easily be brought about.

If such things be crimes, they certainly were not of the kind which troubled Mistress Julia's conscience.

Having settled these abstract points to her own satisfaction, she adjourned to her tiring-room and rang for her maid. She told the wench to prepare that new butter-coloured satin gown with the pink rosebuds broidered thereon—a vastly becoming gown for setting off the fair Julia's style of beauty—and also the colverteen pinner which had the advantage of making any woman look demure. She had her hair redressed in the newest fashion with immense taure and puffs which made her small head look wide and her tiny face more childlike and innocent than ever.

She meant to finish the day at the King's Playhouse, there to witness a vastly diverting comedy by the late Master Shakespeare. She wished to see and to be seen by His Majesty, by the Duke of York, and all London society. Knowing that her name would be in everybody's mouth, she wished to appear radiant with beauty and good spirits, and in no way concerned with the ugly rumours anent the tailor's daughter over in Paris, and the ridiculous cock and bull story that my lord of Stowmaries was other than engaged to wed Mistress Julia Peyton ere the London season had fully run its course.

37

CHAPTER VII

Enquire at London 'mongst the taverns there.

—Richard II. V. 3

You know the place well enough, or failing yourself—if so be that you are less than three-score years and ten—then your father would remember it well.

It was situate in the Strand until that time, close to its junction with Fleet Street and within a pebble's throw from St. Clements. A tall narrow building, raftered and gabled, the timbers painted a dark chocolate colour, with alternate lines of a luscious creamy tint rendered mellow with the dirt and smoke of London. It stood on that selfsame spot two hundred and more years ago, when it was the favourite resort of that band of young rakes who adorned the Court of the Merry Monarch.

It were somewhat difficult to say why my lord of Craye, or Sir Anthony Wykeham, or the Earl of Stowmaries had chosen this very unprepossessing tavern for their evening assemblies. The exterior, as your father could tell you, was certainly not inviting, for the gables were all askew, the stories low and widening one over another, all awry as if ready to fall, the front door, too, was cracked from corner to corner, nor were the public rooms much more alluring. In the coffee room the window with its small panes of bottle glass hardly allowed any daylight to filter in; the floor had once been neatly covered in bricks, but now most of these were broken in half, with pieces of them missing, showing little three-cornered holes which suggested dirt-grubbing insects and storehouses of dust.

There were other disadvantages, too, about the place, which should have scared off any fastidious young man however bent on pleasure he might be, but we have it on M. Misson's own authority— and he was no great admirer of things English and speaks somewhat ill-naturedly of everything he saw during his voyage—that the cellars at the sign of the Three Bears were exceedingly well stocked with Spanish and Rhenish wines and even with French brandies which were heady and vastly pleasing to the palate first and to the temper afterwards.

We are also told by that same highly-critical French traveller that Mistress Janet Foorde, wife of the landlord of the Three Bears, could turn out a better supper than any other cook in London, and fashioned a lamprey pie, or a fricassée of rabbits and chickens, in such a delicious manner that once eaten it could never be forgotten.

Be that as it may, we know it for a fact that in this year of grace 1678 the Tavern in the Strand at the sign of the Three Bears was, every evening after the hour of eight, frequented by the very élite of London society. Supper was served in one of the smaller rooms at a table around which sat those same gentlemen who in the earlier part of the day had graced His Majesty's levee, or the Court of the unhappy Queen, or that narrow circle which stood as a phalanx round the person of the unpopular Duke of York.

The assembly purported to be political. There was more than a mere suggestion of Roman Catholic discontent freely expressed around that congenial board, and it was well known that on more than one occasion the King himself had been present at these gatherings— incognito, of course—his identity known only to his own intimate friends.

But the discussion of the political and social position of Roman Catholics in England, was, we must admit, not the primary object of the nightly reunions in the private room at the Three Bears. Supper after the play in the King's House came first, then dice, hazard or the more fashionable game of Spanish ombre, all well interlarded with the chief gossip and scandals of the day.

Reputations for beauty, wit or morals were made or marred around that table in the small room; the latest fashions were discussed, which to adopt and which to reject. The young fops fresh from the Grand Tour here recounted their impressions, displayed—for approval or disfavour—the latest modes from Paris, the new surcoats, the monstrous periwigs, the very latest notion in lace cravats.

Here, too, the young rakes aired their—oft scandalous—literary efforts, bonsmots unfit for ladies' ears were invented and retailed, and we all know that my lord of Rochester never thought of publishing verse or prose without first submitting it to the censorship of the select party at the Three Bears.

We may take it that Sir John Ayloffe—despite the vicissitudes of fortune which had brought him to the pass of empty pockets and of unavowable shifts—was still a persona grata at the nightly assemblies of the distinguished tavern, for some few hours after his interview with his beautiful kinswoman on this memorable evening of February 8th, 1678, we see him turning his footsteps unhesitatingly in the direction of the "Three Bears" in the Strand.

Closely wrapped in his cloak, for the wind blew bitter gusts, he bent his head against the driving rain as he walked. The rickety door of the tavern stood invitingly open and as one accustomed to the place Sir John with quickened steps entered the narrow passage.

Immediately his nostrils were greeted with the pungent odour of onions and of boiling fat, and his ears with loud shouts of merriment, which raised a boisterous echo in the tumble-down building and seemed to make the walls totter on their insecure foundation.

This hilarious noise, wherein songs, sung in hoarse voices very much out of tune, mingled with violent outbursts of prolonged laughter and with volleys of full-toned oaths, proceeded from behind a door on the cracked panels of which the ten letters of the word Coffee Room tumbled one against the other, like a row of drunken men.

For a moment Sir John paused just outside that door, bending his ear to listen in an attitude of deep attention, like one trying to catch one special sound from out that confused babel which went on within.

The passage in which he stood had been wholly dark but for the dim, uncertain light which came from a brass lanthorn suspended from the blackened ceiling just above his head. Sir John waited a second or two, until a loud and merry shout of laughter rose above the bibulous din. It was the laughter which comes from a young and lusty throat, the laughter of careless irresponsibility and of thoughtless debauchery.

It seemed to be also the sound for which Sir John had been waiting in the ill-lighted passage outside, for now he threw up his head and flung his cloak back with a gesture of satisfaction, whilst a strange laugh, which had but little of merriment in it and a great deal of contempt, broke from his lips as an echo to the light-hearted gaiety beyond.

Sir John now continued his way, past the Coffee Room to a door beyond the stairway at the extreme end of the passage. This he threw open without further ceremony and found himself in that small room of the tavern, wherein Master Foorde—the host—served his more distinguished guests. As a rule merriment and noise, equal at least to that which obtained in the public coffee room, reigned in this private sanctum: many would have said that the great and courtly gentlemen who foregathered here indulged usually in carouses and drunken orgies which would have put the more plebeian merrimakers to shame.

But to-night, at the moment that Ayloffe entered the room, a kind of sullen silence reigned therein. Through the thick haze of tobacco smoke which hung like a grey pall above the feebly flickering light of some half dozen tallow candles, the newcomer could perceive four faces—flushed with wine and heavy meats, dimly outlined against the full greyness of drab-coloured walls, and dark oak wainscotting.

The candles themselves guttering in their sockets threw forth fillets of thick grimy smoke which mingled with the fumes of tobacco, and helped to cast fantastic and trembling shadows on fine cloth surcoats and vests of broidered silk. From the coffee room immediately adjoining the parlour came—echoing faintly through the thick timbered walls—the shouts of laughter, the loudly-uttered oaths, the ribald songs of the merry company, and at intervals, against the tiny panes of the small casement window the dull patter of the rain or the occasional distant call of the watchman challenging an evening prowler.

In the furthest angle of the room, my lord Rochester seated in the chair of honour had apparently been reading aloud to this moody company, the expressions of his latest poetic fancy. He was in the act of rolling up his manuscript and tying it up with a length of rose-coloured

40

ribbon, but his face usually so self-satisfied and so gay bore an expression of keen discontent.

As a rule his poems—highly prized by the king and the ladies—were listened to here among the circle of his intimates with the greatest delight and oft with noisy appreciation. But on this occasion he had been quite unable to hold the attention of his audience, and even whilst he read his most impassioned verses he could not help but notice that all eyes were fixed on the young Earl of Stowmaries, who sat with his head resting in his hand, leaning forward half across the table in an attitude of the deepest dejection.

The young man had arrived late, only joining the convivial party when supper was already at an end, and Mistress Foorde had removed the remains of the finest venison pie which she had ever concocted.

He had taken his place at the table after a curt and sullen nod to the company who had greeted him most sympathetically. He had declared himself unable to eat, but had ordered a bottle of strong sherry and also a bottle of brandy, which expensive liquid—so 'twas said afterwards by some of the company present—he freely mixed with sherry and drank very plentifully.

The story of his unfortunate early marriage and of his hopeless passion for Mistress Julia Peyton had somehow or other leaked out, and before his arrival had been freely discussed in a facetious and irresponsible spirit.

"Old Rowley liked the tale, and was vastly amused thereby," Lord Rochester had said, thus unceremoniously referring to the merry King of England. "I told it him in all its bearings, and he laughed immoderately at thought of a tailor's wench being actually married to my lord of Stowmaries, and expecting to be presented at Court. But after that first outburst of hilarity he looked very grave and said that the matter must presently be arranged to the satisfaction of all those concerned."

"But how can that be done?" queried Sir Anthony Wykeham, who was a strict Catholic and liked not this light talk of breaking marriage vows.

"Bah! money will do a great deal nowadays," sighed Sir Knaith Bullock, a young Irishman but scantily blessed with the commodity.

"As for me," quoth my lord Rochester with easy bonhomme, "I am on the side of the angels. Mistress Julia Peyton is the most beautiful woman in London. She at any rate would be worthy to become chatelaine of Maries Castle and to be our hostess in the many feasts to be given there to my lord of Stowmaries' friends. As for a tailor's daughter!—Bah!—gentlemen, I ask you, can we see ourselves being entertained by a tailor's daughter? She would feed us on pottage and small beer—"

A roar of laughter greeted this exposé of the situation. Lord Rochester had of a truth voiced the opinion of the majority.

41

"But—" protested Sir Anthony Wykeham.

"Tush man," interrupted my lord with scant ceremony. "I know what you would say. The marriage sacrament and all that—Odd's fish! we are none of us heathens, and ye Papists are not the only ones, by my faith! who know how to keep vows. But there are other ways of unravelling an undesired tangle—and old Rowley had no thought of suggesting irreligious measures—"

"Hush!" said one of the others suddenly, "I hear Stowmaries' voice outside. I fancy he'll not be in a mood for jesting over the matter."

It was at this point that Stowmaries had entered the room. There was no doubt that he looked excessively glum, and the first attempts at treating his disappointed love in a hilarious manner were met with such obvious moodiness, that gradually the subject was dropped, and the company, who at supper had been fairly numerous, soon began to dwindle away, each seeking in turn more cheerful society than that of this sober young man who seemed determined to look at his own future life in its very blackest aspect.

Only Lord Rochester remained awhile longer for he wanted an audience for his latest poem, also Sir Anthony Wykeham—an intimate friend of my lord Stowmaries—and Sir Knaith Bullock, an irresponsible youth who seemed to scent an adventure in the romantic child-marriage, and vaguely hoped to find sport therein.

These three gentlemen with Lord Stowmaries himself formed the little group around the table of the private parlour at the "Three Bears" at the moment that Sir John Ayloffe entered it.

CHAPTER VIII

I was a nameless man; you needed me:
Why did I proffer you my aid? there stood
A certain pretty cousin at your side.

—Browning.

With a quick glance thrown on each of the four faces, shrewd Sir John had quickly appraised the mood of this small clique. Stowmaries in sullen rage against the whole world because of this thwarting of his most cherished desire, Rochester and the Irishman, flippant and eager for sport, with Wykeham as the sobering influence, the self-constituted guardian of religious obligations.

It was also obvious to this keen observer of other people's moods that there would be no need for circumlocution. Though silence reigned in the room, the subject of Stowmaries' marriage was uppermost in the minds of his friends.

Sir John therefore, having thrown aside his hat and cloak, went boldly up to the table and greeting the others with easy familiarity, he placed one fleshy hand on Stowmaries' shoulder and said abruptly:

"Tush man! be not so downhearted. My faith on it! have I not seen worse plights even than yours? Yet from which a man of daring and resource soon found a means of extricating himself."

The interruption was a welcome one, for though Sir John Ayloffe was no longer very popular with the gilded clique of young and noble rakes, since he was known to be at his last resources and was oft in sore straits to pay his gaming debts, nevertheless at this moment his lusty, cheery voice helped to dissipate the gloom which was such an unusual atmosphere for these ribald pleasure-seekers to breathe, and one or two voices with obvious signs of relief cordially invited the newcomer to sit.

"Then you, too, know our friend's melancholy story?" queried Lord Rochester as he pushed with hospitable intent a mug of wine in the direction of Ayloffe.

"Yes," replied the latter. "Mistress Julia Peyton is my kinswoman. 'Tis from her I heard the tale."

Stowmaries' frown grew even darker than before. He liked not the suggestion thus implied, the more than obvious hint of this second sentimental complication in his life.

Sir John, in the meanwhile, had selected a chair, which was less rickety than most, and sat down deliberately in such a position that not one of the flickering and uncertain rays of candle light touched his face or illumined its expression.

He took the cup of wine offered him by my lord Rochester and drank it down slowly and at one draught, the while a few ribald remarks flew across the table. Ayloffe's advent seemed certainly to have brought a new atmosphere into the room. Despite Stowmaries' frown and Wykeham's protests, Rochester and Sir Knaith took up the lighter side of the past events; they refused to appreciate the solemnity of the subject or the serious obligations resulting from that solemn sacrament of matrimony performed between children over eighteen years ago.

Sir John waited patiently whilst a volley of somewhat coarse jests was fired at the gloomy hero of the romantic adventure, and until he saw that Stowmaries was on the verge of losing his temper, and Wykeham on the point of quarrelling with Bullock.

Then he pushed the empty cup away from him and leaning forward across the table, he broke in quietly: "Nay Sir Anthony," he said with pleasing urbanity, "we all know what you would say. 'Sdeath! an I mistake not you have harped on that string passing often in the last hour or so, and we all know too that Lord Stowmaries is not

43

desirous of seeing it snap. But I maintain that if a gentleman is placed in so terrible a predicament as is my lord, then it is the duty of all his friends to try and effect an honourable rescue."

The earnestness with which he spoke had silenced the jocose as well as the moody tongues. But Sir Anthony Wykeham now protested hotly.

"That is impossible," he said. "The sacrament of marriage cannot be set aside."

"Only under certain conditions," corrected Sir John.

"Methinks this is braggart's talk," muttered young Bullock who had no love for the older man.

"How will you do it?" queried Stowmaries with moody hopelessness.

"With his tongue chiefly," sneered the Irishman.

But Ayloffe seemed in no way abashed by the hostility, which his statement had evoked; he returned the sarcastic or angry glances levelled at him with a stare of assurance.

Leaning heavily upon the table, his prominent eyes fixed boldly on the over-excited faces before him, he looked a strange contrast to the small, chattering crowd which was grouped around him. Unlike the others, he had supped soberly at home and drunk little or no wine; his head was clear, his tongue glib, and the only uncertainty apparent in his demeanour was that with which from time to time he seemed to be listening to the noise in the next room; then a look of vague doubt would suddenly overshadow his steady gaze and cause a more furtive, more anxious look to creep into his eyes.

"Nay, gentlemen," he resumed after a slight pause vaguely smiling in a condescending manner like one who tells an obvious fact to a child, "'tis no braggart's talk to speak of saving a friend from the most dire calamity that can befall any man. I repeat most emphatically that this can be done, effectually and easily and without interfering with any of those religious scruples which do my lord of Stowmaries and his friend here so much honour."

He spoke so quietly, so confidently and with such an air of certitude that instinctively the sneering tongues ceased to aim their shafts at him and four pairs of eyes were now fixed upon the speaker, who with a calm gesture of indifference was readjusting the lace of his cravat.

He waited thus for awhile like the true entertainer who husbands his effects; he waited until the circle round him drew closer and closer, until four pairs of elbows rested on the table and flagons and mugs were impatiently pushed aside.

Sir Anthony Wykeham was the last to hold aloof, but even he said at last with a distinct ring of excitement in his voice:

"Tell us more fully what you mean, man! Cannot you see that Stowmaries is devoured with impatience?"

"An impatience which I am over-anxious to relieve," rejoined Ayloffe imperturbably, "but firstly let me ask Lord Stowmaries himself—who I assert is a wealthy man—whether he would not give a good tenth of his fortune to be conveniently rid of an unwelcome wife, without hindrance to his belief or conscience."

"I would give half my fortune, good Sir John," sighed Stowmaries dolefully.

"Half is too much, good my lord," responded Sir John blandly. "Popular rumour deems your lordship worth some four hundred thousand pounds in solid cash, besides the rent rolls of half Hertfordshire. Methinks one fourth of that should purchase the freedom which you seek."

"Are you minded to earn that fortune, Sir John?" asked the other not without a sneer.

"Nay, my lord, I am neither young enough, nor sufficiently well-favoured for that desirable task," retorted Sir John imperturbably.

"What have looks or favours to do with it all? Odd's fish!" growled Stowmaries more vehemently, and bringing a clenched fist crashing down upon the table so that mugs and bottles rattled, "meseems that you, Sir John, are trying to fool me, God help me! are even trying to bring ridicule upon my sorrow! By the Mass, sir, if that be so, you'll not find me in a mood to be trifled with."

"Good my lord, I pray you to calm your temper. Am I a man to trifle with your feelings? Have I not professed myself to be your friend? am I not the kinsman of the lady whom you have honoured with your addresses? On mine honour I have her welfare at heart even more so than yours. Can you wonder that I should wish to see you wed her?"

Shrewd Sir John had played a trump card. There was no denying the logic of his statement. He had owned to having much at stake, yet had done so with no lack of dignity. With a certain graciousness not altogether free as yet from his original surliness, Lord Stowmaries owned himself in the wrong.

"You must pardon my evil temper, Sir John," he said with a self-deprecating sigh, "for I am vastly troubled."

This brief interlude had but whetted the curiosity of the others. From Sir John's manner and mode of speech it was fully evident now that his was no empty talk, but that he had assuredly come here this night, with some definite plan for what he termed the welfare of his kinswoman, which no doubt he had much at heart.

The idea pleased these young pleasure-seekers more and more; they cared of a truth but little for the troubles of their friends, but there was now a twinkle in Ayloffe's eyes which vaguely suggested to them the thought of intrigue, mayhap of some adventure, quite unavowable, possibly highly scandalous, which would have that unknown tailor's daughter for its victim.

Such adventures were the delight of the merry monarch who now

45

sat upon the English throne, whose advent had been so earnestly desired, whose personality had been so ardently worshipped. He it was who set the fashion for those gallant episodes which were the boast and delectation of men and the shame and the sorrow of women. But for him and the example set by him I doubt if Sir John Ayloffe would ever have thought of formulating proposals which should have put his present companions to the blush, and which carried subsequently in their train agonies of remorse and of disgrace, wounded honour and more than one broken heart.

CHAPTER IX

Strictly, 'tis what good people style untruth
But yet, so far, not quite the full-grown thing!

—Browning

Sir John Ayloffe leaned back in his chair, and satisfied that he once more held the close attention of the company, he resumed pleasantly:

"Will you, good my lord, and all of you gallant gentlemen grant me five minutes wherein to place before you the situation as it at present stands? Here is my lord of Stowmaries tied by so-called indissoluble marriage vows to a bride whom he doth not desire for wife, and whom he last saw borne away kicking and screaming in the arms of a waiting wench. And there over in Paris is the daughter of a worthy tailor, a girl born in a back shop, presumably ill-favoured and certainly vulgar, but who has pretensions of being Countess of Stowmaries de facto as well as de jure. She it was who eighteen years ago was as aforesaid borne away kicking and screaming in the arms of a waiting wench. She was then not much more than twelve months of age, and has not since that moment seen my lord of Stowmaries here, our gracious, if—momentarily—somewhat troubled friend."

A sneering grunt from Sir Knaith Bullock, a groan from Stowmaries and a murmur of assent from the others were audible whilst Sir John paused for breath.

"The Catholic Church for which we all have deep respect," continued Ayloffe, "doth not allow that the bonds of matrimony thus contracted eighteen years ago shall be severed just because my lord of Stowmaries doth not happen for the moment to have a desire for the tailor's daughter; she having done naught to merit repudiation, since

46

her being carried away kicking and screaming from the presence of her lord when her age had not reached fifteen months, doth not constitute a serious offence in the eyes of the law."

"We know all that, man, we know all that," quoth Stowmaries moodily, "and by the Mass you repeat yourself like a country parson in the pulpit."

"Gently, good my lord," rejoined Ayloffe imperturbably. "What I have to say is a somewhat delicate matter. I am dealing with a Countess of Stowmaries—and if you did not accept my scheme—"

He paused and shrugged his shoulders in token of self-deprecation.

"It may not after all meet with your favour."

"Out with it, man—out with it," came, partly gaily, wholly impatiently from every side.

"'Tis simple enough," said Sir John, "but were easier to say an you, gentlemen, would help me by guessing—My lord of Stowmaries hath not seen his bride, nor was he seen by her, since she was little more than a year old—that is so, my lord, is it not?"

"It is," assented Stowmaries curtly.

"Impressions at that age are not lasting. Infantile memory doth not hold an image. We may assume that if the tailor's daughter were placed in the presence of—er—of any gentleman of noble bearing, she would not know if he were her lord—or not."

There was silence around the table now. Neither assent nor dissent followed Ayloffe's last words. On the face of the young Irishman curiosity still remained impressed. The suggestion so slightly hinted at had not yet reached his inner consciousness; on that of Lord Rochester comprehension had just begun to dawn, a sense of astonishment plainly struggled with one of doubt. But Sir Anthony Wykeham almost imperceptibly drew his chair somewhat away from the table.

Lord Stowmaries in the meanwhile kept his eyes steadily fixed on those of Sir John. They expressed neither doubt nor astonishment, only intense excitement, an obvious desire to hear that hint more fully explained. It was his hoarse mutter "Go on! curse you—why don't you go on?" that first broke the momentary silence which had fallen over the small assembly.

"Nay!" rejoined Ayloffe blandly, "I see that you, at least, my lord, have already taken me. Is not my scheme vastly simple? The tailor's daughter awaits her lord. He comes. She falls into his arms, and after the usual festivities in the back shop of her estimable parents, the bridegroom takes his bride home to far-off England. But mark what hath occurred—it was not my lord of Stowmaries who had gone to claim his bride, but some other man who prompted by his passion for the tailor's beautiful daughter, a passion—we might even suppose—encouraged by the lady herself, had impersonated the bridegroom and snatched the golden prize despite my lord of Stowmaries and the most

47

solemn vows of matrimony contracted eighteen years ago. Imagine the result: the shame, the crying scandal! My lord of Stowmaries is of a surety no longer bound to acknowledge a wife whose very name will have become a byword for every gossip to peck at, and whose virtue hath already been the toy of an adventurer as unscrupulous as he was daring. Not the Catholic Church, not the law of England, nor the decree of the Pope would enforce the original marriage vows after that. I give you my word, gentlemen, that my lord of Stowmaries will be granted leave by every high tribunal, spiritual or temporal, to repudiate the wench who had thus disgraced his name."

Sir John Ayloffe had long finished speaking and silence still reigned all around him. Even the noise in the next room seemed for the moment unaccountably to have ceased. Folk say that when such silences occur in merry company, angels fly across the room, and the flutter of their wings can distinctly be heard. What angels then were these who haunted the private room of the "Three Bears" now? What record of ignominy and dishonour did they mark upon the tablets of infinity when with gentle flutter of wings they passed silently by? To the credit of all these gentlemen here present be it said, that their first feeling was one of shame, when they fully understood the dastardly suggestion which Sir John was making to one of themselves; but the shame was not acute enough to produce horrified repudiation.

Sir Anthony Wykeham certainly still held aloof, but Stowmaries had not winced. That he understood the suggestion to the full, there could be no doubt. His face had flushed to the roots of his hair, his fingers were fidgeting nervously against one another and excitement verging on intoxication caused his eyes to glow with an unnatural inward fire. His thoughts had flown straight back to the prettily furnished parlour in Holborn Row, to Mistress Julia Peyton's violet eyes and the exquisite scent of her white hands when he had pressed them to his lips. His love for her—call it passion or desire an you will—had grown in intensity as the obstacle which separated him from her had seemed more and more insurmountable. In the past few hours that same passion had reached a stage of fever heat, impatient at control, chafing at impotence and longing for satisfaction with all the strength of thwarted desire.

Rupert Kestyon, Earl of Stowmaries and Riveaulx, had been brought up in the hard school of colonial life; in his boyhood he had been denied every kind of pleasure and luxury in which the sense of youth revels, through what he called an unjust Fate; then suddenly he had seen himself thrown in the very lap of Fortune, his every desire satisfied and his every whim made law. The change was sudden enough to throw off its balance a more firm character than that of the son of Captain Kestyon—spendthrift, profligate, a rogue from temperament. Like his father's, Rupert's was essentially a weak nature. He had never attempted to fight Fate, when Fate was against him. When Fortune smiled, he took everything she offered him without attempt at restraint;—and the jade had become very lavish with her gifts to the young outcast who awhile ago had often enough been obliged to tighten his belt against the gnawing pangs of hunger.

He had found friends, followers, sycophants; had been favoured by royalty and smiled on by beauty, but Mistress Peyton was the first passion in his life. He had flirted with her for months, made easy love to her for weeks, but he had not realised that he loved her until twenty-four hours ago when he knew that she was lost to him.

The knowledge that here was the chief desire of his heart, and that this desire he could not gratify, despite his position, his personality and his wealth, almost unhinged his mind. It was two years now since he had exercised any self-denial. He had lost all knowledge of that useful art, and was determined not to learn it again.

The day on which he heard that through an appalling catastrophe, which had swept his kindred into the sea and broken the heart of an old man, he, Rupert Kestyon, the penniless son of a spendthrift father, had become rich, influential, one of the greatest gentlemen in the kingdom, he had said with a sigh of genuine satisfaction: "Now I mean to live!" and with him living meant solely the gratification of his every wish. Now he saw his greatest wish in all the world born only to be thwarted.

It was monstrous, unthinkable! But from that wholesome fear of ecclesiastical authority peculiar in those days to men of his creed, he would have rebelled. Respect for the Church to which he belonged, dread of a scandal which might tarnish the great name he bore, and undermine his pleasant position alone caused him to be submissive.

He was not clever enough to find out a means of freeing himself from irksome bonds, and had drained the cup of despair to its bitter dregs without thinking or even hoping for an issue out of his misery.

But now a man spoke—a man whom in his saner moments he heartily despised, whom he knew to be shiftless, unscrupulous, a born gambler—but yet a man who showed him a way out of the quagmire of despair into a possible haven of hope.

He had not been long in catching Ayloffe's meaning. Whilst the others doubted he had already seen the possibilities of success. His bride had never seen him since consciousness grew into her brain; her parents' only recollections of himself dated back eighteen years! Why indeed should not some other man impersonate the bridegroom, carry the bride away and thus forever after leave on her fair maiden name a stain which would render her unfit to be acknowledged as the wife of any honourable gentleman?

How simple it all seemed!

Unlike his friends here present, Stowmaries saw no shame in the scheme—no shame, let us say to himself! Disgrace to the woman—yes! but he did not know her, and he hated the very thought of her! Disgrace perhaps to the scoundrel who would undertake the ignoble treachery! but to the Earl of Stowmaries who would sit quietly at home whilst the roguery was being carried on by others?—'Sblood! who would suggest such a ridiculous idea?

His eyes wandered round the table. Sir Anthony Wykeham was no longer frowning and Lord Rochester had laughed—a little nervously perhaps—but no one had actually protested.

There was no gainsaying the fact that Ayloffe was a rogue to suggest so profligate a scheme, but profligacy was all the rage now and vastly pleased the King.

"By Gad, a mad notion!—But a right merry one!" quoth Sir Knaith Bullock, himself a rogue and as full of dare-devil schemes as an egg is full of meat.

The remark loudly spoken and accompanied by a blasphemous oath and the loud banging of a clenched fist against the table, eased the tension finally. Even Wykeham began to laugh. Not one of these young men here had wanted to feel ashamed, rather did each one desire to seem a vast deal worse than his neighbour. It was no good allowing the recollections of early lessons in chivalry to mar the enjoyment of the present merry life; not even if those lessons had been taught by a father who had died fighting for King and cause.

Let the ball of pleasure be set rolling; that ball partly made up of love of devilry, partly of ennui seeking for amusement and of contempt for woman's virtue.

"'Twere rare sport!" said Rochester.

Sport! The word acted like magic and shame was completely vanquished by the pleasing sense of excitement.

Bah! what was the virtue, the fair name, the happiness of a tailor's daughter worth, in the face of the vastly pleasing entertainment she herself would provide for her betters.

"An ignoble trick to play on a woman," murmured Wykeham.

But his protest had become very feeble. He saw nothing in the suggestion that shocked his religious scruples, for the rest he cared but little. The victim was only a tailor's daughter after all, and Stowmaries—his friend—would not be the one to repudiate his marriage vows.

"Bah! a tailor's daughter!" was the gist of the argument in favour of the scheme.

"She shall have full compensation," quoth my lord Stowmaries somewhat tonelessly, for his throat felt parched and his tongue seemed to be several sizes too large for his mouth.

He drank down a large bumper full of sherry into which Ayloffe had unobtrusively thrown a dash of raw brandy.

"Have you forgotten, gentlemen," now said gallant Sir John lustily, "that my lord of Stowmaries will give seventy thousand pounds to the friend who will help him in his need. A fortune methinks, which should tempt any young gallant in search of romantic adventure and a pretty wife."

"But the details, man! the details!" came from every side, "surely you have thought of them!"

"And of the risks!" suggested Lord Rochester, who was practical, and who had oft suffered because of his gallant adventures.

"There are no risks, gentlemen," quoth Sir John Ayloffe, "not to us at any rate, nor yet to my lord Stowmaries. As for the tailor and his family, believe me they will be so covered with ridicule, that they will not cause his lordship a moment's anxiety. Just think on it! To give away one's daughter to a man who is not her husband! to greet him with festivities and merrimaking, to kill the fatted calf in honour of the man who brings dishonour into one's home! Nay! Nay! The breeches-maker of Paris will have cause to keep silent after the adventure. The maid perchance will retire into a convent, and the gallant adventurer can brave the world in comfort with seventy thousand pounds in his pocket."

"Bravo! Well said!—But the details?—how will you work, it, Ayloffe?"

Obviously the scheme was commending itself more and more to these over-heated brains. There were no shame-faced looks round the table now. Stowmaries did not speak; his excitement was too keen to find vent in words, and he was shrewd enough to realise at once that Ayloffe did not mean to give away the details of his plans to this trio of young addle-pated rakes.

But cries of "The details, man, the details!" became more and more insistent. Sir John, glass in hand, at last rose in response.

"The details are simple enough, gentlemen, and now that I have your approbation, I will be quick enough in working them out. In the meanwhile let us drink to the gallant adventurer who must help us in our scheme. We do not yet know his name, who he is or whence he comes; the fairy Prince who will free my lord Stowmaries from irksome bondage and the tailor's daughter from the fetters of a respectable home. What we do know is that this Prince must be young, else he could not pass for milor of Stowmaries, he must be well-favoured, else the lady might fight shy of him; but he may be as poor as the proverbial church mouse, since seventy thousand pounds, and the fortune of the richest tailor in Paris are jointly to be his. Come, gentlemen, will you take my toast?"

Loud banging of pewter mugs against the deal table greeted this merry sally. The young men jumped to their feet.

"To him! To the unknown!" they shouted laughing with one accord. There were loud calls for Master Foorde, and confused orders for more Spanish wine. Sir John called for brandy, and anon when the worthy hosteler filled the bumpers all round the table, Ayloffe followed him adding brandy here and there to the wine, laughingly insistent, praising the quality of the liquor for inducing to gaiety and all the elegant qualities of amiable drunkenness so fashionable in a gentleman of the period.

He was quite clever enough not to make any further direct allusions to the scheme, the realisation of which meant the transference of twelve thousand pounds from Mistress Julia Peyton's pocket into his own. So far he had gained the first stake in the game which he had set himself to play, and was content for the moment merely to addle still further the heads of these young reprobates by wild talks of adventure, and sly allusions to the delights of coming scandal, mixed with sweeping sarcasm directed at feminine virtue in general and the morals of the Paris bourgeoisie in particular.

He knew well enough that Stowmaries was at one with him by now, but that he never would have succeeded in persuading the young man to enter into such villainous schemes, if he had been alone with him.

Away from the glamour of his rakish friends, of the atmosphere of the tavern, of the smell of wine and tobacco, Stowmaries' better nature and the inherited instincts of honour would have rebelled against the roguery. Any of these young men here present would individually have repudiated the monstrous proposal whilst collectively they were over-ready to trample on any nascent idea of chivalry, each one ashamed to be called squeamish or Puritanical by the other. There was nothing really depraved in these young men, only a desire to outdo each other in profligacy, in a show of anti-Puritanism, the immediate outcome of the enforced restraint of the past generation.

Ayloffe knew this, and, therefore, he had chosen the supper hour, and the presence of a select number of the worst rakes in London— Rochester and Bullock—for testing Stowmaries' willingness to enter into his own villainous scheme. He wanted the support of confused brains, of rowdy excitement, of shouts and of laughter to drown the preliminary call of conscience. This once smothered, would probably never lift a warning voice again, and details could be comfortably settled in private later on.

"Believe me, gentlemen," he said gaily, "that that tailor's minx will thank us all on her knees for the entertainment which we will provide for her. Odd's fish and I mistake not she hath but little stomach for becoming an honourable British matron, and you may be sure that 'tis only her parents who force her into an unwelcome marriage. We shall be the rescuers of beauty in distress, and will provide the wench with such an adventure as will draw the eyes of half Europe upon her and give her that notoriety which all women prize far beyond those virtues which are only vaunted by the old and ugly ones of their own sex. A bumper on it, gentlemen! I pledge the tailor's minx, ill-favoured though she be—my word on that! she'll become the talk of London—I drink to her adventure—and to the bold man who will share in it—By my halidame, were I but twenty years younger, I'd apply for the post myself."

Ayloffe's irresponsible talk, and the heady wines mixed with alcohol completed the work of destruction. Lord Stowmaries and his friends contrived within the next hour or so to lose more self-respect than their fathers had gained in a lifetime through sublime adherence to a forlorn cause.

CHAPTER X

But indeed words are very rascals since bonds disgrace them.

—Twelfth Night III. 1

I think that we shall have to accept Sir Anthony Wykeham's account of how the proceedings finally terminated. He avers that by the time the church clock of St. Clement's had struck the hour of ten, Sir John Ayloffe was the only man present in that small private room who could at all be called sober.

At that hour my lord of Rochester it seems lay right across the table with flushed face hidden in the bend of the elbow, snoring lustily at intervals and at others lifting a heavy head in order to hurl a bibulous remark at impassive Sir John or over-excited Stowmaries: Sir Knaith Bullock had quite frankly exchanged the rickety incertitude of Master Foorde's chairs for the more solid level of the floor, where after sundry struggles with a tiresome cravat and a persistently wry perruque he lay amidst the straw and the unsavoury postprandial debris that littered it, in comfort and security.

Wykeham, according to his own account, had lapsed into somnolent sulkiness, vaguely listening to the ribald jests and coarse oaths uttered by the others, and to the monotonous murmur of Sir John's voice as he explained the details of his scheme to Stowmaries.

The latter had certainly drunk more brandy than was good for the clearness of his brain. Excitement, too, had wrought upon his blood, with the result that the events of this night took on the garb of some over-vivid dream: but, as soon as he realised that his perceptions were becoming too confused to take in Ayloffe's varied suggestions, he made a vigorous effort to regain possession of himself. He called for a bowl of iced water, and dashed its contents into his face and across his eyes. After that he steadily refused to drink any more, nor did Sir John press him any further.

The insinuating poison had done its work: there was no fear now that Stowmaries would wish to draw back.

"I pray you draw your chair nearer, my lord," said Ayloffe after awhile when of a truth he saw that the rest of the company was quite helpless, "these gentlemen are not like to disturb us now."

With unaccountable reluctance Stowmaries did as the older man bade him, and presently the two men withdrew altogether from out the circle of dim light thrown by the guttering tallow candles.

"Your lordship, I take it then, agrees with the broad basis of my scheme," said Ayloffe, speaking quite low, only just above a whisper. "You are anxious to free yourself from this undesired marriage, and you think that my suggestion is one which will most easily help you to accomplish this purpose?"

"That is so," assented Stowmaries readily.

"On the other hand," continued Ayloffe, "your lordship is prepared to pay the sum of seventy thousand pounds to the man who will impersonate your lordship in the house of M. Legros, merchant tailor of Paris, who will—in your name and person—claim the Legros girl as his wife, and go through the necessary civil and religious ceremonies that will ratify the original marriage; and, finally, who will undertake not to reveal his own identity to the tailor's daughter until you, my lord, will grant him leave. For these services," concluded Sir John with emphasis, "is your lordship prepared to pay the vast sum of seventy thousand pounds?"

"More than that," replied Stowmaries in an excited whisper, which rendered his voice hoarse and his tongue stiff and parched. "More than that and money down: fifty thousand pounds on that day that he signs and seals the bargain with me, and starts on his errand for Paris, and a further seventy thousand on the day that the tailor's daughter leaves her parents' home in his company. A hundred and twenty thousand pounds! mine honour! my life upon it. But where in the name of Hell will you find the man to take it?"

By way of an immediate reply, Sir John placed a warning finger to his mouth, then rose and beckoning to the other to follow him, he went to the door which divided the private parlour from the public Coffee Room, and throwing it open he pointed to the rowdy company who sat assembled each side of the oblong trestle table.

"Amongst that crowd," he whispered with an insinuating smile.

CHAPTER XI

Good-night, good sleep, good rest from sorrow
To these that shall not have good morrow.

—Swinburne

At first when Sir John Ayloffe threw open the door of the public room, Stowmaries was only conscious of an almost Satanic din; he certainly could see nothing through the dense cloud of smoke which filled every corner of the long, narrow hall.

Gradually, however, his eyes, still dimmed from recent libations and acute excitement, became accustomed to this haze-covered gloom, whilst his ears distinguished isolated sounds, drunken songs, loud oaths or hoarse laughter from out the deafening roar which surged towards him like the noise of breakers against a rock.

A narrow deal table ran from end to end of the room, from the main door at the top to the small latticed window at the bottom. The floor was strewn with rushes on which sprawled recumbent figures in various stages of drunken sleep, in the very midst of a litter of debris, broken glasses, overthrown mugs, patches of spilt wine or ale, bones and remnants of pastry and of bread—all evil-smelling and unspeakably dirty. On the table itself the remnants of pies and cooked meats, and a forest of empty mugs and bottles. One by one the tallow candles which had been placed at intervals throughout the whole length of the table had thrown up their last flicker of feeble light, had spluttered their last with a hissing sound and finally died out in a column of grimy smoke.

There were but some half dozen or so left now, which threw uncertain yellow gleams through the thick veil of tobacco fumes, on the prostrate figures that sprawled across the table, on overthrown goblets and jugs, on all the unsavoury debris—remnants of the past orgy.

The rest of the room was in darkness, and through the gloom the figure of a young man, with flushed face and dark brown hair innocent of perruque, moved backwards and forwards to the rhythmic cadence of a boisterous chorus of song.

The draught from the badly-fastened window wafted the strips of cotton which hung in lieu of curtains, straight into the room, with a swishing, moaning sound around which—soft though it was—could be heard like a long drawn-out sigh of pain, in the pauses of lusty laughter and of ribald song.

The storm outside seemed to have ceased, for, as the curtains blew away from the window the pale, ghost-like streaks of moonbeams searched the darkness of that end of the room and found here a fold of satin tattered and frayed, there a broken paste buckle, or rusty sword hilt on which to play its weird gamut of faint and ghoulish rays.

The noise was incessant, merriment mixed with quarrelsome oaths, lively songs alternating with hoarse shouts. All those who were not snoring babbled incoherently, swore or sang; Irish brogue mingling with broad Yorkshire tones, round Scotch oaths striking against Gaelic ones, whilst from time to time, a noisome word loudly flung from end to end of the table like a filthy rag would rouse one of the sleepers and spur him to respond to the challenge with vile blasphemy.

At times the clink of a sword would cut sharply through the buzzing air, the beginnings of a quarrel, a volley of vituperations, a pewter mug or half-empty bottle thrown right across the table scattering its contents over tattered coats and already much-stained vests: then the hoarse admonitions of the peacemakers, the first refrain of a song by way of a diversion, more lively, more out of tune than before, and laughter and jests once more reigned supreme.

Stowmaries gazed on this scene, the while he still felt that somnolent feeling of being in a dream, enveloping his senses. He heard the noise and saw the figures swaying to and fro, moving on unsteady legs, in and out of the narrow circles of yellow light like gnomes dancing the figures of a saraband, in the anteroom of Hell.

The figure of the young man at the extreme end of the room fascinated him. He could not discern the face clearly, only as a flushed mask with the pale moonbeams touching the dark hair with their ghostly rays.

"'Tis your cousin Michael," whispered Ayloffe close to his ear.

Stowmaries gave a sudden start. He understood now why Sir John had shown him this scene, the picture of this rowdy crowd composed of the ne'er-do-well, unclassed profligates who had flooded the country ever since the Restoration, hurrying back to England from Flanders or from Spain, under the guise of Royalist loyalty which had suffered exile for the great cause, and was now eager and ready for reward.

Boisterous, unscrupulous, disrespecters of persons and of dignity, they traded on the people's avowed dislike of the canting Puritans who had ruled in England for so long. Jeering, mocking and carousing they filled London with their noise, the open scandal of their lives, the disgrace of their conduct.

By day they paraded the streets loudly singing licentious songs, dressed in the rags and tatters of cavalier accoutrements long since thrown away, seeking the peaceful citizen with the Puritan leanings, who chanced to find himself in their way and holding him up to ridicule, the butt of their uncontrolled merriment.

By night they filled the taverns and coffee houses of the city and only the small hours of the morning witnessed their final retirement

56

into the small brothels of evil repute where alone they could obtain lodgings.

There were hundreds of these men about the London streets during the few years which followed the Restoration. The great plague had decimated them somewhat, the fire of 1666 had scattered some of them broadcast, but in this present year there were still a goodly number of them about. They were the terror of the night watchmen and the despair of the ill-organised and inefficient police-patrols, and rendered the lesser streets of the city well-nigh impassable to quiet citizens and to decent women.

And it was amongst these men that Michael Kestyon was most often to be found; shouting with them by day, drinking and gambling with them by night. Michael Kestyon, cousin to my lord of Stowmaries and like him descended from those who in mediæval days had writ their name largely on the pages of history: Michael, the ne'er-do-well, the wastrel, the profligate: Michael the idler who strove in such company to forget that he had been born a gentleman, and that he held a claim to the title and estates of Stowmaries which many thought was passing just.

CHAPTER XII

Oh, the strife
Of waves at the stone, some devil threw
In my life's mid-current thwarting God.

—Browning

For Michael Kestyon was a man with a grievance. A just grievance enough since many held that he and not his cousin Rupert should have been the present Earl of Stowmaries.

But possession in those far-off days was even more absolutely an integral part of the law than it is now. Rupert Kestyon was de facto established at Maries Castle, whilst Michael had to begin life by selling his sword or his skin to the highest bidder, and all because his father and grandfather before him had been either very supine or hideously neglectful of their own respective son's interests to enforce the decree of King Edward III anent the family succession.

That the decree existed no one attempted to deny; it was embodied in a document which with other family archives was actually in the possession of Michael Kestyon the pretender. These papers in

57

fact were the only inheritance bequeathed to him by his father, besides a legacy of hatred and covetousness against the usurpers of the name and fortune of Stowmaries. But ye shall judge if the reigning earls were usurpers or not.

It seems that in those distant days when Edward III reigned over England and France, the then Lady of Stowmaries presented her lord with twin boys, born within an hour of another. Fine boys they were, so tradition hath it, well grown and sturdy and as like to one another as two peas lying in the same pod.

The fond mother as she gazed proudly upon these children—who of a truth were each endowed with a powerful pair of lungs—little guessed the mischief which their joint arrival would cause in the ancient and noble family of Kestyon.

According to the laws of military tenure, the eldest of these two boys—older remember than his own brother only by a short hour or so—should have been held to be the heir to the titles, dignities, lands and appurtenances held in fief direct by the Lord of Stowmaries from his suzerain liege Lord Edward III by the Grace of God King of England and of France.

But as evil chance—presided over by some imp of mischief— would have it, the twins—when scarce a few hours old—being placed by my lady's tiring-woman side by side in the bed, presently took to vigorous quarrelling. My lady thereupon was much perturbed and her women were all hastily summoned to her bedside, so that they might administer such soothing draughts as were usual under the circumstances.

When my lady was once more restored to her former quietude she asked for her boys, requesting that the eldest be first placed in her arms.

Alas! the mischief was done! The tiring-woman could not remember which child she had lain on the right side of the bed, and which on the left, nor could her astuteness combined with the adoring mother's searching eyes state positively afterwards which boy was heir to the barony of Stowmaries, and which the mere younger son.

Imagine the confusion which ensued. Stories of innumerable quarrels between the brothers as they grew up to boyhood's estate have been handed down to their posterity. The father himself was at a loss what to do. He had a great love for both his boys, and not knowing which was the elder and which the younger son, he had a vast fear of doing an injustice either to the one or to the other.

What could he do but ask the advice and ascertain the wishes of his suzerain liege? This we are told he did as soon as the children had reached the mature age of ten and owed military service to their lord.

King Edward III we all know was a model of justice and of sound common sense. He declared it impossible that either of the boys should be deprived of what might be his lawful inheritance. Therefore, by a special decree signed by his own hand manual, he declared that on the death of his faithful cousin, the Baron of Stowmaries, the title, estates in fief or military tenure and other lands and appurtenances thereof should devolve jointly on the twin sons of the said lord, and that the first born child in the next generation should then once more reunite in his own person the titles and estates of Stowmaries.

Moreover the King decreed that if at any future time, a Lady of Stowmaries should take it into her gracious head to present her lord with twins, this same rule of succession should apply.

Thus said His Majesty King Edward III, and my lord of Stowmaries was thereby satisfied. The brothers were henceforth brought up as joint heirs of one of the finest baronies in the Kingdom and we hear nothing more of family feuds or dissensions.

That the twins eventually did jointly succeed to their father's title and estates we know from the records anent the twin Barons of Stowmaries who fought under the banner of John of Gaunt in the days of Richard II; and from the fact that King Henry IV in 1410 created the then Baron of Stowmaries, Earl of Stowmaries and Riveaulx we may infer that one of those turbulent twins did have a son who succeeded alone to his father and uncle, and once more united in his own person all dignities and lands belonging to the ancient family.

Thus the carelessness of a tiring-wench had for the time being no further serious consequences on the fortunes of the Kestyons. For some generations to come it seemed that the ladies of Stowmaries had no predilection for twins. But in the year 1552, so the family archives tell us, the wife of John, Earl of Stowmaries—Grand Master of the Ceremonies to King Edward VI—presented her lord with a sturdy pair of boys.

As like to one another as the proverbial peas were these two new scions of the ancient family of Kestyon, and mightily proud of them was their fond mother, but there never was any confusion as to their identity. One of them—Rupert—was born fully two hours before his brother Michael, and was ever after looked upon as his father's heir. Nor, on the death of the Earl, did any one seem to have thought of disputing his sole right to the title and estates of Stowmaries.

Rupert succeeded his father and in his turn was succeeded by his son. But what we do know as a certain fact is that Michael, the younger twin, had a son born to him a full year before his elder brother took unto himself a wife, and that if the decree of King Edward III had been duly enforced by law, Rupert and Michael should have been joint Earls of Stowmaries and it should have been Michael's son—the first born in the next generation—who should have united the title and estates in his own person.

Why Michael did not endeavour to enforce the ancient decree of Edward III we shall never know: there are neither letters nor other documents to explain this supineness, which is all the more inexplicable since it affected the future of his own son even more than his own.

We are concerned with the present generation. With Rupert, Earl of Stowmaries, the direct descendant of the older twin, and with Michael Kestyon, the grandson of the younger.

Such as I have related is the true history of the grievance which this Michael nurtured against his cousin whom he deemed an usurper, and against all his peers, kinsmen and fellow gentlemen for the injustice which they abetted by admitting that usurper as one of themselves.

But unlike his father and grandfather before him Michael was not content to see any one else in possession of the family title and estates, which of a truth should have been his. From his father he had inherited among other family archives the mediæval document embodying the decree of Edward III and bearing that monarch's signature. How and wherefore this had remained as an heirloom in this branch of the family, tradition does not tell us. The fact seems to suggest that the younger twin—Michael—may have had some intention of enforcing his son's claim at a future time—an intention, mayhap, frustrated by death.

The man whom Lord Stowmaries saw at this moment, with flushed face and unsteady voice singing ribald songs to the accompaniment of boisterous laughter, chink of dice and sword, and blasphemous oaths, had at one time taken up his own cause with ardent and heart-whole enthusiasm.

At the age when boyhood first yields to maturity, Michael had lost his father and thereupon had begun to fight for his rights, with all the strength of a turbulent nature, full of instincts of luxury and driven to penury through flagrant injustice. He had spent some of the best years of his life, in a perpetual appeal to the King and to his peers to try his cause and if necessary to find it just. But the King was not fond of settling important questions himself and the Lords' House of Parliament was overbusy re-establishing a number of its own lapsed privileges to bother about a claimant with empty pockets.

Driven from pillar to post, Michael appealed to Common Law, to Chancery and to equity, setting up divers pleas in order to bring his case within the jurisdiction of these respective Courts. He spent all his substance in lawyer's fees, in sworn documents, in meeting constant demands for bribery, the while his kinsman sat comfortably enthroned at Maries Castle paying no heed to a claim, the justice of which one attempted to deny yet which no one was able legally to enforce.

Gradually as his pockets grew more and more empty, as constant rebuffs took the edge off his optimism, Michael carried on the fight with less and less hope if with unabated doggedness.

In the intervals he had sold his sword and his skin to the highest bidder, to Italy or Flanders, to the Emperor or to the King of France.

60

He had led the life of the adventurer, who knows not from day to day whence will come the rations for the morrow, of the soldier of fortune who has neither kindred nor home.

His mother whom he adored—in his own turbulent passionate way—spent a life of humble penury in a remote Kentish village. To this lowly abode of peace Michael returned from time to time from his far-off wanderings in Sicily or Spain; here he would spend some few days in worshipping his mother, until the agony of seeing her patient and serene within measurable sight of starvation drove him frantic from out her doors.

Then he would rush back to London and once more haunt the Courts and the purlieus of Whitehall, swallowing his outbursts of pride in vain supplications for a fresh hearing, in a mad desire to see the King, in licking the dust before the feet of those who might help him to further his cause.

At those times self-deprecation would render him moody; his pleasure-loving nature was swamped beneath the heavy pall of a mother's want, a mother's sorrow and misery. He despised himself for being unable to lift her out of such humiliating penury. She who should be Countess of Stowmaries, one of the greatest ladies in the land, scrubbed her own floors and oft lacked a meal, the while her son, the able-bodied and reckless adventurer, was eating out his heart with the shame of his own impotence.

But what he could not accomplish whilst the scanty means left to him by his father were still at his command, he was totally unable to obtain now that he had not one stiver to offer to those who might have helped him but whose palms seemed forever to be in want of grease.

Blood-money abroad had also become more meagre. The King of France and the Emperor had their own standing armies now, and had less need of mercenary troops than of yore. Michael who in battle sought wounds as another would seek cheap glory, was given but twenty crowns for a sword thrust which he received at Fehrbellin whilst fighting for the Elector of Brandenburg.

He nearly died of the thrust, and afterwards of starvation, for he sent the twenty crowns to his mother, and being considered too enfeebled for active service, he could not immediately obtain further enlistment.

This was but one of the many episodes which had helped to make Michael Kestyon what he now was. A bitter sense of wrong gnawed at his heartstrings, the while he strove to hide his better nature beneath the mask of boisterous gaiety, of a licentious life and reckless gambling.

The buffetings of law officials, the corrupt practises of second rate attorneys, the constant demands on his scanty purse now made up the sum total of his dealings with humanity, when he was not actually in the company of adventurers more profligate, more dissolute than himself.

61

He saw the better world—that world which was composed of his own kindred—turned, as if in arms against him. Not a friend to give him help save at a price which he could not afford to pay. It was money and always money: money which he could not get, and without which he saw the last chance of getting a hearing for his case vanishing beyond his reach.

The descent from those early boyish days full of idealism and of hope, down to the lowest rung of the social ladder, to the companionship of gamesters and of drunkards, had been overcertain and none too slow. Accustomed to the revelries of camp life, to that light-hearted gaiety so full of exuberance to-day and oft the precursor of a bloody death on the morrow, Michael found the England of the Restoration a mercenary and inhospitable spot.

Among his own kind, mockery of his vain endeavours; among the others—the wastrels—a life of boisterous merrimaking which at any rate made for forgetfulness.

CHAPTER XIII

My conscience hath a thousand several tongues
And every tongue brings in a several tale,
And every tale condemns me for a villain.

—Richard III. V. 3

In response to Ayloffe's whisper, Stowmaries had asked hurriedly:

"Is this the man?"

The older man nodded, and Stowmaries gazed long and searchingly upon his cousin, vaguely wondering if Sir John's astuteness had pointed in the right direction, if indeed this were the man most likely to lend himself for a large sum of money to the furtherance of an ignoble scheme.

Stowmaries saw before him a man—still in the prime of life but on whom dissipation, sleeplessness by night and starvation by day had already boldly writ their impress; a man like unto himself in feature, a distinct family resemblance being noticeable between the two cousins, but in Michael Kestyon—the reckless adventurer—the evenly placid expression born of a contented life had long ago yielded to the wild, hunted look, the mirror of a turbulent soul. He wore a surcoat which was obviously of rich cloth though the many vicissitudes of camp life had left severe imprints upon its once immaculate surface: beneath this coat there peeped out innocent of vest, the shirt, which once had been wrought by loving fingers, of fine linen and delicate stitchery, but now presented the appearance of a miscellaneous collection of tatters and darns with here and there a dark stain on it, which spoke of more than one sword thrust in the breast, of the miseries of that life of fighting and of toil, of aches and pains and of ill-tended wounds.

The rest of Michael's attire was in keeping with the surcoat and the shirt: the faded silk sash long since deprived of tassels, the collar free from starch, the breeches a veritable motley of patchwork, and the high boots of untanned leather, stained a dark greenish brown from exposure to constant damp.

This then was the man who was most like to sell himself for so much money, and Stowmaries noting the squalor of Michael's attire, the dissipated yet wearied look in his face, ceased to wonder how it came that Sir John had thought of this wastrel, and in his mind fully approved of the choice.

Suddenly Michael Kestyon caught sight of the two men standing under the lintel of the door. He greeted them at once with a shout of welcome.

"My worthy coz!" he said gaily, "and if I mistake not 'tis gallant Sir John Ayloffe, the finest rogue that ever graced a court. Gentlemen!" he continued mocking, and advancing with mincing and unsteady steps towards the two men, "pray tell us—though by the Mass I call you right welcome—what procures this humble abode the honour of such distinguished company?"

Whilst the young man spoke, most of his companions had ceased both song and laughter; several faces—all flushed with heady liquor— were turned towards the door, whilst glances wherein suspicion fought with the confusing fumes of alcohol, were directed on the newcomers.

But Sir John Ayloffe with determined good humour had returned Michael's greeting with easy bonhomie.

"Nay, friend Michael," he said, the while he prudently closed the door behind him and Stowmaries, lest the noise in the coffee room awaken his sleeping friends, "your amiable cousin and I myself were tired of the sober assembly in the parlour and had desire for more merry company. I hope your call of welcome was no mere empty word, and that of a truth we may join your hospitable board."

With much gravity Michael surveyed Ayloffe and Stowmaries up and down, from the diamond buckles on their shoes to the elaborate curls of their gigantic perruques; then he turned to his friends, who had followed his every movement with that solemn attention peculiar to the drunkard, which tries yet fails to comprehend what is going on before him.

"What say you, gentlemen?" he said, "shall we admit these noble rogues to our table? My cousin here, as you see, has but lately emerged from the surveillance of his keeper, he inhabited a monkey garden for a considerable time, and hath collected a vast amount of hair on his head from the shavings of his many companions."

A terrific and prolonged shout of laughter shook the very walls of the room, the while Stowmaries, who suddenly had became pale with rage, placed a quivering hand on the hilt of his sword.

"Insolent beggar!—" he murmured in a hoarse voice, which, however, was completely drowned in the bibulous noise which had greeted Michael's impertinent sally and which rose and fell in a continuous roar for some considerable time, the while Michael himself, satisfied at the effect which he had produced, struck up the refrain of a drinking song.

"In the name of the lady whom you honour with your love, good my lord," whispered Ayloffe close to Stowmaries' ear and with impressive earnestness, "I entreat you to keep your temper. We have need of this wastrel for the success of our scheme, and a quarrel would of a surety ruin it completely."

Michael Kestyon now turned to his cousin once more.

"I pray you take your seats, gentlemen," he said pointing with unsteady gesture to a couple of empty chairs placed at the head of the table, "though you may not be aware of it, my friends here have shown a desire for the continuance of your presence amongst us. Had they not desired it they would have shown their disapproval by various hints more or less gentle, such as the throwing of a pewter mug at you or the elevation of their toe to the level of your majestic persons. But as it is ye may rest assured, ye are welcome here."

"I thank you, good Michael," said Ayloffe pleasantly, as in response to Michael's invitation he now advanced further into the room and took his seat at the head of the board, followed by Stowmaries who was making vain attempts to conceal his contempt of the proceedings, and to master his ill-humour.

"Indeed," continued Sir John addressing with gracious familiarity the united company present, "I know not what we have done to deserve your favours. Believe me, we came as suppliants desiring to be entertained by the most noted merrimakers in London."

Michael with the same mock gravity once more resumed his place at the table close beside Sir John Ayloffe. He drew two mugs towards him and from a gigantic pewter jug, he poured out full measures of a thick red liquid, which had the appearance of spiced wine.

The beverage certainly exhaled a remarkable methylic odour, which from the nostrils seemed to strike straight into the brain making the blood seethe in the head and the eyes glow as with the heat of running fire. Moreover the mugs which Michael had filled, and then pushed towards the newcomers were not over clean. Even Sir John had much ado to keep his outward show of geniality and to mask his friend's more and more marked impatience and disgust.

"By the Mass, merry sirs," quoth Michael with boisterous hilarity, "an you really desire to be of our company we will grant you admittance. But first must ye pledge us in a full bumper of this nectar, concocted by good Master Foorde for the complete undoing of his most favoured guests. We drink to you, gentlemen, brother rogues an you please. If you are saints do not drink. The liquid will poison you."

"To you all, brother rogues," came in lusty accents from Sir John Ayloffe as he jumped to his feet, bumper in hand, "and may you accept us as two of the worst rogues that ever graced your hospitable board."

He quaffed the sickly, very heady liquid at one draught. He had kept himself uncommonly sober throughout the evening and the potion he knew could not do him a great deal of harm. He had a solid head and was not unused to the rough concoctions made up of cheap wines, of alcohol and sundry spices wherewith these noisy louts were wont still further to addle their over-confused pates.

Stowmaries would have demurred, despite the warning look thrown at him from beneath Sir John's heavy lids, but, looking up, he saw Michael's deep-set eyes fixed upon him with a measure of amusement not altogether free from sarcasm which vastly irritated him and without attempting to hide his disgust he raised the heavy mug with a gesture of recklessness and contempt and he too drank it down at one draught.

There were loud shouts of approval at this, and the occasion was further improved by more drinking and the singing of various snatches culled from the most noted and most licentious songs.

But Michael was now examining Sir John Ayloffe very attentively. The latter having drunk expressed distinct appreciation of the beverage, and even made pretence, as he once more resumed his seat, of asking for more.

"You are looking at me with strange persistence, good Michael," he said at last with unalterable blandness, as he returned the younger man's questioning gaze.

"May not a cat look at a king," retorted the other lightly, "or a beggar gaze on the exalted personality of Sir John Ayloffe?"

"By all means, and welcome. But, on my faith, my personality is in no wise exalted, therefore, I may be permitted to ask again what is the cause of your flattering attention?"

"Curiosity," replied Michael curtly.

"Curiosity?"

"Yes. I was wondering in my mind why you are here to-night, and why you have brought mine estimable if somewhat weak-minded cousin with you here, in the very midst of the most evil-reputed crowd in London?"

"Oh!" protested Sir John gallantly, "'tis not the most evil-reputed

65

crowd by any means. We, who are accustomed to the profligate life of a gentleman, look over leniently on the innocent if somewhat flashy debaucheries of these pleasure-lovers here."

"Yet are we no mere pleasure lovers, Sir John," said Michael with a sudden air of seriousness which contrasted strangely with his flushed face and his slovenly and ragged attire. "You see here before you the very scum of humanity, the bits of flotsam and jetsam which the tide of fortune throws upon the shores of life; tattered rags of manhood, shattered lives, disappointed hopes! This room is full of these wreckages, like morsels of poisonous seaweed or of empty shells that litter the earth and make it foul with their noisome putrefaction. Elegant gentlemen like you and my fair cousin here should not join in this mêlée wherein crime falls against crime, and moral foulness pollutes the air. We are rogues here, sir, all of us," he added bringing his hand open-palmed crashing down upon the table, "rogues that have long ago ceased to blush, rogues that shrink neither before crime nor before shame. Rogues! rogues! all of us—not born so remember, but made rogues because of some one else's crime, some one else's shame!—but damned rogues for all that!"

He drank another bumper full of spiced wine! He had spoken loudly and hoarsely with wrathful eyes gazing straight ahead before him, as if striving through the foul smoke and vitiated air of this den of thieves to perceive that nook in a Kentish village, where in a tumble-down, miserable cottage, a woman who should have been Countess of Stowmaries was often on her knees scrubbing the tiled floors.

But Stowmaries's laugh, loud and almost malignant, broke the trend of Michael's thoughts.

"Ay, ay! Well said!" he shouted as loudly, as hilariously as had done the others. "Well said, Michael, for you at least, an rumour doth not lie, are a damned rogue for all that!"

"Nay! Nay!" interposed Ayloffe with mild amiability, "you do your cousin Michael a grave injustice. I know that my lord of Rochester would back me up in what I say. All these gentlemen here are rogues but in name. They shout and they sing, they parade the streets and make merry, but they are, of a truth, of a right good sort, and if only a pleasing turn of fortune came their way, they would all become peaceful citizens in a trice and forswear all their deeds of profligacy, of which they are often cordially ashamed."

'Twas Michael's turn to laugh. He threw back his head so that the muscles of his neck stood out like cords, and he laughed loudly and immoderately, with a laugh that had absolutely no mirth in it.

"Ashamed of our roguery," he said at last, when that outburst had ceased and he was once more learning forward across the table with dark, glowing eyes wandering from one flushed face to another. "Hark at him, gentlemen! Sir John Ayloffe here would make saints of us! Hark ye, sir," he continued bringing his excited face close to that of

66

Sir John, "I for one delight in mine own roguery. I am what I am, do you hear? what the buffetings of Fate and the injustice of man have made me. The more my mealy-mouthed cousin here exults in his courtliness and in his honour, the more do I glory in mine own disgrace. If that is honour," he said pointing with a trembling hand at Stowmaries who despite his brave attire cut but a sorry figure at the present moment, for he felt supremely ill at ease, "then am I content to be a rogue. The greater the villainy, the prouder am I to accomplish it, and if I am to go to Hell for it, then let my damnation be on the head of those who have driven me thither."

Stowmaries shrugged his shoulders in moody contempt. Sir John looked like one profoundly impressed at an unforeseen aspect of affairs.

"As for me," growled one of the men sulkily, "pay me for it and I'll stick a knife into any person you list."

He was an elderly man with a red face and straggly white hair. He had been a scholar once, drunkenness and an inordinate love of gambling had made him what he now was.

"For ten golden sovereigns I'd poison the King!" quoth another thickly.

"For less than that I'd sell my soul!" added another.

"Thou canst not sell what thou hast not got," comes in a quick reply from the further end of the table.

"And you, friend Michael, what would you do for a fortune?" asked Sir John returning Michael's gaze with a firm, earnest look.

"I'd ask the devil to spare my cousin here!" replied Michael flippantly.

"You would not play the part of an hired assassin, I am sure."

"If I hated any one well enough, I'd kill him without pay," retorted the other.

"Or abduct a woman?"

"An she pleased me, I'd not want money to tell her so."

"Then meseems," sighed Sir John with a deprecating shrug of the shoulders, "that I have come to the wrong man with mine offer."

"There was no offer," quoth Michael curtly.

"Ay! of a fortune," rejoined the other calmly.

"Not a serious one."

"As serious as mine own presence here."

"You have come here prepared to make me an offer?" reiterated the young man now, with contemptuous incredulity.

"The offer of a fortune," reiterated Ayloffe quietly.

"How much?"

"One hundred and twenty thousand pounds."

"One hundred—"

"And twenty thousand pounds," repeated Sir John with slow emphasis.

"Bah!—'tis a stupid and a purposeless lie!"

And Michael striving to look indifferent leaned back in his chair, then fell forward again with elbows resting heavily on the table the while his eyes glowing with the excitement of heady liquor and the vague suggestion only half expressed searched the face of the older man.

"Who would give a ne'er-do-well one hundred and twenty thousand pounds?" he reiterated in an unsteady voice, "and for what purpose? Are you fooling me, Sir John?"

"On my solemn word of honour, no!" asserted the latter calmly.

"Then for what purpose?" repeated Michael, whilst a sneer which looked almost evil for a moment quite distorted his face. "Am I to murder some offending stranger in the dark? bribe the King's physician to poison him, or turn informant against my cousin's co-religionists in England as is the fashion nowadays? Well! tell me what it is? Have I not told you that I am rogue enough to accomplish mine own damnation—at a price."

"My good Michael, you mistake my meaning. I propose no roguery unworthy a gentleman. An you'll accept my offer you'd have no cause to regret it, for you'd be a rich, happy and contented man to the last day of your life."

"An it were so simple as that, man," quoth Michael drily, "you'd have no need to offer a fortune to a rogue in order to get what you want. As for the rest, methinks that most rogueries are unworthy a gentleman. But then you see I am no gentleman, else I were not here now, and probably had long ere this flung my glove in your face. So out with it—you offer me one hundred and twenty thousand pounds—for what?"

Instinctively for the last five minutes or so as their conversation drew into more serious channels, the two men had gradually dropped their voices, speaking almost in a whisper. They had drawn their chairs closely together to the corner of the table, with Lord Stowmaries between them, silent and attentive.

Sir John at this stage was sitting close to the end of the table, the full length of which stretched out on his right. He raised his head now and gave a quick glance at the rest of the assembly.

Those of the revellers who were not wholly incapable, either sprawling across the table, or lying prone upon the floor, had drawn up their chairs in groups. The rattle of dice in boxes was distinctly audible above the snoring of the sleepers, also muttered curses from the gamblers who were losing and the clink of brass money passing from hand to hand. Satisfied that the attention of the company had long since wandered away from himself and Michael, he once more turned to the young man and said quietly in response to that impatient: "For what?"

"For marrying the pretty daughter of an amiable Paris bourgeois, the wench being over-ready to fall into your arms."

Michael made no movement but he studied Sir John's face, as if he thought that the man was not completely sane, or had succumbed to the fumes of spiced wine.

"I do not understand," he murmured quite bewildered.

"Must I repeat my words?" said Sir John imperturbably. "There is a wench over in Paris, as pure and good as the day on which she lisped her first Ave Maria at her mother's knee. For certain simple reasons which you will hear anon, a husband must be found for her within the next fourteen days. An you'll be that happy man there will be fifty thousand pounds for you as soon as you agree to the bargain, and seventy more on the day that you bring home the bride."

"Yes! that sounds simple enough. But now tell me the hitch."

"The hitch?"

"Yes. The hitch which forces you to ask a blackguard like myself to do the work for you. Why do you not become the happy man yourself for instance?"

"Oh! I am not young enough, nor yet well-favoured. The first fifty thousand pounds will help to make of you the most dashing gallant in the two kingdoms."

"But why a blackguard?" persisted Michael with cutting sarcasm. He felt agitated, even strangely excited. He was shrewd enough to see that Sir John was not fooling him, that there was more than a mere undercurrent of seriousness in this extraordinary offer made across this common supper table. His fingers were beating an incessant tattoo upon the boards, and his eyes restless, keen as those of a wild beast scenting a trap, searched the face of his interlocutor.

"Why a blackguard if the wench is a saint as you say, why a blackguard?" he insisted.

"A blackguard? Perish the thought!" said Sir John lightly. "Nay! the reason why your personality commended itself to me and to my lord of Stowmaries was because you are a gentleman, despite the many vicissitudes of an adverse Fate, and that you would render the girl happy and proud to be your wife."

"Ah! my worthy cousin is a party to this game?" queried Michael with a sneer.

"In Heaven's name, man," he added with almost savage impatience, "why cannot you speak up like a man? Cards on the table, by the Mass, or my hand will come in contact with your mealy mouth"

He checked himself, angry at his own outburst of rage which he had been unable to control.

"Have I not said that I am on my way to Hell," he added more quietly, "why should you hesitate to show me a short cut?"

"Cards on the table, friend Michael, since you'll have it so," now said Ayloffe in a quiet impressive whisper, "bear that one hundred and

69

twenty thousand pounds in your mind all the while you listen to me. The wench over in Paris was made to go through a marriage ceremony with your cousin here, eighteen years ago, when she was a babe in arms and he a mere lad, unable to defend himself against this encroachment on his future liberty. Since then my lord of Stowmaries has never met his bride, nor did her parents—worthy yet mercenary tradespeople of Paris—desire him to see their daughter. He was poor Rupert Kestyon then, an undesirable son-in-law if ever there was one: they would have broken the marriage then, only the Church would not allow it. Then my lord became what he now is, rich, influential, desirable, and promptly the Paris shopkeepers changed their tactics. They demanded that your cousin shall acknowledge and take to his heart and home a woman whom he has never seen, whom he can never love; for the affection of his heart, of his whole manhood is pledged to another whom he adores. In his despair my lord hath come to me and I am proud to be his friend. I would help him to regain that liberty which an untoward Fate hath fettered. Is not my lord a wholly innocent victim? He did not ask to wed—for long he was spurned as one unworthy. Now because he is rich, he is to be made the tool of rapacious bourgeois, who would see their daughter Countess of Stowmaries. They have invoked the aid of the Church who spurred by their gold hath threatened anathema and excommunication on my lord. The King—sorely inclined to Catholicism—will not hear of breaking marriage vows which he calls solemn, and which under such circumstances sensible men cannot fail to call a farce. My lord hath come to me and I have thought of a scheme—"

So far Michael had listened with unswerving attention to this long exposé delivered by Sir John in clear, even voice that was hardly raised above a whisper. He had listened, his head resting in his right hand, his left lying clenched and motionless on the table. But now he interrupted Ayloffe's placid flow of eloquence.

"You need not tell me your scheme, man," he said, "I have guessed it already. I know now why you had need of a rogue for the furtherance of your project. I, Michael Kestyon, am to go to Paris and there impersonate my love-sick cousin, carry away the bride by that trick, and thus forever so shame her, that a dissolution of that child-marriage will readily be granted by Church and State."

"And that for the sum of one hundred and twenty thousand pounds, friend Michael! one hundred and twenty thousand pounds—a fortune that would tempt a King!" added Sir John earnestly.

Michael made no comment, and there was thus an instant's silence at this end of the table where sat the three men: only a second or two mayhap during which a blasphemous oath uttered at the further end of the room seemed in some strange and occult way to mark the descent of a soul one step further down on its way to Hell. One instant during which the tempter watched the tempted, and from the giddy heights of future satisfied ambition showed him the world conquered at the paltry price of momentary dishonour.

One fitful ray of a ghoulish moon searched, through a narrow slit between swishing curtains, the fleshy face of Ayloffe, the descendant of the Hebrew bondswoman; the thickly-lidded eyes fixed like those of some poison-giving reptile upon the trapped victim. It played weird and ghost-like upon the dull scarlet of his cloak, and made strange shadows beneath his heavy brows, giving him an eerie, satanic expression, which Stowmaries—whose brain was on fire—was quick to note.

He shuddered and instinctively drew away. But Michael Keyston who had not stirred a muscle, who had scarce breathed during that moment's solemn pause, now leaned forward and said quietly:

"For the sum of one hundred and twenty thousand pounds, I will do what you wish."

Then noting that the look of satisfaction on Stowmaries' face was not wholly unmixed with contempt, he added with a quick return to his flippant mood:

"Nay, Cousin, look not so loftily from adown the giddy heights of supposed integrity. 'Tis useless at this stage to despise the hand that will help you in your need. Methinks that my share in the intrigue is no more unavowable than your own. 'Tis you are married to the lady and owe her protection, yet you offer money to further treachery against her. Now I have never seen the wench and am no traitor to her since I do not know her. I owe her no allegiance; she is but one woman out of a million to me. Have you never tried to win a woman by trickery, good Coz?"

He spoke lightly, even gaily, only Sir John—the keen observer of his fellowmen—noted that the laugh which accompanied this tirade had a hollow ring in it, also that Michael after he had spoken drank down one after another two large goblets full of wine.

"Do not let us split hairs, gentlemen, over the meaning of a word," said Ayloffe pleasantly. "Friend Michael, my hand on it. I devised the scheme, and confess that my thoughts flew to you for its accomplishment." He put out his hand, but Michael seemed to ignore the gesture. With a shrug of the shoulders indicating good-tempered toleration, the other continued glibly, "Let us own to it, gentlemen, we are all rogues, every one of us here present; I, who made the proposal, my lord of Stowmaries who pays the piper, and Michael who takes a fortune in exchange for a trick. Bah, gentlemen, 'tis but a merry jest, and, on my honour, no harm can come to any one. Is not Michael Kestyon henceforth rich, as well as highly-connected and amiable of mien. By Gad the practised hand of his future father-in-law together with that of a court barber, would soon turn him into the most gallant gentleman in the two kingdoms."

"A truce on this nonsense," interposed Michael with a quick

return to his impatient mood. "Tell me what you expect me to do, and I'll do it; but there's no cause for such empty talk. I am being paid to act and not to listen."

"We'll be serious, old sobersides," quoth Sir John with imperturbable good humour, "and think of the best schemes to bring our scheme to a successful issue. My lord of Stowmaries, have I your leave to place the details of our plan before our friend here?"

Scarce waiting for the impatient assent of the other, Ayloffe continued, speaking directly to Michael:

"Firstly, then: to-morrow as soon as the shopkeepers have taken down their shutters you shall go to the King's tailor in Holborn and there order yourself various suits of clothes, befitting the many occasions when you shall have need of them in Paris and on your honeymoon. Once the bargain sealed between us, by word of honour as between gentlemen, your gracious cousin will place fifty thousand pounds in your hands. You will be a rich man to-morrow, friend Michael, and can attire yourself in accordance with your whim. From the tailor's in Holborn you had best proceed to the barber's in Fleet Street, who will provide you with the most fashionable perruques—"

"I know all that, man," interrupted Michael with ever-growing impatience. "I know that the monkey hath to be tricked out for parade. When I have been made to look like a fool in motley garb, what further shall I do?"

"You'll hie over to France as soon as may be; for already at break of day to-morrow you—in your temporary name of Earl of Stowmaries—will write a letter to M. Legros, merchant tailor of Paris apprising him of your intentions no longer to disobey the decrees of the Church, or the dictates of your own heart, which of a truth has ever been true to your baby bride; also you will tell him of your desire to proceed forthwith to Paris in order to claim your wife, to have the marriage ceremony of eighteen years ago formally ratified and finally to bring her back in state and solemnity to her new home in England."

"Am I to write all these lies myself?" asked Michael.

"Nay! I'll constitute myself your secretary," replied Ayloffe, "you need only to sign 'Stowmaries.' As I mistake not, 'tis a name you would gladly sign always, 'twill not come amiss for once. You may have to sign papers over there, 'twere better that your handwriting be known at once."

"When do I start for Paris?"

"What say you to a fortnight's hence from this day? 'Twill give you ample time for the completion of your toilet. An you will allow me I will provide you with a retinue worthy of your rank. It must be composed of men whom we can trust, and men who do not know my lord of Stowmaries by sight and are not like to guess that something is amiss. Three will be sufficient. I will engage them at the last, so that there may be no fear of our secret reaching their knowledge."

"Clothes, men, money," quoth Michael, "methinks, Sir John, you have thought of everything. Once I am in Paris?"

"You will act as judgment guides you."

"And no doubt seventy thousand pounds is a good guide to judgment."

Michael's somewhat defiant manner seemed completely to have vanished. He appeared to be yielding himself quite freely to the delights of the promised adventure; at least this was what good Sir John hoped whilst congratulating himself on the remarkable attainment of his fondly-cherished desire.

But remember that this same good Sir John was no superficial observer of human nature. He was not altogether deceived by Michael's outward show of flippancy. That excitement had got hold of the adventurer's imagination was undoubted and probably the obstinacy of an untamed nature would prevent his drawing back from a promise once given.

At the same time the glint of excitement in Michael's eyes had but little genuine merriment in it. It was more like the unnatural fire produced by fever-heated blood.

It was the money which had tempted Michael—so concluded Ayloffe in his own mind. The money which mayhap would help the claimant to bring forward his cause once again into the light of day. Money which would mean bribes, high enough to tempt corrupt judges or even—who knows—a pleasure-loving King.

What Michael thought of the adventure itself, what it cost him to acquiesce in it with an outward show of careless gaiety even the astute Sir John could not have said: he himself had achieved his own ends and personally he cared little what Michael felt so long as the young man fulfilled his share of the ignoble contract.

Was it so ignoble after all? Sir John with a smile of self-contempt found himself wondering in his mind whether any one would indeed be the loser by it. Stowmaries? certainly not!—he could well afford to pay twice a hundred thousand pounds for the gratification of his most ardent desire: his freedom to marry the woman whom he loved. Michael?—of a truth Michael would lose a little more self-respect than he had already done, but then he must have so little left—and he would become passing rich.

As for the tailor's wench, bah!—one husband was as good as another, concluded Sir John with a splendid cynicism, and if Michael Kestyon was not actually Earl of Stowmaries, by Gad he was mighty near to it, and—who knows?—with one hundred and twenty thousand pounds in his pocket might yet oust his cousin from that enviable state.

And he—Sir John Ayloffe—gambler on his beam ends, would henceforth look forward to a comfortable old age with Mistress Julia Peyton's twelve thousand pounds carefully placed at interest so that there might be no temptation to dribble it away.

All was for the best in the best possible world!

CHAPTER XIV

Like a hell-broth boil and bubble.

—Macbeth IV. 1

But there was one more card which Ayloffe, the gambler, desired to play ere he lost sight momentarily of the man who was to be his tool in the carving of their respective fortunes.

He now rose from the table and went up to the door which gave on the private parlour. This he opened and looked in. Just as he had anticipated, there was but little change in the attitude of the three gentlemen whom he had left in the room.

Sir Anthony Wykeham still sat moodily leaning back in his chair, a shade more confused in his brain than he had been before, his eyes more shifty and uncertain in expression. A couple of empty bottles in front of him mutely explained the reason for this gradual change in the emphatic moraliser of a while ago.

Sir Knaith Bullock was still lying on the floor, in the midst of the straw which with idle hands he had gradually heaped up all round him, so that he seemed reclining in a nest. But he was not asleep now; he was singing chorus to the songs of my lord Rochester, who—frankly tipsy—made as much noise and sang as thoroughly out of tune as any of the plebeian revellers in the coffee room.

"Hello, Sir John!" he shouted lustily, "where in the devil's name have you and Stowmaries been hiding yourselves?"

His tongue was thick and the words fell inarticulately from his quivering lips. Sir Knaith Bullock rolled over in the straw in order to have a good view of the intruder.

"Where the devil—sh—sh—Stowmaries?" he babbled as incoherently as his friend.

"We have been busy finding an alternative husband for the tailor's daughter," said Sir John gaily.

"And have you found one?" queried Wykeham with vague, somnolent eyes fixed upon the speaker.

"Ay! that we have! And I pray you gentlemen to join the merry company in the coffee room and to pledge the bold adventurer in a monster goblet of wine."

"Egad!—you—you don't mean—that—hic!—" hiccupped Bullock who had rolled right over in the straw and now looked like a giant and frowzy dog with prickly wisps standing out of his perruque and sticking to his surcoat and velvet breeches. He contrived to work himself about until he got onto his feet, whereupon he stood there tottering and swaying the while his bleary eyes tried to take in what was going on around him.

74

A great shout issuing from the coffee room, great banging of mugs against the boards, loud laughter and the first verse of a song, roused Rochester from his apathy and Wykeham from his moodiness.

"They are passing roisterous over there!" remarked the latter, gazing covetously toward the open door.

"They are toasting the gallant adventurer," said Sir John; "I pray you, gentlemen, come and join us. Let us drink to the future husband of the tailor's daughter, the future possessor of one hundred and twenty thousand pounds in solid cash and of my lord Stowmaries' eternal gratitude. Let us drink to Michael Kestyon."

"Michael—Kesh—Keshtyon is it?" babbled Sir Knaith.

"The damned blackguard—" murmured Wykeham.

"I say hurrah for Michael Kestyon!" roared my lord Rochester lustily, "the beggar hath pluck. By Gad! won't old Rowley laugh at the adventure? Would I'd had the impudence to go through with it myself!—I say hurrah for Michael Kestyon!"

He lurched forward in the wake of Sir John who had once more turned towards the coffee room, and closely followed by the others, all four men shouting: "Hurrah for Michael Kestyon! Hurrah for the tailor's daughter!"

Their advent was greeted by more vigorous shouting, more singing and cries of: "Hurrah!" which issued from out the darkness. For by now only one last tallow candle was left spluttering and dripping, its feeble yellow rays illumining but one narrow circle of light wherein the remnant of a pie, an overturned bottle and a pool of red wine, stood out as the sole objects actually visible in the room.

In this total darkness, the noise of hoarse shouts, of cries for "Michael Kestyon!" of blasphemies and of oaths sounded weird and satanic, like a babel of ghouls exulting in the realms of the night.

Sir John paused at the door. He had wished to see Michael Kestyon commit himself finally before these other three gentlemen, who were almost partners in the conspiracy. He wanted to see the bond sealed with the word of honour of the rogue who—as Ayloffe well knew—would never break a pledge once given.

Therefore, he called loudly to Michael, and listened for the cheery tones of his voice. But no response came, only from out the gloom a curt answer from Stowmaries:

"Oh! 'tis no use calling for Michael! He hath gone!"

CHAPTER XV

Still his soul fed upon the sovereign hour
That had been or that should be:

—*Swinburne*

Michael in the meanwhile was running through the deserted streets like a man possessed. Cloakless and hatless he ran, bending his head to the gusts of wind which tore down the narrow byways in the neighbourhood of the Strand.

Fitful clouds chased one another over his head, obscuring the moon, and from time to time descending in sharp showers of icy rain.

But Michael loved the wind and cared naught for the wet. The rags he wore were soon soaked through, but he did not attempt to take shelter beneath the various yawning archways which he passed from time to time; on the contrary he liked the cold douches of these winter showers which seemed to cool his head, burning with inward fever.

Michael Kestyon, the gambler, the adventurer, the wastrel, had begun the fight against his own soul.

For the space of a few seconds, there in the over-heated tavern room in the midst of all those drunkards, those profligates—scums of humanity—dying honour had called out in its agony: "Wilt sell me for gold?" but Michael had laughed out loud and long, and smothered those warning cries with the recklessness of the soldier of fortune who stakes his all on the winning card.

His claim, his rights! His and those of that patient old soul dying of want in a lonely cottage, the while she should be living in the lap of luxury and of ease.

She was dying of want, of actual hard, bitter starvation. Michael knew it and could do naught to help, and in the midst of the dissolute life of the town had vainly striven to forget that even at the cost of his life's blood, which he would have given gladly drop by drop, he could not purchase for her a soft bed on which she would finally go to her eternal sleep.

His claim! His rights! Her happiness! The happiness of the one being in the whole wide world who had clung to him, who loved him for what he was and did not despise him for what he had become: this he could purchase for one hundred and twenty thousand pounds.

Had not Sir John Ayloffe himself said that 'twas a fortune which would tempt a king.

The lawyers had told Michael that only money was wanted to bring his claim before the Lords' House of Parliament now, and once publicly debated, justice could not stand against it.

Michael had oft laughed at those two words, "Only money!"

76

Only money! and when he sought and got a sword thrust that nearly killed him, he was given twenty crowns as blood-money. He reckoned at this rate that his miserable body would have to be as full of holes as a sieve, before he obtained enough money wherewith to satisfy the first lawyer who would condescend once more to take up his case.

But now all that—lawyers' fees, fees for a first hearing, for a second and for a third, for pleadings, interrogatories and affidavits, for petitions to the King and for briberies to obtain a private audience—all that would be within his reach.

The price? A woman's honour and his own self-respect.

Once—very long ago, these would have mattered to him a great deal; in those days he had believed in men's honour and in women's virtue.

But now? He had lost so much self-respect already—what mattered if a few more shreds of it went the way of all his other ideals.

He had once boldly said that he would give his life's blood drop by drop, endure every agony, undergo every torture to see his mother installed at Maries Castle, her rightful and proper place.

Well, that had been easy to say! These things were not asked of him, and he had gone through so much, suffered often so terribly from hunger, wounds and fatigue that the sacrifice of his life or the endurance of most bitter tortures would have been an easy sacrifice. He was hard and tough—what nerves he had had been jarred beyond all sensibility long ago.

But now something was asked of him. Fate had spoken in no uncertain accents. She had said: "Make a sacrifice of thine honour, and thy most cherished wish will be gratified!"

If those former bold words—offers of blood and life—were not the talk of a weak-kneed braggart, then, Michael Kestyon, thou shouldst not hesitate!

Dost prize those paltry remnants of self-respect so highly that thou wouldst see thy mother starve ere thou sell them?

Starve, remember, starve!—in the direct, absolute, unmitigated sense of the word. If thou canst not provide her with the necessities of life, she must starve sooner or later, in a month, in a year, in two mayhap, that would depend how charitably inclined the neighbours happened to be. But starve she must, if thou, her son, dost naught for her.

And Fate had whispered: "Money, power, justice await thee, at the price of thy self-respect and the honour of a woman who is a stranger to thee."

The subtle temptation had entered into Michael's heart like an insinuating poison which killed every objection, every argument, every moral rebellion in his soul. And the temptation assailed him just at this time when his whole being ached with the constant buffetings of life, when he longed with all the maddening strength of defiant impotence

77

to hit right and left at the world which had derided him, to begin again a new life of action, of combat, of lofty aspirations.

Try and pity him, for the temptation was over-great; pity him because Fate had struck him one blow after another, each more and more difficult to bear since his soul, his mind, his entire self had scarcely time to recover from one before the next came crashing down, leaving him with one hope the less, one more ideal shattered, one more misery to bear.

One hundred and twenty thousand pounds!—Michael kept repeating the half dozen wonderful words to himself over and over again as he walked.

Thus tottering, buffeted by the wind, drunk with the magic of the thought which the words evoked, he reached his lodgings at last.

He rapped loudly at a low door with his knuckles, but had to wait some time before it was opened. A gnome-like figure wrapped in a tattered dressing gown and wearing a cotton night-cap appeared in the doorway. It was difficult to distinguish if the figure was that of man or woman. In brown and wrinkled hands it held a guttering tallow dip which threw a trembling light on the dank walls of the narrow passage and feebly illumined the approach to the rickety stairs beyond.

Michael paid no heed to the muttered grumblings of the creature, but walked straight past it along the passage, and then up the creaky stairs which led to the garret above. As he reached the several landings he nearly fell over various prostrate bundles made up of human rags from out of which issued sleepy oaths, as Michael's foot stumbled against them.

His own garret was not much better than those open landings across which he had tottered and fumbled in the dark. Here the roof sloped down to the tiny dormer window, innocent of curtains, and made up of some half dozen tiny panes, mostly cracked and covered with thick coatings of grime.

Along the low wall opposite the window a row of ragged bundles—human only in shape—and similar to those which encumbered the landings, told their tale of misery and of degradation. There were some half dozen of these bundles lying all of a row against the wall. They were Michael's room companions, the wreckages of man and womankind, with whom he had lived now for close on eighteen months.

Snores and drunken oaths, blasphemy too and noisome words spoken in sleep came from these bundles, greeting Michael's somewhat stormy entrance into this den.

He shut the rickety door behind him, and made his way to the little window, through which the light of some street lanthorn opposite came shyly peeping through.

Michael threw the casement open, allowing that feeble light to enter more fully, then he turned and surveyed his surroundings,—those

78

bundles along the floor, the wooden boards across which a crowd of vermin were scrampering out of sight, the two chairs, innocent of seats, the wooden packing case in lieu of table, the walls dank and grey, covered with obscene writing scribbled with shaky fingers dipped in grime!

Michael looked at it all, as if he had never seen it before. In an angle of the room was the straw paillasse still empty which awaited him, and around which the dying instincts of gentle birth had caused him to erect a kind of unseen barrier between that corner and the rest of the room. Here the floor was clean, the straw was fresh; above the paillasse the wall had been carefully wiped clean and rubbed over with lime, and on an overturned wooden case beside the miserable bed there were one or two books, and a small metal crucifix which profane fingers had apparently never dared to touch.

But these very trifling attempts at cleanliness were the only luxury which had come within Michael's reach, ever since he came home from that last campaign in Brandenburg and sent his last crown to his mother in Kent. And remember that such garrets, such degrading propinquity, such misery and such dirt represented the only kind of life which London offered in those days to the poor, to the outcast and the homeless. There was nothing else except the gutter itself.

Michael stood in the centre of this garret and looked upon the picture—his life! His life such as it had been for the past eighteen months, such as it would continue to be until he became too old and too feeble to drag himself up from that straw paillasse in the corner. Then he would lie there sick and starving until he was taken away feet foremost down the rickety stairway to the paupers' graveyard out beyond St. Paul's.

With arms akimbo, hands resting on his hips and feet firmly planted on the dust-covered floor, Michael looked and laughed; not bitterly or mirthlessly. Bitterness had gone—strangely enough—at sight of the picture. He laughed, mocking himself for the few scruples which had assailed him awhile ago, for having conjured up—yes! conjured up himself—those phantoms of honour which accused him of selling his self-respect.

Was this self-respect, this den of rogues, this herd of miserable ne'er-do-wells, these filthy walls, this life of misery, of wretchedness, of shifts—growing day by day more unavowable for obtaining bread for the morrow? Was this manhood to stand against such odds? Was this honour to endure such a life?

Bah! if it was, then far better sell it for the price of oak boards sufficient to make two coffins: one for the man, the other for the old woman living the same life and enduring the same misery.

Michael turned back to the window and with a brusque, impatient gesture tore open the second casement. A gust of wind found its way into the musty corners of the garret and scattered the vitiated air, the while the moon emerging triumphantly from her long imprisonment behind the clouds searched with bluish and ghostly rays the grey walls opposite, the drunken sleepers on the floor, the vermin scuttling between those litters of straw more fit for cattle than for human beings.

The blustering wind, as it tore at the rickety casements roused some of the sleepers from their dreams. Volleys of oaths were flung at Michael, but he heard nothing now. He leaned out of the narrow window—as far out as he could—and looked on the forest of chimney stacks, the irregular roofs and tall spires of this great and heartless city.

How peacefully she lay beneath the cool kiss of the moon! Invisible arms seemed to be stretched out toward the lonely watcher bidding him to come and conquer.

There was no longer any compunction in Michael's heart, and certainly no shame.

"I am a man," he said speaking to those unseen shadows, "and what I do, I do!"

The freshness of the air came as a bath of moral cleanliness to his soul; he felt an excitement, too, akin to that of a war horse when scenting the coming battle. To Michael now the whole transaction—to which on the morrow he would affix the seal of his pledged word—was but a mighty combat wherein a powerful weapon would be placed in his hand.

He would at last be able to hit right and left, to be even with that world which had buffeted him, which had scorned his efforts, but allowed his mother to starve.

Aye! He was a turbulent soul; a soul created to fight and not to endure.

And if at moments during that lonely watch above the chimney stacks and roofs of London there came floating to his mind the thought of the girl who was nothing to him, the stranger whom he would so bitterly wrong, then with a proud toss of the head, a joy which literally lighted up his whole being, he would send an unspoken challenge up to those swiftly-flying clouds which tended southwards, towards Paris.

"Go tell her!" he murmured, "that whoever she may be Michael Kestyon will serve her with gratitude and love all the days of his life. On his knees will he worship her, and devote his life to her happiness. And," he added mentally, whilst a quiver of excitement shook his broad shoulders, "tell her that an she desires to be Countess of Stowmaries, even that desire Michael Kestyon will gratify, for he will make her that—tell her—tell her that before next December's snows cover the earth there will be two Countesses of Stowmaries in England: Michael Kestyon's mother and Michael Kestyon's wife."

He did not attempt to go and rest on his miserable couch, but leant for hours up against the window watching the moon slowly drawing its peaceful course along the dark firmament, seeing the fleecy,

80

silvered clouds fly madly across the sky, lashed by the wind into fantastic shapes of witches' heads and of lurid beasts. He watched the roofs and towers of many churches as gradually they were wrapped in the mist-laden mantle of approaching dawn.

He watched until far away above chimney stacks and pointed steeples a feeble rosy glow precursed the rising sun. He was too weary now to think any more, too weary to dream, too weary he thought even to live.

And through the gathering mist it seemed to him that the ghostly spectres of his tumultuous past came to him enwrapped in white palls, monstrous and majestic, towering above mighty London, and that walking slowly in their wake, tottering and shy was his mother, enfeebled by starvation and the wretchedness of her life. She held out emaciated arms to him in a mute appeal for help, whilst the ghosts of the past spoke with unseen lips of all that he had suffered, of the great sorrows and the tiny pin-pricks.

And with every word they uttered his soul sank more and more to rest, and even as his aching head sank down upon his outstretched arms, and his eyes closed in a dreamless sleep, his lips murmured with final defiance:

"I am a man! and what I do, I do."

CHAPTER XVI

Now mark! To be precise—Though
I say "lies," all these, at this first stage
'Tis but for science' sake.

—Browning

In the meanwhile my lord of Stowmaries had been allowed to spend a happy hour in the tiny withdrawing room at Holborn Row, kneeling at Mistress Julia Peyton's feet.

He had been so excited, so full of Sir John's proposals and their more than probable success that like Michael Kestyon he had no desire for rest. He had soon wearied of the crowd in the coffee room, and presently had allowed Ayloffe to lead him out into the streets.

Instinctively his footsteps turned in the direction of Holborn Row, the while he lent a somewhat inattentive ear to what Sir John was saying to him. Ayloffe was talking of the details of his scheme; of the payment of the money to Michael on the morrow, if the latter finally pledged himself to the bargain; fifty thousand pounds then, and a further seventy on the day that the tailor's daughter left her home in her husband's company.

"We must be as good as our word, my lord," said the astute Sir John. "A word misplaced, the faintest suggestion of withdrawal on any point might upset Michael's curious temper and turn his acquiescence into obstinate refusal."

Ayloffe had no doubt of Stowmaries' integrity, only the sum was such a vast one—and the worthy baronet was so unaccustomed to the handling of thousands—that he could not help dreading the fact that the young man had mayhap overestimated his power of paying away such large sums at such short intervals, and that, when the time came for disbursement, a hitch might occur which would rouse Michael's antagonism and upset the perfectly-laid scheme once and for all.

Stowmaries, however, seemed to attach very slight importance to this question of money.

"I am a man of my word," he said curtly. "I have no wish to draw back. What I've said, I've said."

What cared he if it cost him twice one hundred thousand pounds, if indeed he were free to wed the beautiful Julia?

He was over-eager to be at her feet now and showed marked impatience to rid himself of Ayloffe's company.

"My hand on it, Sir John," he said, halting at the corner of Holborn Row, for he did not want the older man to see whither he was going, the while the latter was well aware that my lord was on his way to Mistress Peyton's house. "My hand on it; and to-morrow Michael Kestyon shall have his fifty thousand pounds, if he finally agrees to do what we want."

"This he must do in the presence of witnesses—my lord of Rochester or Sir Knaith Bullock would favour us as much. Yet have I no fear that the rogue will play us false, 'tis the money he wants, and fifty thousand were not enough to tempt him; 'tis that further seventy that he'll crave for most."

"I know, I know," said Stowmaries, impatiently anxious to get away, now that he had perceived—as he thought—a light in one of the windows of his fair Julia's house. "He shall have that, too. The money is at interest with Master Vivish the diamond merchant. I can get it at any time."

"We promised it to Michael on the day that the tailor's daughter leaves her father's home," urged the over-prudent Sir John.

"On that day he shall have it," rejoined the other.

"Then your lordship would have to journey to France in order to fulfil that promise."

"I'll to France then," retorted the young man who had come to the end of his tether, "an you'll go to Hell now and leave me in peace."

Ayloffe laughed good-humouredly. Usually prone to quarrel he was determined to keep his temper to-night; and as he felt that nothing further would be gained now by talking whilst Stowmaries was so obviously waiting to be rid of him, he said nothing more, but gave his friend a cordial Good-night and turned on his heel in the direction of Lincoln's Inn Fields.

Stowmaries—as soon as the other was out of sight—walked down Holborn Row, and had soon reached the familiar door.

In response to his loud knocking the East Anglian serving-man came to open it. With the stolidity peculiar to his race, he showed no surprise at the untimely visitor, and with solemn imperturbability held out his furrowed hand even before Stowmaries had produced the small piece of silver which alone would induce the old man to permit that visitor to enter.

The piece of silver being deemed sufficient to overcome the man's scruples, he shuffled along the flagged passage without uttering a word, leaving Stowmaries to follow as he liked, and presently he threw open the door which gave on the small parlour.

Though it was close on midnight, Mistress Peyton was not abed. She had been to the Playhouse, and was still attired in that beautiful cream-coloured brocade which had been the envy of the feminine portion of the audience there; but though she was tired after the many and varied emotions of that eventful day, yet she felt that she could not have slept. Her proposals to Sir John Ayloffe, the schemes which she well knew that the gambler would concoct, the possibility or probability of ultimate success, harassed her nerves and fired her brain.

She had spent the last two hours in that narrow room, now pacing up and down like a caged rodent, now throwing herself down in a chair in an agony of restlessness.

The advent of my lord Stowmaries occurred in the nick of time, for she was on the verge of hysterics.

He knelt at her feet, adoring and excited. He told her all that had occurred during that momentous evening, humbly begging her pardon for having betrayed the secret of their mutual love, his own passion and his despair, to some of his most intimate friends.

Mistress Julia whose flushed face when my lord entered might have been caused by shyness at his stormy entrance, or by anger at the untimeliness of his visit, looked adorable in her obvious agitation. She chided him gently for his impetuosity, and for disclosing her tender secret to those who mayhap would sneer at her hopeless love.

Then my lord told her of Sir John Ayloffe's scheme, the proposed public disgrace of the tailor's daughter which would render the dissolution of the child-marriage not only probable but certain. Mistress Julia looked quite sad and shed sympathetic tears; she was so sorry, so very sorry for the poor dear child.

But when she heard that my lord had actually promised one hundred and twenty thousand pounds to his cousin Michael Kestyon

83

for rendering him this service, the fair Julia frowned and checked an angry exclamation which had risen to her lips.

"The sum seems overvast," she remarked with affected indifference.

"The bribe had to be heavy, Mistress," replied my lord. "Michael was the only man who could help us. He might have refused for less. It had to be a fortune worth a gentleman's while to accept. Michael is a gentleman despite his roguery, and we were asking him to do a mighty villainous action. He had to be well paid for it," repeated the young man decisively, "methinks that for less he would have refused."

Mistress Peyton allowed the subject to drop for the moment and her lover to wander back into the realms of dithyrambic utterances, of vows and of sighs. But anon she recurred to the question of the money, showing a desire to know how and when it would be paid over.

"To-morrow when we have Michael's final acquiescence," said Stowmaries, eager to dismiss this question, "I will hand over fifty thousand pounds to him, and another seventy thousand the day on which Rose Marie Legros leaves her father's shop in company with mine adventurous cousin."

"You talk lightly of such vast sums, my lord," said Julia.

"Would I not give my fortune to win you?" he rejoined.

She continued for a long time afterwards to listen shyly and adorably to my lord's continued protestations, and when these became too violent, she rang for her tiring-wench and with many charmingly-timid blushes dismissed her adorer, promising to receive him again on the morrow.

He went away quite happy, vowing that he would gladly have given not only his entire fortune, but also his family estates and titles to Michael for enabling him to regain his freedom and to marry the most adorable woman in the whole world.

But Mistress Julia Peyton was not quite so content as all that. After my lord's departure, she went up to her sleeping room and exchanging her stiff brocade for a loose and easy wrap, she sat down in order to think various matters out.

Agitation and restlessness had gone from her, but not the frown of disapproval.

Her impetuous lover had been a fool, and Sir John a traitor to have allowed such monstrous promises to be made to Michael Kestyon. Surely her own kinsman should have known that her ardent love for my lord of Stowmaries consisted in the main of an overmastering desire to become a countess. Now with one hundred and twenty thousand pounds in Michael's hands and given that claimant's obstinate temperament and determination to carry his cause through, was there not a grave danger that the wretch would win his case after all and that my lord would presently have to yield his title and estates to the cousin whom he had so needlessly rendered rich?

It was monstrous, silly and childish! Sir John of course must have been well under the influence of liquor ere he allowed such a bargain, without realising the danger which threatened his kinswoman's ambitious desires.

She was mightily angry with Sir John, who should have been more shrewd, and could not understand how it was that so astute and so unscrupulous a schemer had overlooked the eventuality which she herself had foreseen in a flash.

The first fifty thousand, well and good!—Julia supposed that so vast a sum would certainly be required to bribe even a broken-down gentleman to enter into Ayloffe's dishonourable schemes.

But the further seventy thousand, was unnecessary, she felt sure of that and moreover it was dangerous.

Would it not be the most bitter irony of which Fate was capable if the tailor's daughter became Countess of Stowmaries after all?

Such a thing had become possible now, nay, probable, thanks to the blunder made by Sir John. As for my lord, he seemed unaware of the danger—he was too fond of laughing at Michael Kestyon's pretensions, and was ever inclined to dismiss them as puerile and beneath contempt; mayhap, too, that he was fatuous enough to think that even without wealth or title his adored one would become his.

But the adored one had no such intention.

Like unto the adventurer himself up in that squalid garret above the roofs of London, Mistress Peyton could not rest that night. Her active mind was troubled with plans of how to undo the blunders of the past hour.

And whilst Michael dreamed of future glory, of power and of wealth, Julia racked her woman's brain to find a means to bring him back to the dust.

PART III

CHAPTER XVII

Her eyes were deeper than the depth
Of waters still at even:
She had three lilies in her hand,
And the stars in her hair were seven.

—*Dante Gabriel Rossetti*

"No, no, my cabbage, I do not find that plain gown becoming, of a verity thou must remember that thou art an English Countess and must henceforth adorn thy person with proper grandeur."

And worthy Mme. Legros, whilst vainly trying to express disapproval, gazed with obvious admiration at the dainty apparition before her.

"Let be, Maman, let be!" interposed Papa Legros soothingly, "the chit is well enough as she is. When she is over there in England, she may well look grand and stately; for the present she is still a tailor's daughter and I'll challenge the world to produce a daintier bale of goods. Par ma foi! were I not thy father, my pigeon, I were tempted to envy that profligate young scoundrel, thy noble lord and husband. 'Tis a mightily succulent morsel he will bite into the nonce."

Rose Marie striving to hide the confusion, which her kind father's broad allusion caused in her sensitive young heart, buried her face in the bouquet of snowdrops which she held in her hand.

No wonder that her adoring parents were proud of her. She looked a picture on this cold winter's morning, standing there in her little room beneath the eaves, clad in pure white like the snow which lay thick on the narrow window sill and along the streets of Paris.

She had fashioned her gown herself, of white grogram with a beautiful openwork lace pinner and delicate kerchief demurely folded across her young bosom. Her fair hair was dressed in small curls all over her small head, her neck was bare, as were her arms and hands, and in colour as delicate as the snowdrops which she carried.

The spring was still in its infancy and snowdrops were very scarce; worthy M. Legros had paid a vast sum of money in order that Rose Marie should carry a bouquet when first she met her lord.

All white she looked—almost like a little snow image, only that her cheeks glowed with the excitement in her blood, and her bosom rose and fell with unwonted rapidity beneath the filmy folds of her muslin kerchief.

86

My lord of Stowmaries had arrived in Paris the evening before, and had sent one of his serving-men round to say that he would come and pay his respects before midday.

Oh! there seemed no laggardness about him now. The influence of Monseigneur the Archbishop and no doubt his own better nature had prevailed at last, and since a fortnight ago when his letter arrived announcing his coming, he seemed to have lost no time in useless preparations.

Now he was here in Paris and Rose Marie had put on her pretty gown in order to receive him. She did so mightily desire to please him, for she on her side was quite ready to give him that respectful love which husbands demand of their wives. Mme. Legros had fussed round the child all the morning, and though she grumbled at the simplicity of the gown, she could not help but admire the exquisite picture of innocent girlhood which her daughter presented with such charming unconsciousness.

Rose Marie had been singularly silent all the while that she dressed. She was very anxious to be beautiful, and thought that this could not be accomplished without much care and trouble. This she bestowed ungrudgingly on every curl as she twisted and pinned it up, on every fold of her kerchief, on the tying of her shoe.

She had taken over two hours in completing her toilet, selecting with scrupulous care each article of dainty underlinen, which her own fingers had embroidered months ago, in anticipation of this great day: the white stockings, the silken garters, the beribboned shift and petticoat.

When she was ready, she called to maman to come and inspect, and oh! to criticise if there were any fault to find, which maman of a surety would detect. Mme. Legros determined not to let affection blind her, had turned the snow-white apparition round and round, seeking for defects, where none existed, readjusting a curl here, a ribbon there, and finally calling to good M. Legros to come and give his verdict on the picture.

But good M. Legros was far too adoring to do aught but admire. So now Rose Marie, if not quite free from doubt, was at any rate satisfied that everything which could be done to render her beautiful and desirable, had of a truth been done.

"We had best go down, Maman," said Legros at last, when he had finished feasting his eyes on the beauty of his daughter, "and make ready to receive milor. The child had best remain up here, and not enter the parlour until her lord is there, ready to greet her as she advances."

The worthy tailor was more agitated than he cared to own. He felt fussy and could not manage to sit still. It still lacked nearly an hour to midday, and he was ready and over-ready to receive milor. He

87

bustled maman out of the room, then ran back to have a final look at Rose Marie.

"Keep calm, my treasure," he said agitatedly, "par Dieu! There's no need for excitement. Thou art not the first and only bride who has ever been claimed by an unknown husband. 'Tis milor, no doubt, who feels flustered. He has been in the wrong and comes to make amends. Not a very pleasant position for a proud English lord, eh, my pigeon? But thou art within thy rights, and wilt receive him with becoming dignity."

With gentle, insinuating gestures Rose Marie contrived to lead her father out of the room, and finally to close the door behind him.

Time was hurrying on and she did so want to be alone and to think. This was the end of the old life, the beginning of the new: the new with all its hopes, its fears, its mysteries. She had put it very pertinently to her mother when she said that nothing, nothing would ever be quite the same again.

Now that dear Papa Legros' heavy footsteps had died down the steep staircase, Rose Marie could sit by the open window and just think of it all, for the last time, before these mysteries of the new life were revealed to her.

I think that what struck her as most curious in the future was the idea that she would never be quite alone again. For she had—despite the loving care of adoring parents—been very much alone. We must remember that there is never complete harmony between the young and the old. The former live for the future, the latter for the present, oft times only for the past. Papa and Maman Legros found their joy in seeing Rose Marie grow up and live, like some beautiful flower, carefully tended, guarded against the tearing winds of life, nourished, fed and caressed. But Rose Marie thought she cherished her parents, dreamed of the time when she would be a woman with another home, with other affections, with other kindred. Therefore she was lonely even in the midst of her happy home. There was a great deal that Rose Marie did not understand in life, but there was an infinity which maman would never comprehend.

Would this newcomer, this stranger understand better than maman, she wondered. Would he know what ailed her when in the very midst of joy she suddenly felt inclined to cry? Would he then know just the right word to say, the right word to soothe her, and to fit in with her mood?

There were other thoughts that flew through Rose Marie's mind during this, the last lonely hour of her girlhood, but these she would not allow to linger in her mind, for they caused her cheeks to blush, and her heart to beat with sudden, nameless fear. She had seen the girls and boys of Paris wandering arm in arm in the woods of Fontainebleau, she had seen a fair head leaning against a dark head, and lips meeting lips

88

in a furtive kiss, and now in her innocent heart she wondered what it felt like thus to be kissed.

Hush!—sh!—sh!—No, no! Maman was not there to see the quick blush which at the thought rose to the girlish cheek. Maman would not understand. She would say gaily: "Pardi my cabbage! but thy husband shall kiss thee of a truth and right lustily on thy fresh cheeks or thy budding mouth. A good, round, sounding kiss an he loves thee, which of course he will!" And the girls, too, in the woods at Fontainebleau, they usually laughed after that furtive kiss snatched behind some tree, when they thought that no one was looking.

But Rose Marie did not think that she would laugh when my lord kissed her. It seemed to her so strange that girls should make light of such wondrous moments in their lives. Rose Marie thought that when my lord kissed her she would probably cry, not in grief, oh, no! but with a strange exultant joy because of his love for her.

And that was what she hoped that he would understand.

CHAPTER XVIII

And a bird overhead sang "Follow"!
And a bird to the right sang "Here";
And the arch of the leaves was hollow
And the meaning of May was clear.

—Swinburne

But good M. Legros could not contrive to sit still.

He had gone down into the parlour and worried maman, until, poor soul, she had put milk into the metheglin, in mistake for ale, and had to brew the mixture all over again, quite a quantity of good Spanish wine having been completely spoilt, owing to the fidgety temper of her lord.

He hung round her whilst she evolved the fresh bowl of posset, and made her so nervous that in desperation, fearing that more waste of expensive liquid would ensue, she ran upstairs loudly calling to Rose Marie to come down and help keep papa quiet by engaging him in a game of cribbage.

Therefore it was that when with loud clatter of hoofs on the rough pavement of the Rue de l'Ancienne Comédie, my lord and his retinue drew rein outside the tailor's shop, Rose Marie was sitting in the room above playing cribbage with her father.

She heard the noise of the horses, the brief word of command as the small party halted, but not for all the treasures of this world could she at this moment have risen in order to peep out of the window and thus get a glimpse of her future husband.

Papa rose in great agitation. Maman ceased fussing round the room and there was silence for a time, the while no doubt my lord dismounted. Then M. and Mme. Legros went out of the room in order to welcome the distinguished guest. But Rose Marie sat quite still, with her trembling fingers clasped tightly round the tiny bouquet of snowdrops. Through the window behind her the spring sun peeped in, pale and tender, and searching the remote corner of the homely parlour found the dainty, white-clad figure of the girl and touching her fair hair with the magic of its kiss turned it into an aureole of gold.

The door opened and Michael entered. Thus he saw her for the first time—she, the woman whom he had been paid to wrong.

He realised this the moment he saw her. In all the whirl of riotous thought which had assailed him during the past three weeks since that night which he had spent in self-communion, the impression of the woman had never been a lasting one. He had never thought of her as a distinct personality, as a creature of flesh and blood with thoughts and feelings mayhap as deep as his own.

To his mind so far she had only been a tool, a sexless means to his ends: and this man who had such a passionate attachment for his mother, such a sense of her worth and importance, had given but a very cursory thought to her who was to become his wife by a trick.

In this we must do him justice, that he did not dream of wronging the woman, who was the channel which Fortune had selected for her welcome course towards him. His cousin Stowmaries would of course repudiate her, that was understood. Undoubtedly he would be allowed to do this: but he—Michael Kestyon—would atone for his kinsman's villainy, he would keep, honour and respect her as his wife and the future mother of his children, and make her—by the will of God, the King and the Lords' House of Parliament, and by the power of his newly acquired wealth—Countess of Stowmaries despite the rogues who had planned to oust her from that place.

Because of all these good resolutions, Michael had therefore anticipated his meeting with his future wife with perfect equanimity. I do not think that during the many preparations for his journey which he had to see to in the past three weeks, he ever tried even for a moment to picture to himself what she would be like.

Now she stood before him, in the full charm of her innocent girlhood, clad all in white, with her little hands clasping that bunch of flowers, the pale rays of an April sun touching her fair hair with gold. Her blue eyes were raised shyly to him just for an instant as she rose to meet him. He thought her elegant and pretty, stately, too, in her prim white gown.

90

"She was born to be a great lady," he thought to himself with an inward chuckle, "and by Gad I'll make her one."

In his mind—which seemed all in a whirl now—he compared her to Mistress Julia Peyton, and thought his cousin a mighty fool for preferring the latter.

He bowed very low as Rose Marie advanced and at an encouraging word from maman, she placed her hand on his, and he kissed the tips of her ice-cold fingers.

"A snow-maiden, by my faith!" he thought to himself. "Michael, thou rogue! Thou'lt of a surety have to infuse warmth into those pale cheeks."

She felt almost paralyzed with shyness, and very angry with herself for seeming so gauche and stupid. The while she curtsied to my lord in the most approved and primmest of fashions, the little bouquet of snowdrops escaped her trembling fingers. My lord stooped and picked it up, and she held out her hand for it, but he met her swift and timid glance with a bold challenge, and raised the bouquet to his lips before he hid it in the folds of his surcoat.

Rose Marie thought her future lord picturesque in his elegant accoutrements; the fine cloth of his coat, of a dull shade of red, the cut of his garments, the delicate bit of lace at throat and wrist set off the massive strength of his figure: she was not quite sure if he were really handsome, for there was a curious look in his eyes, especially when they met hers which she had never seen in any man before, and a strange setting of mouth and jaw which did I not suggest the love-sick husband.

But she liked his easy bearing as he talked to maman with an easy familiarity that proclaimed high birth and, gentle breeding. He had declined for himself Mme. Legros' offers of refreshment in the shape of mead or aromatic wines, but accepted gratefully when she offered to take mugs of steaming ale out to his men.

Rose Marie felt as if this were all a dream, and as if she would wake anon in her narrow bed behind the cotton curtains in her room under the eaves. She took several furtive glances at her future lord, and felt not a little piqued that he took so little heed of her. After that first hand kiss, and that quick flash of his deep-set eyes, when he hid her bouquet in his coat, she had not caught him once looking at her—was it because he did not think her fair?

Papa talked incessantly, and presently maman came back, and in that same vague dream-like way Rose Marie seemed to hear them talking about the wedding ceremony. My lord seemed impatient and anxious to get through the necessary formalities prescribed by the Church, and then to take his bride away with him to England as quickly as possible. Obviously she was not to be left alone with her future husband just now; and though in her young heart, she had looked forward to the moment when she would be alone with my lord, she now felt relieved at the thought that it was not to be.

Poor Rose Marie was bitterly disappointed. It had all been so very, very different—this first meeting—to what she had anticipated. She felt very angry with herself indeed for being so childish and so timid—no doubt by now my lord had set her down as a silly goose quite unfit to be a great English lady. At this thought she felt tears of shame welling to her eyes, and was infinitely relieved when maman took hold of her hand and led her out of the room.

She bowed to my lord, and then held her head very erect as she walked past him to the door; she wanted to look proud and defiant now, for she had felt those strange deep-set eyes of his fixed upon her with an expression she could not define.

And when she was alone in her room, she went straight to the image of the Virgin Mary which hung against the wall close to her narrow bed. She knelt on the prie-dieu beneath it, and she begged the Holy Mother of God to teach her not to be rebellious, and to be ready to obey her lord in all things, to give him love and respect, "And O holy Mary, Mother of God!" she added with a pitiful little sigh, "if it be in your power to make my lord love me, then I humbly pray you tell him so to do; and whisper to me from on high what I must do to please him and to find favour in his sight."

CHAPTER XIX

Smiling, frowning, evermore
Thou art perfect in love-lore.

—Tennyson

"My cabbage," said Maman Legros in that decisive tone, which she only assumed on great occasions, and which then no one dreamed of contradicting, "what thou dost ask is entirely out of the question. It is not seemly for a maiden to be left alone in company with her lord. Why! every one down the street would know of it—thy father's 'prentices would make mock of thee—and thy reputation would be as surely gone as is thistle-down after a gale."

"But, Maman," hazarded Rose Marie, bold for the first time in her life, in the face of maman's stern refusal, "my lord is not my future husband. He is my husband, and surely I have the right to talk to him alone sometimes."

"Rose Marie, thou talkest like a goose, that cackles without understanding," replied maman sternly, "though my lord is thy husband by law and by the will of the Church, he will not be thy true lord until the day after to-morrow, when thou wilt ratify thy vows to love, honour and humbly obey him, which vows I, thy mother, took in thy name eighteen years ago. Before thou hast spoken them with thine own lips, after High Mass on Wednesday, thou dost an unseemly and unmaiden-like act in wishing to be alone in his company. Truly thy guardian angel must be veiling his face with the shame of thee at the present moment."

But Rose Marie refused to look upon the troubles of her guardian angel with proper compunction. She still felt rebellious and argumentative; but she changed her tactics. The sly young damsel realised that she had taken maman the wrong way and that she would gain nothing by controversy. She, therefore, brought forth her other weapons of attack, certain methods of pressure on the parental will which hitherto she had never known to fail.

She commenced proceedings by allowing her blue eyes to be veiled in tears, then seeing that maman turned her face away so as not to be forced to look on those pathetic dewdrops the rogue went close up to her mother and kneeling beside her put two loving arms round the old woman's shoulders.

"Maman!" she whispered with quivering lips.

"'Tis no use," retorted maman obdurately.

"Only one very tiny, short quarter of an hour, Maman chérie—after dinner—when papa goes downstairs to set the afternoon work to the 'prentices—you could be busy in the kitchen—accidentally—just for one quarter of an hour—Maman chérie!"

The pleading voice was hard to resist. Maman tried to steel her heart and obstinately turned away from those liquid eyes, drowned in tears.

"But in the name of the Holy Virgin, child," she said gruffly, "what is there that thou wouldst say to my lord, that thou canst not do in thy mother's presence?"

"'Tis not what I would say, Maman—" rejoined Rose Marie in a soft murmur quite close to maman's ear.

"Then what?"

"I want to hear him speak to me, Maman chérie—oh, I am sure that he will say naught that is unseemly—he is too proud and too rigid for that—but, when you and papa are in the room he never, never speaks to me at all—I have oft wondered if he thought me a goose. When he comes, he greets me of a truth as if I were a queen, he kisses my hand—and bows in the most correct manner—then, when I sing to him and play on the harpsichord, he praises my voice, and coldly thanks me for the entertainment—"

"And 'tis right and proper conduct on the part of a great

93

gentleman," retorted maman hotly, "thou wouldst not have him kiss thee, as if thou wert a kitchen wench."

But Rose Marie did not commit herself into saying what she did wish in this matter, but continued with seeming irrelevance.

"When I go out of the room, after the frigid and stately adieux which my lord bestows upon me, I oft hear his ringing, merry voice echoing up the stairs, right through the walls to my room. I hear papa and you laughing, in obvious response to his sallies—and once—it was yesterday—I stayed peeping over the bannister until my lord departed—"

"Very unseemly behaviour," growled maman whilst an obvious blush rose to her fat cheeks, and her little, beady eyes seemed to twinkle at a certain recollection.

"I saw my lord take thee in his arms, Maman," continued Rose Marie with stern reproach, "and he imprinted two such kisses on thy cheeks that literally raised the echoes in the house and must have been heard in the 'prentices' shop."

Maman made great efforts to preserve her gravity.

"Well!" she said, "and if he did—I am old enough to be his mother—and would it had pleased God to give me a son like him! Those merry eyes give joy to my heart when I look into them, and he has such funny ways with him—such amusing sallies—why not later than yesterday, he said, speaking of Mme. Renaud, the cobbler's wife down the street, that—"

Maman caught Rose Marie's blue eyes fixed eagerly upon her—there were no tears in them now—only excitement and curiosity—Maman promptly checked her own flow of eloquence and suddenly resumed her gruff, stern voice.

"But that is naught for thee, my pigeon—and now, enough of this talk—the pot-au-feu will be boiling over."

She wore a great air of finality now and would have risen but for Rose Marie's clinging arms.

"Maman darling," pleaded the girl.

"Nonsense!" retorted Mme. Legros decisively.

"One little, tiny, very, very short quarter of an hour."

"Nonsense."

"I want so to know what he would say when we are alone—he could not sit before me mute as a carp, and stiff as papa's wooden measure. I want to hear his merry voice myself. I want to see—what he looks like—when he laughs."

"Nonsense," reiterated maman for the third time.

But even as she spoke the word, she looked down upon the beautiful upturned head, the glowing eyes, the quivering lips parted in earnest pleading, and like the thistle-down in a gale, which she herself had quoted, the worthy old woman's resistance fell away.

"Of a truth thou'rt a rogue," she said more gently.

94

"Fifteen minutes, Maman."

"Thy father would not hear of it."

"He need not know. When he goes down after dinner—to set the work for the 'prentices."

Maman hesitated one moment longer, but that final hesitation was useless by now. The fortress had yielded to the powerful weapons of the loved one in tears.

"Very well," she said. And Rose Marie jumped to her feet with a little cry of triumph. "But remember," continued maman with stern, upraised finger, "it shall be ten minutes and no more."

CHAPTER XX

—So that hour died
Like odour rapt into the winged wind
Borne into alien lands and far away.

—Tennyson

Thus it was that this day, after maman had cleared the debris of dinner, and papa went downstairs to set the 'prentices to their afternoon's work, that no sooner had Rose Marie sat down to her harpsichord and begun to sing:

"La nuit écoute et se penche sur l'onde
Pour y cueillir rien qu'un souffle d'amour,"

then maman gave a slight cry of surprise, and jumped to her feet exclaiming:

"Oh, mon Dieu! I had forgot the pot-au-feu—it must be boiling over," and incontinently ran out of the room.

Rose Marie continued her song. She was sitting with her back to the light, and my lord straight in front of her: and as her young voice rose and fell to the simple cadence of the old song, she was able to throw many a veiled look in his direction.

At first when maman ran away, he had made a movement as if he would follow her, then seeing that Rose Marie remained at the harpsichord, he seemed to think that mayhap courtesy compelled him to remain with her. He sat down again in the high-backed arm chair and rested his head in his hand. Every time that Rose Marie looked up she caught his deep-set eyes fixed upon her. Strangely enough the look in them seemed quite sad—indeed if it were possible in one so rich and in so high-born a gentleman—Rose Marie would almost have imagined that my lord's whole attitude was one which made appeal to her tenderness and even to her pity.

Then when the last note of her song died away in a soft murmur, my lord rose and came up to her.

"What a sweet voice you have, Rose Marie," he said in that even, gentle voice with which he usually addressed her and which seemed to her veiled with studied coldness, "and 'tis a tender song which you sang."

"It pleases me, my lord, that it should find favour with you," she replied demurely, the while she allowed her long lashes to veil the light of excitement which danced in her eyes.

"Nay! who am I that you should try to please me, dear heart?" he said a trifle sadly, "rather is it I who with my whole mind and soul and strength should strive to make you happy."

"That were not very difficult, my lord."

She would then and there have liked to give her excitement fuller rein, to jump up, to clasp her hands together and to look up into his grave face and say: "Only, only be kind and gentle to me, give me as much love as ever you can—I am prepared to be the truest, most devoted, most loving wife that e'er strove to be a joy to her lord. Give me sunshine, and gaiety and laughter, and what meed of love you are able to give."

But she did not quite dare to say and do all that, for maman's admonitions were still fresh in her mind, and her guardian angel would of a surety have had to veil his face again before this unseemly behaviour on the part of his turbulent charge.

Therefore she added somewhat tamely:

"I have been taught to be easily contented, and meseems that by honouring me with your love, you, my lord, would be doing all that God doth ask of you."

Though she had spoken lightly, almost flippantly, for her heart was glad, and her mind free from any presage of sorrow, his face, which all along had been passing grave now looked deeply troubled at her words.

"Doing all that God doth ask of me," he exclaimed with sudden vehemence, whilst a tone of bitterness, which she could not understand, rang through his usually clear and fresh voice. "Nay, little snowdrop, therein you wrong divine justice—if indeed there be one. Dear heart, were I from this time forth to shed drop by drop all the blood of my veins, were I to give my life inch by inch, my flesh piece by piece to secure your happiness, even then I would not be doing all that God would ask of me."

He had turned from her and while he spoke he paced up and down the narrow room like some untamed creature fretful of its cage;

96

then he broke into a laugh—not the merry laugh which she had so oft heard ringing through the house, but a harsh outburst of passionate sarcasm, which had an undercurrent in it of deep and hidden sorrow. Rose Marie felt a wealth of pity surging in her heart, when she heard that mirthless laugh. Yet was it not passing strange that she, an humble tradesman's daughter, with no knowledge of that great world in which lived my lord, that she should thus dare to pity this noble, high-born and rich English gentleman? But she could not combat the feeling and her innocent blue eyes watching his restless movements, and that troubled look on his face, were filled with the tears of womanly compassion.

She looked divinely pretty thus, sitting at the harpsichord, one delicate hand idly resting on the ivory keys, from which almost unconsciously she had just evoked one sweet and melancholy chord from out the soul of the old instrument, like a long-drawn-out sigh of unspoken sorrow. Her young bosom rose and fell beneath the folds of the primly folded kerchief, and her upturned face showed the white column of her throat round which nestled a string of pearls, large and translucent—his bridal gift to her.

He paused beside her, and in his expressive face the signs of a great inward combat became strangely visible. Then he knelt down, close to her, and with a curious gesture half masterful and half appealing he took both her hands and imprisoned them in his own. He looked straight into those tear-dimmed eyes, with a questioning look that seemed to probe the very depths of her soul.

"My lord you are troubled," she said gently.

"Ay, little snowdrop," he replied, "deeply troubled at sight of the exquisite purity which speaks to me with such mute eloquence from out the depths of your blue eyes. How dare I, miserable wretch, drag you from out that secluded garden of innocence wherein you have grown to such perfect beauty. How dare I with impious hand guide you toward that great outer world which lies so far beyond the glorious land of your girlish dreams? It is a world, dear heart, wherein great monsters dwell, pollution, sin and evil and that canker of corruption which will inevitably mar the calyx of the snowdrop and cause her white petals to droop at its touch."

"I have no fear of that great world, my lord," she rejoined simply, "since I will enter it in your company."

"No, no, you must not talk like that, dear heart," he said with strange persistence, "you must not trust me so. What do you know of me or of my life? You so young, so pure, so exquisite, and I—"

He paused and pushing her hands away with a rough, impetuous movement he jumped to his feet and once more resumed his restless wanderings up and down the room.

"Have you ever wandered, little one, in the forests round Cluny," he asked with one of those sudden transitions in voice and manner which puzzled her so, "and paused beside that pool which the country folk about there call the Lake of Sighs? Yes, I see from your telltale eyes that you do remember it. Well then, you must oft have seen it lying silent and stagnant beneath the shades of the overhanging willows, whilst on its smooth, dark surface water lilies as white as snowdrops rear their stately heads in June. You should see these in the spring tall and majestic, with graceful upright stems and fragrant, wide-open buds, which seem to invite with a kind of cold aloofness the rough caresses and kisses of the bee. Tall and majestic like you, dear heart, pure and coldly innocent like your soul—the spring, coy and cool, smiles and passes by, leaving those lilies to face the scorching breath of awakened summer. Have you stood beside the Lake of Sighs, little one, when dying a summer draws out her last sigh of agony? When rank weeds and poisonous plants begin to grow apace from out the slimy ooze which encircles the pool, and throw out sinewy, death-dealing arms along its peaceful surface? Then noisome trails of slugs and grime skim the once pure waters of the pond and rank growths of coarse weeds cover the slender stems of the lilies, and drag them down, down until the stately flowers, weighted with mud-scattering rain bend their proud heads to the mire, the while in their slimy hovels, loathsome toads croak their chorus in unison. The world to which I must take you, little snowdrop, is just such another pool, you the lily and I the weed—and men and women the loud-voiced croakers who are always ready to proclaim triumphantly the pollution of a work of God."

Whilst he spoke he halted opposite to her and looking down into her face he studied every line of it, watching for the first look of horror which would mar its perfect peace. He was conscious of a strange desire to see her afraid of him, to feel that at his words her innocence would rebel, that if after what he had said he attempted to touch her, she would shrink away in unexplainable horror.

Now that he was alone with her for the first time, and could study at leisure every line of her graceful form, the perfect shell which contained a perfect soul, the first poisoned fangs of remorse fastened themselves into his heart, and impatient of the monster's attack, he strove to smother it, and thus longed to see her less trustful, less innocent, even—God help him—less pure!

Already he was searching for justification for that great wrong which he was about to commit, nay which he did commit with every word of gentleness which he spoke to her, with every moment that he spent in her company. Therefore he tried to make his voice harsh and rough, he did not want the child's regard, her trust, her allegiance. He would have had her ambitious, sordid and grasping for in this he could satisfy her by and bye, when he had all the promised riches in his hands, and had made her Countess of Stowmaries. He would have had her look on him as a necessary means to her own ends, as a man who

98

would at best be wholly indifferent to her, or if that could not be, then as a man whom she would hate.

But in spite of all he said, in spite of his harsh words, and strange imageries, the meaning of which she scarce understood, yet almost feared to guess, her face remained perfectly calm, and her eyes—still tender and compassionate—met his in absolute, childlike serenity.

"I am not afraid of entering that world, my lord," she said, "with you to guide me."

"What a brave snowdrop," he said, "nay, you foolish little daughter of the frosts, you'll want an angel to guard you and to stand 'twixt you and me. I begin to think that cold ice-maiden though you be, you must at some time of your brief terrestrial existence have offended the God who made you, since He has thought fit to punish you so severely by giving you for husband the most abandoned sinner that ever defiled His earth. Or was it in a former existence, dear heart, when you dwelt amidst the snows that you roused the ire of devils to such an extent that they swore to be revenged on you, once you were a woman and could understand and feel. 'Twas a cowardly revenge of a surety, for there were other men—less vile, less corrupt, less contemptible than he in whose hand you so trustfully place yours. God forgive me, but meseems that I do feel tempted to draw aside the veil of ignorance which lies before your blue eyes, and to show you pictures of evil and of wretchedness from which your calm soul would shrink in horror, and even your serene virginity would recoil in fear. See the abandoned wretch that I am! I would rouse terror in those eyes—which hitherto have been the blue and opaque windows through which a placid soul hath gazed upon the devilries of mankind—and gazing hath not seen. Dear heart, how will you bear it, this first contact with pollution, and with sin; my hand to guide you, my finger to be the one to point the hideous way?—Broad the priests call it, and an easy descent to Hell, lined with the grinning faces of monstrous ghouls, one of which is called drunkenness, the other licentiousness, whilst blasphemy is the constant companion of both—and right and left from the road itself stand those hideous booths where poverty and degradation shrink out of sight in the dark hours of the evening gloom, and where hovers—like a gigantic bat with black and loathsome wings outspread and claw-like feet that grip and tear—that cruel Titan, called Remorse. Little snowdrop, snow-white and so pure, how will you trust after that, the hand that would guide you still further on the way, the voice that in its agony of shame would yet murmur in your ears promises of a turning out of the hideous road, a turning which leads to happiness and peace?"

His voice broke in a sigh which was almost a sob. Gradually as he spoke he had drawn nearer to her, until his knee touched the ground, and his head was bowed in his hands. But had he looked at her face even now he would not on any line of it have seen the slightest sign of the fear which he wished to evoke, nor of the loathing which he would have conjured up, yet would dread to see.

Only her eyes as pure, as childlike as before, were veiled in the tears of infinite pity. There was silence for awhile in the little parlour, her hands had fallen away from the keys of the harpsichord. Only the old clock ticked solemnly on, marking the brief minutes wherein these two souls met each other in this their first communion. Then as she did not speak, his whole soul recoiled at thought of losing her and a great dread seized him, lest after all she had understood, and in understanding, turned away from him in fear.

And humbly, gently, not daring to look up, and murmuring scarce above a whisper, he said:

"Little snowdrop, would you trust me still?"

And whilst despite iron will, obstinacy and pride hot tears would surge to his eyes and sear his aching lids, he suddenly felt a light touch, soft and cool as a snowflake, a tiny hand resting upon his shoulder.

"I trusted you ere this, my lord," she said simply, "trusted and honoured you, mayhap a little feared you as my lord and master. But now, methinks that a great sorrow lies buried in your heart—you choose to call it sin—mayhap it is—that I do not know—I am a woman—soon to be your wife, but never your judge, my lord. And if you have sinned, then you stand nearer to me, who am so far from that perfection which, alas! you see in me. If I feared you before, my lord—meseems that I could love you now."

To Michael Kestyon, with a life of insubordination behind him, a life of debauchery, of loneliness and lovelessness, it seemed as if some unknown Heaven had opened and he had his first vision of what paradise might be. A paradise wherein voices of angels spoke to him of love, and cool white hands, cold as snowflakes yet infinitely gentle, led him towards that open door. That tiny snowflake fell from his shoulder onto his own burning hands, and to his vague astonishment it did not melt at the contact, but lay there cool and soft, mayhap a little trembling, having suddenly changed into some fairy bird.

Michael pressed his hot forehead against it, his eyes and then his lips. His whole soul cried out mutely now in a passionate longing for happiness. Womanly tenderness, womanly pity awaited him in that paradise, the door of which stood open, and if honour long since dormant called out loudly against treachery and against a trick, who shall pronounce judgment on this man, if he had not the strength at this moment to respond to that call?

With his own hands now, with one word spoken by his own lips, he could shut against himself those glorious gates of Heaven, and deliberately turn his back on that brief vision of paradise, and walk once more down that hideous path which leads straight to Hell.

There were but the two courses open to him. The one was to take this trusting, loving woman to his heart, to guard and keep her in

100

happiness and peace, whilst showering on her all the gifts which her weaker nature might desire. He was rich now, would be richer still, he could satisfy her ambition, and by constant love and tender care, he could win her heart and her inner self in time, even though he had won her person by a trick.

The other course was the rugged path to which the inexorable hand of almost barbaric honour pointed relentlessly, to tell her all and to lose her forever. To throw back in his kinsman's face the price of this girl's innocence, and then to go back to that life in London, the drinking booths, the degrading hovels, the propinquity of abandoned reprobates as despicable as he had been himself before he met her.

Pity him if you can!—judge him not if you've never been tempted to chose 'twixt life and living death, 'twixt happiness and degradation, 'twixt the hand of an angel and the gripping tentacles of devils.

Pity him for he was only a man, with a burning thirst for happiness, a mad longing for love and for peace.

Michael Kestyon kissed the little hand which had confirmed the promise of love spoken by the girl's pure lips. He looked up then and met her eyes. Heaven alone knows what he would have said or done the next moment. The Fates who in their distant, rock-bound cavern spin the threads of destiny decreed that these two people should —ere another word was spoken between them—be incontinently hurled from out the realms of romance wherein they had wandered hand in hand for over ten minutes.

For that—as we know—was the time limit set by maman, for allowing her daughter to be alone in the company of my lord. And Michael had only just time to free the small imprisoned hand so that it might wander back to the keys of the harpsichord ere Mme. Legros—rubicund, fussy and prosy—made irruption into the room.

Thus it was that for Michael Kestyon the gates of paradise remained for the nonce invitingly open, nor did the Fates give him another chance to close them against his own happiness.

CHAPTER XXI

Love took up the Harp of Life and smote on all the chords with might;
Smote the chord of Self, that, trembling, pass'd in music out of sight.

—Tennyson

The old, majestic Church of St. Gervais had been made quite gay with flowers. Good M. Legros was passing rich, thank God! He could gratify his only child's every whim—however trivial—on this her wedding day.

She had expressed a great desire to see the church quite full of flowers—as many flowers as it could hold, and Papa Legros had spent—so the gossips said—enough money in indulging this wish as would have kept a dozen poor families in comfort for a dozen years.

'Twas mid April and there were white roses from the King's conservatories in Versailles, white hyacinths from Fontainebleau and white violas from the walled-in gardens at Blois, there were white violets and snowdrops and sweet-scented narcissi. They lay everywhere in heavy fragrant bunches and wreaths fashioned by loving hands, untutored in the art of decoration. The high altar groaned beneath the weight of huge brass pots wherein old-fashioned stocks reared their sweet-scented heads. The Virgin in her niche, the saints upon their altars almost disappeared beneath their monster crowns of violets and of roses.

The central nave was filled with a motley crowd, attired in holiday clothes, come to see the tailor's daughter wedded to the English milor. A few simple folk there were—gaffers and cronies who had watched Rose Marie as she grew up in her father's back shop, and who came with shaking heads and ominous murmurs to see the last of the poor child, who of a surety would be drowned when she sailed upon the sea or if she did survive that calamity, would certainly be most unhappy in a land of evil-doers, and of cruel, red-haired, large-toothed men. But there were others, too, mere idlers these, who had never before set eyes on an English milor, and were curious to know if what was said of these English were true, namely that they were big as giants and like them ferocious, with fangs instead of teeth, and fists as heavy as bullocks.

Under one of the arches, quite close to the chancel, special places had been reserved and chairs covered with red cloth. Here a small group of gaily-dressed ladies and gentlemen had assembled, gilded butterflies flown from out their silken nets over in the St. Germain quarter and even from the Louvre and Versailles; gentlemen of the court and of His Majesty's bedchamber with their ladies in stiff brocaded paniers and silken skirts which made a soft swishing sound as the wearers turned to right or left to lend an ear to the whisperings of a gallant or to murmur a word of scandal in that of a friend.

They had crossed the river and wandered into this abandoned quarter of the city from idle curiosity. Rumours had reached the Court that the Earl of Stowmaries, one of the richest young gallants of London, had come to wed the daughter of the Paris breeches-maker, a man well-known to all. His Majesty had deigned to seem interested, Mme. de Montespan expressed a desire to see this milor, whom gossip had reported as handsome and had endowed with the romantic history of early life spent in distant lands, where he was kept in poverty and exiled by a rapacious kinsman, who robbed him of his inheritance.

Gossip as a rule had mingled truth with fiction, but the marquise was interested and brought her brilliantly decked-out sycophants in her train—gentlemen and ladies who sunned themselves in the sunshine of her graces,—to witness the ceremony of St. Gervais. From this group beneath the archway came the constant murmur of fluttering fans, the rustle of silks, the creaking of chairs on the flag-stones of the floor—also at times a giggle quickly suppressed, a cry of astonishment or amusement held in check only by the solemnity of the surroundings.

The atmosphere was waxing oppressive, despite the cold April breeze which found its way into the edifice through the chinks of many cracked window panes. The scent of the poet's narcissus, heavy and intoxicating, filled nostrils and brain with its overpowering savour; the roses already inclined to droop added their faded fragrance to the air, mingling, too, with the penetrating odour of white Roman hyacinths and the pungent smell of primroses and of violas, whilst through it all the heavy fumes of incense rose upwards to the high-vaulted roof and wrapped the statues of saints, the small side altars and tall embroidered banners in their mystery-creating clouds.

Monseigneur the Archbishop of Paris had just entered, robed in gorgeous cope and mitre and followed by the clergy of St. Gervais and the band of acolytes clad in scarlet and white. Behind heavy curtains, a band of skilled musicians from His Majesty's own opera house were playing an Introit from one of M. Lulli's most exquisite scores.

All necks were craned to catch sight of the man and woman who were kneeling on crimson cushions at the foot of the chancel steps.

The bride could scarce be seen though her figure looked dainty in her simple white gown; but her golden head was hidden beneath a filmy veil of delicate Mechlin lace, which fell right over her face and far back to the edge of her gown.

But every one could see milor well, for his dark head towered above those of the spectators. And he held his head very erect, some folk thinking that on this occasion a man should look less proud and certainly less defiant. He was gorgeously clad in surcoat and vest of delicate ivory-tinted silk, with exquisite embroideries of gold and silver which the gaffers thought must have cost a mint of money. But then English milors were all so rich, and this one—so 'twas said—was one of the richest amongst all; he certainly was one of the most handsome. Goodly to look at was the verdict of the women, with his dark hair innocent of those monstrous perruques which the jeunesse dorée of Paris and Versailles had lately affected. He wore neither beard nor moustache and every one could see what a firm, strong mouth and jaw he had—an obstinate one murmured some of the ladies, a masterful one, sighed the others.

Mme. de Montespan enthroned on a velvet-covered armchair made vain attempts to draw his dark, deep-set eyes to hers.

But milor looked straight before him, and his arms were crossed over his broad chest. When Monseigneur kneeled at the foot of the altar and began to recite the first verse of the Introibe, milor knelt too, beside his bride, and buried his face in his hands.

M. and Mme. Legros clad in their Sunday best, knelt quite close to the bridal pair. Maman in rich puce-coloured brocade, her scanty locks hidden beneath a remarkable confection of lace was frequently mopping her eyes, the while M. Legros, master tailor to the Court of Paris, tried to conceal the inordinate pride which he felt at seeing his only child wedded to so great a lord.

Now Monseigneur bent his broad shoulders and sotto voce murmured the Confiteor. Rose Marie in the innocence of her heart prayed to the Virgin to make her quite, quite perfect, as good as my lord thought her to be, lest he be deceived and disappointed in her. She had not spoken to him alone again after that happy yet sad quarter of an hour when she had seen his proud head bent before her, and felt that unutterable pity for him, which so quickly then became unutterable love.

That his self-accusations were only the result of an over-sensitive conscience she firmly believed, and if in his early youth my lord had sinned as other young men sin from thoughtlessness and want of a guiding hand, who was she that she should judge him, now that he had honoured her with his love?

And as Monseigneur at the altar read the Holy Gospel wherein the Good God himself enjoins man and woman to cleave to one another, Rose Marie's whole heart went out to the man by her side, and the magnetism of her enthusiastic sacrifice of her whole self to him drew his dark eyes down to hers.

Michael, as in a dream, saw the exquisite white-clad figure close to him; never—he thought—had he beheld aught so lovely, so pure, so worthy of love. Then looking from her to the great altar before him, he saw through the moving clouds of incense phantom figures and objects from out his past.

There in that dark recess, beside the niche of that mitred saint, faces of men who had sneered at his misfortunes, the men of law who had plundered him, and a forest of outstretched palms, oily and smooth awaiting the bribes. There again high up in the groined roof, his companions in those far-off days in Flanders, faces red with the excesses of the day, hands soiled with the evil deeds of night; the miserable camp followers in the wake of a starving mercenary army, dissolute men and intemperate women; and all around him the poor, miserable scum of London, the men with whom he had herded, beasts like himself, no more human since wretchedness had killed all manhood in that perpetual, that degrading search after forgetfulness.

104

All these monsters and ghoulish phantoms grinned at Michael now, polluting the sacred edifice with their imaginary presence. They floated corpse-like on the shifting clouds of the ever-rising incense and taunted Michael with their grinning faces, daring him now to turn from the broad path of happiness whither the snow-white hand of an ignorant girl was so trustingly leading him.

"Follow the path of honour, follow truth and loyalty now, Michael, and to-morrow thou'lt be one of us again: one with the grinning and dishonest sceptics, one with the profligate crowd of mercenary soldiers, one with the flotsam and jetsam of criminal London, the drunkards, the roisterers, God's damned upon earth. Truth leads the way to perdition, follow truth now, Michael, an you can."

And as, up high on the altar steps, Monseigneur now held up for the adoration of the multitude the sacred mysteries which no brain of man can understand, Michael bowing his head and looking within himself with searching, conscience-stricken eyes, saw nothing but loyalty to the girl who was thus unwittingly snatching him from out the yawning abyss of misery and degradation, of humiliation for himself and starvation for his mother.

Anon Monseigneur whispered the Pater Noster, and after that he turned and with hand upheld, three fingers pointing upwards to the mystery-hidden vault, he pronounced the solemn benediction on Michael Kestyon and Rose Marie his wife. Not a sound stirred in the vast and ancient church, save the voice of the Archbishop as it rose high above the chancel, and the blessing spoken by him seemed to descend with unseen wings on the bowed heads of the two young people whom so strange a fate was linking together.

To her—the girl—it was a Sacrament—this confirmation of the vows spoken in her name when she was too young even to lisp them; for him it was the word of honour of a man who throughout a rough life had never succeeded in burying honour out of sight.

Both pronounced their vows without thought of ever rebelling against them. Both pronounced the solemn "I will" with fervour as well as gladness. The assistants almost held their breath. Instinctive awe had silenced every chattering tongue, stilled every careless laugh.

My lord's voice rang out clear and distinct in the midst of that hushed reverence, and more than one fair dame accustomed to the insipid gallantries of the Court of Versailles sighed for the latent and rugged passion which rang out through that firm "I will."

Rose Marie's young heart gave a great leap for joy.

"He loves me," she whispered exultantly to herself, despite the solemnity of the moment, the sacredness of her surroundings, "he loves me, he loves me. I can tell it by the sound of his voice."

And she had to press her bouquet of roses to her lips to suppress the little cry of joy which almost escaped her throat. Perhaps she did not altogether understand at this moment what she herself meant when she thought "he loves me!" Mayhap some of those ladies in the stiff brocades, who cast admiring glances at my lord knew and guessed much more of what went on in his mind than did the simple tradesman's daughter with the innocent mind and the pure heart of childhood still undefiled within her.

And now Monseigneur came right down the altar steps and my lord and Rose Marie had to rise, and to pass through the wrought-iron gates of the rood screen, then pause, standing just below the communion rail. Monseigneur stood there awaiting them, and the good curé of St. Gervais was near him holding a jewelled salver whereon rested two circlets of gold. My lord took one of these between his fingers and some one whispered in Rose Marie's ear to hold out her hand.

From far away came in sweet muffled sounds the opening bars of Lulli's Beati Omnes exquisitely played on the string instruments. All round Rose Marie's feet lay a carpet of white roses which sent their last dying fragrance into the air. She felt my lord's strong hand grasping her own and the tiny band of gold being slipped on her finger—the sign of her bondage to her lord; she was so happy that she could have cried for joy, so happy that she longed to kiss that cold little circlet which now irrevocably bound her to him.

She raised her eyes and saw his dark head bent just over her hand, and it seemed as if a magnetic fluid ran from his veins into hers, for she felt the passion which quivered in his pulse, and though she might not wholly understand it as yet, she nevertheless responded to it with all the strength of her young nature full of the joy of love and of life.

"May the God of Abraham, the God of Isaac, the God of Jacob be with you and remain with you always."

Monseigneur had begun to speak the final prayer. Bride and bridegroom had partaken of the Sacrament together, and Monseigneur had declared that the other sacrament, that of matrimony, had indissolubly now renewed the ties which already bound them to one another since childhood. This was not a marriage, he said, but the repetition of solemn vows made in their name when they were too young to understand, the consecration by the Church of those bonds which she forged for them eighteen years ago.

The solemn Amen was pronounced and sung; the King's musicians played the first bars of a stirring wedding march specially composed for this great occasion by Maître Colasse of His Majesty's orchestra. There was a general movement amongst the spectators, a great sigh of excited satisfaction as Monseigneur having stood for a few moments whispering final admonitions to milor, now turned and walked with slow steps out through the chancel door.

One by one the glittering group of gorgeously-clad priests and acolytes disappeared out through the narrow opening. The strains of the hidden orchestra swelled in glorious volume until they filled every corner of the vast building, like a pæan of triumph and of joy. There was a general frou-frou of silken skirts, a clink of swords, a scraping of chairs against the flagged floor, as my lord now led his young bride down the nave. He pressed her trembling hand against his side, the while he frowned—despite himself—at this crowd of peering faces, this sea of importunate looks which made him restive and impatient. He longed to take his snowdrop away with him, out of this indifferent throng, far, far away to some hidden nook among the Kentish hills, there where the lime trees were just beginning to unfold their delicate leaves of emerald tinged with gold, where lying on a carpet of primroses and violets, beneath a cool, grey sky, his burning head fanned by the cold, spring breezes, he could kneel at her feet and tell her that with her small icy tendrils she had already twined herself around his heart; that her blue eyes, cold and pure as those of a forget-me-not beside a brook, had taught the miserable reprobate his first lesson of love.

Then when the pale tints of the limes turned to a more vivid green, when primroses had paled beneath the shadows of brilliant Lent lilies, then he would try his hand at the great miracle of which he dreamed, the transmutation of the white snowdrop into a glowing, crimson rose.

CHAPTER XXII

Sometimes lurk I in a gossip's bowl.

—A Midsummer Night's Dream

"By the Mass, but the blackguard bears himself bravely! And you, my lord, have no cause to be ashamed of your substitute."

It was Lord Rochester who spoke. He, together with Lord Stowmaries and Sir John Ayloffe, was standing on the top of the steps beneath the ancient stone portcullis which surmounts the porch. They formed a compact little group, which gained distinction from the rest of the motley throng, by the sober cut of the English-made clothes, and by the drooping plumes of the hats—a fashion long since discarded in France.

Michael Kestyon with his bride on his arm had just come out of the church. She, wrapped in cloak and hood—for the spring day was chilly and the east wind keen—looked little more for the moment than a small bundle of humanity desirous above all of escaping observation.

But Michael for all the world looked the picture of the soldier of fortune, defiant and conscious of danger, ready to walk straight into that yawning abyss, at the bottom of which lurks a mysterious death, yet disdainful to evade it, too proud to halt, too obstinate to turn back.

As he came out of the porch, a violent gust of wind caught the folds of his cloak, and lashed him in the face, whipping up the swiftly-coursing blood which the solemnity of the religious service, the drowsy influence of faded roses had lulled into temporary somnolence. The glare of the young April sun dazzled him, after the sombre, grey tones of the majestic chancel; the pupils of his eyes contracted to a pin's point, making the eyes themselves seem pale in colour, and tawny as those of a wild beast sweeping the desert with great savage orbs. There was altogether for the moment in the man's expression a strange look of dreamy aloofness. His eyes wandered over the crowd but obviously they recognised no individual face.

No wonder that Lord Rochester—essentially a man himself and a despiser of the other sex—gazed with ungrudging admiration at this splendid blackguard, who bore the stamp of virility on every line of his massive frame, and who seemed to defy contempt and dare contumely to reach him. Looking at Michael now it seemed impossible to think that he could ever regret any action which he had set his mind to do. Compunction is for the weak who is led astray, who fears gibes and dreads humiliation, but this man had donned an armour of pride and of ruthless ambition which neither sneers nor contempt could ever penetrate.

He might be a blackguard—he was one by every code of moral or religious civilisation, but in his most evil moments he was never paltry and never vile.

"I feel no longer any sorrow for the girl," continued Lord Rochester after awhile. "Odd's fish! Were I a woman I would not complain at the bridegroom. And withal she looked vastly pleasing as a bride, and methinks Michael Kestyon, too, is overmuch in luck's way. What say you, Ayloffe? are you not grieved that you did not take the entire business on your own shoulders, rather than depute that good-looking young reprobate to earn a fortune and an exquisite bride to boot?"

Sir John frowned. Some thought, such as the one expressed by Rochester, had mayhap crossed his own mind during the past three weeks—but this was not for other people to see. He, too, watched Michael's tall retreating figure, as he led Rose Marie down the stone steps, giving it ungrudging admiration and also the tribute of secret envy, until a crowd of friends and servants closed in round the bridal pair and hid them both from view.

Then Sir John turned to his friends and said drily:

"My lord of Rochester is ever ready for a joke. I desired this scheme to succeed, and obviously the worthy tailor yonder would never have mistaken me for a man who was seven years old eighteen years ago. But I'll confess, an it'll please you, my lord and also my lord of Stowmaries, that I do deem Michael Kestyon a lucky dog. One hundred and twenty thousand pounds and such a bride! By Gad, had I been able to put back the hand of time some twenty years—"

"The bride would have loathed you," retorted Stowmaries with an unpleasant snarl. "She'll fall in love with Michael and clear me of remorse."

"Surely my lord of Stowmaries is not troubled with any such unpleasantness?" said Ayloffe imperturbably. "'Tis too late now to give way to remorse. By to-morrow's dawn, my lord, you'll be as free as air to wed whom you please. That simpering tailor's daughter will not have a rag of reputation left to her name, and you can repudiate her whenever you feel so inclined."

"And that will be at once," replied Stowmaries, who, of a truth, was not experiencing the slightest pricks of conscience. The thought of this mock wedding which he had actually witnessed to-day had been dwelling in his mind for close upon a month. He had envisaged it from every point of view and had completely exonerated himself from blame in the matter. The image of his fair Julia had quite succeeded in screening from his mental vision all thought of the unfortunate girl whom he was thus condemning to disgrace and to shame, and whilst he steadily looked on Michael as a miserable blackguard he firmly believed that when once he had paid over the price of an innocent girl's betrayal he himself would remain absolutely free from blame.

"I have made all enquiries," now continued Sir John drawing his two friends out of earshot of the crowd. "I understand that there are to be rare doings to-day in Master the tailor's back shop—a banquet, dancing and I imagine a good deal of wine drinking and licentious entertainment. These French bourgeois have no knowledge of decency and Michael Kestyon, methinks, did not learn to be squeamish whilst herding with the scum of mercenary armies in Flanders and Brandenburg. At five o'clock however a coach is to take the bridal pair as far as St. Denis—"

He paused a moment, then added with a cynical smile, almost cruel in its callousness:

"The first stage of their journey to Havre."

Lord Rochester laughed loudly. He had all along only seen the humour of the adventure. A woman's reputation destroyed, a woman won by a trick, by Gad! these were of every-day occurrence in the life of a fashionable gentleman. Indeed he thought that both Stowmaries and Ayloffe were making far too much of the whole business, and though he, too, called Michael Kestyon a rogue, yet he admired him for his pluck and envied him for his good fortune.

In his heart of hearts he much regretted that on the memorable night when the adventure was proposed, he had been too drunk to accept its terms or to enter the lists for it himself.

"Nay then!" he said lustily, "we'll all call on the turtle doves at St. Denis to-night, and whilst my lord of Stowmaries pays up like a man for all that he gains by Michael's roguery, Sir John Ayloffe and I will entertain the bride by hoodwinking her still further into the belief that she is of a truth Countess of Stowmaries forever and ever Amen, as the Archbishop told her this day."

"I should be glad to get to St. Denis to-night," rejoined Stowmaries. "I owe Michael seventy thousand pounds, which according to promise I should pay him to-day. The draft for it on Master Vivish the goldsmith is in my pocket now. The sooner I am rid of it the more pleased will I be."

"Then will I at once and see about a coach," said Sir John. "We can make a start at about six o'clock, one hour after the dove hath flown out of the paternal cote."

"Nay, old Daniel Pye will see about the coach," rejoined Stowmaries. "He hath met a crony who speaks English and knows his way about Paris better than we do. He'll get us what we want."

"Daniel Pye!" exclaimed Sir John in astonishment. "What doth my kinswoman's faithful henchman in this depraved city?"

"Mistress Julia Peyton desired him to do certain commissions for her here in Paris. When she heard that I was making the journey she requested that I should allow her servant to travel in the company of my men, since he was unversed in foreign ways, and knew nothing of the French language."

Sir John made no further comment, but he wondered vaguely in his mind as to why the fair Julia had sent old Pye over to Paris. The question of commissions was of course nonsense. Daniel could no more choose a length of silk or even of grogram, than he could trim a lace coif or fashion a pinner.

"Mayhap my fair coz is jealous," was Sir John's mental comment and the conclusion to which he arrived with that convenient cynicism of his, with which he usually disposed of any problem wherein feminine motives or feminine actions played an important part. "She hath mayhap deputed that old sinner, Daniel Pye, to watch over young Stowmaries and to make report in case the wiles of this wicked city make my lord forget his allegiance to herself."

Thus content with his own explanation of the circumstance, Sir John dismissed the old serving-man from his mind, but not without deciding to question Pye closely as soon as he had an opportunity so to do.

Most of the crowd had dispersed by now. The bridal pair with good M. and Mme. Legros were being escorted by a merry crowd of 'prentices, servants and friends as far as the worthy tailor's house in the

Rue de l'Ancienne Comédie. This cortège had already turned the angle of the street, and the noise of laughter and of songs sung to the accompaniment of flute and hautbois was gradually dying away in the distance.

The few laggards who remained behind were discussing the chief actors in the pageant which they had witnessed. Mme. de Montespan and her gaily chattering court were gossiping whilst waiting for their chaises.

"Ah!" sighed Madame provokingly, "are all these English milors as handsome as that? I vow our gallants of Versailles have much to learn from them, if indeed they all look like milor of Stowmaries."

And while the gallants there present protested in dismay an ill-concealed jealousy, Madame's roving eyes had discovered the small group of Englishmen close by, and amongst them had recognised Lord Rochester.

"Ah, milor," she exclaimed, "I pray you approach. I did not know you were in Paris! What brings you hither, I pray?"

Lord Rochester, obedient to the call, had already advanced, and was duly allowed to kiss those finger tips whereon royal lips were ever wont to linger. Englishmen were in high favour with Madame for the next half hour at least.

"Why are you in Paris?" she repeated.

"To catch a glimpse of the most beautiful woman in Europe," replied my lord of Rochester with bold gallantry.

"Then you'll come see her in Versailles," she replied, drinking in the full measure of his flattering speech, the obvious falseness of which would not have deceived a child.

"Nay, now that I have seen her!" he retorted, "I must hie me home to England again."

"So soon! Then why did you come? Nay!" she added with mock severity, "Do not repeat your pretty lie again. You could not imagine to see me in this old church to-day. I came out of curiosity, to see this strange, ill-assorted marriage. Tell me what makes the rich Earl of Stowmaries wed a tailor's daughter?"

"He was not always rich, nor always Earl of Stowmaries. The ceremony was not a marriage. It was a confirmation."

"And you came to witness it?"

"And to take part in an adventure."

"I might have guessed. Who is the lady?"

"The bride of half an hour ago."

"I do not understand," said Mme. de Montespan with a frown. "Pray explain."

"I'll do even more than that, Madame la Marquise," retorted Lord Rochester as he stepped a little to one side and disclosed the person of my lord of Stowmaries. "I will with your permission present to you my friend the Earl of Stowmaries and Rivaulx, the only Earl of Stowmaries

111

whom I or His Majesty the King of England would ever acknowledge as such."

The Marquise looked very bewildered, her great violet-hued eyes opened wide and wandered in puzzlement from the face of Lord Rochester to that of his friend.

"The only Earl of Stowmaries!" she exclaimed in astonishment. "I vow milor that you have vastly puzzled me. Then who was that handsome young milor who just now swore to love the tailor's daughter, the while the hearts of two Duchesses, and one other Marquise besides myself were pining for his glance."

My lord of Rochester, however, kept Madame on the tenter-hooks of expectation, whilst he affected the elaborate presentation of his friend which the etiquette of the time demanded. He introduced my lord of Stowmaries to Madame la Marquise de Montespan, and performed a like service for Sir John Ayloffe. Then only did he partly satisfy Madame's curiosity.

"The young reprobate," he said airily, "whom the most beautiful Marquise in Christendom has honoured with a glance of her Myosotis eyes is—well! just a young reprobate, whom my lord of Stowmaries here is paying handsomely to take an unwelcome bride from off his shoulders. My lord of Stowmaries was seven years old when he wedded the tailor's daughter—now he has other matrimonial views—also a handsome cousin who was not averse to stepping into his shoes for this occasion which we have all witnessed to-day. He'll be well paid—neither bride nor bridegroom will have much to complain of—the bridegroom was a wastrel ere my lord of Stowmaries proposed this adventure—and the bride is only a tailor's daughter. She will have a handsome husband, if Michael Kestyon chooses to acknowledge her—if not there is always the nunnery handy for those saintly women like herself who have made a temporary if not wholly voluntary diversion from the strict paths of decorum and virtue. Et puis voila!"

Mme. de Montespan had listened attentively to this tale so cynically told; her friends, too, had closed in round her. Every one was vastly interested and I assure you not the least in the world shocked. The Court of le Roi Soleil abounded in such adventures, the convents of France were filled with the grief-stricken victims of the dissolute idlers of the day. Lord Rochester's story evoked nothing but amusement, and Lord Stowmaries at once became the centre of an admiring little crowd.

"But par ma foi!" commented Madame with a sigh not altogether free from envy, "you English gentlemen are mighty blackguards!"

"We do our best, Madame," rejoined Rochester lightly, "to emulate our confrères in France."

"His Majesty shall hear of your gallantries this very night. I pray you, Lord Rochester, do not leave us yet, nor you, my lord of Stowmaries, nor you, Sir Ayloffe. His Majesty would delight in your company. He so loves a bold adventure. And I am much mistaken he'll

112

wish to see our handsome young reprobate, too—Michael Kestyon, did you say?" she added, prettily mispronouncing the English vowels, "'tis an ugly name—but oh! he hath fine eyes and a manly bearing—and did he really do it for money?"

She called Lord Stowmaries to her side and closely questioned him, until she knew the entire discreditable story from beginning to end. Her amusement in the recital of the tale, her appreciation of the adorable wickedness which had prompted the scheme for the cruel hoodwinking of another woman, did much to dissipate once and for all any lingering thoughts of remorse which Stowmaries may still have been troubled with.

Nothing would do but the imperious beauty's decree that after the call at St. Denis—which was the call of honour since it meant the paying of money for services rendered—the three English gentlemen must straightway back to Versailles, where they would be sure of a cordial welcome from His Majesty and from every lady and gentleman at his Court.

"And," urged Madame, when at last she was installed in her chaise and was bidding farewell to her array of courtiers, "if you can bring that adorable young blackguard with you, you'll earn a gratified smile from the lips of King Louis, and I'll promise not to do more than turn his head and make him forget that he was paid in order to wed the daughter of a tailor—brrr—the thought makes me shudder. The rogue is an Apollo, milors, else a Hercules—and has just that wicked look which makes us poor women tremble and which we adore."

And with this parting shot levelled at those who would have fought to the death for praise such as this, Madame ordered her serving-men to bear her away.

Rochester, satisfied that he had sown the seeds of the most amusing and most comprehensive piece of scandal that had ever amused the jaded monarchs of two rival kingdoms, turned to his friends for final approval. Ayloffe was distinctly appreciative of the new move, but Stowmaries with that shiftiness peculiar to weak characters was not quite sure if it had been premature.

Anyhow the draft for seventy thousand pounds on Master Vivish seemed to burn a hole in the pocket of his elegant surcoat. He was longing to be rid of all obligations in the matter, firmly convinced as he was when he had made Michael richer by one hundred and twenty thousand pounds and himself poorer by that vast sum, this tiresome feeling of uncertainty would leave him, and he could once more enjoy life in its full—life with the prospect of adorable Mistress Julia as a constant companion by his side.

He and his friends walked back to the hostelry where they had put up for the night. There Stowmaries called for Daniel Pye in order to give him instructions about getting a coach ready for the trip to St. Denis.

But it seems that Daniel had gone out earlier in the day and no one knew whither he had gone. But there was no difficulty about the coach. The amiable host of the uncomfortable little inn assured MM. les milors that one would be ready by half-past five of the clock and that the journey to St. Denis could be accomplished in something less than three hours.

CHAPTER XXIII

The man was my whole world all the same
With his flowers to praise or his weeds to blame
And either or both to love.

—Browning

The workshop of Master Legros, tailor-in-chief to His Majesty the King of France, had been transformed into a vast assembly-room. The big central tables whereon usually sat cross-legged the 'prentices and stitchers, had been pushed to one side, right along the wall where it now groaned beneath the weight of pasties, and of pies, of a lamb roasted whole, of dishes of marrow bones, of prawns and of cheese, amongst which dishes and platters, the bottles of good Burgundy and of wine of Navarre, and the jugs of metheglin and hypocras reared their enticing heads.

The centre of the room was given over to dancing. The wooden floor had been greased and polished until it had become slippery to the feet, whilst in a corner raised upon a wooden platform covered with crimson cloth a band of musicians were playing good lilting, swinging measures for a dance. None of your simpering minuets or slow-going pavanes for these young people; but something with a good lively tune in it, and plenty of noise and banging of the small drum and cymbal, so that a youngster could have a chance of gripping a wench well round the waist and of turning her round and round until she became so giddy, so breathless and so hot that she had to cry for mercy even at the price of a sounding kiss.

For close upon an hour now the musicians had played the same rousing tune, and for close upon an hour indefatigable feet—some clad in shoe leather, others with hard bare soles beating the polished floor— had been raising up a mighty cloud of dust which settled on pasties and on cheese, on the big drum and on perspiring faces. Cheeks were crimson from the exertion, short hair and long hair, curly and straight hung limply over sweating, greasy foreheads. Pinners were getting awry, displaying more bosom than prudery would otherwise allow. To right and left surcoats and vests were being cast aside and flung across the room leaving bare arms and chests to view, or else a shirt more full of tatters than of stitches.

Daylight still came streaming in for it was only four o'clock and les mariés would not be leaving for at least another hour. In the meanwhile M. Legros had much ado to keep the curious, the idle, the impertinent from his doorstep, for, look you! though the hospitable abode of the goodly tailor was open on this great occasion to all and sundry friends and acquaintances who wished to eat and drink and to make merry, yet there was no intention of permitting every shiftless vagabond to come and partake of the cheer.

Good Papa Legros had planted two of his most stalwart assistants at the door, with orders to admit no one who did not bear a familiar face, and if any one prove importunate, why then the end of a whip-lash or even a stout stick should drive impudence away.

Thus it was that when Master Daniel Pye—the faithful henchman of fair Mistress Peyton—presented himself at the tailor's shop in the Rue de l'Ancienne Comédie, he was incontinently refused admittance.

"I desire to speak with M. Legros, tailor to His Majesty the King of France," growled Daniel Pye in excessively bad French, for he knew nothing of the gibberish and had only learnt this phrase off by heart like a parrot that jabbers without understanding.

"Then thou silly lout of a buffle-headed Englishman, thou'lt have to wait with thy desire until to-morrow."

"I desire to speak with M. Legros, tailor to His Majesty the King of France," repeated Pye mechanically. It was the only sentence which he knew, and he had been assured by his crony that the magic phrase would ope the doors for him without any difficulty.

"Get thee gone, and come back to-morrow," retorted the stalwart sentinel.

"I desire to speak with—"

"An thou'lt not go at once," shouted the tailor's irascible cutter, "I'll give thee a taste of a French stick across thy English shoulders."

"I desire—"

Bang! came the stout stick crashing down on worthy Pye's broad back, quickly bent in order to check the strength of the blow.

But he held his ground.

"Thou'lt go to Paris in company with my lord," the mistress had said to him peremptorily, "and on the day on which the daughter of Master Legros, tailor-in-chief to His Majesty the King of France weds an English gentleman, thou'lt to the house of that same Master Legros, and thou'lt deliver him this letter—to him and to no one else—and without saying whence thou comest, nor who it was that sent thee. Thou'lt go to him one hour after the religious ceremony of matrimony

115

shall have been performed in the church and before the newly-wedded pair have quitted the bride's parental home."

Daniel Pye had presented himself according to instructions. He had safely hidden in his breast pocket the letter which he was to deliver to the tailor of his Majesty the King of France, and to no one else. If he failed in the discharge of his duty, he knew that his fair mistress would punish him mercilessly, probably dismiss him from her service altogether and send him—old and unfit for other work—to starve in his remote East Anglian village.

At best there were plenty of subordinates in Mistress Peyton's household who would only too gladly wield the lash on him who never spared it to others. Therefore Daniel Pye held his ground. The more blows he received, the more sure would he be of the indulgence of his own mistress. He had a tough hide, and after all is said and done, one does not die of a beating. So he bore the blows of the stick on his back, and the stinging swish of whipcord round his legs. He knew quite well that on occasions such as marriage-feasts or other merrimaking days, 'prentices and young assistants would have their bit of fun.

He had had his own many a time. So when his back ached overmuch, and his legs were more sore than he could stand, he gave up all further attempts to force his way into the house and beat a retreat in the rear of the good-natured crowd.

He would, he thought, find a means to speak to Master Legros a little later on, when every one's attention would be more fully concentrated on merrimaking, and the door was not so closely guarded.

When Papa Legros heard of the incident he was vastly amused, then he bethought himself that mayhap the persistent English lout had some command for him for some rich clothes on behalf of one or other of the elegant milors who were in Paris at this moment—friends of my Lord Stowmaries, mayhap. Master Legros was vastly perturbed, and sent one of his 'prentices to search for the Englishman in the crowd, and to bring him hither forthwith. But Master Daniel Pye with that stolidity peculiar to his race had gone very quietly off to a neighbouring coffee house to nurse his sores, to drink mulled ale and to await events.

In the meanwhile within the house itself much time had been spent in eating and drinking, as the debris which at this hour littered Mme. Legros' kitchen could well testify. The banquet had lasted for nearly two hours and had gone on at intervals ever since. M. Legros had made a speech which had caused his fair young daughter to blush and made every one there clap mugs against the table and shout: "Long live! long live!" until the old rafters and beams shook with the mighty echo.

One or two buxom maids of all work, with muscular, bare arms and streaming, red faces had since then brought in fresh relays of victuals, and any number of bottles of wine—quite enough for every 'prentice in the shop to get as drunk as any lord.

116

The noise in the back shop was now incessant and the shouting of the dancers, the screams of the girls, the laughing and hooting of the boys, almost drowned the cymbal, hautbois and big drum. The intoxication of pleasure had whipped up the blood of all these youngsters. Ay! and of the sober folk, too, for behold Mme. Legros in her beautiful puce silk footing it with good M. Dumas, the shoesmith, and displaying a length of stockinged leg such as no decent matron should show except to her husband.

But what would you? This is an occasion such as only occurs once in a lifetime: the marriage of an only daughter, and that to the handsomest, richest, most noble seigneur that ever dwelt at the Court of the King of England.

Then vogue la galère! Let us dance and make merry! Dance until every sinew in the body aches and clothes slip off dripping shoulders.

"Mais va donc! vieille tortue!" shouted some of the young 'prentices to the musicians as these poor wretches, perspiring profusely, straining their arms and puffing out their cheeks tried to keep up the measure to the required rapidity.

"C'est un enterrement par Dieu!" yelled another, as he whirled his partner round until both her little feet gave way and she and the indefatigable youth collapsed with a violent thud upon the hard floor.

A terrific shout of laughter greeted the catastrophe. The musicians, in response to vigorous shouts, struck up the measure with renewed quickness. They blew and puffed at such a rate now that no foot of man could have kept up with the tune, at least not after an hour of this same exertion.

"Assez! assez! not so fast morbleu!"

But the players evidently had resented the previous comments anent their slowness, and now would listen to no admonition in the contrary direction. Faster and faster they played, the exhausted, sweating 'prentices tripped it with frantic efforts; the girls loudly clamoured for the music to stop. They were giddy, they were toweringly hot, the young men's breath almost burned their cheeks.

"Enough! enough! par tous les diables! These musicians have the devil in them!"

The couples fell back one by one panting against the wall, only one pair remained in the centre now twirling and twisting in a cloud of dust. The girl's white skirts flew out all round her like a thousand wings which seemed to lift her off her feet. The man held her tightly, his strong arms twined round her as if he never would let her go again, but meant to dance and turn, to whirl her through space even to eternity.

His head was bent for he was over-tall and towered above every one else in the room. He was a head taller than she was, but he looked straight down at her as he held her, straight into her eyes, those beautiful blue eyes of hers which he had thought so cold. They were dark now, almost as dark as his own, and flashed with curious purple lights, and deep velvety shadows; her lips were parted with the effort of breathing, they were red and full, and showed glimpses of small pearly teeth, and the red moist tongue between them.

The man's heart gave a great bound of joy. This was no ice-maiden wrapped in a mantle of snow, the tips of whose chaste fingers he had hitherto hardly dared to touch with his lips. No! this was a living, breathing woman full of passion, full of the joy of life, a woman moreover who was ready to love him, to return passion for passion, and kiss for kiss.

Ye gods! Michael, but thou'rt a happy man!

He held her close in his arms, for is not God's most glorious, most perfect creation upon earth a woman who is pure the while she burns with passion? And that priceless treasure was his. Fate had given her to him, Fate and his own damnable action.

Nay, Michael, thou blackguard, if thine action be damnable, then by all the Saints in Heaven and by all the devils in Hell, do thou go and be damned, but hold this woman first.

And wild, mad thoughts went coursing through his brain, thoughts of himself and of her:

"I am a man, and what I do, I do. With mine honour did I buy thee, with mine own humiliation and shame have I conquered thee. Thou who art no snow-maiden but living lava melting at my touch, thou whom I adore, for whom were it to be done again, I would lie and I would cheat, I would descend to Hell or conquer paradise. I am a man and what I do, I do! Perish honour, perish life itself and eternal salvation if to gain honour mean to forsake thee."

These were the tumultuous coursings of his excited brain the while he held her thus, swirling and whirling in his arms, swaying as a reed in the embrace of a blasting wind.

The cloud of dust enveloped them, as, on the Brocken, the steam from unseen cauldrons envelops the witches in their revels. Through this haze Rose Marie saw nothing but his face and in it she read mayhap something that was passing in his mind, something of that passion which her mind as yet could not understand, even though her blood and heart were so ready to respond.

But strangely enough she was not afraid. The child whose life boundary did not extend far beyond the walls of the parental home looked out on a limitless horizon of men's passions and men's sins, but even beyond that horizon the personality of the man to whom she had given her innocent love stood out clear and pure: the master to obey, the hero to worship. That she had roused a great love in him, she could not fail to see; of that she was proud, for her feminine instinct whispered that the greatness of his love transcended any sin which he ever might commit.

How it all happened she never afterwards could say; but it was all so different to what had been prearranged by mother and father, and

118

by all the friends. Rose Marie had not heard the pawing of horse's hoofs outside, nor yet the rumble of the coach. Truth to tell she was so lost in the wild dream of the moment that she had forgotten all about what was to come: the farewell to maman and papa, the noisy "good-bye" to friends, the conventional departure accompanied by shouts and cheers and showers of rose leaves which all richly-dowered brides have to experience.

In her case, too, it had all been duly planned, but it happened so differently!

She had been dancing with her lord, looking up like a fascinated bird into his face glowing with ardent love. Then the room began to spin round and round, she could see nothing very clearly, yet a delicious languor stole into her every limb, she closed her eyes, and gave herself over limp and motionless into his embrace. Suddenly she felt herself lifted off her feet and carried by strong protecting arms through door and passage, until the cold April wind struck her cheeks and forced her with the power of his frolicsome will to open her eyes once more. She saw as in a quick vision a rearing horse, two or three men in sad-coloured surcoats, one of whom clung to the horse's bridle, whilst the other held the stirrup, and then as a background of curious faces the crowd of street gaffers standing gaping round. Behind her the dense throng of 'prentices and wenches, of friends and serving-maids pressed forward down the narrow passage, shouting, clamouring cheering to the echoes; in the forefront of these papa and maman half laughing, half crying, waving hands and mopping tears.

But it was only a vision swift and sudden, for everything happened so quickly—and she was still so dizzy with the frantic whirl of the dance that she hardly remembered being lifted up on to the saddle and landed safely in the strong arms of her lord. The words of command had been so quickly spoken, my lord had jumped with such rapidity into the saddle, no wonder that she did not know exactly how she came to be where she was, clinging to him with all her might, and making herself very, very small lest she hindered him in the guiding of his horse.

She knew exactly how to hold on, and how to sit, for she had oft sat thus ere now, on her father's saddle when he took her with him for a ride—he bent on some business errand, she enjoying the movement, and the fresh air as soon as the grime and smoke of Paris had been left behind.

But no other ride had ever been quite like this one, for soon the horse settled down to an easy, swinging canter in the soft mud of the road, and there was an infinite sense of security in the clasp of the sinewy arm which held her so deliciously close.

Just one slight shifting of her lissome body to settle herself more comfortably, one little movement which seemed to bring her yet a little nearer to him.

119

"Is it well with you, my snowdrop?" he asked, bending his head in a vain endeavour to catch sight of her face.

He only could see the top of a small, fair head, from which the hood had slipped off, disclosing the wealth of quaint curls and puffs, the formal bridal coiffure since then somewhat disarranged.

The wealth of curls shook in obvious assent, and presently a shy voice murmured:

"Why do you call me snowdrop?"

"Because I was an ignorant fool," he replied, "when I first beheld you, a blind and senseless lout who did not distinguish the lovely crimson rose that hid so shyly within a borrowed mantle of ice."

"They call me Rose Marie," she whispered.

"Rosemary to me," he said fervently, "which is for remembrance."

"Tu m'aimes?" she asked, but so softly that whilst she wondered if he would hear she almost hoped that the April breeze would fail to carry her words to his ear.

Of course he did not reply. There is no answer to that exquisite question when it is asked by the loved one's lips, but his right arm tightened round her, until she felt almost crushed in the passionate embrace.

CHAPTER XXIV

Love that keeps all the choir of lives in chime
Love that is blood within the veins of time.

—Swinburne

You all know that funny little inn at St. Denis, on what was then the main road between Paris and Havre; it stands sheltered against north and east winds by a towering bouquet of mighty oaks, which were there, believe me—though mayhap not quite so gnarled and so battered by storms of wind and thunder as they are now—in the April of that year 1678.

The upper story gabled and raftered hung then as now quite askew above its lower companion, and the door even in those days was in perpetual warfare with its own arched lintel, and refused to meet it in a spirit of friendly propinquity. The Seine winds its turgid curves in the rear of the building with nothing between it and the outer walls only the tow path always ankle deep in mud.

120

The view out and across the winding river is only interesting to the lover of colour and of space, for there are no romantic hills, no rugged crags or fir-crowned plateaus to delight the eye. Only a few melancholy acacias sigh and crackle in the wind and tall poplars rear their majestic heads up to the vast expanse of sky.

Now elegant villas and well-trimmed gardens fill the space over which two hundred and forty years ago the eye wandered seeking in vain for signs of human habitation. Rank grass covered the earth, and close to the water's edge clumps of reeds gave shelter to water rats and birds.

Through the small dormer window just beneath the gable, Michael Kestyon looked out upon the melancholy landscape and found it exquisitely fair.

The wind howled down the wide chimney and sighed drearily through the reeds, whereon the spring had not yet thrown her delicate tints of green; but Michael thought the sound divine, for it mingled in his ear with the tones of a fresh, young voice which had prattled gaily on throughout supper-time, of past and of future—not of the present, for that was sacred, too sacred even for her words.

She was a little tired at first, when he lifted her off the saddle, and the amiable hostess of the ramshackle inn took charge of her and saw to her comforts. But after a little rest in her room, she came and joined him in the stuffy parlour, the window of which gave on that far horizon, beyond which lay the sea, England and home.

She seemed a little scared when she found herself quite alone with him, without maman or papa to interrupt the tête-à-tête. She was so young, and oh! how tender and fragile she appeared to him, as she came forward a little timidly, with great, blue eyes opened wide, wherein her pure love fought with her timidity.

Her whole appearance, her expression of face as she yielded her hand to him, and allowed him to draw her closer ever closer to his heart, made appeal to all that was best, most humbly reverent within him.

Rose Marie was home to him, she was joy and she was peace, and he, the homeless, the joyless, the insubordinate wastrel, felt a wave of infinite tenderness, a tenderness which purified his love, and laid ardent passion to rest.

He led her to the window, and throwing it wide open, he knelt down beside her there in the embrasure. She sat on the narrow window seat, looking out on that vast expanse of sky and land whereon the shadows of evening had thrown a veil of exquisite sadness and peace. The bare branches of the acacias as yet only tipped with tiny flecks of green moaned softly beneath the kiss of the breezes. Banks of clouds lashed into activity by the wind hurried swiftly past, out towards the unseen ocean, now obscuring the moon, now revealing her magic beauty, more transcendent and glorious after those brief spells of mystery conquered and of darkness subdued. Michael said very little. There was so little that he could say, which was not now a lie. He could not speak to her of his home, for home to him had been a miserable garret under the grimy roof of a house of disrepute, shared with others as miserable, as homeless as himself. He could not speak to her of friends, for of these he had none, only the depraved companions of a dissolute past, nor could he speak of kindred, unless he told her that it was because his mother was dying of hunger in a wretched hovel that he had spoken the mighty lie and taken payment for speaking it.

I would not have you think that even now Michael felt any remorse for what he had done. He was not a man to act first and blush for his actions afterwards. He knew his action to be vile, but then he had known that ere he committed it, and knowing it had deliberately taken his course. Were it to be done all over again, he would do it; since she never could be his save by the great lie and the monstrous trick, then the lie must be spoken and the trick accomplished. For she meant love and purification; she meant the re-awakening of all that was holy in him and which the Creator infuses in every man be he cast into this world in a gutter or upon a throne.

And he would make her happy, for he had gained her love, and a woman such as she hath but one love to give. She would never have loved Stowmaries, and not loving, she would have been unhappy. He had taken upon himself the outer shell of another man, and that was all; just another man's name, title and past history, nothing more. But it was his personality which had conquered her, his love which had roused hers. She loved—not an Earl of Stowmaries, the plighted husband of her babyhood. No! she loved him, Michael, the blackguard, the liar, the cheat an you will call him so; but she loved him, the man for all that.

Therefore he felt no remorse, when he knelt beside her and during that exquisite hour of evening, when shadows flew across the moon, and the acacias whispered fairy tales of love and of brave deeds, he listened to her innocent prattle with a clear mind and a determined conscience, and the while she spoke to him of her simple past life, of her books and of her music, his ambition went galloping on into the land of romance.

The title of Earl of Stowmaries which he had assumed, he could easily win now; the riches, the position, everything that could satisfy a woman's innocent vanity he would shower upon his snowdrop. She would have all that her parents wished for her, all and more, for she would have a husband who worshipped her, whose boundless love was built on the secure foundation of a great and lasting gratitude.

It was in this same boundless gratitude that he kissed her hands now; those little hands which had been the exquisite channels through which had flown to him the pure waters of love and of happiness.

How quaint she looked, with her fair hair almost wild round her little head. The dance first, then the ride through wind and space had loosened most of the puffs and curls from their prearranged places. That tired look round the eyes, the ring of dark tone which set off the pearly whiteness of her skin, the beads of moisture on her forehead, these gave her a strangely-pathetic air of frailty, which most specially appealed to Michael's rugged strength.

Her white gown was torn here and there—Michael remembered catching his foot in it in the mazes of the dance—it was crumpled, too, and hung limply round her young figure, showing every delicate curve of the childlike form, every rounded outline of budding womanhood.

Think you it was an easy task for Michael to keep his tempestuous passion in check, he who throughout his life had known no control save that of cruel necessity? Think you he did not long to take her in his arms, to cover those sweet lips with kisses, to frighten her with the overwhelming strength of his love and then to see fright slowly changing to trust and the scared look give way beneath the hot wave of passion.

But with all that mad desire coursing through brain and blood, Michael knelt there at her feet, holding her hands, and listening to the flow of talk which like a cooling stream rippled in his ear. She asked him about England and about his home, and wanted to know if in springtime the white acacias were in bloom in Sussex, and if rosemary—her namesake—grew wild in the meadows.

In the woods round Fontainebleau the ground was carpeted with anemones; were there such sweet white carpets in the English woods? Then she looked about her in the ugly, uninteresting little room and saw a broken-down harpsichord standing in a corner.

She jumped up gay as a bird and ran to open it. There were several broken keys, and those that still were whole gave forth quaint, plaintive little sounds but she sang:

"Si tu m'aimais, tu serais roi de la terre!"

and he remained beside the window, with the cold breeze fanning his cheek, his head resting in his hand, and his eye piercing the gloomy corner of the room from whence came the heavenly song.

Indeed! was he not king of all the world?

Thus passed a delicious hour. Anon the coach—which originally should have brought the bridal pair hither, had not milor carried off the bride in such high-handed fashion—came lumbering up to the door.

Prudent maman had despatched it off in the wake of the impetuous rider. It contained a bundle of clothes and change of linen for Rose Marie and had my lord's effects, too, in the boot.

Rose Marie gave a little cry of delight when she realised maman's forethought, and then one of dismay for she suddenly became conscious of her disordered dress.

123

The worthy hostess—fat, greasy and motherly, had entered, candle in hand, to announce the arrival of the coach.

"Me and my man expected Monsieur and Madame to arrive in it," she explained volubly. "Monsieur's servant came yesterday to bespeak the rooms and to arrange for the stabling. I was so surprised when Monsieur arrived on horseback, so much earlier, too, than we had anticipated—else I had had supper ready ere this, for Monsieur and Madame must surely be hungry."

"But supper must be ready by now, good Madame Blond," said Rose Marie blushing to hear herself called "Madame," "and I pray you have my effects taken to my room."

"They are there already, so please you, my pigeon," said the amiable old soul, "and there is some water for washing your pretty face."

"And will supper be ready soon?" she reiterated insistently for she was young and healthy, and had eaten very little for sheer excitement all day.

"While you smooth out your golden curls, ma mignonne, I'll dish up the soup. Nay! but Monsieur is in luck's way!" she said, shaking her large round head. "Madame is the comeliest bride we have seen at St. Denis for a long time past. And they all come this way, you know—away from the prying eyes of kindly friends. Me and my man are so discreet!—especially if the bride be so pretty and the bridegroom so good to look at."

She would have babbled on a long time, despite Monsieur's look of fretful impatience, but fortunately just then the hissing sound of an overflowing soup-pot came ominously through the open door.

"Holy Joseph, patron of good housewives, defend us!" exclaimed Mme. Blond, making a dash for the door, "the croûte-au-pot is boiling over."

Rose Marie made to follow her.

"Need you go, my snowdrop?" he asked, loth to let her go.

"Just to change my crumpled gown, and smooth my hair," she replied demurely.

"You are so beautiful like this, I would not wish to see one single curl altered upon your head, or one fold changed upon your gown."

She was standing against the table, the fingers of one hand resting lightly upon the blackened oak, her head bent slightly forward the while her blue eyes half sought, half shrank from his gaze.

He went up to her, and drew her to him. The desire was irresistible and she almost called for that first kiss by her beauty, her innocence, her perfect girlishness which was so ready to give all bliss and to taste all happiness.

He kissed her fair hair, her eyes, her delicate cheeks now suffused with blushes. Then with a look he asked for her lips and she understood and yielded them to him with a glad little sigh of infinite trust.

124

The hand of time marked these heavenly minutes; surely the angels looked down from their paradise in envy at this earthly heaven. Outside the wind sighed amid the branches of the acacias, wafting into the room something of the pungent odour of this spring air, of the opening buds of poplars and of beeches and the languorous odour of newly-awakened life.

Gently she tried to disengage herself from his arms.

"I must go now," she whispered.

"Not yet."

"For a moment and I'll come back."

"Not yet."

"Let go, dear lord, for I would go."

"Not till I've had another kiss."

Happiness and the springtime of the earth, joy and life and love dancing hand in hand with youth! O Time, why dost not stop at moments such as this?

The sighing of the reeds on the river bank came as the sound of a fairy lullaby, the scent of the spring reached the girl's nostrils like an intoxicant vapour, which clouded her brain. The room was quite dark, and she could scarcely see his face, yet she felt that his eyes perpetually asked a question, to which she could only respond by closing her own:

"Tu m'aimes?" he whispered, and the heavy lids falling over ardent eyes made mute response to him.

A confused sound of horses' hoofs outside, of shouts and calls from within roused them both from their dream. She succeeded now in disengaging herself from his arms, and still whispering:

"I'll come back!" she retreated toward the door.

Just as she reached it, the moon so long obscured burst forth in full glory from behind a bank of clouds, her rays came straight into the narrow room and lighted on the dainty figure of the girl standing with crumpled white dress and hair disarranged, cheeks rosy red and eyes full of promise and love against the dark background of the heavy oaken door.

Michael looked upon her with longing, hungry eyes, drinking in every line of that delicately-moulded form, the graceful neck, the slender hands, the firm girlish shoulders on which the prim kerchief had become slightly disarranged. Then as she retreated further into the next room, she vanished from his sight; the door fell to behind her with a heavy, ominous sound, shutting out the radiant vision of Michael's cherished dream, leaving him on the other side of the heavenly portals, alone and desolate.

Thus he saw her in full light, and lost her in the shadows. Something of the premonition of what was to come already held his heart as in a cold and cruel vice. When the door closed upon his dream, upon his Rose Marie, he knew by an unerring and torturing instinct that he would never, never see her quite as she had been just now. The Rose Marie who had left him was for remembrance.

125

CHAPTER XXV

Though doom keep always heaven and hell
Irreconcilable, infinitely apart;
Keep not in twain for ever heart and heart
That once, albeit by not thy law, were one.

—Swinburne

The next moment the door which gave on the landing was thrown open, and Michael stood face to face with M. Legros.

Thus premonition had come true. Thus would nothing remain of the past delicious hour only remembrance and bitter, bitter longing for what could never be.

The light of the one candle fell full upon the unromantic figure of the good tailor, on his pallid face whereon beads of perspiration told their mute tale of anxiety and of fulsome wrath. His eyes, dilated and tawny in colour were fastened full upon the reprobate, demanding above all things to know if the outraged father had perchance arrived too late.

The man's gay wedding clothes were torn and awry; mud covered his shoes and stockings for he had not even stopped to be booted and spurred. The old English serving-man who had vainly tried earlier in the day to gain speech with the master tailor, had reached the august presence at last, and had handed to M. Legros the letter which was to be given to him and to no one else. It was written in a bold, clear hand and in scholarly French for the better understanding of Monsieur the tailor to the king. Mistress Peyton having penned a few ill-scrawled, ill-spelt words had bethought herself of a young Huguenot clerk of French parentage who earned his living in London by the work of his pen; and being desirous above all that M. Legros should fully comprehend her letter, she caused it to be translated and writ clearly by that same young clerk, ere she finally entrusted it to Daniel Pye for delivery.

Thus it was that that which was written in the letter did not fail to reach the understanding of good Papa Legros. It was a full and detailed account of the treachery which had been perpetrated on the tailor's daughter by one Michael Kestyon, who was naught but a dissolute profligate, a liar and a cheat, since his own cousin was Earl of Stowmaries, and no one else had any right to such title but he.

Papa Legros did not trouble to ask many questions, and since the English lout knew not a word of French, the good tailor took no further heed of him. He spoke to no one, not even to his wife. The letter said something which must be verified at once—at once—before it was too late. He gave orders that no one—least of all Mme. Legros—was to be disturbed, the merrimaking was to go on, the dancing, the eating and drinking, the speech making and all.

126

Then he slipped out by the back door and reached the small outbuilding where he kept a horse, which served him on occasions when he had to go to Versailles to try on a pair of breeches for His Majesty the King. It took good M. Legros no time to saddle his horse, and a ride of over three hours had no terrors for him beside the awful fear which gripped his paternal heart.

Before he left his home he detached from a nail on the wall of the shed an enormous stick with heavy leather thong, with which he at times administered castigation to refractory or evil-minded 'prentices.

Then he mounted his horse and rode away in the fast-gathering twilight.

He knew his way to St. Denis and to the inn whither he wished to go. He put his horse to a gentle canter and it was just past nine o'clock when he saw the light in the old tower of the Church of St. Denis.

He was tired and stiff from riding, but he had sufficient control of himself to speak quietly to the host of the little inn, and to ask cheerfully of good Mme. Blond which room his daughter was occupying.

The amiable old soul pointed the way up the stairs, then returned to her stock-pot with the cheerful comment that she would serve the soup in a few moments.

Then Papa Legros went upstairs and pushing open the door stood face to face with Michael. With one hand he gripped the heavy stick with the stout leather thong on it, with the other he fumbled in the pocket of his surcoat until he found the letter again—the letter which was penned in such scholarly French by the Huguenot clerk, and which revealed such damnable treachery.

But Papa Legros wanted above all to be fair. During the long, monotonous ride in the silence and darkness of this spring evening he had had time to collect his thoughts somewhat, to weigh the value of the anonymous writing, to think of milor as he had known him these past three weeks: gallant and plucky to a fault, proud, generous and brave; and now that he stood before the man, saw the noble bearing of the head, the fine dark eyes, the mouth that was so ready to smile or to speak gentle words, his terror fled from him, and though his voice still shook a little from the intensity of his emotion, he contrived to say quite quietly, as he held the crumpled letter out toward Michael:

"My lord—you will forgive me—I know you will understand—but it is the child's happiness—and—and—my lord, will you read this letter and tell me if its contents are true?"

Michael took the paper from him quite mechanically, for of course he had guessed its contents, but mayhap he had a vague desire to know who it was that had so wantonly destroyed his happiness. He went to the table and drew the flickering candle a little nearer, then bent his tall figure to read that cruel letter.

127

The handwriting told him nothing, but the tale was plainly told. The avenging angel of God was already standing with flaming sword at the gate of his paradise, forbidding him ever to enter. He looked up from the letter to that black door behind which she was; it almost seemed as if his aching eyes could pierce the solid oak. She was there behind the door and he could never, never again go to her, he could never, never again hold her in his arms.

Heaven had vanished and at his feet now yawned merciless, illimitable Hell.

"My lord," and the trembling voice of the outraged father broke in upon his thoughts, "my lord, I still await your answer—I'll not believe that nameless scrawl—I ask your word—only your solemn word, my lord, and all my fears will vanish. Swear to me, my lord, on the innocent head of my darling child that this letter holds nothing but calumnies and I'll believe you, my lord—if you'll swear it on her golden head."

Do you know that hush that to the imagination seems to fall upon the whole world just when a human heart is about to break? Michael felt that hush all around him now; the April wind ceased its moaning in the boughs of the young acacia trees, the reeds by the river bank sighed no longer in the breeze, awakened nature just for one moment fell back into winter-like sleep, and a shadow—blacker and more dense than any that can fall from an angry heaven over the earth—descended on Michael's soul.

To swear—as he had sworn this morning at the foot of the altar? To swear by that most sacred thing upon God's earth, her sweet head?—no!

"Will you swear, my lord, that this letter is but vile calumny?"

And Michael gave answer loudly and firmly:

"It is the truth!"

Less like a man than like an infuriated beast, the meek man— now an outraged father—literally sprang forward with upraised arm wielding the heavy dog-whip, ready to strike the miscreant in the face.

The proud, defiant head, noble even now in its humiliation, was bent without a murmur. Michael made no movement to avert the blow.

"Will you not kill me instead?" was all the protest which he made.

Legros' upraised hand fell nerveless by his side. He threw the stick away from him. He, poor soul, had never learned to control emotion, he had gone through no hard school wherein tears are jeered at, and sorrows unshared. He had never learned to be ashamed either of joy or of grief, and now, face to face with this man who had so deeply wronged him, and whom, despite his wrath, he was powerless to strike, he sank into a chair, and buried his face in his hands whilst a pitiful moan escaped his lips.

128

"The child—the poor child—how shall I ever tell her? The shame of it all—the cruelty—the shame—how shall I tell her?"

And Time's callous hand marked these minutes of terrible soul-agony, just as awhile ago it had marked the fleeting moments of celestial joy. Michael was silent, the while he wondered almost senselessly—stupidly—if Hell could hold more awful agony than he was enduring now.

Yet through it all his turbulent soul rebelled at the situation, the sentimental parleyings, the pitiful grief of the father and the enforced humility of his own attitude. He knew that he had lost his Rose Marie, that the parents would never give her to him now; the solid and indestructible wall of bourgeois integrity stood between him and those mad, glad dreams of triumph and of happiness.

It was characteristic of the man that he never for a moment attempted to guess or to find out the channel through which his own misery had come to him. He certainly never suspected his cousin of treachery. Fate had dealt the blow cruelly and remorselessly and sent him back to a worse hell than he had ever known; a hell which Satan reserves for those he hates the most—the way to it leads past the entrance to heaven.

"Good M. Legros," said Michael at last, striving to curb his impatience and to speak with gentleness, "will you try and listen to me? Nay, you need not fear, 'tis not my purpose to plead justification, nor yet leniency—I wish that you could bring yourself to believe that though I wooed and won your daughter by what you think is naught but an abominable trick, I had one great thought above all others and that was that I would make her happy. This I do swear by the living God, and by what I hold dearer still, by the love which I bear to Rose Marie. And as there is a heaven above me, I would have made her happy, for I had gained her heart, and anon when the bonds of mine own boundless love had rivetted her still more closely to me, I should have taught her to forgive my venial sin of having entered heaven by a tortuous way. The name which I bear is mine own, the title which I have assumed is mine by right, I would have conquered it for myself and for her. You say that it is not to be—yet I swear to you that she will not be happy if you take her from me. This I know; if I did not I would go to her myself and tell her that I have lied to her. If despite what you know you will still confide her to me, you will never regret it to your dying day, for apart from the life of love and happiness which will be hers, I will lavish upon her all the treasures of satisfied ambition, far surpassing anything which you—her father—have ever wished for her."

M. Legros despite his grief which had completely overmastered him for awhile, raised his head in absolute astonishment. Surely these English were the most astounding people in all the world! Here was this man who of a truth had committed the most flagrant, most impudent act of trickery, that had ever been perpetrated within

129

memory of living man—he had done this thing and been ignominiously found out. By all the laws of decent and seemly behaviour he should now be standing humble and ashamed before the man whom he had tried to injure. And yet what happened? Here he stood, in perfect calm and undisguised pride, not a muscle of his face twitched with emotion, and his neck was as stiff as if he were exulting in some noble deed.

Had these English no sense of what was fitting? had they no heart? no feelings? no blood within their veins? The man—so help us the living God!—was actually suggesting that his trickery be condoned, that an innocent child be entrusted to him, who stood convicted of falsehood and of treachery! Good M. Legros' Gallic blood boiled within him, overwhelming grief gave place to uncontrollable wrath. He rose to his feet, and pulled up his small stature to its uttermost height.

"You will make her happy!" he thundered, throwing an infinity of withering scorn into every word. "You—who like a prying jackal came to steal the fledgling from its nest? You who took money with one hand, the while you snatched a girl's honour with the other? With lying lips and soft, false words you stole our child's heart—even until father and mother were forgotten for the sake of the liar and the cheat who—"

Michael held up a quick warning hand, and instinctively the insults died on the other man's lips. Rose Marie—white as the clinging, crumpled gown which she had hastily refastened when anon she heard her father's voice raised in angered scorn—Rose Marie silent and still, and with great eyes fixed on Michael Kestyon, was standing in the doorway.

At sight of her good M. Legros' grief swept over him with renewed force. Once more he sank into a chair, and buried his face in his hands whilst a moan of painful soul-agony escaped his lips.

"The child!—the child! My God how to tell her!"

But Rose Marie's voice came quite clear and distinct, there was no catch in her throat, nor tremor in the gentle tones as she said quietly:

"Nay! my dear father, an there is aught to tell—milor will best know how to say it to me."

CHAPTER XXVI

As the dawn loves the sunlight, I love thee.
—Swinburne

Papa Legros at first had been too dazed to protest. Truly his loving heart had been for hours on the rack at thought of the awful task which lay before him—the opening of his child's eyes to the monstrous trick played upon her by the man to whom her innocent heart had turned in perfect love and in perfect trust. He, the father, who worshipped this dainty, delicately-nurtured daughter, who had spent the past twenty years of an arduous life in trying to smooth away every unevenness from the child's pathway of life, now suddenly saw himself like unto the scarlet-clad executioner, rope and branding irons in hand, forced to bind his beloved one on the rack, and himself to apply the searing torture of sorrow and of shame to her soul.

The child's calm words as she stood confronting the miscreant had almost brought relief. Why indeed should not the villain accomplish his own unmasking? Papa Legros hating the man who had done him and his child an infinite wrong, had a sufficiency of perception in him to realise, with that subtle cruelty of which the meek are alone capable, that he could not inflict more exquisite torture on his enemy than by forcing him to stand self-convicted before the child.

Just for the moment—and truly he may be forgiven for it—all that was good and kind in the gentle nature of the tailor had been ousted by his wrath as a father and as a man. He had found himself unable to strike the liar just now; but he longed for the power to torture his very soul, to bring him to the dust in sorrow and humiliation, to see the proud head down in the mud of abject shame. Great God! did you not know that Papa Legros had learned to love this man like he would his own son, and that the grief which he felt was in part for Rose Marie and in part for the miscreant who had twined himself around his heartstrings, and whom he cherished the while he longed to chastise him with infinite cruelty?

"Father dear," said Rose Marie after a slight pause, "will you not allow me to speak with milor alone?"

"I would not trust thee one second in his keeping, child, now I know him for what he is."

"You need have no fear, dear," she rejoined calmly, "and 'twere best methinks for us all if milor were to tell me himself all that I ought to know."

The candle flickered low, and Michael stood back amidst the shadow; thus the good tailor failed to see if his own shaft had gone home—if it had pierced that armour of stolid English indifference which the descendant of Gallic forebears found so difficult to comprehend.

Certain it is that Michael raised no protest, and that not even a sigh escaped him as this final insult was hurled at him with the utmost refinement of vengeful cruelty.

Rose Marie went up to her father and placed her small cool hands on his. Then with gentle persuasion she drew him up. He yielded to her, for vaguely at the bottom of his heart, he knew that he could trust the man whom he loved and hated, yet even now could not wholly despise. For one moment as father and daughter stood side by side, he took her in his arms and kissed her forehead. She rested against him

131

cold and placid, and when he released her from his embrace she took his rough toil-worn hand and kissed it tenderly. Then with supreme yet irresistible gentleness she led him out of the room.

As he passed close to Michael he held out the fateful letter to him.

"You will show her that," he almost commanded.

"An you wish it," replied the other, as he took the letter from him.

A curious instinct prompted Michael to blow out the flickering light, just as Rose Marie, having closed the door behind her father, turned back into the room. He went up to her, but she retreated a step or two at his approach, and of her own accord went to the window seat, there where a brief hour ago she had sat with him in perfect communion and perfect happiness.

The casement was still open, and the moon which had been so fitful throughout the evening poured her cold radiance straight on the dainty silhouette of the girl, just as she had done awhile ago, ere the gates of paradise were closed and the angels had ceased to sing their glad hosannas! Outside, the sighing of the reeds and the moaning of the wind in the young acacias made a sound as of innumerable feet of restless spirits stirring the dead leaves of an unforgettable past.

"That letter, milor," said Rose Marie, "will you give it me—since my father hath so commanded."

Without a word he handed the paper to her, and when he saw that she could not read it—for the room was dark and the rays of the moon not sufficiently bright—he took out his tinder-box and relighted the guttering candle. Then as the wind blew the feeble flame hither and thither he shielded it with his hand, and held the candle so that she might read and yet not move from that window seat.

She read the letter through to the end, and while she read he could see the top of her head bent down to the paper, and the wealth of those fair curls which he would never again be allowed to kiss.

When she had finished reading, she looked up and he threw the candle far away out through the window.

"Then you had lied to me," was all that she said; and she said it so calmly, so quietly, like the true snow maiden which she had once more become, now that he who alone had the power to turn the snow to living fire, was proved to be treacherous and false. Then she folded up the letter and slipped it under her kerchief.

Stately and tall as the water lilies on the pond which he had once described to her—she drew up her slender figure and held her little head erect. She did not look in his direction but rose slowly and turned to go out of the room.

"Rose Marie," he called out to her in an involuntary moan of agony.

Instinctively his hand went out to her as she passed, and

132

clutched the crumpled wedding dress which seemed to wrap her in, now like a shroud. She tried to disengage her gown, but as he held it tight she desisted, standing there cold and impassive, a woman turned to ice.

"Rose Marie!" he whispered, "my own little snowdrop, will you be so unyielding now? Awhile ago do you remember, you yielded to the sweetness of a first kiss?"

"And yet you lied to me," she said slowly, tonelessly, the while her eyes sought the distant horizon far away, where astride on the cold grey mists unreached by the tender light of the moon, her dreams of happiness were fleeting quickly away.

He drew himself up and caught her to him with a masterful gesture of possession. He felt her body rigid and impassive at his touch, stiffening in a backward motion away from him behind that massive stone wall of awful finality which had so mercilessly risen between her and him. He felt that he was losing her, that she was slipping away from him—slipping—up, up to some cold and unresponsive heaven, peopled with stern angels, whose great white wings would soon enclose her and hide her from him forever. He felt that he was losing her, not with that same bitter-sweet sense of sadness as he did just now when the savour of her exquisite lips still clung to his own, and she retreated out of his sight like a perfect vision of beauty.

Now an almost savage longing was in him not to let her go, to keep her to him at any cost, any sacrifice, even that of his own self-control. There was enough power in his own ardent love for her so to bind her to him that she could never, never leave him.

"My beautiful crimson rose," he murmured, drawing her closer, closer, even while he felt that with her whole gentle strength she opposed an icy calm to the warm glow of his passion, "turn your dear eyes to me, just for one brief moment. Oh! think, think of the past few days when first our hearts, our souls, our entire beings met in perfect accord. Look at me, my dear, sweet soul, am I not the man to whom you have listened so oft, sitting at your harpsichord, the while he whispered to you the first words of love? Look, look, my dear, mine eyes, are they not the same?—my lips have they not met yours in one sublime, unforgettable kiss? You were a child, ere your soul met mine—now you are a woman, 'tis I who applied the magic fire to your heart, 'tis I who kindled the flame of your pure love; you are no longer a child now, Rose Marie, you are an exquisitely beautiful woman, and I love you with every fibre of my body, with every aspiration of my soul—"

"And yet you lied to me."

"And would lie again, would sin again a thousand times, since my sin gave you to me. Sweetheart, if I have sinned, yet have I expiated already—one cold look from your dear eyes hath caused me more acute agony than the damned can ever suffer in Hell. My love—my love—do you understand what you mean to me? Have you realised the exquisite gift—your perfect womanhood—which you would snatch from me? I was a wastrel, a thief, a miserable degraded wretch—awhile ago when I held you in my arms I was king of all the world. By my sin I won you! Great God, then is not my sin the greatest, grandest and most glorious deed ever accomplished by man—in order to gain a heaven?"

But with all his ardour, all his savage strength of will and of purpose, Michael was but bruising his heart against a solid stone wall. Perhaps if Rose Marie had been a little older, a little more sophisticated, a little more wearied in the ways of men, she might have yielded to the love of the man, and closed her eyes to the deeds of the sinner. Whatever else he had done, she would easily have forgiven— nay! she would never have judged—but it was the betrayal of her trust which turned her heart to stone. Of course she had not had time as yet to think. In the letter which he had given her she had read the awful account of that transaction wherein she appeared as a mere chattel tossed from one hand to another, paid for with money like a bale of goods.

Oh! the shame of it! And he, to whom she had given her entire heart and soul, to whom she was ready to yield herself absolutely and completely had bought her at a price. Love? She no longer believed in it. If he had lied to her, then neither love nor purity nor manhood existed on God's earth—and this was no vale of tears but one of infinite shame.

She looked down on him with just such a cold look in her eyes as he had compared to the infliction of the tortures of the damned. She knew that physically she would be too weak to resist him, and she would scorn to call out to her father. This she tried to convey to him by that cold look and by the perfect placidity of her demeanour.

For one moment he was conscious of the wild desire to snatch his happiness from out the burning brand even now, and to take her in his arms and ride away with her into the land of forgetfulness. The wind in the trees seemed to call out to him not to let her go, and the reeds murmured as they bent their heavy heads that she would forgive everything after another kiss.

"Rose Marie!"

Something of what was passing in his mind must have reached her inner consciousness. She was quite woman enough to know that here was no ephemeral passion, no flame of desire extinguished as soon as born. He loved her and she loved him, that was as true, as incontestable as that—in her understanding—the treacherous act which he had committed now stood irremediably between them, whilst to his wild and rugged sense of the overwhelming grandeur of love, nothing could or should ever part him from her.

In her eyes the betrayal was greater than the love which—in his— had by its very existence atoned for everything. But throughout her deeply resentful feeling of wrong done to her and hers there was

134

mayhap an unconscious sense of weakness, a desire to bring forth a greater array of will power and set it up against the insinuating persuasion of his voice, the insidious magic of his touch. Certain it is that she felt suddenly compelled to break the rigid silence which throughout his impassioned pleading she had so deliberately imposed upon herself.

Held in his nervy grip, she could not altogether withdraw from him, but her eyes, cold and calm sought his in the gloom.

"My lord," she said quietly and firmly, "since I know you by no other name, therefore still my lord to me, I would have you recall the day when sitting in my father's house, you whiled away an idle afternoon by telling a foolish maid the pretty allegory of water lilies growing on the weedy pond at Cluny, and of the slime which oozes from unclean things and pollutes the white petals of the flowers. 'Twas a pretty tale and no doubt it afforded you much amusement to see the look of puzzledom in the eyes of an ignorant tailor's wench. Well, my lord! the wench is no longer ignorant now—she understands the rude imagery, her eyes have seen such pollution, such miserable corruption as will forever leave them tainted with the villainy which they have seen. Whoever you are, sir, I know not—what other deeds of evil and disgrace you may have committed I care not—I only pray God that we may never meet again. You no doubt will find pleasures elsewhere, some other flower to pollute with your touch, some other heart to break. That you brought shame upon me, mayhap God will one day forgive you, I could perchance have forgiven you that had your sin rested there, but you tried to bring dishonour on my father's house. You did succeed in bringing sorrow and shame into it. My father and mother, who loved you almost as a son, will never again hold their heads high among their kind; a dishonoured daughter—for I am that now, for my true husband will cast me off as a woman unfit to be his mate—a dishonoured daughter is a lasting curse upon a house. That is your work, stranger, whoever you are; and this deed like unto the treachery which by a kiss brought the beloved Master to death upon the Cross, cries out to heaven for punishment; it is writ on the very front page in the book of the recording angel, and all the tears which you may shed, all the blood and all the atonement could not now wipe that front page clean. All this I do know, and yet one thing more: and that is that you do err when you speak of my love for you. To you who have lied, who with soft words and false pretences did enter my father's house and stole that which is most precious to us humble folk, our honour and the integrity of our name, to such as that, I gave no love. 'Tis true that I did love a man once—for one brief hour he lived in my heart but nowhere else. He was true and loyal, too proud to lie, too noble to steal. He has vanished like the mist, leaving no trace of his passage, for my heart wherein he dwelt is broken, and even his memory hath faded from my ken—"

Her voice died away like a long-drawn-out sigh, mingling with the murmur of the reeds and the moaning as of lost souls gliding through the branches of the acacias in their restless wandering through infinite space.

The next moment she was gone, leaving in Michael's trembling hands a scrap of torn lace, a tiny shred of her gown.

All that was left of her—and the savour of a bitter memory— rosemary for remembrance!

CHAPTER XXVII

Such a deal of wonder is broken out within this hour
That ballad-makers cannot be able to express it.

—*A Winter's Tale V. 2*

It was about an hour later that a hired coach brought three English gentlemen to the small inn at St. Denis.

M. Blond was much perturbed. He was not accustomed to foreigners at any time and he held the English theoretically in abhorrence, and now here were four of these milors actually under his roof at one and the same time.

The three who had last arrived in the coach from Paris carried matters off in a very high-handed fashion and seemed ready to throw money about in a manner which was highly satisfactory to the bedraggled and seedy married couple who—besides the landlord and his spouse—formed the sum total of the personnel at the Sign of "Three Archangels" in St. Denis.

Sir John Ayloffe had assumed the leadership of the small party. He gave his own name to the landlord, and added that he and his two friends had come to pay their respects to my lord of Stowmaries, but lately arrived with his young bride.

Now can you wonder at good M. Blond's perturbation? The incidents which had crowded in at the Sign of the "Three Archangels" in the past half hour were enough to furnish food for gossip for many a long evening to come. In point of fact M. and Mme. Blond had just started talking the whole sequence of events over from the beginning when the coach arrived with the three English milors, nor had the worthy couple had any chance of comparing impressions on these same mysterious events.

Firstly there had been the extraordinary arrival of the bride and bridegroom, who of a truth had been expected, since relays for the next day's journey had been sent to the "Three Archangels" the day before, but they certainly had not been expected under such amazing circumstances, the English milor's horse covered with lather, and the bride in her wedding gown all crumpled and soiled, clinging to her newly-wedded husband in front of his saddle, and in a vastly uncomfortable position.

This astonishing arrival of a bride and bridegroom who were reputed to be passing wealthy had of course vastly upset mine good host and his amiable wife. But then English milors were known to be eccentric, in fact most folk who had travelled in the fog-ridden country vowed that all the people there were more or less mad. 'Twas but lately that they had cut off the head of their king and set up a low-born soldier to rule them. No wonder that King Louis—whom le bon Dieu preserve!—was greatly angered with these English, and only forgave them when they returned to their senses and once more acknowledged the authority of him who was their king by right divine.

Worthy Monsieur Blond had explained all these matters to his buxom wife in an off-hand yet comprehensive manner, the while the latter made haste to hurry on the preparations for supper, for the pretty bride and the English milor—deeply in love with one another though they were, as any one who looked could see—had shown a very sensible and laudable desire to have some of Mme. Blond's excellent croûte-au-pot to warm the cockles of their young hearts.

The second incident on this eventful evening was of minor importance, and tended greatly to minimise the eccentricity of that romantic arrival. The coach which should have brought the bridal pair to the "Three Archangels" did come in due time—even whilst Mme. Blond was preparing her bit of fricandeau garnished with fresh winter cabbage, which was to be the second course at the bridal supper.

The thoughtful mother of the love-sick bride had had the good sense to send her daughter's effects along, and all recollection of the curious arrival on horseback was forgotten before the prosy advent of boxes and bundles of clothes.

Mme. Blond, moreover, became fully satisfied that everything was right as right could be, when she went upstairs to announce the arrival of the coach. The bride's pretty face was as pink as the eglantine in June, and her eyes brighter than the full moon outside, whilst milor—ah, well, Mme. Blond had seen many a man in love in her day, Blond himself had not been backward when he was courting her—but never, never, had she seen a man so gloating on the sight of his young wife, as that eccentric mad milor had done, the while the pretty dear was prosily asking for supper.

All then had been for the best at nine of the clock that evening, but mark ye, what happened after that. Less than ten minutes later a rider—obviously half exhausted from a long and wearying journey—

drew rein outside the "Three Archangels." M. Blond who more than once had been in Paris, had no difficulty in recognising in the belated traveller Master Legros, tailor in chief to His Majesty the King, and the father of the pretty bride upstairs.

Master Legros undoubtedly did not look like himself, though he did try to assume a jaunty air as he asked to be shown the room wherein his daughter and milor would presently be supping.

It seemed a fairly simple incident at the time, this late arrival here of the bride's father, though Mme. Blond in thinking over the matter afterwards distinctly remembered that the fact did strike her as odd. What should good M. Legros be doing at St. Denis at this tardy hour, when most good citizens should be in bed, and when he had given his paternal blessing to the young couple fully four hours ago?

"Milor's best suit of clothes had not been finished in time for the departure, and Maitre Legros brought it along himself," suggested M. Blond placidly.

But he scratched his dark poll while he made this suggestion knowing it to be nonsense.

Mme. Blond's premonitions proved to be correct. Half an hour elapsed, the while she and Blond took turns on the upstairs landing to try and hear something of what was going on inside that room, wherein awhile ago the turtle doves had been cooing so prettily. The croûte-au-pot had been ready ages ago but no one had asked for it. No sound penetrated through the heavy oaken doors; only once had Mme. Blond heard a voice raised in what seemed most terrible anger. She then fled incontinently back to her kitchen.

A quarter of an hour later M. Legros gave orders that the coach which had brought his daughter's effects an hour previously, be got ready at once, and that those horses be put to it that had been sent down the day before with a view to the continuance of the journey to Havre. He gave no explanation, of course, nor answered any of the discreet questions put to him by Mme. Blond. He tried to swallow some hot soup, but gave up the attempt after the third spoonful; he looked as white as a sheet, and trembled like a poplar leaf in the breeze. Presently the young bride came down the stairs. She still wore her wedding gown under her thick dark cloak. Mme. Blond noticed how crumpled it looked and that a great piece of the beautiful lace was torn off.

But she wore her hood closely wrapped round her head, so neither Monsieur nor Madame could see anything of her face; nor did she speak any words, save a short "Thank you!" to Mme. Blond, and this she said in a curious, husky voice as if her throat were choked.

Maitre Legros paid lavishly for everything. The bride's boxes and bundles were once more stowed away in the boot of the coach; then she and her father stepped into the vehicle, the postillion cracked his whip, there was a scraping of iron hoofs on the rough paving stones, a clanking of chains, a shout or two and the lumbering coach turned out toward the highroad and was quickly lost to sight in the gloom.

After that nothing!

Not a sound came from the room where the English milor had remained alone. Mme. Blond at her wits' ends what to do or how to interpret the remarkable series of incidents which had occurred beneath her roof, had thought of knocking at milor's door and asking him if he would have some supper.

Her mind—which as her good man was wont to say—was ever inclined to romance, had seen horrible visions of a bleeding corpse lying prone upon the parlour floor. Suicide must have followed this forcible abduction by an infuriated father, of the ardently worshipped bride.

Great was her astonishment, perhaps also her disappointment, when in answer to a peremptory "Come in" she went into the room and saw milor standing there by the open window looking out upon the moonlit landscape for all the world as if nothing had happened.

"There he was," she explained somewhat irately to her man, for she felt almost as if she had been cheated out of the most thrilling chapter of her romance, "dressed in his beautiful bridal clothes, with arms folded across his chest, and not a hair on his head the least bit ruffled. Ah! these English! they have no heart. I thought to find him either with a sword thrust through his heart, else a man mad and raving with grief. Holy Virgin! Had my father taken me away from thee, my Blond, on the very night of our wedding day, wouldst thou not have been crazy with rage, even if thou hadst not actually committed suicide? There's heart for thee! There's love! But not in these English! And wilt believe me that when I said something to milor about supper, he did not even curse me, but said quite quietly that he had no hunger."

Well now! does not all that give furiously to think?

Milor had no hunger, the bride had gone and the supper was ready. What could Mme. Blond do better than to dish up the croûte-au-pot and the fricandeau with the winter cabbage and to serve it to her man?

Monsieur Blond took off his heavy boots and donned a pair of cloth slippers, he covered his dark hair with a warmly-fitting cap and drew the most comfortable chair to the table, preparatory to enjoying a supper fit for an English milor.

But he was not destined to enjoy more than a preliminary sniff at the succulent croûte-au-pot. Mme. Blond had been very talkative and the dishing-up process consequently slow, and at the very moment when good M. Blond was conveying the first spoonful of soup to his mouth there was a loud noise of wheels grating against the slipper, the cracking of a whip and a good deal of shouting; all of which were unmistakable signs that more mysterious travellers had chosen this eventful night for their arrival at the "Three Archangels."

CHAPTER XXVIII

What whisperest thou? Nay, why
Name the dead hours? I mind them well:
Their ghosts in many darkened doorways dwell
With desolate eyes to know them by.

—Dante Gabriel Rossetti

Michael Kestyon had paid no heed to the noise of this last arrival. Indeed he had heard nothing since that one awful noise, the departure of the coach which bore her away from him. How long ago that was he could not say. It might have been a moment or a cycle of years. Just before it he had had his last glimpse of her. She crossed the room in company with her father, who had come up to fetch her. She was wrapped from head to foot in cloak and hood; all that he could see of her was her torn wedding gown.

He made no movement as she walked past him, and though his whole soul called out her name, his lips uttered no sound. What were the use? If she did not hear the silent call of love, no words could move her.

"Even his memory hath faded from my ken."

Michael vaguely remembering the sacred tale told him in his childhood by his mother of how God had hurled His sinful angels from Heaven down to Hell, could not recall that in His anger He had used words that were quite so cruel.

Well, that page in life had been written, the book was closed. One brief glimpse at possible happiness, one tiny chink open in the gates of paradise, and then once more the weary tramp along the road which leads to misery on this earth, to perdition hereafter.

The gambler had staked his all upon one venture and had lost. But Michael Kestyon was not made of the mould which rots in a suicide's grave or harbours a brain which goes crazy with grief.

A weaker man would have felt regrets, a better man would have been racked with remorse. Michael with her words ringing in his ears thought only of redemption.

"My father and mother, who loved you as their son, will never again hold their heads high among their kind—for a dishonoured daughter is a lasting curse upon a house. That is your work, stranger—it is writ on the front page in the book of the recording angel, and all the tears which you may shed, all the blood and all the atonement could not now wipe that front page clean."

The gambler in losing all had, it seems, involved others in his ruin; innocent people who had loved and trusted him. The debt which he had thus contracted would have to be paid to them, not in the coin which Michael had tendered—since it had been dross in their sight—but in coin which would compensate them for all that they had lost.

And it was because of the future redemption of that great debt, because of all that there was yet to do, that Michael held such a tight rein over his reason, the while it almost tottered beneath the crushing blow. Nor did he allow the thought of suicide to dwell in his mind. Yet madness and death—the twin phantoms born of cowardice—lurked within the dark shadows of the low-raftered room, after Rose Marie's last passage along the uneven floor when her torn wedding gown swept over the boards with a sighing and swishing sound, which would reverberate in Michael's heart throughout eternity.

From beneath the lintel of that oaken door which had clanged to behind her, the spectre of madness grinned into the deserted room, and beckoned to the man who stood there in utter loneliness; and on the window-sill whereat she had sat awhile ago the gaunt shadow of suicide whispered the alluring words: Rest! Forgetfulness! Rest! Forgetfulness!

Michael did not flee from the twin demons. He called them to his side and looked fully and squarely at their hideous, alluring forms.

Madness and Death! Destruction of the mind or of the body. Both would blot her image from his soul. Madness enticed by drink would mean the bestial forgetfulness of heavy sleep and addled intellect. Death would mean infinite peace.

The struggle 'twixt devils and the man was fierce and short. Anon the crouching spectres vanished into the night; and the man stood there in splendid isolation with the memory of a great crime and of a brief joy for sole companion of his loneliness. But the man was a man for all that; body and mind were still the slaves of his will, not for the carving of his own fortune now, not for the spinning of the web of Fate, but bound and fettered under the heel of an iron determination to wipe out the writing on that front page in the book of the recording angel; not by tears, not by blood and cringing atonement, but by deeds and acts dark if necessary, heroic always, by vanquishing the wrongs of the past with the triumphant redemption to come.

In this mood the good landlady of the "Three Archangels" found him and marvelled at British indifference in the face of a love tragedy. And he was still in this selfsame mood half an hour or so later when my lord of Stowmaries and his friends came upon the solitary watcher in the night.

Michael had not eaten, nor had he relinquished his place by the open window, for it seemed to his over-sensitive mind as if the sound of those wheels which bore his snowdrop further and further away from him echoed against the distant bank of storm-portending clouds, and though the heartrending sound reverberated within him like unto the grinding of the rack which tears the limbs and martyrizes the body, yet it still seemed something of her, the last memory, the final farewell.

141

It was past ten o'clock now, and of a surety Michael thought that he must have fallen asleep, dreaming by that open window, when the sudden noise of several familiar voices, a loud if somewhat forced laugh, and the peremptory throwing open of the door brought the dreamer back to the exigencies of the moment.

The aspect of the room was almost weird, dark and gloomy with only the slanting moonbeams to touch with pale and capricious light the tall, solitary figure in the window embrasure.

For a moment the three men paused beneath the lintel, their volatile imagination strangely gripped by the picture before them, that dark silhouette against the moonlit landscape beyond, the total air of desolation and loneliness which seemed to hang like a pall even in the gloom.

Sir John Ayloffe was the first to shake himself free from this unwonted feeling of superstitious awe:

"Friend Michael, by the Mass!" he shouted with somewhat forced jocoseness. "Still astir, and like the love-sick poet contemplating the moon."

The loud words broke the spell of subtle and weird magic which seemed to pervade the place. Michael Kestyon gave a start and turned abruptly away from the window.

"Are we welcome, Michael?" added Lord Rochester pleasantly. "Or do we intrude?"

Michael whose surprise at seeing the three men had been quite momentary, now came forward with outstretched hands.

"Not in the least," he said cordially, "and ye are right welcome. I had thoughts of going to bed and yet was longing for merry company, little guessing that it would thus unexpectedly fall from heaven. And may I ask what procures St. Denis the honour of this tardy visit from so distinguished a company?"

"The desire to see you, Cousin," here interposed Lord Stowmaries, "and if you'll allow us, to sup with you, for we were not invited to your wedding feast, remember, and have not enjoyed the worthy tailor's good cheer."

"We have not tasted food since the middle of the day," added Ayloffe, "and that was none of the best."

"But mayhap Michael hath supped," suggested Lord Rochester, who contrary to his usual freedom of manner and speech seemed unaccountably reticent for the nonce.

"Nay, nay! And if I had I could sup again in such elegant company," rejoined Michael. "But I was dreaming indeed since I was forgetting that we were still in the dark. Our amiable host must bring us light as well as food. It will give me much pleasure to see your amiable faces more clearly."

Even as he spoke he went to the door, and soon his calls to Mme. Blond for lights and supper echoed pleasantly through the house.

The three others were left staring at one another in blank surprise. They had not thought of putting questions to mine host on their arrival, but had merely and somewhat peremptorily ordered M. Blond to show them up to the room occupied by their friend, the English milor. They, therefore, knew nothing of what had happened, but all three of them vaguely felt—by a curious, unexplainable instinct—that something was amiss, and knew that Michael's attitude of serene indifference was only an assumed rôle.

"Strike me dead but there's something almost uncanny about the man," said Lord Rochester, forcing a laugh.

"Something has happened of course," rejoined Ayloffe, "but nothing to concern us. Mayhap an early quarrel with the bride."

"'Tis strange, forsooth, to find the bridegroom alone at this hour," added Stowmaries, whilst the refrain of a ribald song rose somewhat affectedly to his lips.

But Rochester quickly checked him, for Michael's footstep was heard on the landing. The latter now entered, closely followed by M. Blond who carried a couple of candelabra of heavy metal and fitted with tallow candles.

These he soon lighted and the flickering yellow flames quickly dispersed the gloom which lingered in the corners of the room. They threw into full relief the faces of the four men, three of whom retained an expression of great bewilderment, whilst the fourth looked serene and placid, as if the entertaining of his friends was for nonce the most momentous thing in his existence.

Michael went to the window and with a quick, impatient gesture he pulled the curtains together, shutting out the moonlit landscape and the silhouette of the trees, whose soft sighs had been the accompaniment to the murmur of her voice; mayhap he had a thought of shutting out at the same time the very remembrance of the past.

Then he turned once more to the others and his face now was a perfect mirror of jovial good-humour as he said gaily:

"I hope, gentlemen, that you are anhungered. As for me I could devour a wilderness of frogs, so be it that it is the only food of which this remarkable country can boast. I pray you sit. Supper will not be long—and in the meanwhile tell me, pray, the latest gossip in London."

The company settled itself around the table. Every one was glad enough to be rid of the uncanny sensation of awhile ago. M. Blond in the meanwhile had bustled out of the room but he soon reappeared bearing platters and spoons, and, what was more to the purpose, pewter mugs and huge tankards of good red wine. Close behind him came his portly spouse holding aloft with massive, outstretched arms, the monumental tureen whence escaped the savoury fumes of her famous croûte-au-pot.

Loud cheers greeted the arrival of the worthy pair. Mme. Blond

143

quickly fell to, distributing the soup with no niggardly hand, the while her man made the round, filling the mugs with excellent wine.

Gossip became general. Rochester as usual was full of anecdotes, bits of scandal and gossip, retailed with a free tongue and an inexhaustible fund of somewhat boisterous humour. The soup was beyond reproach and the wine more than drinkable.

"Gad's 'ounds," he cried presently when Blond and his wife had retired, leaving the English company to itself, "this is a feast fit for the gods! Michael Kestyon, our amiable host, I raise my glass to thee! Gentlemen, our host!"

He raised his glass, Stowmaries following suit; but Ayloffe checked them both with a peremptory lifting of his hand.

"Nay, nay!" he said, "my lord Rochester you do forget—and you, too, gentlemen! Fie on you, fie, I say! Not a drop shall pass your lips until you have pledged me as you should. 'Tis I will give you the first toast of the evening. Gentlemen, the bride!"

There was loud clapping of mugs against the table, then lusty shouts of "The bride! the bride!" The three men raised their bumpers and drained them to the last drop, honouring the toast to the full. Sir John looked keenly at Michael, but even his sharp, observant eyes could not detect the slightest change in the calm and serene face. Michael, too, had raised his mug, but Ayloffe noted that he did not touch the wine with his lips.

Shrewd Sir John ever alive to his own interests fell to speculating as to what had gone amiss, and whether any event had been likely to occur which would affect his own prospects in any way. Mistress Peyton's twelve thousand pounds had not yet—remember,—been transferred to Cousin John's pocket, and no one was more profoundly aware of the truth of the old dictum that "there's many a slip—" than was Sir John Ayloffe himself. But there was naught to read on Michael Kestyon's placid face, only the vague suspicion of carefully concealed weariness; and in Ayloffe's practical mind there was something distinctly unnatural in the serene calm of a man who was richer to-day by one hundred and twenty thousand pounds, not even to mention an excessively pretty and well-dowered bride.

Sir John, relying on his own powers of observation, had every intention of probing this matter to the bottom, but in the meanwhile he thought it best not to let the others see, too clearly, what he himself had only vaguely guessed, therefore it was he again who shouted more lustily even than before:

"Now the bridegroom, gentlemen! I give you the bridegroom! Long live! Long live I say!"

He was on his feet waving his mug with every lusty shout. Then he drained it once more to the last drop, Stowmaries and Rochester doing likewise, for time-honoured custom demanded that such toasts must be responded to right heartily. Michael however made no acknowledgment as he should have done. He sat quite still with slender, nervy fingers idly toying with the crumbs on the table.

"Respond, Michael, respond," cried Lord Rochester who seemed to have quite shaken off his former diffidence. "Man, are you in the clouds?—Of a surety," he continued with a knowing wink directed at his friends, "'twere no marvel on this eventful night, and with a pretty bride awaiting her lord not thirty paces away on the other side of that door. We saw her in church, Michael, and by Gad, man, you are a lucky dog! But we did drink to the bridegroom and—"

"And I, too, drink to him," interposed Michael loudly, as he rose to his feet, bumper in hand and turned directly to his Cousin Stowmaries, "to you, my lord and cousin do I drink—the only bridegroom worthy of such a bride."

To say the least of it, this speech was vastly astonishing. No one quite knew how to take it, and as Michael drained his cup Stowmaries broke into a forced laugh.

"You do flatter me, Coz," he said, feeling strangely uncomfortable under the other's steady gaze, and realising that some sort of reply was expected of him, "but of a truth the flattery is misplaced. The bride is yours and you have won her by fair means; and I, in my turn, will add something to my lord Rochester's toast—something which, an I mistake not, will be vastly acceptable to you—a draft for seventy thousand pounds on my banker, Master Vivish of Fleet Street. The final payment of my debt to you."

And Stowmaries took a paper from the pocket of his surcoat and handed it to Michael, who made no movement to take it.

"Cousin," he said, "when I accepted the bargain which you offered me, I was more deeply in my cups than I myself had any idea of. Let us admit that 'twas an ignoble bargain, shameful alike to me and to you. Now I would pray you to return that draft to your pocket; 'tis but little I have spent of that first fifty thousand pounds, the balance of what remains you shall have on my return to London, as for the rest— that which I have so foolishly spent—I pray you to grant me a few months delay and I will repay you to the full. Thus we two who made the bargain, and these two gentlemen who witnessed it, will cease to have aught but a dim recollection of the shameful doings of a mad and roisterous night."

Silence greeted this strange speech. The beginning of it had at once awakened surprise, the end left the three men there present in a state of complete puzzlement. Stowmaries frankly gazed at Michael with wide-open eyes wherein good-humoured contempt fought with utter amazement.

Then as no one spoke, Michael added quietly:

"I await your answer, Cousin."

"Tush, man, you are joking," retorted Stowmaries with a shrug of the shoulders.

"I never was more serious in my life," rejoined the other with deep earnestness, "and 'tis a serious answer that I ask of you."

"But I know not to what your lengthy speech did tend, how can I give it answer?"

"I asked you to put that draft for money yet unpaid into your pocket; I propose to repay you in full every penny of that which this folly hath already cost you, and you on the other hand can fulfil your obligations to the lady who, of a truth, is still legally your wife."

"Hold on, man, hold on!" cried Stowmaries almost in dismay, for it seemed to him that his cousin was bereft of his senses. "Odd's fish! But you talk like a madman—and a dangerous one, too, for you use words which, were I not your guest, I could not help but resent."

"There is naught to resent, Cousin, in what I say, nor is it the act or speech of a madman to ask you to rescind a bargain which tended neither to your honour nor to mine own."

"But, by the Mass, Cousin, the bargain good or bad, righteous or shameful, is no longer in the making. Even were I so minded—which by our Lady I vow that I am not—I could not now release you of your pledged word to me. What is done, is done, and you have fulfilled your share of the bargain. Now 'tis my turn as an honourable gentlemen to acquit myself of my debt to you. So I pray you take the money—it is justly yours—but do not prate any further nonsense."

"Ay! ay! friend Kestyon," added Ayloffe with his habitual bonhomme, through which nevertheless the cloven hoof of sarcasm was quite perceptible, "do not allow your over-sensitive conscience to persuade you into refusing what is justly your due."

"Odd's fish, man, you have won the bride and thereby rendered Stowmaries an incomparable service," quoth Lord Rochester decisively, "and—"

He was about to say more but Michael interrupted him.

"I pray you, gentlemen," he said, "grant me patience for awhile; I fear me that my gentle cousin did not altogether grasp my meaning. Cousin," he added, turning once more fully to Stowmaries, "will you put your money back into your pocket and instead of fulfilling your engagements to me, fulfil them toward the lady who hath first claims on your loyalty?"

"Tush, man!" retorted Stowmaries, who was waxing wrathful, "cannot you cease that senseless talk? The thing is done, man, the thing is done. Gad! We none of us want it undone, nor could we an we would."

"My lord of Stowmaries is right," concluded Lord Rochester decisively, "and you, Kestyon, do but run your head against a stone wall. An you feel remorse, I for one am sorry for you—but what has been, has been. You no more can withdraw from your present position than you could erase from the Book of Life all that has passed to-day. So take your money, man, you have the right to it. Odd's fish! A

146

hundred and twenty thousand pounds, and you talk of flinging it as a sop to your perturbed conscience."

"Who talked of conscience, my lord?" rejoined Michael haughtily, "or yet of remorse? Surely not I. We have all been gambling on an issue, and I now offer my cousin of Stowmaries his own stakes back again an he'll pay his just debt to his wife rather than to me."

"My wife, man, are you joking!" retorted Stowmaries hotly. "After what has occurred, think you I would take for my countess—"

"The purest, most exquisite woman, Cousin, that ever graced a man's ancestral home," interposed Michael earnestly. "To say less of her were blasphemy."

"Pshaw!" ejaculated Stowmaries with ill-concealed contempt.

"Cousin, I swear to you," reiterated Michael with solemn emphasis, "by all that men hold most sacred, by all that I hold most holy, that the lady is as pure to-day as when her baby hand was placed in yours eighteen years ago, in token that she was to be your wife. She is as worthy to be the wife of a good man, the mother of loyal children, as I am unfit to tie the laces of her shoe. An you'll do your duty by her, you'll never regret it—all that you will regret will be the memory of that turbulent night when in your madness you thought of wronging her!"

"By God, man, I swear that you are crazy!" cried Stowmaries whose impatience had been visibly growing and who now gave full rein to his exasperation. "Are you a damned, canting Puritan that you talk to me like that? Nay, an you wish to be rid of yon baggage, send her back to the tailor's back shop whence she came,—throw her out into the streets,—I care not what you do with her, but in G—d's name I tell you that you shall not palm off on to my mother's son a cast-off troll whom you no longer want."

But even before the words had fully escaped the young man's lips Michael had lifted his glass and thrown its full contents in the face of the blasphemer.

Sickened and blinded with his own fury and the pungent odour of the wine which poured down his face into his eyes and mouth, Stowmaries uttered a violent oath and the next instant had sprung upon his kinsman like an infuriated and raging beast, and had him by the throat even before Ayloffe and Rochester who had quickly jumped to their feet were able to interfere.

The onslaught was vigorous and sudden and Stowmaries' fury hot and uncontrolled. But Michael who throughout the wordy warfare had kept his own temper in check, who had foreseen the attack even when he threw the wine in the younger man's face, had already grasped Stowmaries' wrists with a steel-like pressure of his own nervy hands, causing the other to relax his grip and forcing an involuntary cry of pain to escape his throat.

"Nay, Cousin," he said, still speaking quite quietly, but with a slight tone of contempt now, "in a hand-to-hand struggle you would

147

fare worse than I. Have I hurt your wrist? Then am I deeply grieved—but 'tis not broken I assure you—and you know, dear Coz, that since you are still my debtor, you could not in honour kill me until you had acquitted yourself of your debt to me. I have offered you a fair way of paying that debt, not to me but to her to whom you really owe it. An you'll keep your money now, and take back all you've given me, an you'll fulfil your sacred promise to take Rose Marie for wife, you'll be the happiest man on God's earth. This I swear to you, and also that I'll serve you humbly and devotedly as servant or as slave to the last day of my life and with the last drop of blood in my veins. After that an you wish to kill me—why, my life is at your service. Will you do it, Cousin? God and his army of saints and of angels will give you rich reward."

But Stowmaries who with a sulky look on his face was readjusting the lace ruffles at his wrist whilst glowering at the man whose physical strength he had just been made to feel, turned on him now with an evil sneer.

"You seem to be intimately acquainted with the heavenly hierarchy, Cousin," he said, "but, believe me, I have no intention of entering those celestial spheres which are of your own imagining and of which you seem to be the self-constituted guardian."

"Sneer at me as much as you will, Cousin, but give me answer," urged Michael and for the first time his voice shook as he uttered this final, desperate appeal, "'Twere best for you—this I entreat you to believe. Best for you and right for her. As for me, I no longer exist; the ignoble bargain has never been; wipe it out, Cousin, even from your memory. Take back your money and with it your honour. She is worthy of your love, of your faith and of your trust; take her to your heart, Cousin, take her for she is as pure as the Madonna and you will be richer by all that she can give, the priceless guerdon of her exquisite womanhood."

The other two men were silent. They had taken no part in the discussion and had listened to it each with vastly divers emotions. Rochester, a noble gentleman despite his many extravagances, could not help but admire the man who thus stood up boldly to right a wrong, fearless of consequences, fearless of ridicule. But Ayloffe merely hoped that Michael's rugged eloquence, his earnest, passionate appeal would fail to reach the armour of selfishness and vanity which effectually enveloped Stowmaries' better nature.

Now after this last appeal there was a pause. The storm of turbulent passions was lulled to momentary rest, the better to gather strength for the final conflict.

"Take her to your heart, Cousin," Michael had urged, and no one there could guess the infinity of renunciation which lay in this appeal. Stowmaries was silent for awhile. His glowering eyes expressed nothing but unyielding obstinacy. Otherwise he was totally unmoved.

Then, keeping his gaze rivetted on Michael, he pointed with

outstretched finger to the paper which lay on the table—the draft for seventy thousand pounds on Master Vivish of Fleet Street.

"That is my answer, Cousin," he said loudly and firmly. "You have rendered me a service; for this now I pay you to the full as agreed. Let there be no more of this crazy talk, for what is done is done, and you above all should be satisfied."

Once more there was silence in the low-raftered room. A gust of wind blew the thin curtains way from the open window and caused the scrap of paper to stir with a soft sound as of a spirit voice that murmured a warning "Hush!"

Michael had neither moved nor spoken, not a line of his face betrayed the conflict in his soul. But three pairs of eyes were fixed upon him. He did not seem to see them, for his own were fixed on the fluttering curtain which had whispered spectral words to him; between the gently swaying folds there peeped cold gleams of moonbeam radiance, and from far away the sighing of the young acacia boughs which had mingled with her voice awhile ago.

Then he turned his gaze back to the paper which lay before him, still gently stirring under the soft breath of the evening air. Deliberately and with a firm hand he took it up, folded it across and across and slipped it in the inner pocket of his coat.

"You know best, Cousin," he said in a quiet, unmodulated voice. "As you say, I have rendered you a service. You have paid me in full according to our bond. We should both be satisfied. And now, gentlemen, shall we proceed with supper?"

PART IV

CHAPTER XXIX

And do you ask what game she plays?
With me 'tis lost or won;
With thee it is playing still; with him
It is not well begun;
But 'tis a game she plays with all
Beneath the sway o' the sun.

—Dante Gabriel Rossetti

Mistress Julia Peyton felt a trifle worried. Matters had not turned out exactly as she had anticipated; it is a way peculiar to matters over which we have no control.

She had been quite aware of the fact that my lord of Stowmaries, with Sir John Ayloffe and Lord Rochester, had made the journey over to Paris in order to be present at the marriage of Michael Kestyon with the tailor's daughter, and it had been with the intention of frustrating my lord's desire to pay his final debt of seventy thousand pounds to Michael that she had sent old Daniel Pye over in the gentlemen's company, armed with the letters writ in scholarly French by the exiled Huguenot clerk and intended for good M. Legros' personal perusal.

Mistress Peyton had no special wish to save the susceptibilities of a tailor's wench, and cared little whether the fraud was discovered by her before she had left her father's home or afterwards, but—she had argued this out in her own mind over and over again—if the girl never actually left her father's house, my lord would not in honour be bound to pay Michael the additional seventy thousand pounds, since the latter would not have accomplished his own share of the bargain to the full. On the other hand there would be quite enough public scandal and gossip round the girl, as it was, to enable my lord of Stowmaries to justify his repudiation of the matrimonial bonds, contracted eighteen years ago, on the grounds that the future Countess of Stowmaries no longer bore a spotless reputation.

That had been Mistress Peyton's subtle argument, and on the basis of this unanswerable logic she had laid her plans. Caring nothing for the girl, she cared everything for the money, and above all for the power that so vast a sum would place in Michael's hand for the furtherance of his own case.

Daniel Pye had returned to England about a week after the wedding at St. Gervais. He was an unblushing liar, both by habit and by temperament. Therefore, when he presented himself before his mistress, he assured her that he had handed her letter over to the master tailor even while the wedding festivities were in progress in the back shop, and long before the coach bore the bridal pair away.

When Mistress Peyton heard the circumstantial narrative of how her faithful henchman had fought his way into the tailor's house at peril of his life, and had given the letter into M. Legros' own hands, the while his own poor shoulders were bruised and well-nigh broken with the blows dealt to him by cruel miscreants who strove to hinder him from performing his duty—when the fair Julia heard all this, I say, she was vastly pleased and commended Master Pye very highly for his faithfulness, and I believe even rewarded him by giving him five shillings.

The wedding it seems had been the talk of Paris, ladies and gentlemen from the Court had been present thereat, and Mme. de Montespan had loudly praised the handsome presence of the bridegroom. All this was passing satisfactory, and Mistress Julia was quite content to think that the tailor and his family would—after such an esclandre—be only too willing to hide their humble heads out of the ken of society wherein they had become a laughing stock.

On legal grounds my lord of Stowmaries could readily command the nullity of the child-marriage now; as for the religious grounds which had been the chief stumbling-block hitherto—"Bah!" argued the fair Julia naïvely to herself, "His Holiness the Pope of Rome is a gentleman; he will not expect an English grand seigneur to acknowledge as his countess the cast-off plaything of an adventurer."

The disappointment came some three or four days later when Cousin John in his turn presented himself at the little house in Holborn Row. Of course he had known nothing of his fair cousin's treacherous little scheme, and although he had greatly wondered at Master Pye's presence in Paris at the time of the wedding, yet he had been far from suspecting the truth with regard to its purport. All that good Sir John knew was that the bridal pair did leave the house of M. Legros in a somewhat unconventional style, for this he had been told by the gaffers of the neighbourhood.

He had not seen the departure, but had heard glowing accounts of it all from one or two of the spectators whom he had closely questioned.

There was no doubt that it had been a fine departure: romantic and epoch-making. No fear now of the scandal being in any way hushed up. "Milor the Englishman," as that rascal Michael had been universally called in that quarter of Paris wherein his prowess had been witnessed, was a magnificent horseman, so the gossips declared with one accord. The way he had jumped on his horse, using neither stirrup nor bridle, was a sight good for sore eyes, then two of his English serving-men had raised the bride to his saddle bow, and after a lusty shout of farewell milor had ridden away with her, and soon his horse was head galloping at maddening speed. Never had such a spectacle been witnessed in the streets of Paris before; the gaffers were still agape at the remembrance of it, and it had all seemed more like a vivid and exciting dream than like sober reality.

But no sooner had milor and the bride disappeared round the bend of the narrow street than the first breath of gossip rose— apparently from nothingness—in their wake. Whence it originated nobody knew, but sure it is that within an hour the whole of the quarter was agog with the scandal. Cousin John prided himself on the fact that he had contributed more than his share in spreading the report from one end of Paris to the other that the daughter of the mightily rich and highly-respectable tailor-in-chief of His Majesty the King of France had eloped with an adventurer, who was even kinsman to her own husband, my lord of Stowmaries and Rivaulx.

"The scandal is quite immense, fair Cousin," quoth Cousin John lustily, and with a merry guffaw the while he sat sipping sack-posset in Mistress Peyton's elegantly furnished boudoir. "Personally I see naught for the tailor's wench but the inevitable nunnery, although Michael— but of this more anon. In the meanwhile Mme. de Montespan dotes on the adventure. Lord Rochester retailed it all to her outside the church porch, and you may well believe that it hath lost naught in the telling. She quite fell in love with Michael's handsome presence, and His Majesty the King of France vows that English gentlemen are the primest rogues on this earth; and even sober diplomatists aver that Michael's prowess and Michael's romantic personality have done more to cement international friendship than a whole host of secret treaties. From the Court the scandal hath reached the lower classes of Paris, all thanks to your humble servant, so I flatter myself; the tailor and his family are the butt of every quip-maker in the city. There is a rhyme that goes the round which—nay, your pardon, fair Cousin, I could not repeat it for fear of offending your ears, but let me assure you that the heroine thereof is not like to petition Monseigneur the Archbishop of Paris or His Holiness the Pope to assert her rights to be Countess of Stowmaries—Countess of Stowmaries," added Sir John with another prolonged guffaw, "Countess of Stowmaries! Odd's fish! In Paris they sing of her: 'Une vertu ingulière—' your pardon—your pardon again, dear Coz, I was forgetting—"

And Cousin John had indeed to stop in his narration, for he was choking for very laughter and the tears were streaming down his ruddy cheeks.

Mistress Peyton had listened to the cheerful tale with but ill-repressed impatience, and had not Sir John been so absorbed in what was his favourite topic of conversation—the tearing to shreds of a woman's reputation—he would not have failed to notice that his kinswoman was far from sharing his own hilarity.

Of a truth, the fair Julia's impatience soon gave place to great anger, for it was by now quite clear to her that Daniel Pye had failed in his trust, that he had not only lied like a consummate rogue, but had actually by his unforgivable delinquency caused his mistress' most cherished and carefully-conceived counter-intrigue to come absolutely to naught.

Michael Kestyon had carried off the bride and Lord Stowmaries could not now as a man of honour refuse to pay him that final seventy thousand pounds; a fortune, forsooth, wherewith the adventurer, the wastrel, the haunter of brothels and booths could now make good his claim to the title and peerage of Stowmaries and Rivaulx.

Given a dissolute, money-grabbing king on whose decision the claim for the peerage rested, given this adventure which rendered Michael interesting to those who had the ear of Charles Stuart, and what more likely than that the present lord of Stowmaries should find himself in the terrible position of having paid for his own undoing?

And all because a fool of a serving-man had failed in doing what he had been ordered to do, and this in despite of the most carefully thought-out plans, most ardent wishes and most subtle schemes. We may take it that visions of a terrible retribution to be wreaked on that rascally Daniel Pye already found birth in his mistress' inventive brain; and whilst good Cousin John was wiping the tears of laughter which his own narrative had called to his bulgy eyes, his fair cousin was meditating on the best pretext she could employ for ordering Pye to be lawfully and publicly flogged.

At last Mistress Peyton's sullen silence brought Cousin John back from the pleasing realms of gossip and scandal. Looking into her face he saw anger, where he had expected to witness a smile of triumph; he also saw two perfect lips closed tightly in obvious moodiness, the while he had looked forward to unstinted praise for his own share in the furtherance of her desires.

Cousin John, therefore, was vastly astonished. Puzzlement in its turn yielded to speculation. Mistress Julia was angered—why? She had desired the scandal; now she seemed to resent it. Something had gone amiss then—or had she veered round in her intentions?

Women were strange cattle in Sir John Ayloffe's estimation. Had his ambitious cousin perchance nurtured some counter-scheme of her own, which had come to naught through the success of the original intrigue? It almost seemed like it from the wrathful expression of her face.

The presence of Daniel Pye in Paris came back to Sir John as a swift memory. There had been a counter-intrigue then?

Of a truth this would trouble him but little, provided that such intrigue did not affect the due payment to himself of the twelve thousand pounds promised by the capricious lady. But of this guerdon he felt fully assured. Which is another proof of the truth of the ancient adage which says that there's many a slip 'twixt cup and lip, and also of the fact that women are far keener diviners of such untoward slips than are those who belong to the sterner and less intuitive sex.

Even while the prospect of those pleasing thousands was flitting—all unbeknown to him—further and further from his future grasp, Sir John, studying his cousin's unaccountable mood tried to make some of his wonted cynical maxims anent the motives and emotions of the other sex fit the present situation.

Mistress Peyton was angered when she should have been pleased. Had she perchance conceived an attachment for the romantic blackguard? Such things were possible—women's tastes ever erred on the queer side—and this would certainly account for Julia's impatient anger when she heard of Michael's interesting departure with the beautiful bride in his arms.

Nay then! if this was the case, good Cousin John had still the cream of his narrative in reserve, and the final episode which he had to relate would of a surety satisfy the most rancorous feelings of revenge harboured against a hated rival by any fair monster that wore petticoat.

And at the moment that Mistress Peyton finally decided in her own mind that an accusation of theft preferred by herself against Daniel Pye would bring that elderly reprobate to the whipping post and the stocks, Cousin John's mellifluent voice broke in upon these pleasant dreams.

"Odd's fish, fair Coz," he said loudly and emphatically, for he desired his words to rouse her from her absorption, "imagine our surprise, nay, our consternation when on our arrival at St. Denis we found one solitary turtledove mourning over the absence of the other"

The effect of these words was instantaneous. The fair Julia's thoughts suddenly flew from prospective vengeance to present interests, and though the frown did not disappear from her brow, her eyes flashed eagerness now rather than anger.

"What nonsense is this?" she queried with a show of petulance. "I pray you, Cousin, speak with less imagery. The matter is of serious portent to me as you know—and also to yourself," she added significantly, "and I fear me that my poor wits are too dull to follow the circumlocutions of your flowery speech."

Sir John smiled complacently; he was quite satisfied that he once more held his cousin's undivided attention, and resumed his narrative with imperturbable good-humour.

"I crave your pardon, fair lady," he said, "but on my honour 'tis just as I have told you. My lord of Stowmaries, Lord Rochester and your humble servant did journey by coach to St. Denis, for we knew that thither was the bridal couple bound. We drove in the lumbering vehicle on God-forsaken roads all the way from Paris, and never in all

154

my life did I experience such uncomfortable journeying. 'Milor the Englishman,' quoth Rochester as soon as his feet had touched the ground, 'is he abed?' For you must know that it was then nigh on ten of the clock and the hostelry of the Three Archangels looked as dark as pitch from within and without. 'Milor is upstairs,' exclaimed mine host who, of a surety, looked vastly bewildered at our arrival. He seemed like a man bursting with news, and as if eager to explain something, but we were too impatient to pay any heed to him at the time and ran helter-skelter upstairs in the wake of Lord Rochester who, as you know, is ever in the forefront in a spicy adventure, and who moreover was eager for another peep at the bride, whom he had greatly admired during the religious ceremony in the church. We none of us had any idea that anything could be amiss, and as I have had the honour of assuring you, our consternation was great when on entering the parlour we found Michael standing by the open window, staring moodily out into the dreary landscape, the room itself in total darkness, and—as we learnt afterwards—the bride gone back to Paris by coach in company with her father."

"Impossible," ejaculated Mistress Peyton, feigning surprise which of a truth she did not feel. What had been and still was a mystery to Sir John was clear enough to his fair cousin, and there was, it seems, some slight attenuation to Daniel Pye's monstrous delinquency. The letter, by some idiotic blunder on the part of old Pye, had reached Master Legros just a trifle too late, but it had reached him at last, and the infuriated father had contrived to reach St. Denis in time to snatch his daughter away from the arms of the adventurer—who thus stood prematurely unmasked.

"Impossible!" she reiterated the while Sir John like a true raconteur, having succeeded in capturing her interest, made an effective pause in his narration. He could not complain of her moodiness now, for she seemed all eagerness and agitation.

"True, nevertheless," he asserted quietly, "the bride was gone and Michael—left desolate—seemed inclined to act like a man bereft of his senses."

"How mean you that?" she asked.

"He had, it seems, fallen madly in love with the tailor's daughter, and had no doubt during his hours of loneliness been assailed with remorse at what he chose to call a shameful bargain."

Again Cousin John paused; his large, prominent eyes were fixed once more upon his cousin. Clearly there was an undercurrent of intrigue going on here of which he did not as yet possess the entire secret, for he had distinctly noted that at his last words the deep frown which had still lingered on Julia's snow-white brow now vanished completely, giving place to an excited look of hope. Something of the inner workings of her mind began to dawn on him, however, a vague, indefinable sense of what had gone before, what she had feared, and

155

what she now hoped. Therefore he waited awhile, watching her eager, impatient face, the play of her delicate features, the nervous movements of her hands, ere he resumed with well-simulated carelessness.

"Ay! my dear Coz, the more I think on it, the more am I convinced that Michael in his love-sickness became bereft of reason, for you'll scarce believe it when I tell you that when my lord of Stowmaries desired to acquit himself like an honourable gentleman of his debt to his kinsman, and held out to him the draft for seventy thousand pounds, Michael refused to take it."

This time there was no mistaking the look of pleasure which lit up the fair Julia's face. A less acute observer than was Sir John would have realised at once that this last item of news was essentially pleasant to the hearer. Mistress Peyton of a truth, found her anxieties vanishing away, and was at no pains to hide the pleasure which she felt. Hope was returning to her heart, also gratitude towards Fate who, it seems, had been kind enough after all to play into her hands.

Psychologically the situation was interesting, and we may assume that Cousin John was no longer at sea now. He might not yet possess the key which opened the magic gate into his fair cousin's secret orchard, but he was essentially a gambler, an unscrupulous schemer himself; money, to him, was the all-powerful solution of many an obscure puzzle.

The mention of money had brought on the beautiful face before him the first smile of satisfaction since the beginning of his narrative; ergo, argued Cousin John, the fair mistress entered into a private, villainous little scheme of her own, of calling the tune without paying the piper. Women have no sense of honour, where debts between gentlemen are concerned.

Once on a track, Sir John was quick enough to follow the puzzle to its satisfactory solution. But he was not pleased that his cousin, and partner in the whole enterprise, should thus have intrigued without his knowledge or counsel. Heavens above, if conspirators did not work together, every plot, however well laid, would speedily abort. Women were ever ready for these petty infamies; they seemed to revel in them, to plan and scheme them even if—as in this case—they were wholly superfluous.

He was angry with his pretty cousin, and showed it by keeping her on tenter-hooks, dropping his narrative and ostentatiously draining a mug of posset to its last drop. He would force her, he thought, to disclose her treacherous little hand to the full.

And he succeeded, for as he did not speak she was quite unable to curb her impatience.

"Then—the money—" she asked with obviously affected indifference, "what became of it?"

"The money?" he asked blandly "What money?"

"The seventy thousand pounds," she said, "which Michael Kestyon was to receive and which he refused to take."

Cousin John looked at her over the top of his goblet, his round, bulgy eyes told her quite plainly that he had read her through and through, and that he for one was not sorry that her little counter-scheme had failed, since she had not thought fit to ask his advice. But he said quite lightly, as one who speaks of a trifle too mean to dwell in the memory:

"Oh! the seventy thousand pounds! They are where they should be, dear Cousin, in Michael Kestyon's pocket. The just reward for his services rendered to his kinsman, your future lord, fair Coz!"

"But you said just now—" she stammered on the verge of tears, for the sudden sense of disappointment had been very bitter to bear.

"I said that Michael had been smitten with remorse, and had at first refused to take the money, but Lord Stowmaries soon overcame his scruples and—"

"Lord Stowmaries is a fool!" she interrupted hotly.

Sir John feigned great astonishment.

"A fool? For acquitting himself of a debt of honour?" he asked in tones of mild reproof.

"Ay! a fool, and thrice a fool," she reiterated with increased vehemence, for she was no gaby and was not taken in now by Cousin John's blandness. He had divined her thoughts, and guessed something of her aborted plans; there was no occasion therefore to subdue her annoyance any longer. "An Michael Kestyon was such a dotard as to refuse a fortune," she continued, "why should my lord Stowmaries be the one to force it upon him. Nay! The whole bargain was iniquitous or worse. Ridiculous it was of a truth—one hundred and twenty thousand pounds to a man who would have done the trick for so many pence. I marvelled at you, Cousin, for lending a hand to such wanton waste and did my best to circumvent your folly, but thanks to that dolt Daniel Pye, and apparently to my lord Stowmaries' idiocy, Michael Kestyon is now in possession of the means whereby he can divest the cousin who paid him so well not only of his title but of all his wealth. A blunder, Cousin, an idiotic, silly blunder," she added as she jumped to her feet, unable to sit still, tramping up and down the room like a raging wildcat, lashing herself into worse fury by picturing all the evils which the unfortunate business would bring in its train, chief amongst these being my lord Stowmaries' undoing, for which she really cared naught only in so long as it affected her own prospects.

"The silly adventure is already the talk of the town; the king has asked to see Michael Kestyon. Bah! The man sold his kingdom, the liberty and dignity of England for a sum not much larger than what Michael can now offer him for a favourable decision in a peerage claim. Ye saints above! what fools men are! what blind, blundering, silly fools, the moment they begin to prate of honour!"

157

Cousin John had allowed his fair cousin's vehement vituperations to pass unchallenged over his humbled head. That there was some truth in her argument he himself could not deny, and it was a fact that fears very akin to her own in the matter of the money had more than once crossed his mind. Feeling, therefore, that the reproof, though exceptionally violent, was not undeserved, he dropped his bland, cynical manner, and when at last the fair Julia paused in her invectives, chiefly for lack of breath, and also because tears of anger were choking her voice, he spoke to her quite quietly and almost apologetically.

"Indeed, Coz," he said, "I would have you believe that I am deeply touched by your reproaches, which, alas, I may have merited to a certain extent. Zeal in your cause may have rendered me less far-seeing than I really should have been, considering what we both have at stake. But let me tell you also that I have not been quite such a dolt as you seem to think. You are quite wrong in supposing that Michael Kestyon would have acted the part which he did for a less sum than we have given him. Nothing but a real substantial fortune would have tempted Michael. Nothing," reiterated Sir John emphatically, seeing that Julia made a contemptuous gesture of incredulity. "He is a curious mixture of the wastrel and the gentleman; if we could not satisfy his ambition, we could not attack his sense of honour. Where we made the mistake was in thinking that a substantial sum would satisfy him in itself. No one guessed that his dormant claim to the peerage of Stowmaries was still of such vital importance to him. He had ceased to move actively in the matter partly through the lack of money, but also in part through the moral collapse which he has undergone in the past two years. I confess that I did think that when he was possessed of his newly-acquired fortune, he would continue the life of dissolute vagabondage which we all believed had become his second—nay, his only nature. It seems that we were all mistaken—"

"What do you mean? Has anything occurred already?" asked Julia, who found all her fears increased tenfold at Cousin John's seriously-spoken words.

"No! No! No!" he said reassuringly, "nothing at present, save that Michael Kestyon has made no attempt to return to his boon companions in the various brothels which were wont to be his haunts. Rumour hath it that he is oft seen in the company of my lord Shaftesbury, and there is no doubt that the king was vastly amused by the adventure. Some say that royal smiles are the sure precursors to royal favours. But between entertaining Charles II with tales of spicy adventures and obtaining actual decisions from him in important matters lie vast gulfs of kingly indifference and of kindly indolence. There is nothing that the king hates worse than the giving of a decision, and, believe me, that he will dilly-dally with Michael until that young reprobate will have spent every penny of his new fortune, and will have none left to offer as a bribe to our merry monarch. It is not cheap, believe me, to be a temporary boon companion to Charles Stuart, and a great deal more than a hundred thousand pounds would have to pass through Michael's fingers in keeping up a certain gentlemanly state, in tailor's accounts, in bets and in losses at hazard, before the king would think of rewarding him in the only manner which would compensate him for all the money expended in obtaining the royal smiles."

"You may be right, Cousin," said Mistress Peyton, somewhat reassured, "at the same time a great deal of anxiety would have been saved me, if that old liar Daniel Pye had done as he was bid. But he shall rue his prevarications, and bitterly, too."

"You may wreak what vengeance you will, fair Cousin, on the varlet who hath disobeyed you. But I entreat you to keep your favours for those who have tried to serve you to the best of their poor abilities. As for the rest, let me assure you now that Michael Kestyon refused the seventy thousand pounds and even offered to repay the first instalment of fifty thousand on terms which were wholly unacceptable to Lord Stowmaries. The chief condition being that my lord should rescind the whole of the bargain, and take the tailor's wench back into his heart and marital bosom. You see, fair Coz, how impossible it was to treat with Michael at all, and we certainly were not to blame. My lord of Stowmaries is still the happiest man on earth; glad enough to have purchased his happiness for one hundred and twenty thousand pounds. An I mistake not he is in Rome now, awaiting the Pope's decision—but that is a foregone conclusion. Monseigneur the Archbishop hath assured him of his cooperation. Soon my lord will receive that for which he craves: religious dispensation to avail himself of the civil law of England which will readily grant him nullity of marriage, and the blessing of the Pope himself on his remarriage with the fairest beauty that e'er hath graced an ancestral home. Until then I entreat you, Cousin," added Sir John with elaborate gallantry, "to smooth away those frowns of anxiety which ill become the future Countess of Stowmaries. Let me see you smile, dear Coz, ere I take my leave, having, I trust, assured you that you have no truer servant than your faithful kinsman, the recipient of your favours, and, I trust, of many more in the not very distant future."

There was no resisting Cousin John's assurance and his smile of confident encouragement. Mistress Peyton did allow the wrinkles of anger to fade from her smooth brow. But complete peace of mind was not restored to her in full; she was almost glad that "the happiest man on earth" was away from her just now. She wanted to think matters over in absolute quietude, away from her good cousin's bland platitudes. It almost seemed as if Fate had reshuffled all her cards; she and her partners in the great life-gamble, Lord Stowmaries, Sir John and Michael Kestyon, too, had had fresh hands dealt to them. They needed sorting and the game mayhap reconsidering.

It was even doubtful at the present moment what was the chief trump card. Daniel Pye with his clumsy fingers had abstracted one out of his mistress' hand. At thought of that the frown returned and the "fairest beauty that e'er graced an ancestral home" looked not unlike a vengeful termagant gloating over the petty revenge which—in a small measure—would compensate her for all anxieties past, present and to come.

CHAPTER XXX

How! Old thief thy wits are lame;
To clip such it is no shame;
I rede you in the devil's name,
Ye come not here to make men game.

—Swinburne

Daniel Pye, having arrived at that corner stone in Holborn Row which afforded him a full view of the house whence he had just been ignominiously dismissed, turned and shook a menacing fist in its direction. His body ached, he was smarting in every limb, and he had a grievance which clamoured loudly for revenge.

In Paris he had endured, whilst executing his duty, the buffetings and blows of a crowd of rowdy apprentices; this he had done not from any deep-rooted attachment to a capricious and exacting mistress, nor from any very exalted notions of abstract duty, but chiefly for the sake of the commendations and the rewards which the due fulfilment to Mistress Peyton's commands would naturally bring in its train.

The fact that, in order to allay the futile anxieties of a pretty woman, good Daniel Pye subsequently went in for a somewhat highly-coloured tale of his adventures was, after all, a venial sin, and surely the minor transgression which he had committed in delivering the letter, half an hour later than he should have done, did not call for such malignant and cruel treatment as his ungrateful mistress had thought fit to impose upon him. Under a paltry accusation of theft, which the lady herself must have known was totally unfounded, she had handed him over to the magistrate for punishment. Convicted of the charge on the most flimsy evidence, he had been made to stand in the pillory two hours, and been publicly flogged like some recalcitrant 'prentice, or immoral wench.

Nay, worse! For Mistress Peyton herself, accompanied by Sir

160

John Ayloffe, had gone down to Bridewell to see her serving-man whipped, under the pretence that she wished to see justice properly tempered with mercy, since she only desired merited chastisement for him and not wanton cruelty.

And yet when he, Daniel Pye, was howling at the whipping post like one possessed, the while a crowd of young jackanapes—among whom were some of Pye's fellow servants—stood hooting and jeering, Sir John Ayloffe at Mistress Peyton's special command had ordered that an additional ten strokes with the lash be dealt him with no lenient hand. And when Daniel anon stood in the pillory, bruised, sore, every limb in his body aching with the heavy blows, Sir John had caused baskets full of rotten eggs and scraps of tainted fish and meat and decayed vegetable to be distributed among the spectators so that the ribald youngsters might throw this evil-smelling refuse at the unfortunate man whose sole crime had been a tiny lie spoken in order to reassure an ungrateful mistress.

Finally Pye was dismissed from Mistress Peyton's service, despite his abject entreaties. He was kicked out of the street door by a young lacquey whom he himself had oft flogged for impertinence and who now had already assumed the comfortable shoes of office which Daniel had worn for so long.

To the last the mistress had persisted in her unfounded and cruel accusations. To the last she coldly asserted that Daniel had robbed her of seventy thousand pounds.

Seventy thousand pounds! By Heaven! Daniel was not aware that such a vast sum existed in the world, nor if he had stolen it—which of course he had not—would he have known what to do with all that money!

No wonder, therefore, that the man felt mentally as well as bodily sore—nay, that he swore to be revenged on the cruel lady who had so wantonly wronged him. What form his revenge would take he could not at first determine, but these were days when it was not over-difficult for a man to make his petty spite be very uncomfortably felt, provided he had nothing more to lose and possessed neither conscience nor fear of ulterior punishment.

Now Daniel Pye, we know, had no overwhelming regard for truth; as to punishment, by the Lord, he had had all the punishment that any menial could possibly receive. He could sink no lower in the hierarchy of respectable domesticity; he had nothing more to lose, nothing more to gain. A serving-man who had been publicly flogged for theft was an outcast as far as gentlemen's houses were concerned. All the service that a branded thief might obtain in future would be in mean taverns or places of doubtful reputation where the master could not afford to be over-particular in the choice of his henchmen.

Pye had indeed shaken a menacing fist at the house in Holborn Row. Though he had not thought out the exact form which his revenge might take, he knew by instinct in what quarter to seek for guidance in this desire.

His steps led him almost mechanically in the direction of Whitefriars. When he himself was still a respectable lacquey; he would have scorned to set foot in this unhallowed spot where cheats, liars and other reprobates rubbed shoulders with the wastrels of aristocratic descent who had sought sanctuary here against their creditors.

In a corner of the narrow street, and in what had once been the refectory of white-robed monks, there now stood a tavern of evil fame—one or two low-raftered rooms, wherein light and air penetrated in such minute particles that these had not the power to drive away the heavy fumes of alcohol, of rank tobacco, of vice and of licentiousness which filled every corner of this dark and squalid spot.

Here the informer, the perjurer, the cheat, held his court unmolested, here the debtor was free from pursuit, and the highway robber safe from the arm of the law.

Whitefriars was sanctuary! Oh, the mockery of the word! For it was the brawlers and the bullies, the termagants and hags that inhabited these once holy and consecrated precincts, who enforced this self-ordained law of sanctuary. Neither townguard nor soldiery would dare to enter the unhallowed neighbourhood save in great numerical strength, and even then the flails of the lawless fraternity, the bludgeons of the men and stew-pans and spits of the women oft gained a victory over the musketeers.

To this spot now Daniel Pye unhesitatingly turned his footsteps. The servant kicked out of house for theft, the henchman who had been flogged and had stood in the pillory, naturally drifted towards those who like himself were at war with law and order, who had quarrelled with justice or were nursing a grievance.

It was then late in the afternoon. Outside the beautiful May sun was trying to smile on the grimy city, on all that man had put up in order to pollute God's pure earth: the evil-smelling, narrow streets, the pavements oozing with slimy, slippery mud, the rickety, tumble-down houses covered with dirt and stains. All this the sun had kissed and touched gently with warmth and promise of spring, but into that corner of Whitefriars where Daniel Pye now stood, it had not attempted to penetrate.

Overhead the protruding gables right and left of the street almost met, obscuring all save a very narrow strip of sky. Underfoot the slimy mud, fed by innumerable overflowing gutters, hardly gave a foothold to the passerby.

But the door of the brothel stood invitingly open. Daniel Pye walked in unchallenged; scarce a head was turned or a glance raised to appraise the newcomer. He looked sulky and unkempt, his clothes were soiled and tattered after the painful halt in the pillory. In fact he looked what he was—a rebel against society like unto themselves.

162

Men sat in groups conversing in whispers and drinking deeply out of pewter mugs. One of these groups, more compact than the others, occupied the centre of the room. In the midst of it a man with thin, long, yellow hair straggling round a high forehead, his thin shanks encased in undarned worsted stockings, his stooping shoulders covered by a surcoat of sad-coloured grogram, seemed to hold a kind of court.

Daniel slouched toward that group; the man in the sad-coloured coat raised a pair of pale, watery eyes to him, and no doubt recognising by that subtle instinct peculiar to the great army of blackguards, that here was a kindred spirit, he made way for the stranger so that the latter might sit on the bench beside him.

After a very little while Pye found himself quite at home in that low-raftered room, wherein the air surfeited with evil-smelling fumes was less foul than the sentiments, the lies, the blasphemies that were freely emitted here.

The group of whom Mistress Peyton's ex-henchman had now become a unit, and over which presided the lanky-haired, pale-eyed youth, consisted of men who had neither the enthusiasm of their own villainy nor the courage of their own crimes; they were the spies that worked in the dark, the informers who struck unseen. False oaths, perjured information, lying accusations were their special trade. It did not take Daniel Pye very long to learn its secrets.

The man with the yellow hair was called Oates. He had once been a priest, now he was a renegade, a sacrilegious liar, and maker of false oaths. Close to him sat another man, outwardly very different to look at, for he was stout and florid, and his eyes were bleary, but the perversion of the soul within was equal in these two men. Oates and Tongue! What a world of infamy do their very names evoke! They were the leaders of this band of false informers who lived and throve by this infamous trade. Oates soon made a fortune by those very schemes which he propounded to his henchmen on this memorable day when Daniel Pye drifted into their midst.

The East Anglian peasant torn from his primitive home amongst the wheatfields of Norfolk, transplanted into the vitiated atmosphere of the great city, there to learn the abject lessons which the service of a capricious woman and the bribes of her courtiers do so readily teach to a grasping nature, now fell a ready slave to the insidious suggestions of these perjurers. Pye at first had listened with half an ear. His thoughts were still centred on vengeance and on his own aches and pains, and the denunciations against Papists which was the chief subject of discussion between Oates and his audience seemed to him of puerile significance.

But the eye of the other, of him with the florid complexion, was constantly fixed on Daniel Pye. Gradually he drew the latter into conversation. A vague question here, a suggestion there, and the whole history of that day's bitter wrongs was soon poured into overwilling ears: the accusation of theft, the whipping post, the pillory.

Pye felt no shame in retailing these humiliating woes to a stranger. Ever since he had been kicked out of the house by that insolent subordinate he had longed to tell the tale to some one. Truly he would have gone raving mad with compressed rage if he had had to go silently to bed. The stranger was a sympathetic listener:

"Strike me! but 'tis a damnable tale," he said, "misdeeds that cry loudly for revenge. Cannot you, friend, be even with a woman who hath treated you so ill?"

"How can I?" growled Pye, moodily. "A woman! She is rich, too, and hath many friends—"

"Well-favoured, too, mayhap," suggested the other.

"Ay, she's counted pretty—"

"And her friends are mostly gentlemen, I imagine."

"Mostly," replied Daniel impatiently, for he liked not this digression from the all-absorbing topic of his own woes.

Tongue said nothing more for the present, but anon he called for mulled ale, and made Pye draw nearer to the table and partake largely of his lavishness.

The ale had been strengthened with raw alcohol, and made heady with steaming and the admixture of spices. It had special properties— as all blackguards in search of victims or confederates well knew—of loosening tongues and addling feeble minds.

Daniel Pye had had no desire to be reticent. He was already over-ready to talk. But the spirituous ale which soon got into his head killed that instinctive native suspicion in him, which in more sober moments would have caused him to look askance at the easy familiarity of his newly-found friend.

Pye was quite unaware of the fact that Tongue was really questioning him very closely, and that he himself gave ready answer to every question. Within half an hour, he had told the other all that there was to know about Mistress Peyton and her household, but still Master Tongue was disappointing in his offers of advice. Daniel was under the impression that the man with the florid face would help him to be revenged on his spiteful mistress, and yet time went on and Daniel had told his story over and over again in every detail and yet nothing had been suggested that sounded satisfactory.

He wanted to dwell on his troubles, those final ten lashes specially ordered, the rotten eggs thrown at him one by one by that damnable little scullion whom he himself had so often thrashed. Yet Master Tongue would no longer dwell on these interesting facts, but always dragged the conversation back to Mistress Peyton's household, or to the gentlemen who formed her court.

"Surely, friend," he said somewhat impatiently at last, "you must have known some of these gentlemen quite intimately. If as you say

164

your mistress was a noted beauty, she must have had many admirers, some more favoured than others—some of these must have been Papists. The Duke of Norfolk now—did he come to see your lady?"

"No," replied Daniel Pye, sulkily. "But just as that rascally scullion hit me in the eye—"

"Never mind about that now," interrupted the other. "Try and tell me the names of those gentlemen who most often visited this Mistress Julia Peyton."

"There was Sir John Ayloffe—"

"He is no Papist—who else?"

"Sir Anthony Wykeham—"

"Oh!" said Tongue eagerly. "Did he come often?"

"No. Only once. But as I was telling you, there was a youngster in that crowd—"

But the other again broke in impatiently:

"You only saw Sir Anthony Wykeham once? When was that?"

"He came with my lord of Stowmaries."

"My lord Stowmaries? You know my lord Stowmaries? Did he come often?"

"Every day nearly. Mistress Peyton is like to marry him, now that he's rid of his first wife."

To Daniel Pye's utter astonishment, this simple fact—which he himself considered of very minor interest in comparison with the story of his own troubles—seemed to delight his newly-found friend.

Master Tongue jumped up with every sign of eager excitement.

"You knew my lord Stowmaries?" he reiterated insistently. "You knew him well?"

Then as Pye, somewhat bewildered, assented, he ejaculated:

"By G—d! the best man we could ever have hit upon, under the circumstances."

He now slipped his hand confidentially under Pye's arm, forcing him to rise, then he dragged him away from the group, and into a distant corner of the room.

"Friend," he whispered eagerly, "let me tell you that you are in luck to-day. You want your revenge; you shall have it, and much more yet to boot, and your spiteful mistress will yet have cause to rue the day when she turned you out of doors. Listen to me, man! Are you desirous of securing a good competence as well as of being even with her who had you whipped and pilloried?"

"Ay!" replied Daniel Pye with a fervour which was too deep for a longer flow of words.

"Then do you go out of here now and find means to kill time in some other tavern close by. But at ten of the clock this night return here. You will find me and my friend Oates, and one or two more of these gentlemen who have a vast scheme in hand for our own good fortune, wherein we will ask you to participate. Nay, ask me no more

165

now!" added the man with the bleary eyes. "It were too long to explain, and there are several pairs of ears present in this room at this moment who are not meant to hear all that I say. But I tell you, friend, that if you be willing, my friend Oates will help you to your revenge, and in addition there will be at least £30 in your pocket, and the chance of earning more. Well, what say you?"

"That I'll come," said Daniel Pye simply.

CHAPTER XXXI

Love's wings are overfleet
And like the panther's feet
The feet of Love.

—Swinburne

When Mistress Peyton had finally dismissed Daniel Pye from her service, after having seen him flogged and pilloried, she felt somewhat more at ease.

She did not see his gesture of menace, nor would it have perturbed her much if she had. Her spite against the man had been cruel and petty; she knew that well enough, yet did not strive to curb it. Daniel Pye's howls at the whipping post had momentarily served to alleviate the anxieties which as day succeeded day grew in intensity.

The recollection of what she had made the man suffer was a solace, even now when the awful truth had begun to dawn upon her that in striving to gain too much, she had very likely lost all.

Rumour was overbusy with Michael Kestyon; his popularity with the king, my lord Shaftesbury's interest in the long-forgotten peerage claim, Michael's long conferences with Sir William Jones, the Attorney-General, who was said to know more about peerages, genealogies and legitimacies than did His Majesty's heralds and poursuivants themselves.

On Sir William's report would the king ultimately base his decision as to Michael Kestyon's claim to the title and estates of Stowmaries and Rivaulx. The matter would not be referred to the Lord's House of Parliament. It was absolutely one for the Crown to decide, nor were the noble lords like to go against the king's mandate.

Already gossips averred that Michael had paid the Attorney-General one hundred thousand pounds for the report which was ready to be submitted to the king, and which, needless to say, was entirely in favour of the claim. It was also said that my lord Stowmaries—financially somewhat straitened for the moment, through a recent highly-interesting adventure—was unable to cap his cousin's munificent gift to Sir William Jones by one more magnificent still.

All these rumours were quite sufficient forsooth to cause the fair Julia many an anxious hour and many a sleepless night. Small wonder that when she thought of Daniel Pye and of that hundred thousand pounds paid to the Attorney-General, which could not have been forthcoming if the miserable reprobate had delivered his mistress' letter to M. Legros in good time, no wonder, then, I say, that her small teeth, sharp as those of a wildcat, set against each other in an agony of impotent rage. She would have liked to have got hold of her serving-man again, to have had him flogged again and again, ay, and to have had him deprived of his right hand for his disobedience and his lies.

The "might-have-beens" were becoming positive torture to the beautiful Julia; and my lord Stowmaries had not yet come home. He had gone to Rome for the dispensation, which he told her in an ardent and passionate missive, he had at last obtained. Julia laughed, a cruel, callous, bitter laugh when she read that letter. Of a truth the man must be mad who could for a moment think that she would wed him in poverty and obscurity, just as readily as she would in riches.

Cousin John did his best to console her. He vowed that rumour lied, that Michael was spending his money in a vain endeavour to retain his popularity with the king, in which he was rapidly failing, and that no sensible-minded person did believe that His Majesty would uphold the preposterous claims of a sworn adventurer, wastrel and soldier of fortune, against so elegant a gentleman as was my lord of Stowmaries.

After one of these visits from Cousin John, Mistress Julia always felt temporarily relieved of her anxiety. She had thought it best for the moment to keep aloof from the society of London; she was nowhere to be seen in public, not even at the playhouses where she had once been the cynosure of all eyes. She wanted to see her future fully assured before she again encountered the admiring glances of the men, or the oft ill-natured comments of the women.

When at last Lord Stowmaries, back from his journey to Rome, was once more at her feet, glowing with loving ardour, triumphant in his success, Mistress Peyton remained cold and unresponsive. He did not notice this, for he was full of projects and happy that the path which led him to her arms had at last been made quite clear.

"Madly as I longed for your sweet presence, my best beloved," he said whilst he covered her little hands with kisses, "I would not return until I knew that I was free—quite free to place mine all, my name, my fortune at your feet. I journeyed to Rome, dear heart, immediately after the esclandre in Paris. I paid Michael his due, then flew to His Holiness. When I returned homewards I was eager to know how the

167

scandal had spread. Nay, there is no fear now that the tailor will strive to interfere with me. There are various rumours current about the wench, one of them being that she will go to a nunnery, the other, which gains far more credence, being that King Louis, vastly interested in her adventure hath cast eyes of admiration on her and that Mme. de Montespan is deadly jealous. Be that as it may, Monseigneur the Archbishop of Paris is now wholly on my side. He gave me letters to His Holiness, whom I saw in Rome."

"And what said His Holiness, the Pope?" queried Julia, feigning eagerness which she was far from feeling.

"He has granted me religious dispensation to contract a fresh marriage, provided the courts of England do dissolve my present bonds, which is a foregone conclusion," said the young man triumphantly. "My man of law tells me that it will be but a matter of a few weeks, and that the case will be decided as soon as heard, provided the tailor's wench doth not defend it, which under the circumstances she is not like to do. I am free, dear heart, free to marry you as soon as you will consent."

Then, as she did not reply, he added reproachfully:

"You are silent, my Julia; will you not tell me that you are glad?"

She made no effort to smile.

"Indeed, my lord, I am glad," she said calmly, "but I would not have you hasten matters too much."

"Why not? To me every day, every hour that separates me from you, seems like weary cycles of dull and deadly years. Methinks that if you would but allow me to proclaim you to the whole world as my future countess, I could wait more patiently then."

"Not yet, my lord, not yet," she said with a slight show of petulance.

"Why not?" he urged.

"The times are troublous for your co-religionists, my lord," she said vaguely.

"Bah! the troubles will not last, and they do not affect me."

"Are you quite sure of that, my lord? One by one the Papists in the kingdom fall under the ban of public hatred."

"We are much maligned, but the king is on our side," interposed Stowmaries with an indifferent shrug of the shoulders.

"Mayhap, mayhap," she rejoined impatiently. "But nevertheless, the Papists are in bad odour. There is talk that the Duke of York will soon be sent abroad. The outcry in London is loud against what is called a Papist intrigue to sell England to France and to place her people under the yoke of Rome."

"What hath all that to do with our love, dear heart?"

"Everything," she said, angry with him for being so obtuse, not liking yet to show him her hand, the cruel hand which would dismiss him without compunction, were his fortunes on the wane. "You forget

168

that by disgracing the tailor's wench, you have made Michael Kestyon, the claimant to your title, passing rich."

"Bah! He hath spent half that substance already, so 'tis said. The king soon tires of his friends, and his affections are an expensive luxury to keep."

"Rumour goes on to say that Michael Kestyon hath paid the Attorney-General one hundred thousand pounds that he may send a favourable report of his case to the king," asserted Mistress Peyton, relentlessly, almost spitefully.

Lord Stowmaries made no direct reply. Truth to tell, he thought his fair Julia's anxieties futile, but at the same time, with unvarying optimism and self-sufficiency, he had attributed these anxieties on his behalf to her great love for him. Everything so far had gone well with him; for years now his every wish in life had been gratified; even the child-marriage, that great obstacle to the desires of his heart, had been swept away from before his path, leaving it clear and broad, to lead him straight to gratification and to happiness.

With characteristic vanity he would not see that Julia, who had been all eagerness and ardour awhile ago, had suddenly become cold and well-nigh hostile. In every word which she uttered, in every inflection of her voice—even when it became petulant and spiteful—he heard but the echo of the overmastering emotions of a tender heart, whose sole object, himself, was in imaginary peril.

He loved her all the better for her fears, though he felt none himself. He knew quite well that a wave of fanatical hatred against the Roman Catholics was passing over Puritan England; that the nation tired of a king's treachery had turned in deadly bitterness against those whom it held responsible for the constitutional faithlessness of a Stuart.

But Titus Oates had not yet come forward with his lies, and Lord Stowmaries and his co-religionists were the last to foresee that the abject terror and malignant intolerance of the whole nation were already being directed against them, and that these would anon culminate in those shameful accusations, mock trials and scandalous verdicts which have remained to this day a dark and ineradicable blot on England's integrity and on her sense of justice.

We must not suppose for a moment that Mistress Peyton foresaw the ugly black cloud which was looming on the not very distant horizon. Her intuition in political matters only went so far as these affected her own prospects. But no one who lived in London in this year of grace could help but see that Papists were held in abhorrence and in fear. The terms of the treaty of Dover had, despite strenuous efforts on the part of my lords Clifford and Arlington, become public property. England, with eyes rendered unseeing by abject fear, saw herself the minion of France, the slave of the Papacy. It only needed the tiny spark to kindle these smouldering ashes into raging flames.

Mistress Peyton, keenly alive to her own interests, did not wish to tie her future irrevocably to a man who within the next few months might find himself divested of title and wealth and mayhap in the dock for treason. Therefore, all Stowmaries' ardent entreaties received but little response.

"There is time and to spare," was all the hope which the fair beauty chose to give to her adorer; "as you say, this wave of anti-Romanism will pass away; Michael Kestyon will dissipate his newly-acquired wealth in riotous living; then you, my lord, will be free to think once more of marriage. I' faith the bonds are scarce broken yet; your nullity suit, my lord, hath not even been tried; the tailor may prove more obstinate than you think, and give you trouble yet. On my soul, 'twill be better to wait till all anxiety is removed from you, until Michael Kestyon is sunk back in obscurity and the tailor's baggage hid in a nunnery. Then, my lord, you may claim my promise—but not before."

My lord of Stowmaries had perforce to be satisfied for the present, though he chafed under this further period of incertitude. But the fair Julia would grant him no more for the present, although after her cold declaration that she herself would not be tied by a promise, she did exact from him a holy and solemn pledge that he considered himself bound to her irrevocably and whatever might betide, so help him God.

CHAPTER XXXII

They said that love would die when Hope was gone
And Love mourned long, and sorrowed after Hope;
At last she sought out Memory and they trod
The same old paths where Love had walked with Hope,
And Memory fed the soul of Love with tears.

—Tennyson

M. Legros walked out backwards from the august presence of Monseigneur the Archbishop of Paris with head reverently bent to receive the benediction not altogether ungraciously given.

Through the close ranks of gorgeously attired, liveried servants he passed, then across the courtyard and through the gilded gates out into the street.

Then only would his sense of what was due to Monseigneur allow him to give vent to his feelings. He sighed and shook his head and muttered vague words of despondency.

Of a truth how different had been this interview to-day to that other one a brief while ago, when with light elastic step, good M. Legros had left Monseigneur's presence with his heart full of elation, of triumph and of hope.

It had been November then; the kindly tailor remembered how cold had been the night, with that penetrating drizzle which sought out the very marrow of the unfortunate pedestrian who happened to be abroad. But M. Legros had not heeded the cold or the wet then, his heart had been warm with the joyful news which he was about to bring into his home. Now the warm glow of a late September sun was in the air; not far away in the gardens of the Queen Mother's palace the last roses of summer were throwing their dying fragrance into the air even as far as the dismal streets which Legros traversed, oh, with such a heavy heart!

Indeed, he paid no heed to the scent of the flowers, the last tender calls of thrush and blackbird which came from the heavy bouquets of the Luxembourg, and he almost shivered despite the warmth of this late summer's afternoon. Monseigneur had not been encouraging; and even the tailor's philosophical temperament had shown signs of inward rebellion at the cold manner in which the Archbishop had received his just plaint. Wherein had he sinned, either he or his wife? They had been deceived, nothing more. Would not any one else have been deceived in just the same way, by the soft words and grand manner of that splendid blackguard?

And Rose Marie, the innocent lamb? Was it not a sin in itself even to suggest that she had been to blame? Yet Monseigneur would not listen, despite good M. Legros' entreaties. "You should have guarded your daughter's honour more carefully," His Greatness had said very severely.

Prayers for help had been of no avail.

"I cannot help you now," Monseigneur had reiterated with marked impatience; "the matter rests with your daughter's husband. My lord of Stowmaries is the gravely-injured husband; he may choose to forgive and forget, he may take his erring wife back to his heart and home, but I cannot interfere; the Holy Church would not enforce her decree under such circumstances. It would be cruel and unjust. If the law of England will grant the suit of nullity, the Holy Father will not— nay, he cannot, object. My lord of Stowmaries hath the right to his freedom now, an he choose."

"But my child is as pure and as innocent as the Holy Virgin herself," M. Legros had protested with all the strength of his poor broken heart; "will not the Church protect the innocent, rather than the guilty? My lord of Stowmaries himself was a party to the infamous trick which—"

"Into this discussion I cannot enter with you, sirrah!" His Greatness had interrupted with overwhelming severity. "The matter is one which doth not concern the Church. What doth concern her is that my lord of Stowmaries, who is a devout Catholic, hath asked for leave to appeal to the civil courts of his country for a dissolution of his marriage with a woman who no longer bears a spotless reputation. This leave under the unfortunate circumstances and the undoubted publicity of the scandal around your daughter's fame, the Holy Father hath decided to grant. I can do nothing in the matter."

"Your Greatness, knowing the real facts of the case—" hazarded the timid man rendered bold by the excess of his sorrow.

"I only know the facts of the case, such as I see them," interrupted the Archbishop haughtily, "but since you are so sure of your daughter's innocence, go and persuade my lord of Stowmaries to view it in the same light as you do. Transcendent virtue," added Monseigneur, with a scarce perceptible curl of his thin lips, "is sure to triumph over base calumny. I promise you that I will do nothing to fan the flames of my lord's wrath. My attitude will be strictly neutral. Go, seek out Lord Stowmaries. Let your daughter make a personal appeal. My blessing go with you."

M. Legros was dismissed. It had been worse than useless now to try and force a prolongation of the interview. Monseigneur's indifference might turn at any moment to active opposition. The tailor had made discreet if lavish offers of money—alms or endowments; he would have given his entire fortune to see Rose Marie righted. But either my lord of Stowmaries had forestalled him, or the matter had become one of graver moment beyond the powers of bribery; certain it is that Monseigneur had paid no heed to vague suggestions and had severely repressed any more decided offers.

No wonder, therefore, that despair lay like a heavy weight on the worthy tailor's heart, as he made his way slowly along the muddy bank of the river, crossed the Pont Neuf and finally turned in the direction of the Rue de l'Ancienne Comédie.

Now as then, a girlish hand opened the door for him, in response to his knock; now as then a pair of confiding arms were thrown around his neck. But it was a sigh which escaped his throat, and to the sigh there was no response from those girlish lips turned grave in sorrow.

Maman, with unvarying optimism, insisted on hearing a full account of the interview with Monseigneur; she weighed every sentence which was faithfully reported to her, queried indefatigably and commented with somewhat forced cheerfulness on what she heard.

Rose Marie sat—silent and absorbed—at her father's knee. She had never harboured any hopes from this long-projected audience; the result therefore in no way disappointed her.

Not even maman knew what went on in the girl's thoughts, nor how complete and sudden had been the transformation from the child

172

into the woman. Rose Marie, when she returned home with her father on that never-to-be-forgotten night in April, had gone to bed tired and submissive. When she rose the next morning at her accustomed hour she took up the threads of her former uneventful life, just as if they had never been snapped by that strong and treacherous hand.

She studied her music, and delved deeply into her books, she read aloud to her father out of holy books, and oft sang to him whilst playing on the harpsichord. M. and Mme. Legros oft wondered exactly how much she felt; for they loved her far too dearly to be deceived by these attempts at indifference.

Something of Rose Marie's girlishness had gone from her, never again to return, something of the bird-like quality of her voice, something of the deer-like spring of her step. The blue eyes were as clear as ever, the mouth as perfectly curved, but across the brow lay— all unseen save to doting eyes—the ineradicable impress of a bitter sorrow.

But the child never spoke of those three weeks that were past, nor was Michael's name ever mentioned within the walls of the old house in the Rue de l'Ancienne Comédie. "Milor" had come and stolen the girl's heart and happiness, wrecked the brightness of a home, and sown disgrace and shame. And yet to all these three people who should so ardently have hated him, his name seemed to have become through the intensity of that grief which he had caused, almost sacred in the magnitude of his sin.

It was as, when to a fanatic, the name of Lucifer becomes as unspeakable as that of God.

The news that the real lord of Stowmaries had appealed to His Holiness for leave to contract a fresh marriage had not been long in reaching the tailor's house. For the past five months now M. Legros had exhausted every means of persuasion and of bribery to obtain an audience of Monseigneur.

The Archbishop had been overbusy with grave affairs of state, so the wretched man was invariably told whenever he tried—most respectfully—to press his claim for an early audience. It was only after the terrible news which came direct from Rome that at last Monseigneur consented to see the stricken father.

Now that interview was over—on which so many feeble hopes had of a truth been built—His Greatness had been haughty and severe, and the only consolation which he had deigned to offer was advice which was indeed very hard to follow.

At the first suggestion, somewhat hesitatingly put forward by Papa Legros to his daughter, she rose up in revolt.

"Make appeal to my lord Stowmaries?" she said indignantly. "Never. How could Monseigneur suggest such a course?"

Papa was silent, and even maman sighed and shook her head.

173

Rose Marie had gone to the window, and her cheeks aflame now, she was staring out into the street.

"Are we beggars," she murmured, proudly defiant, "that we should be bidden to sue for grace?"

From where she sat, could her vision but have pierced through the forest of houses, and thence through the sunlit distance, she might have beheld the forest of Cluny, and that silent pool whereon the water lilies reared their stately heads. Here she had sat, just by this same window, when with bitter words—cruel in that irresistible appeal which they made to her heart—he had told her about that pool, the lilies stained with mud, the slimy weeds that spread and girt the graceful stems, the ineradicable smirch of contact with the infamies of this world.

Even now his captivating voice seemed to ring in her ears. The blaze of wrath fled from her cheeks, and the terrible, awful pain gripped her heart which she knew would never find solace whilst she lived.

At the other end of the room her parents were conversing on the ever-present topic.

Maman's hitherto indomitable optimism was at last giving way. She had held up bravely throughout these five weary months of waiting, hoping—almost against hope, sometimes—that everything would come right in one audience with Monseigneur.

With unvarying confidence she waited for the summons for Papa Legros to appear before His Greatness; once the Archbishop heard the truth he would soon put the matter to rights, and His Holiness himself would see that the child was righted in the end.

But now the long-looked-for audience had taken place, and it was no longer any use to disguise the fact that the last glimmer of hope had flickered out behind the gilded gates of Monseigneur's palace.

Maman, too, had felt indignant when first she heard the Archbishop's callous advice to Papa Legros. Her mother's heart rebelled at the very thought of seeing her child a suppliant; she would not add fuel to the flames of outraged pride by showing what she thought on the matter, but when Rose Marie rose in revolt with the indignant outcry of "Are we beggars?" she, the mother, quietly went up to her stewpot and kept her own counsels to herself, the while she stirred the soup.

Anon when the first wave of angry rebellion had subsided, when Rose Marie sat quiescent by the open window, Maman Legros put down her wooden spoon and went up to her husband, putting her heavy, rough hand on his shoulder, with a motherly gesture of supreme consolation.

"Perhaps Monseigneur is right, Armand," she said with her own indomitable philosophy; "why not make appeal to Lord Stowmaries, he may not be a bad man after all."

174

"You have heard what the child said, Mélanie," replied M. Legros sadly. "Are we beggars that we should be bidden to sue?"

A great sob rose in Rose Marie's throat. It was the sorrow, the humiliation of these two dearly-loved folk that was so terrible to bear. They had been stricken in what they held most dear, in their integrity and in their child. Self-reproach, too, played no small part in their grief, and they had not even a memory on which to dwell.

She—Rose Marie—had had her glorious three weeks of perfect happiness, before she had known that the man she loved was a liar and a cheat.

For the sake of those few brief days of unalloyed joy, because of the memory of that unclouded happiness, she had endured such an intensity of pain, that at times she felt—nay! hoped that death or madness would end the agony. But she had been happy! Remembrance brought an overwhelming shame, but she had been happy!

Sometimes she thought that her whole soul must have become perverted, her sense of virtue warped, for bitter as was the pain of it all, she dwelt oft and oft in her mind on those three exquisite weeks of perfect happiness.

Her heart, starved and aching, now lived on that memory. Her ears seemed to catch again the timbre of his voice vibrating with passion, her eyes rendered dull and heavy with all the unshed tears, seemed, in closing, to see him there, standing near her with his arms held ready to enfold her, and that burning, ardent look in his dark eyes which had shown her visions of an earthly heaven, such as she had never dreamed before.

Was it wicked to dwell on it all? Sinful, mayhap!—and surely not chaste, for he had lied to her when he said—

And then an insidious spirit voice would interrupt this train of thought and whisper in her ear: "No, he did not lie when he said that he loved thee, Rose Marie!" and the girl—just a suffering woman now— would in response feel such an agonizing sense of pain that she cried to God—to the blessed, suffering Lord—to take her away out of this unbearable misery.

But they—the dear old folk—had no such bitter-sweet memories on which to dwell, nothing but blank, dull sorrow, with no longer now any hope of seeing the load lifted. It would grow heavier and heavier as the years went by. Rose Marie had noticed that the streaks of grey on maman's smooth hair had become more marked of late, and Papa Legros seldom rose from a chair now without leaning heavily on his stick, with one hand, and on the arm of the chair with the other.

Yet maman still strove to be cheerful, even now she said with that new touch of philosophy in her which seemed to have taken the place of her former optimism:

"Ah, well, Armand! if the child will not go, we cannot force her,

175

poor lamb! but 'tis not saying that we are beggars and I cannot help thinking that Monseigneur may be right in his advice after all."

Then as Papa Legros sighed and shook his head, staring in mute depression straight out before him, Rose Marie rose from the window seat and came close to where her parents sat. Kneeling beside the kind father, whose every sigh cut into her heart, looking up at those streaks of grey in her mother's smooth hair, she said simply:

"We are beggars, Father, Mother dear, beggared of happiness, of joy, of pride. Father, we'll to England when you will. We'll seek out my lord of Stowmaries and make appeal to him, that he may restore to us that which in wantonness he hath taken away."

"The child is right, Armand," said maman, and like a true phœnix from out the flames, her optimism rose triumphant:

"I do verily believe," she said cheerfully, the while she surreptitiously wiped her eyes with the corner of her apron, "I do verily believe that the young man when he sees our Rose Marie will repent him of his folly and will be joyful to take her to his heart."

CHAPTER XXXIII

Brute worshippers or wielders of the rod
Most murderous even of all that call thee God!
Most treacherous even of all that called thee Lord!

—*Swinburne*

No one—not even her parents—knew what the proposed journey cost the girl in bitter sense of shame. She had, in order to consent to this pilgrimage of humiliation, to put aside all thoughts of her own feelings in the matter. She as a sentient, thinking, suffering woman must for awhile cease to be; her individuality must sink into nothingness, her pride, alas, must be broken on the wheel of her filial affection, crushed out of all desire for rebellion.

If the dear folk thought that a personal appeal to Lord Stowmaries was a possible loophole out of the present abyss of sorrow and disgrace, then she—Rose Marie—would lend herself to that appeal: and that not as a martyr, a saint going to the rack, but as readily, as cheerfully, as if the meeting with the man who had despised and discarded her, who had sold her to another man, as if seeing him face to face was at least a matter of indifference to her.

Once having made up her mind to the sacrifice, Rose Marie

would not allow herself to think of it. She set to her little preparations for the journey with well-feigned eagerness. Even maman was at times deceived, for the child would sing whilst she put a few stitches to the clothes which she was to take away.

Only when she was quite alone, or lying awake in the narrow little bed in the wall, would that sinful and rebellious pride rise up in arms, and Rose Marie would almost have to cling to the woodwork of her bed lest she found herself jumping up and rushing to her parents with a frantic cry of revolt: "I cannot go! I cannot do it!"

One word of protest from her even at this eleventh hour, and the journey would have been abandoned. But she made no protest, and the day for the voyage was fixed.

It was some two or three days before the projected departure that M. Legros, going down at his accustomed hour, to see the last of his 'prentices and cutters ere they left the workshop, found that two strangers were waiting to speak with him.

One of them was not altogether a stranger, for Papa Legros looking—with the keen eyes of a successful business man—on the unkempt and slouchy figure that stood expectantly in the doorway soon made up his mind that he had seen the face before. A second look decided the point, and brought back with a sharp pang the bitter memory of that gay wedding festivity which the advent of this same stranger, then the bearer of a fateful letter, had so rudely interrupted.

Daniel Pye and his companion, a meek-faced young man who looked like a scholar very much out at elbows, were kept humbly standing in the doorway, the while the 'prentices filed out past them, on the close of the working-day. We may assume that these rowdy youngsters did not make the two men's halt there any too pleasant for them. But Pye had learnt patience in the past two months, ever since he had ceased to be the dreaded majordomo in a pretty woman's household. He did not understand the gibes aimed at him by the impertinent crowd, and the pin-pricks, covert pinches and other physical inconveniences to which he was subjected left him passably indifferent.

As for the young student who accompanied him, he certainly looked well accustomed to buffetings from whatever quarter these might descend upon him.

The two men stood stolidly still, twirling their soft felt hats in their hands, never moving from the spot where they had been told to wait until such time as Maitre Legros might condescend to speak with them. Maitre Legros for the nonce was engaged in counting out his 'prentices as they filed past him and then out by the door, lest one of them bent on nocturnal mischief remained behind in safe concealment until time was ripe for pranks. After the 'prentices, the cutters and fitters filed out—more soberly for they were older men, but every man as he passed threw a curious look at the visitors, more especially at the shaggy, grimy face of Daniel Pye.

When the last of the crowd of workers had passed out into the street, Papa Legros turned to his foreman cutter, who had introduced the strangers into the shop.

"What do these men want?" he asked. "Have they told you their business, Master Duval?"

"No, M'sieu," replied the foreman, "one of them does not understand French, the other one only seems to be here as interpreter. The one with the shaggy beard is the principal, he asked for M. Legros with great insistence and as he has been here before—"

"Ah!—You do recognize him then?"

"I have seen his face before, M'sieu—I'd take my oath on that— though when that was I could not say."

"Bien, my good Duval, I'll speak to the stranger anon," rejoined M. Legros. "I shall not require you any more to-day. You may go now. I'll lock the back doors."

Whilst Duval obeyed, Legros studied the face of his visitor very attentively. He had no doubt in his mind that this was the same man who had brought him that fateful letter on Rose Marie's wedding day, just an hour after the child had gone away with that cruel and treacherous blackguard. Undoubtedly the face was very much altered; it had been trim and clean-shaved before, now an unkempt beard hid the mouth and jaw. The eyes, too, looked more sunken, the nose and forehead more pinched, and a shifty, furtive expression replaced the former obsequious manner peculiar to the well-drilled lacquey.

Obviously this man was the principal in this new affair, and at a curt word from M. Legros he came forward into the room with a certain air of sulky defiance, the while his companion followed meekly in the rear.

Papa Legros would have not owned to it for worlds, but as a matter of fact his heart was throbbing with anxiety. Instinctively he looked on the shaggy figure of Daniel Pye as on a bird of ill-omen. It was through the agency of those same grimy hands that the first terrible blow of a crushing misfortune had fallen on the tailor and his family. What other misery would this unwelcome visitor bring in his train?

"You have business with me, my masters?" asked M. Legros at last. He settled himself down resolutely in the high-backed chair, which he always used when talking to his inferiors—but he left the two men standing before him; there were no other chairs in the room.

Daniel Pye had grunted a surly assent.

"And of what nature is that business?" continued M. Legros, keeping up an air of haughty indifference.

"It is of a private nature, Master," here interposed the younger of the two men. He was evidently impressed by the great tailor's august

178

condescension and spoke timidly with a slight impediment in his speech.

"Then you may speak of it freely," said M. Legros. "No one can overhear you. All my men have gone. So I pray you be brief. My time is much occupied, and I have none to waste."

The young student no doubt would have hemmed and hawed very hesitatingly for some little while to come. But Daniel Pye, moody and impatient, gave him a vigorous nudge in the ribs.

"Go it, Master Clerk," he said gruffly in English. "By G—d, man, I am not paying you to toady to this old fool, but to state my business clearly before him. Let me tell you that that business will be highly welcomed in this house, so there is no cause for this damnable shaking of your body, as if you were afraid."

"What does your friend say to you, sirrah?" asked the tailor peremptorily, for he did not like this conversation carried on in a language which he did not understand.

"He says, my Master," replied the clerk, "that I must speak up boldly, for his business will be pleasing to your graciousness. I am but the poor, ill-paid interpreter, who—"

"Then I pray you interpret both boldly and briefly," interposed M. Legros impatiently. "What is your friend's business? Out with it, quick, before I have you both kicked out of this door."

The clerk did not think it necessary to translate the tailor's last words into English.

"The business concerns my lord the Earl of Stowmaries and Rivaulx," he began.

"Then 'tis none of mine," retorted the tailor coldly.

"Ay, but of a truth it is, good Master," rejoined the other more boldly, "and my friend here, Master Daniel Pye, by name, a worthy and independent Englishman, hath journeyed all the way from London to speak with you on this business. The noble Earl of Stowmaries hath greatly wronged you, sir, and your family. You have suffered great humiliation at his hands. Your daughter through his neglect is neither wife nor maid—"

"And you, sirrah, will be neither alive nor dead, but near to both estates, an you do not hold your tongue," said M. Legros bringing an angry fist crashing down on the arm of his chair. "Out of my house this instant!—How dare you speak my daughter's name without my leave, you dirty paper-scraper, you bundle of quill feathers, you—"

Good M. Legros was choking with wrath but he did fully intend to put his threat into execution and to kick these two impertinent rascals out of his house. Ere he could recover himself, however, the clerk forcibly egged on by Daniel Pye had interposed quietly but firmly:

"Nevertheless, sir, it is my duty to be the mouthpiece of my friend who hath come all this way to tell you that God himself hath taken up your cause against the great and noble Earl of Stowmaries, whose pride will soon be laid in the dust, who will become an abject, cringing creature, dependent mayhap on your bounty for subsistence, dispossessed, disinherited, nay worse, tried for treason, and hanged, sir, hanged as a traitor! Is not that a glorious revenge, sir, for the wrongs which he has done to you?"

"Nay, and by the Mass, sirrah," said M. Legros who had recovered sufficiently from his blind wrath to be justly indignant at this mealy-mouthed harangue, "if you do, value your shoulders and if your friend cares for his skin, you can have thirty seconds wherein to reach that door, after which the toe of my boot and the stout stick in yonder corner shall accelerate your footsteps."

"Sir," protested the clerk, prompted thereto by Daniel Pye, "my friend here desires to remind you that he was driven away by blows from your doors in this like manner just five months ago. Had you given him more ready access to your august person, the letter which he bore and which was written by my hand at a kind lady's bidding, would have been delivered into your hands one hour the earlier, and thus would have averted a misery which you yourself would now give your life's blood to undo."

The words were well chosen. The Huguenot clerk had interpreted Daniel Pye's promptings in a manner which could not fail to bear impress on Master Legros' mind. The shaft had been well aimed. It had struck a vital nerve centre. The tailor, feeling the justice of the reproof, curbed his wrath. He was silent for a moment or two, while the two men watched and waited.

Suddenly the touch of a hand which he loved, roused Master Legros from his moody incertitude and a girl's voice said with firm decision:

"These men are right in what they say, Father. There is no harm in hearing what they have to say. If they bring lying news or empty scandal 'twill be ample time then to turn them out of doors."

"You have not heard all their impertinent canting harangues, my jewel."

"I heard enough to understand that these men have come here to tell you of some evil which is about to descend on my lord of Stowmaries, my husband before God. That is so, is it not?"

And she turned great inquiring eyes on Daniel Pye and on the clerk.

"That is so, Mademoiselle."

"My mother and I heard my father's voice raised in anger against you. She bade me come down to see what was amiss. The matter which concerns my lord of Stowmaries also concerns me, so I pray you tell my father all about it in my presence, and have no fear of his wrath, for he will listen to you for my sake."

"Then, sirrah, an my daughter desires it, I pray you tell your story!" rejoined Legros. "But do so briefly; I'll patiently hear of the evil

180

which hath befallen my lord Stowmaries, but will not listen to any impertinent comments on his actions past or in the present."

"Tell them the whole tale just as you did write it out," whispered Daniel Pye to his interpreter. "Damn you, sir, how much longer will you be about it!"

"Then hear me, master tailor, for it began this wise," now said the clerk with a great effort at composure. "My lord of Stowmaries hath a kinsman, one named Michael Kestyon, whom you know, and on whose conduct I am not permitted to make comment. Michael hath for years held—on grounds which it would take too long now to explain—that he and not his cousin should own the titles and estates of Stowmaries and Rivaulx. But hitherto he hath had no money wherewith to press his claim. The law as administered in England is a vastly expensive affair, my master, and Michael Kestyon was a poor man, poorer even than I; he was a wastrel and many called him a dissolute reprobate."

"Enough of Michael Kestyon," interrupted Legros gruffly. "Have I not told you to be brief."

"Michael Kestyon's affairs form part of my tale, Master. You must know that he is now passing rich. Many and varied are the rumours as to the provenance of his wealth, and many the comments as to the change in the man himself. Armed with money Michael Kestyon hath obtained the ear and attention of the high dignitaries of the law and the favour of the King himself. The fact hath become of public knowledge that only His Majesty's signature to a document is needed now to instate Michael Kestyon in the title and dignities which are declared to be legally his. My lord of Stowmaries, therefore, is, as you see, no longer secure in his position and his wealth, and though you may not permit the humble clerk to make comment on the doings of his betters, yet Master Daniel Pye hath come all the way from England to bring you this news, which must be vastly gratifying to you, whom that same lord of Stowmaries had so wantonly injured."

Daniel Pye and his mouthpiece both looked at the tailor with marked assurance now. Of a truth they were quite confident that the Legros thirsting for revenge would receive the news with every sign of exultation. But the master tailor was silent and moody, and it was Mademoiselle who spoke.

"And is this all the news which you, sir, came all the way from England to impart to my father?" she asked, addressing Daniel Pye in his mother tongue.

"No, not altogether all, Mistress," he replied; "I have better news for you yet."

"Anent my lord Stowmaries' troubles?"

"Ay, something you will be still more glad to hear."

"What is it?"

"My lord of Stowmaries is a Papist—or—saving your presence he is a Catholic, and Catholics are in bad odour in England just now—they are said to be conspiring to murder the King, and to place the Duke of York on the throne—to sell England to France, and to place the English people under the yoke of the Pope of Rome."

"Hath my lord of Stowmaries thus conspired?" she asked coldly.

"I think so," replied Daniel Pye.

"How do you mean? That you think so is no proof that he hath done it."

"I can soon bring forward the proofs," said Pye with a knowing leer directed at her from under his shaggy brows, "if you, Mistress, will help me."

Rose Marie felt a shudder which was almost one of loathing creeping up her spine, at sight of the expression in the man's face.

It told such an infamous tale of base thoughts and desires, of cupidity and of triumphant revenge, that her every nerve rebelled against further parleyings with such a villain.

But there was something more than mere feminine curiosity in her wish to know something definite of what was really passing in the mind of Daniel Pye. That shrewd instinct and sound common sense— which is the inalienable birthright of the French bourgeoisie—told her that the man would not have undertaken the arduous and costly journey from England to France unless he had some powerful motive to prompt him thereunto, or—what was more likely still—some reward to gain.

The desire to learn the truth of this motive or of this hoped-for gain remained therefore paramount in her mind, and she did her best not to give outward expression to her sense of repulsion when Daniel Pye drew nearer to her in an attempt at confidential familiarity.

He was far from guessing that his last words had done aught but please this wench and her father, both of whom had as serious a grievance against Lord Stowmaries as he himself had against Mistress Peyton.

It had not taken the dismissed serving-man very long to learn the lesson of how he could best be revenged on his past mistress. The easiest way to hit at the ambitious lady was undoubtedly—as Master Tongue had pointed out to him—by bringing the man she desired to marry to humiliation and ruin. Michael Kestyon's successful claim to the peerage of Stowmaries had paved the way for the more complete undoing of my lord, and Daniel Pye soon knew the lesson by heart which the informers of Whitefriars had taught him.

Oates was ready with his lies; he and his confederates had soon mustered up a goodly array of names of Papist gentlemen against whom these lies could most easily be proved. The first spark had been set to the tinder which presently would set the whole of England ablaze with the hideous flame of persecution. But to make their villainous perjuries more startling, and at the same time to obtain better pay for uttering them, they wanted to add to their list a few more high-sounding names which would have the additional advantage of proving the far-reaching dimensions of the supposed Popish plot. Amongst these names that of Stowmaries would be of great moment. Daniel Pye with his intimate acquaintance with my lord became a valuable addition to the band.

Soon he was taught to concoct a plausible story; information against Papists was being richly rewarded already by the terrorised Ministry and Parliament. But Pye, grafting his own wits onto the lesson given, bethought himself of the rich tailor over in Paris who surely would not only help him actively in the telling of his lies, but also pay him passing well for bringing Lord Stowmaries to humiliation and disgrace—if not to the gallows.

Tongue—who had remained Daniel Pye's guide and leader in all his villainies—fully approved of the plan; we may take it that he intended to levy a percentage on what the more ignorant peasant would obtain from Master Legros.

It was felt among that vile band of informers that foreign witnesses, especially those of French nationality, would be a valuable help to the success of the accusations, and to all these men of low and debased mind, it seemed quite natural that the tailor—whose daughter had been the heroine of a public scandal brought about by Lord Stowmaries' repudiation of her—would out of vengeful malice be only too ready to swear to any falsehood against the young man.

Thus Daniel Pye went over to France, accompanied by the good wishes of an infamous crowd. The few pounds which he had saved whilst he was in Mistress Peyton's service were rapidly dwindling away. The journey to Paris had been expensive, too, and he had therefore much at stake in this interview with the tailor, and watched with greedy eyes the face both of Legros and of his daughter, now that the latter was silent and that the old man resolutely took no part in the conversation.

Of a truth Legros had been listening moodily to what this uncouth stranger was saying, trying to comprehend the drift of all his talk. But the worthy tailor had only a very scanty knowledge of the English tongue, only so much in fact as enabled him in his business to make himself understood by the cloth manufacturers and button makers of England with whom he came in contact. Therefore he had only made vague guesses as to what Pye was saying to Rose Marie. Once or twice he tried to interpose, but every time his daughter checked him with a gesture of firm entreaty, and then a whispered: "Chéri, allow me to speak with him!"

Now after that first instinctive movement of recoil quickly suppressed, Rose Marie, keen to know what ugly schemes were being nurtured in the man's brain, feeling, too, that to know might mean the power to avert or to help, turned with well-assumed cordiality once more to Daniel Pye.

"Meseems, sir," she said, "that you have more to tell me. In what way can I help to prove that my lord of Stowmaries hath conspired against the King of England?"

"You need not do much, Mistress," rejoined Pye confidentially. "I will do most of the work for you. But I am a poor man and—"

"I understand. You want some money. You wish to be paid. For what?"

That sense of repulsion almost overmastered her again. Was she not lending herself—if only with words and with seeming acquiescence—to some abominable infamy? Swiftly her thoughts flew back to the pool of Cluny, the water lilies smirched with the slime. How true had been those words he spoke: contact with what is depraved, what is mean and base, soils and humiliates ineradicably very soon.

"You have come to my father to sell him some information against Lord Stowmaries. Is that it?" she reiterated impatiently as Daniel Pye was somewhat slow in replying.

"I can bring Lord Stowmaries to the gallows, by just saying the word," replied the man. "I thought Master Legros would wish me to say the word—that he would help a poor man who tried to do him service."

"My lord of Stowmaries is not at the mercy of false accusers," she said almost involuntarily.

"Papists in England do conspire," retorted Pye phlegmatically, "and I and my friends know a vast deal of their doings—Hark 'ee, Mistress," he added, drawing nearer to her, "and you too, my master, for methinks you understand something of what I say. It is all as simple and as clear as daylight. Papists are in very bad odour in England, and the Ministry and Parliament are all in blue terror lest the country be sold to France or to Rome. Now my friend Titus Oates and some other equally honourable gentlemen bethought themselves of a splendid plan whereby we can all render our own country a great service by exposing these Papist conspiracies. We are being well paid already for any information we get, and information is quite easy to obtain. Look at Master Oates! He hath invented a splendid tale whereby the Duke of York himself and certainly his secretary—one Coleman—and a number of others do find themselves in dire trouble. Lord Stowmaries is a Papist, too. I know him well. You know him passing well. We can readily concoct a famous story between us, which will vastly please the Privy Council and Parliament. Lord Stowmaries, I feel sure, would wish to see England Catholic like himself. He wishes to see the King put away, and the Duke of York reigning in his stead. Well! all that we need do, good Master and Mistress, is to write out a statement wherein we all swear that we overheard my lord of Stowmaries express a desire to that effect, and the man who did you both so great a wrong, the man, Master, who first married your daughter and then cast her away from him as if she were of evil fame, will dangle on the gallows to your satisfaction and to mine."

184

Daniel Pye paused, viewing his two interlocutors with a glance of triumph. He had absolutely no doubt in his mind that the rich tailor would within the next second or two—as soon, in fact, as he had recovered from the first shock of pleasant surprise, jump up from his chair, and with the impetuous fervour peculiar to Frenchmen, throw himself on the breast of his benefactor. The transference of a bag full of gold from the pocket of the grateful and rich tailor to that of good Master Pye would then be but a matter of time.

But no such manifestations of joyful excitement occurred, and the expression of triumph in the informer's face soon gave place to one of anxiety.

M. Legros had looked up at his daughter, who stood beside him, pale and thoughtful.

"I have not understood all that this man hath said, my jewel."

"'Tis as well, Father dear," she replied, "for methinks you would have thrashed him to within an inch of his life. Nay!" she added coldly as the Huguenot clerk—suddenly realising that matters were taking a dangerous turn all unbeknown as yet to his companion—gripped the latter's arm and began to talk to him volubly in English, "you, sir, need not warn your friend. I will tell him, myself, all that he need know."

"Miserable perjurer," she continued, now speaking directly to Pye, "go out of my father's house forthwith, ere he understands more of your villainies and breaks his stick across your back, as he would over that of a mad and vicious cur. I have listened to your lies, your evil projects, your schemes of villainies only because I wished to know the extent of your infamy and gauge the harm which your perjuries might cause. Now, with the help of God, I can yet warn him, who though he may have injured me, is nevertheless my husband in the sight of Heaven. Your perjuries will do you no good—they will mayhap lead you and your friends to the gallows. If there is justice in England your lies will lead you thither. Now you can go, ere I myself beg my father to lay his dog-whip across your back."

Daniel Pye's surprise was quite boundless. It had never for a moment entered his head that the tailor and his family would not join readily in any project for the undoing of my lord Stowmaries. He blamed himself for having been too precipitate; he would have liked to argue and mayhap to persuade, but though he did not understand the French language, he guessed by the expression in the master tailor's eyes, as his daughter now spoke with cold decision to him, that the moment was not propitious for a prolonged stay in this inhospitable house.

The look of terror on his interpreter's face also warned him that a hasty retreat would be the most prudent course; already M. Legros was gripping his stick very ominously.

But by the time the old man had struggled to his feet, Daniel Pye and his companion had incontinently fled. They had reached the door, torn it open and were out in the street even before M. Legros had time to throw his stick after them.

CHAPTER XXXIV

A saint whose perfect soul
With perfect love for goal
Faith hardly might control,
Creeds might not harden.

—Swinburne

When Legros was alone once more with his daughter he asked for a fuller explanation.

"I wish, my jewel, that you had not interfered," he said reproachfully, "when first I desired to kick those rascals out of doors. My first instinct was right, you see."

"Nay, but, Father dear," she said gently, "I am glad that you yielded to me in this. If we had not listened to what these men said, we should know nothing of the villainies which they are concocting, and could not warn those whom they attack."

"Methinks that were no concern of ours," retorted her father gruffly.

"They are proposing to bring false accusations of treason against Lord Stowmaries," urged Rose Marie, almost reproachfully.

"And what is that to us, my child?"

"Lord Stowmaries is my husband, Father; to-morrow we set out on a journey in order to ask him to render me justice—and this we do on Monseigneur's advice."

"There is no obligation on our part to undertake the journey."

"There was none yesterday, Father dear, but there is to-day."

"To-day? Why?"

"Because to-day we know that Lord Stowmaries—my husband— is in danger of his life, and that we can, mayhap, give him timely warning."

"Lord Stowmaries is so little thy husband, child, that even to-day when thou thinkest of saving him from these perjurers, he goes about carrying in the pocket of his coat the dispensation to repudiate thee, which he hath obtained from His Holiness by a misrepresentation of facts."

Even as he spoke these harsh words—and he spoke them

roughly, too—the good tailor took his daughter's hand tenderly in his, and stroked it, as if to mitigate by this loving touch the cruelty of the words. But the child who had been once so yielding and submissive was now an obstinate woman.

"All the more reason, Father dear," she said, "for proving to my Lord Stowmaries that he hath deeply wronged me, and that I am worthy to be his wife."

He was wholly unaccustomed to this new phase in his daughter's character. She had always been of a meek, gentle disposition, still a child in her expressions of loving obedience, in her tender, clinging ways. Now, suddenly she seemed to have a will of her own. She it was who had decreed that Monseigneur's advice should be followed, she it was now who refused to give up all thoughts of the journey.

Let us confess that worthy M. Legros was now for awaiting events. If the rascals spoke true, God Himself had provided a glorious vengeance against the dastardly young reprobate who had so ill-used Rose Marie. Papa Legros of a truth did not see that she—the injured wife—was called upon to move a finger in the cause of a man who had paid another to dishonour her. There are times and circumstances in life when the meekest of men become as ravenous tigers. The kindly tailor had a heart of gold, a simple mind and an adoring fondness for his child. He would never have done the meanest man any hurt. Yet in this case, and because of the terrible wrong done to his Rose Marie, he almost gloated on the thought of the troubles which were about to descend on Stowmaries. Vaguely the hope wormed itself into his heart that my lord would cease to exist—painlessly if possible—still that he would cease to be, and then Rose Marie would be free, a child-widow, who might yet find happiness in the arms of a good man.

But not one thought of Michael in all this! Legros himself would not let his mind dwell on that reprobate whom he had loved as a son. And Rose Marie? Did she perchance, when thinking of her journey to England, feel a vague thrill of hope that she might see him there?

Who shall pry into the secret orchard, the key of which lies hid in a young girl's heart. Those who knew Rose Marie both before and after the tragic episode of the mock marriage, declared that she had a great desire to see Michael Kestyon again.

If only to tell him that she had not forgiven him—that she would never forgive—and never, never forget.

CHAPTER XXXV

Steep and deep and sterile, under fields no plough can tame,
Dip the cliffs full-fledged with poppies red as love or shame.

—Swinburne

And it was in consequence of Monseigneur the Archbishop's advice, and of maman's desire that this advice be acted upon, that anon we see Master Legros, tailor-in-chief to His Majesty, the King of France, journeying with his daughter to England.

But this was chiefly, too, because of what Daniel Pye, the informer, had gone over to Paris to say. Nothing would take it out of Rose Marie's head that it was her duty now, if ever, to be loyal to the man who was still her husband in the sight of God. He could repudiate her—if His Holiness gave him leave—but two great wrongs could never make one simple right.

She, Rose Marie, had no dispensation to break the marriage vows of eighteen years ago. She had done no wrong to justify a dissolution of that marriage. Her husband was her husband; he was in danger of losing his honour and his life. She could at least give him timely warning.

If she failed in this, her duty, then indeed would she deserve the scorn of the world, the repudiation and the disgrace which pertains to the unfaithful wife.

On a beautiful sunny day early in October, Master Legros and his daughter first caught sight of the white cliffs of England gleaming beneath the kiss of the radiant sun. Rose Marie had sat silently, meditatively, in the prow of the boat; she had gazed during the past few hours into that distant horizon whereon trembled a heat-laden mist. The titanic band of gilded atoms had long hidden from her view the shores of that mysterious country wherein he dwelt.

England to her meant the land where Michael Kestyon lived, and with aching eyes and throbbing heart she watched and watched, waiting for that first view when the mist would part and reveal to her the soil on which his foot was wont to tread. How starved was her heart that even that thought was a solace; the sensation of putting her foot down on the selfsame land whereon he dwelt was almost a consolation.

She gazed at the white cliffs like one anhungered, and as the slowly-moving boat drew nearer to this new land of promise, the sun slowly setting in the west changed with a touch of the fairy wand the white cliffs into gold.

She thought England beautiful both in the long twilight when mysterious veils of grey and mauve soften the outlines of the distant landscape, and in the glory of noon when tiny clouds chase one another

188

across a sky of tender sapphire blue. She loved the early morning when every blade of grass on the crest of the cliffs at Dover was adorned by a tiny brilliant diamond, and she loved the midday sun which had drawn the breath of the dew until its soul had passed into delicate golden vapours.

She loved the quaintly-arrayed army of fruit trees in the orchards, the tender green of the lawns, the ruddy tints of early autumn which clothed the hillside with a brilliant mantle of gold. No! She could not believe that in this land of beauty, of peace and of plenty, all men were born traitors, all men were liars and thieves of honour.

Some subtle change came over them, no doubt, and their bravery, their loyalty, passed away from them, revealing the devil which had taken possession of their soul. She would persist in thinking that Michael, whom she had loved, was a different man to the one who stood before her, accused and self-convicted—more shamed than she whom he had wronged.

Thus her thoughts kept her body alert and she scarcely felt the fatigue of that long, lumbering drive on the stage-coach between Dover and London. There was so much to see and so much to think on and to plan. The very next day her father should seek out my lord of Stowmaries and tell him all that was brewing against him. It was surely more than likely that my lord would be grateful and in his gratitude strive to undo the mischief which his own wantonness had created.

What this would mean to Rose Marie she had not even dared to ask herself. A strong sense of right and of justice and an overwhelming love for her parents had prompted her to offer herself a willing sacrifice for their happiness. Her own poor heart was already so bruised, so battered, almost broken in its agony of sorrow, what mattered a little more humiliation, a few more tears, another pang?

Rose Marie sighed with regret when in the gloaming the stage-coach finally left behind it the orchards and green pastures of Kent and rattled over the cobblestones of the big city. At seven o'clock, with much rattle of chains and billets, many shouts from driver and ostler and much champing of bits, the big vehicle swung through the gates of the yard at Savage's Bell Inn near Lud Gate. Here the tailor and his daughter meant to put up, the hostelry having been warmly recommended to him by several business friends who travelled to and fro from London to Paris.

As Rose Marie climbed down from the top of the coach, it seemed to her that despite the fast-gathering gloom within the enclosed yard, she could recognise the face of Master Daniel Pye among the crowd who were assembled to witness the arrival of the coach.

The face disappeared in the crowd almost as soon as she had recognised it, but the brief vision left her with a great sense of satisfaction that obviously the journey had not been undertaken in vain. The man had taken the trouble to watch and to wait, obviously fearing that his nefarious plans might be frustrated by those whom he had hoped to enlist on his side.

Neither Rose Marie nor good M. Legros slept much that night. The fatigue of the journey, the sound of many voices jabbering in a tongue unfamiliar to their ear, chased sleep resolutely away. Only toward early morning did father and daughter, each in their respective very uncomfortable beds, fall into troubled slumber.

Master Legros dreamt of the morrow's meeting with his lordly son-in-law, and Rose Marie fell asleep wondering in what quarter of the great city dwelt the man whose very image she would wish to blot out of her memory.

CHAPTER XXXVI

These tardy tricks of yours will, on my life,
One time or other, break some gallows back.

—*2 Henry IV. IV. 3*

Master Daniel Pye had certainly thought it wiser—after that precipitous exit from the master tailor's house—to watch and to await events. He had been wholly taken by surprise at M. Legros' reception of his news, and staggered at the thought that where he had sought a patron, or at least an ally, he had found an active enemy.

He soon learned that preparations were being actively pushed forward in the house of the Rue de l'Ancienne Comédie for the journey of the master and his daughter to England. Pye and his interpreter, therefore, well-disguised and travelling as the poorest of men in the wake of their betters, reached Dover by the same packet boat that had brought the Legros hither. While the latter took rest at a small hostelry in the town, awaiting the day when a stage-coach would take them to London, Pye made his way straight to the great city, using what humble conveyances he contrived to hire for some portions of the road.

The yard of Savage's Bell Inn near Lud Gate was the halting place of the stage-coach from Dover, and thither Pye repaired on those afternoons—three days in the week—when a complement of voyagers from France were expected. It was quite simple, and within forty-eight hours Pye found his patience rewarded and his worst fears justified. The good tailor had obviously come to London in order to warn Lord Stowmaries of the mischief that was brewing against him.

Fortunately Pye had his false information against my lord ready, even before he had set out for Paris. His friend, the Huguenot clerk, had writ out the deposition in a good round hand, and Daniel Pye had sworn to it before a commissioner. All he had to do now was to lodge it with Sir Edmund Berry Godfrey, who had already received the sworn depositions of Titus Oates and of Tongue.

Lord Stowmaries' name also figured on the Oates indictment as one of those who were said to have been present at the famous "consult" whereat the Duke of York was offered the crown of England by the Catholic peers of this realm at the express desire of the Pope of Rome.

Daniel Pye had incontinently sworn to everything that had been asked of him. He pretended a close intimacy with my lord of Stowmaries, and was prepared to take all the solemn oaths that were required to the effect that he had overheard my lord express loudly every kind of treasonable wish—notably that of seeing the king duly poisoned by his physician.

But for all these false accusations, Pye presently discovered that he could only get about £20 as a reward, and that only if the indictment was proved on evidence. The commissioners had already told him that in order to bring his accusations home it were better that another witness came forward to swear to the same story. This is where the help of the French tailor or of the wench would have been so useful for—as luck and his own eagerness would have it—Pye had declared in his original affidavit that he had overheard my lord Stowmaries' treasonable conversations at a hostelry in Paris.

Pye had thought thereby to give more verisimilitude to his story, and even Master Tongue had approved of this plan, when he heard the man declaring emphatically that the tailor's daughter would only be too ready to swear away the life of the man whom she must hate with all the bitter sense of an overwhelming wrong.

Thus therefore did the accusation stand. Master Daniel Pye had sworn that when he was at the hostelry of the "Rat Mort," in Paris, on April 19th of this same year of grace, he had overheard my lord of Stowmaries talking—with one of the ministers of the King of France—of the terms of a treaty whereby the Papist peers of England would acclaim the Duke of York as King of England and vassal of the Pope, and receive a subsidy of five million livres from King Louis for their pains.

It was indeed a splendid story. No wonder that Master Pye was over-pleased with it; he had added the final touch of apparent truth to it by stating that M. Legros—a French subject—and his daughter—the reputed and repudiated wife of the accused—were also present at the "Rat Mort" on that occasion and had also overheard this conversation, and would testify as to the verity thereof.

Imagine the disappointment, the vexation, nay, the grave fears now engendered in Master Pye's mind at thought that the tailor and his

191

wench meant to frustrate his schemes completely, and not only to throw discredit on the elaborate accusation, but even mayhap to prejudice the payment of that meagre reward of £20.

When Master Legros, accompanied by his daughter arrived at the Bell Inn, Daniel Pye was at first seized with a mad desire to try and influence them yet once again in his own favour. Remember that Pye was little more than an uncouth peasant, with just as much knowledge of other people's natures as he had gleaned through daily contact with his own underlings.

He could not get it into his head that the Legros really meant to forego the happy sensation of a complete revenge, and half thought that, mayhap, they had misunderstood the whole scheme during that stormy interview in the back shop, when there was so much talk of stick and of dog-whip, and not nearly enough of just reward for a great service rendered.

At the last moment, however, when Legros had alighted from the coach and had somewhat impatiently ordered beds and board, Daniel Pye's heart misgave him, and he felt afraid to encounter the irascible little tailor's wrath.

Once more he sought out his friend, the needy and out-at-elbows Huguenot clerk, and offered him a shilling to go the next morning to the Bell Inn and to watch the Legros' movements. Quite a goodly amount of Master Pye's savings were now dwindling away in this direction.

"Do you try and get speech with the tailor," he said to the young scribe, "and try by your great skill to make him believe that you would wish to serve him, seeing that you have quarrelled with me and are now penniless. These people must of a truth be friendless and lonely in London; who knows but that they may take you as their guide, in which case all you need do is to try and prevent by every means in your power that they have speech with Lord Stowmaries for the next few days. Once my lord is duly arrested on our information, strangers will, of course, have no access to him; the trials we know are to be hurried through very quickly and there would then be no fear of our losing our just rewards."

Well schooled in the part which he had to play, the Huguenot clerk duly installed himself just outside the gates of the yard of the Bell Inn on the following morning, and by ten o'clock he had the satisfaction of seeing Master Legros obviously bent on obtaining information, and wandering for that purpose somewhat disconsolately about the yard, seeing that no one there was able to converse with him in his own tongue.

This was the clerk's opportunity. He slipped through the gate, and doffing his soft cap, humbly accosted the foreign gentleman.

"Can I be of service, Master?" he said in French. "I am an interpreter by trade."

"And if I mistake not," replied the tailor suspiciously, "you are one of two damned blackguards who came to my house in Paris with some lying tale of Papist conspiracy against my lord Stowmaries, some few days ago."

"Hush, hush, good Master, I entreat you," quoth the clerk with well-feigned alarm, and throwing quick, furtive glances around him; "the subject is not one which must be discussed aloud just now."

"And why, sirrah, must it not be discussed aloud?"

"Because to call yourself a Papist just now, my Master, is synonymous to proclaiming yourself a traitor. Your very life would not be safe in this yard. A reign of terror hath set in in England. The peaceful citizens themselves go about the streets carrying flails hidden in the pockets of their breeches to defend themselves against the Jesuits. Nay, Master, an your business is not urgent, I entreat you to return to France, ere you or your daughter come to any harm."

"My business with my lord Stowmaries is urgent," said Legros with characteristic hot-headed impulsiveness; "an you'll direct me to his house, there'll be a shilling or mayhap two for you."

"In the name of Heaven, good Master," ejaculated the clerk in an agonised whisper, "do not speak that name aloud. My lord is in very bad odour. His arrest is imminent and all his friends are like to fare as badly as himself."

"All the more reason why I should speak with him at once. So now, sirrah! Wilt earn that shilling and direct me to his house, or wilt thou not?"

"Alas, kind sir, I am a poor man, a starving man since that traitor, Daniel Pye, hath turned against me, seeing that I would not aid him in his conspiracies. And I'll gladly earn a shilling, kind sir, and direct you to the house of my lord Stowmaries, an you will deign to place yourself under my protection."

Truly Master Legros had no cause not to accept the clerk's offer. However villainous the man's conduct might or might not be, there could be no harm in accepting his escort in broad daylight as far as the house of my lord of Stowmaries.

Legros was a complete stranger in the English city, which he thought overwhelmingly vast and terribly dirty. He had heard many tales of the plague in London, and though this had occurred thirteen years ago, he still thought the place infected and mistrusted the hackney coaches and carrying chairs which were plying the streets for hire.

After hurried consultation with his daughter, he decided that no harm could come of being escorted by the clerk through the streets of London. The latter spoke French and would be vastly useful, and he could easily be dismissed, once my Lord Stowmaries' house had been reached.

Good M. Legros was suffering from an unusually severe attack of

193

chronic fussiness. He could not have sat still another hour, and was for starting immediately for my lord's house. Rose Marie had no reason for wishing to put off that interview, the thought of which she abhorred more and more strongly as the time for its occurrence drew nigh.

She was conscious of a desire to get it over, to put finality between the inevitable and her own ever-rebellious hopes. For her parents' sake she wanted to see Lord Stowmaries grateful and yielding; for her own she almost wished that he remained obdurate. She would gladly have purchased her freedom at the price of more bitter humiliation than she had yet endured, yet she had set herself the task of purchasing the content and happiness of those she cared for at the price of her freedom and the most bitter of all humiliation.

These contradictory thoughts and wishes fretted her and rendered her nervous and agitated. But at her father's bidding, she was ready to make a start.

When Legros once more came down into the courtyard, dressed for the momentous visit, and with his daughter on his arm, the Huguenot clerk was nowhere to be seen. He soon reappeared, however, almost breathless from fast running, but seemingly ready to accompany the distinguished foreign visitors withersoever they wished to go.

He had just had time in the interim to consult with Master Daniel Pye as to what had best be done.

"If I do not take that accursed tailor over to my lord Stowmaries, some one else will for sure," he said disconsolately.

"Let me think for a moment," quoth Pye, with an anxious frown on his lowering brow. "I understand that the arrest of my lord is imminent—if only we can put off this meddlesome Frenchman for to-day, I do verily believe that all will be well. For the nonce you had best tell him that my lord Stowmaries is from home, but is expected daily, hourly, to return. Thus we might gain twenty-four hours, for you would tell the same tale again in the afternoon—after that your wits should give you counsel. Am I not paying you that they should be of service to me?"

Thus it was that when the clerk arrived breathless in the yard of the Bell Inn, where Master Legros was impatiently awaiting him, he excused himself for his absence on the grounds that he had—surely with commendable forethought—taken the precaution to make enquiries as to whether my lord of Stowmaries was at home.

"My lord's house is some distance from here," he explained, "and I thought to save you and the fair mistress a fruitless walk through the city."

"Then 'twas mightily officious of you, sirrah?" quoth the irascible tailor, "to meddle with what doth not concern you."

"Zeal in your service prompted me, good master, and as my lord of Stowmaries is from home, I have the honour of saving you much fatigue."

194

"My lord is from home, did you say?" queried Legros in a tone of obvious disappointment.

"Ay, good master; but his servants expect to see him back to-morrow."

"We will find out for ourselves, Father dear, when my lord is expected home," here interposed Rose Marie, with her usual quiet air of decision; "no doubt there are others in London besides this same officious clerk who will guide us to his house."

We may imagine that at this point the pious young Huguenot formulated an inward but very emphatic "Damn!" cursing the interference of young damsels and their impatient ways.

Not having his principal to consult with, he was momentarily thrown on his own resources of wit and of readiness. This was certainly an occasion when the devil should aid those who serve him well. The clerk had only a very slight moment of hesitation, then a brilliant idea seemed to strike him, for his wizened face brightened up visibly.

"Fair Mistress," he said in tones of respectful reproach, "far be it from me to shirk my duty toward you. An you'll permit me I'll escort you to the house of my lord of Stowmaries forthwith."

"Then, why so much talking, sirrah," rejoined Papa Legros. "March, and briskly, too. I have a convenient stick which oft works wonders in making laggards walk briskly. Go ahead; my daughter and I will follow."

CHAPTER XXXVII

"I will hold your hand but as long as all may,
Or so very little longer."

—Browning

After half an hour's continuous walking—for the roads out of London were over-bad after the heavy rains during the past week—the Huguenot clerk, closely followed by Master Legros, who had his daughter on his arm, turned into the new parish of Soho, where a number of fine houses had been recently erected, and a few more were even now in process of construction.

The clerk had at first seemed desirous of imparting various scraps of topographical information to his compatriots, but to his interesting conversation the tailor only responded in curt monosyllables. He still harboured a vague mistrust against his guide.

The latter part of the walk through the ill-paved, muddy and evil-smelling streets of London was therefore accomplished in silence. Rose Marie's nerves were tingling with excitement, and she shivered beneath her cloak and hood, despite the warmth of this fine summer afternoon.

Soon the little party came to a halt before a newly-built house, fashioned of red brick with a fine portico of stone, richly carved and tall, arched windows set in flush with the outside walls and painted in creamy white.

"Here lives my lord of Stowmaries," said the clerk, as without waiting for further permission he plied the brass knocker vigorously. "Shall I ask if he hath come home?"

The tailor nodded in assent. He, too, was now getting too excited to speak. The next moment a serving-man, dressed in clothes of sober grey, opened the front door, and to the clerk's query whether my lord was at home, he replied in the affirmative.

Master Legros and Rose Marie were far too troubled in their minds to notice the furnishings and appointments of the house. Rose Marie threw the hood back from her face, and asked whether they could speak with my lord forthwith.

"Will you tell him, I pray you," she added, "that Monsieur Legros from Paris desires speech with him."

Legros dismissed the clerk—who was eager enough to get away—by bestowing a shilling upon him, and after that he and his daughter followed the serving-man through the hall into a small withdrawing room where they were bidden to wait.

A few moments of suspense—terrible alike to the girl and to the father—then a firm tread on the flagged floor outside; a step that to Rose Marie's supersensitive ear sounded strangely, almost weirdly familiar.

The next moment Michael Kestyon had entered the room.

"You have come to speak with me, good M. Legros—" he said even as he entered. Then he caught sight of Rose Marie and the words died on his lips.

They looked at one another—these two who once had been all in all one to the other—parted now by the shadow of that unforgettable wrong.

Instinctively—with eye fixed to eye—each asked the other the mute question: "Didst suffer as I did?" and in the heart of each—of the defiant adventurer, and the unsophisticated girl—there rose the wild, mad thrill, the triumphant, exulting hosanna, at sight of the lines of sorrow, so unmistakable, so eloquent on the face so dearly loved.

Rose Marie saw at once how much Michael had altered—that tender, motherly instinct inseparable from perfect womanhood told her even more than that which the sunken eyes and the drawn look in the face so pathetically expressed.

Yet outwardly he had changed but little; the step—as he rapidly

196

crossed the room—had been as firm, as elastic as of old; he still carried his head high, and his manner—as of yore—was easy and gracious. When he had first entered, there was even an eager, joyful expression in his face. He did not know, you see, that M. Legros' visit to him was the result of a mistake, the freak of a mischievous clerk. He really thought that the good tailor had come here to see him, Michael, and the news had brought almost joy to his heart and had accelerated his footsteps as he flew down to greet his visitor.

No, the change was in none of these outward signs. It was the spirit in him which had changed. The dark eyes once so full of tenderness had a cold, steely look in them now, which was apparent even through the first pleasurable greeting. The mouth, too, looked set in its lines; the lips, which ere this were ever wont to smile, were now tightly pressed as if for ever controlling a sigh or trying to suppress a cry of pain.

Michael—with the eyes of a man hungering for love—gazed on his snowdrop and saw the change which the past dark months had wrought on the former serenity of her face. And if he had suffered during that time the exquisite pangs of mad and hopeless longing, how much more acute did that pain seem now that he saw her, looking pale and fragile, almost frightened, too, in his presence, cold as she had been ere that mad glad moment when he had held her—a living, loving woman—in his arms, with the hot blood rushing to her cheeks at his whispered words of passion, and the light of love kindled in her eyes.

Can brain of man or of torturing devils conceive aught so cruel as this living, breathing embodiment of the might-have-been; this tearing of every heart-string in the maddening desire for one more embrace, one last lingering kiss, one touch only of hand against hand, one final breath of life—after which, death and peace?

As in a dream, good Master Legros' diffident voice struck on Michael's ear:

"It was with my lord of Stowmaries that we wished to speak."

And directly after that, Rose Marie's trembling tones, half-choked with sobs resolutely suppressed:

"Let us go, Father—we—we must not stay here—let us go—"

She had drawn close to her father, and was twining her hands round his arm trying to drag him away.

The sad pathos of this appeal—this clinging to another as if for protection and help, whilst he—Michael—stood by—nothing to her, less than nothing, a thing to fear, to hate, mayhap, certainly to despise—struck him as with a whip-lash across his aching breast. But it woke him from his dream. It brought him back to earth, with senses bruised and temples throbbing, his pride of manhood brought down to the dust of a childish desire to keep her here in his presence if only for a moment, a second; to hear her speak, to look on her, to endure her scorn if need be, only to have her there.

Therefore, he turned to Papa Legros and almost humbly said:

"Will you at least tell me, good Master, if I cannot serve you in any way?"

"No, sir, you cannot," replied Papa Legros gruffly. "I would have you believe and know that we came here under a misapprehension. A miscreant interpreter brought us hither, though he was bidden to take us to the house of Lord Stowmaries. We did not know that this was your house, sir, or believe me, we had never entered it."

"This is not my house," rejoined Michael gravely. "It is that of my mother, who hath left her Kentish village in order to dwell with me. For the rest, the misapprehension is most easy of explanation; nor is your interpreter so very much to blame."

He paused for the space of a second or two, then fixing steady eyes on the face of Rose Marie and throwing his head back with an air that was almost defiant in its pride, he said:

"You asked to speak with my lord of Stowmaries—'tis I who am the lord of Stowmaries now."

Then, as Legros, somewhat bewildered, stared at him in blank surprise, he added more quietly:

"You did not know this, mayhap?"

"No—no—my lord," stammered the tailor, who of a truth felt strangely perturbed, "we—that is, I and my daughter did not know that—"

"His Majesty gave his decision late last night."

There was a moment's silence in the room. It seemed as if Michael was anticipating something, waiting for a word from Rose Marie. His very attitude was an expectant one; he was leaning forward, and his eyes had sought her lips, as if trying to guess what they would utter.

"Then the title which you borrowed from your cousin awhile ago, and to some purpose, you have now succeeded in filching from him altogether?" said the girl coldly.

If she had the desire to hurt him, she certainly did succeed. Michael did not move, but his cheeks, already pale, turned to ashy grey; the eyes sank still deeper within their sockets, and in a moment the face looked worn and haggard as that of a man with one foot in the grave.

Then he said slowly:

"Your pardon, Mistress; I have filched naught which was not already mine, mine and my father's before me. That which I took was my right; it is also my mother's, who for years had been left to starve whilst another filched from her that which was hers. For her sake did I claim that which was mine, because during all those years of starvation, misery and degradation—her misery and mine own degradation—she kept up her faith in me. And also for mine own sake did I claim my right, and in order to mend a wrong which, it seems, I had committed.

198

Good Master Legros," he added, turning to the vastly bewildered tailor, "as Lord of Stowmaries I entered your house and, methinks, your heart. Of this I am not ashamed; the wrong that I did you is past; the righting thereof will last my lifetime and yours. I was Lord Stowmaries then by the word of God—I am that now by the word of the King and Parliament. That which seemed a lie I have proved to be true. Will you give me back your daughter, whom the caprice of a wanton reprobate would have cast from him, and whom I have justly won, by my deeds, by my will, by my crime if you call it so, but whom I have won rightfully and whom I would wish to render happy even at the cost of my life."

Gradually, as he spoke, the tone of defiance died out of his voice and only pride remained expressed therein—pride and an infinity of tenderness. There was no attempt at mitigating the fault that was past, no desire to excuse or to palliate. The man and his sin were inseparable; obviously had the sin to be again committed, Michael would have committed it again, with the same determination and the same defiance.

"I am a man, and what I do, I do. I won you by a trick. I fought for your love and won it. Mine enemy put a weapon in my hand. With it I conquered him; I conquered Fate and you. Had I been ashamed of the act, I had never committed it. I looked sin squarely in the face and took it by its grim hand and allowed it to lead me to your feet. To you I never lied; you I do not cheat."

These thoughts and more were fully expressed in his eyes as they rested on Rose Marie, and so subtle is the wave of sympathy that she understood every word which he did not utter; she understood them, even though she steeled her heart against the insidious whisperings of a drowsy conscience.

We may well imagine that on the other hand, good M. Legros, though he did not altogether grasp the proud sophistries of such a splendid blackguard, nevertheless quickly ranged himself against the whole array of all the grim virtues. Would you blame him very much if you knew that within the innermost recesses of his kindly and simple heart he no longer greatly desired to speak with the man whom he had come all the way from Paris to supplicate and to warn?

Was it very wrong, think you, very self-interested on the part of this amiable little tailor to be now cursing those very necessities engendered by an ultrasensitive sense of loyalty which imposed on him the task of cleaving to that man who was now dispossessed, beggared, a most undesirable husband for his beautiful daughter?

Truly the situation, from the point of view of conscience and of decency, was a very difficult one. Is it a wonder that the doting father was quite unable to grapple with it?

Here was a man who was a terrible scoundrel, yet a mightily pleasing one for all that. He was now rich, of high consideration and power; he professed and undoubtedly felt a great and genuine love for

Rose Marie. On the other hand, the other—his daughter's rightful lord—only too ready, nay, anxious, to repudiate her—who truly was a far greater blackguard and not nearly such an attractive one—he was now poor and insignificant—always providing that Michael Kestyon's story was true and—and—

Good M. Legros' conscience was having such a tough fight inside him that he had to take out his vast, coloured handkerchief and to mop his forehead well, for he was literally in a sweat of intense perturbation. He would not meet Michael's enquiring eyes, lest the latter should read in his own the ready assent which they proclaimed. The worst of the situation was that good M. Legros was bound to leave the ultimate decision to his daughter, and alas, he knew quite well what that decision would be. And God help them all, but he was bound to admit that that decision was the only right one, in the sight of the Lord and of all His self-denying and uncomfortably rigid saints.

Even now Rose Marie's clear voice, which had lost all its childlike ring of old and all its light tones of joy, broke in on her father's meditation.

"Sir, or my lord," she said coldly, "for of a truth I know not which you are, meseems you do a cowardly thing by appealing to my father. He would only have my earthly welfare in view, and even in this he might be mistaken if he thought that my earthly welfare could lie there, where there is disloyalty and shameless betrayal. For all your pride, good sir, and for all your defiance, you cannot e'en persuade yourself that what you do is right. As for me, I am a wife—not yours, my lord—despite the trick wherewith you drew from me an oath at the altar. I swore no love, no allegiance to any man save to him whom you have now wholly despoiled and beggared—nay," she added with a look of pride at least as great as his own, "I need no reminder, sir, that I stand here, a cast-out wife, repudiated for no fault of mine own, but through an infamy in which you bore the leading hand. But, nevertheless, I am a wife, and as such God hath enjoined me to cleave to my husband. Since you have beggared him, I, thank God, can still enrich him. Never have I blest my father's wealth so sincerely as now, when it can go to proving to a scoffer that there is truth and loyalty in women, even when sordid self-interest fights against truth and justice. And if all the world, his king and country, turned against my lord, I, his wife, good sir, his wife in the sight of God, despite dispensations, despite courts of law and decrees of popes or kings, I, his wife, for all that would still be ready to serve him."

Gradually her voice as she spoke had become more steady and also less trenchant; there was a quiver of passion in it, the passion of self-sacrifice. And he—poor man—mistook that warm, vibrating ring in the sweet, tender voice for the expression of true love felt for another.

"I did not know that you loved him, Rose Marie," he said simply.

She bent her head in order to hide the blush which rose to her

200

cheeks at his words. Was she thankful that he had misunderstood? Perhaps! For of a truth it would make the battle less hard to fight, and would guard against defeat. But, nevertheless, two heavy tears rose to her eyes, and strive as she might she could not prevent their falling down onto her hands which were clasped before her.

He saw the tears, and heard her murmur:

"He who was my lord of Stowmaries is a beggar now."

"No, not a beggar," he rejoined quietly, "for he is rich beyond the dreams of men."

"Good sir—or—or my lord," here interposed Papa Legros, who was still in a grave state of mental perturbation, "you see that the decision doth not rest with me—Heaven help me, but with all your fault I would—somehow—somehow have entrusted my child in your keeping with an easy heart."

"And may God bless you for these words, good Master," said Michael fervently.

"But you see, kind sir—I mean my lord—that this cannot be. My lord of Stowmaries—if so be that he is that no longer—yet as lord of Stowmaries he did wed my daughter. She feels—and rightly, too, no doubt—that she owes fealty to him. God knows but 'tis all very puzzling and I never was a casuist, but she says this is right and no doubt it is. It had all been much easier but for this additional grave trouble which threatens my lord."

"What additional grave trouble? I know of none such," queried Michael.

"A scoundrel, liar and perjurer hath laid information against my lord, that he did conspire against the King of England."

"Impossible."

"Ay! 'tis true, good my lord. The damned ruffian came to Paris to inform me of all the lies which he meant to tell against Lord Stowmaries, hoping that I would be pleased thereat and would reward him for his perjuries. I kicked him out of my house, and my daughter and I came to warn my lord of the mischief that was brewing against him."

A frown of deep perplexity darkened Michael's brow.

"Good master tailor, I pray you leave me to see my cousin forthwith. The trouble, alas, if your information be correct, is graver than even you have any idea of. England is mad just now! Terror hath chased away all her reason, and, God help her, all her sense of justice. It may be that I shall have to arrange that my cousin leave the country as soon as may be. An you return to France soon he could travel in your company."

"I would wish to see my lord myself," said Rose Marie.

"Because you do not trust me?" he asked.

She would not reply to his look of reproach. How strange it is when a wave of cruelty sweeps over a woman, who otherwise is tender and kind and gentle. Rose Marie felt herself quite unable to stifle this longing to wound and to hurt, even though her heart ached at sight of the hopeless misery which was expressed in Michael's every movement, in the tonelessness of his voice, and the drawn look in his face. Who shall probe the secrets of a woman's heart, of a woman who has been cheated of a great love even at its birth, of a woman who thought that she had reached the utmost pinnacle of happiness only to find herself hurled from those giddy heights down, down to an abyss of loneliness, of lovelessness, and of bitter, undying memories.

"The child is unstrung, good my lord," here interposed Papa Legros gently. "I pray, do not think that we do not trust in you. It were better mayhaps that you did see Lord Stowmaries—er—your cousin—alas! I know not how to call him now—and we'll to him this afternoon. He can then best tell us what he desires to do."

"Come, Rose Marie, we had best go now," he added with a pathetic sigh, which expressed all the disappointment of his kindly heart.

He picked up his soft felt hat and with gentle, trembling movement twirled it round and round in his hand. Rose Marie drew the hood over her hair and prepared to follow him.

It was all over then! The seconds had flown. She had come and would now go again, leaving him mayhap a shade more desolate even than before.

It was all over, and the darkness of the past months would descend on him once more, only that the darkness would be more dense, more unbearable, because of this one ray of light—caused by her presence here for these few brief moments.

Of a truth he had not known until now quite how much he had hoped, during these past months whilst he fought his battle with grim and steady vigour, winning step by step, until that last final decision of the king, which gave him all that he wanted, all that he desired to offer her.

Now she was going out of his life—for the second time—and it seemed more irrevocable than that other parting at St. Denis. She was going and there would not remain one single tiny spark of hope to light the darkness of his despair.

Nothing would remain, only memory! Memory, on which the tears of Love would henceforth for ever be fed. Her words might ring in his ears, her image dwell in his mind, but his heart would go on starving, starving, athirst for just one tiny remembrance on which to dwell until mercifully it would break at last.

"May I not kiss your finger tips once more, Rose Marie?" he pleaded.

The words had escaped his lips almost involuntarily. The longing for the tiny remembrance had been too strong to be stilled.

A kiss on her finger tips, one crumb of bread to a man dying of hunger, the sponge steeped in water to slake a raging thirst.

She turned to him. The tears had dried on her cheeks by now, and her eyes were seared and aching. She looked on his face, but did not lift her hand. Papa Legros, who felt an uncomfortable lump in his throat, busied himself with a careful examination of the door handle.

"It will probably be a long farewell," said Michael gently. "Will you not let me hold your hand just once again, my snowdrop? Nay, not mine, but another's—a king now amongst men."

Then, as very slowly, and with eyes fixed straight into his own, she raised her hand up to his, he took it, and looked long at each finger tip, tapering and delicately tipped with rose.

"See the epicure I am," he said, whilst a quaint smile played round the corners of his lips; "your little hand rests now in mine. I know that I may kiss it, that my lips may linger on each exquisite finger tip, until my poor brain, dizzy with joy, will mayhap totter into the land of madness. I know that I may kiss this cold little hand—so cold! I know that it will chill my lips—and still I wait—for my last joy now is anticipation. Nay, do not draw your hand away, my beautiful ice-maid. Let me hold it just one little brief while longer. Are we not to be friends in the future? Then as a friend may I not hold and kiss your hand?"

She could not speak, for sobs which she resolutely suppressed would rise in her throat, but she allowed her hand to rest in his; there was some solace even in this slight touch.

"Is it not strange," he said, "that life will go on just the same? The birds will sing, the leaves in autumn will wither and will fall. Your dear eyes will greet the first swallow when it circles over the towers of St. Gervais. Nature will not wear mourning because a miserable reprobate is eating out his heart in an agony of the might-have-been."

"I pray you, milor, release my hand," she murmured, for of a truth she no longer could bear the strain. "My father waits—"

"And the husband whom you love—nay, he must be a good man since God hath loved him so—"

"Farewell, my lord."

"Farewell, Rose Marie—my rosemary—'tis for remembrance, you know."

He tasted the supreme joy to the full—all the joy that was left to him now—five finger tips, cold against his burning lips, and they trembled beneath each kiss. Then she turned and followed her father out of the room.

For a moment he remained alone, standing there like one drunken or dazed. Mechanically his hand went to the inner pocket of his coat and anon he pulled out a withered, crumbling bunch of snowdrops, the tiny bouquet which she had dropped at his feet that day in Paris, when first he saw her, and her blue eyes kindled the flame of a great and overwhelming passion.

Nay! thou art a man, and of what thou doest, thou art not ashamed; but, proud man that thou art, there is thy Master, Love; he rules thee with his rod of steel, and if thou sin, beware! for that rod will smite thee 'til thou kneel humbly in the dust, with the weakness of unshed tears shaming thy manhood, and with a faded bunch of snowdrops pressed against thy lips, to smother a miserable, intensely human cry of awful agony.

CHAPTER XXXVIII

What be her cards you ask? Even these:—
The heart, that doth but crave
More, having fed; the diamond,
Skilled to make base seem brave;
The club, for smiting in the dark
The spade, to dig a grave.

—Dante Gabriel Rossetti

The one supreme moment of complete and abject weakness was soon past; it had gone by in solitude. No one saw the fall of the defiant reprobate brought to the dust by the intensity of his grief. No one but God and triumphant Love.

Within a few minutes Michael had gathered together his scattered senses. What avail were tears and the bitter joys of lingering memories when there was still so much to do? Of a truth, Rose Marie's firm attitude of loyalty towards her rightful husband had not so much astonished Michael, for to a man who loves, the adored one necessarily possesses every virtue that ever adorned the halo of a saint; but he did not know that she loved her husband, and the warmth of her defence of the absent one had, in Michael's ears, sounded like the expression of her love. He did not stop to reason, to visualize the fact that Rose Marie did not know Stowmaries, that the passion in her voice had the ring of tragic despair in it, coupled with the sublime ardour of heroic self-sacrifice.

A man in love never stops to reason. Passion and the dormant seeds of ever-present jealousy still the powers of common sense.

The thought that Rose Marie loved him, the remembrance of that day when he had held her in his arms, feeling her young body quivering at his touch, seeing her eyes glowing in response to his ardour, her exquisite lips moist with the promise of a kiss, these had been his life during the past few months; they had been the very breath of his body, the blood in his veins, the strength which bore him through all that he had set himself to do.

The winning of name and estate, and then a reconquering of his snowdrop, with a foregone certainty of victory ahead, that had been his existence.

A foregone certainty of victory! How oft had he exulted at the thought, drugging his despair with the intoxicating potion of hope, and now one brief word from her and defeat had been more hopeless, more complete than before.

"I am his wife," she said; "his wife in the sight of God; his wife despite the infamy in which you bore the leading hand!"

Michael had thought of everything, had envisaged everything save this: that Rose Marie would turn from him, because she loved the other. Loyalty and love, love and passion, were all synonymous to the impatient ardour, the proud defiance of this splendid blackguard—splendid in this, that he never swerved from the path into which he had once engaged his footsteps, never looked back with purposeless longing, and neither cursed Fate nor ever gave way to despair.

Even now, he pulled himself together, and within half an hour of the Legros' departure from his house he was on his way to see his friend Sir William Jones, the Attorney-General, first, and thence to his cousin's house on the outskirts of Piccadilly.

Rupert Kestyon—by the king's mandate no longer Lord of Stowmaries now—still occupied the same house into which he had made triumphant entry some two years ago on the death of the old earl. It was an ancient family mansion built a century and a half back, with gigantic and elaborate coat of arms carved in stone above the majestic porch. The serving-man who in response to Michael's peremptory knocking opened the massive door to him, gave no outward sign that so great a change had come, and with appalling suddenness, in the fortunes of his master.

He even addressed Michael as "sir" and spoke of "his lordship" being still in his room upstairs.

Impatiently waving the man aside, Michael threw hat and cloak down in the hall, and not waiting to be formally announced he ran quickly up the broad staircase. He knew the house well, for in childhood he had oft been in it, when his mother, holding him by the hand, came to ask for pecuniary assistance from the wealthy kinsman.

Without hesitation, therefore, Michael went up to the door of the principal bedroom and gave an impatient rap with his knuckles on the solid panel.

A fretful "Come in!" from within invited him to enter.

Rupert Kestyon was lying on the monumental four-post bedstead stretched out flat on his back and staring moodily into the glowing embers of the wood-fire which was burning in the wide-open grate.

At sight of his cousin he jumped up to a sitting posture; a deep frown of anger puckered his brow, and lent to the face a look of savagery. He stared at Michael for awhile, more than astonished at this unlooked-for appearance of his triumphant enemy; then he blurted out in his overwhelming wrath:

"Out of my house! Out of my house, you thief—you—out of here, I say—the men are still my servants—and I am still master here."

He put his feet to the ground, and made straightway for the door, but Michael intercepted him, and gripping the young man's wrists with his own strong fingers, he pushed him gently but firmly back.

"Easy, easy, Coz!" he said with kindly firmness; "by our Lady, but 'tis poor policy to harass the harbinger of good news."

"Good news," quoth Rupert, who was boiling over with rage, "good news from you, who have just robbed me of my inheritance!"

"'Twas an even game, good Coz," retorted Michael good-naturedly. "My father, my mother and I had all been robbed in the past, and left in a more pitiable plight, believe me, than it was ever my intention to leave you."

"Prate not of your intentions, man. You used my money, the money I myself did give you, in order to wage war against me, and press a claim which you never would have made good but for that money which I gave you."

"Let us be fair, good Coz. I offered you the whole of that money back on that memorable night in April at the inn of St. Denis."

"Ay, on a ridiculous condition to which I cared not to agree."

"The ridiculous condition," said Michael gravely, "consisted in your acknowledging as your lawful wife, an exquisitely beautiful and virtuous lady who already had claim on your loyalty."

"The exquisitely beautiful lady," retorted Rupert with an ugly sneer, "had, an I mistake not, already dragged her virtue in the wake of your chariot, my friend."

"Silence, man," said Michael sternly, "for you know that you lie."

"Will you attempt to deny that your magnanimous offer at St. Denis was made because you were in love with my wife?"

"I'll not deny it, but what my feelings were in the matter concerned no one but myself."

"Mayhap, mayhap, but e'en you admit, good Coz," quoth Rupert with obvious spite, "that a wife's conduct—"

"Your wife's conduct, Cousin, is beyond reproach," broke in Michael calmly, "as you know right full well."

"Pardi! Since she is in love with you—"

"That, too, is a lie—She loves no one but you."

"Mayhaps she told you so?" queried the young man, as with a yawn of ostentatious indifference he stretched himself out again—on a couch this time, with one booted leg resting on the ground and tapping it impatiently, whilst the other kicked savagely at an unoffensive sofa-cushion, tearing its silk cover to shreds.

"Yes!" replied Michael calmly, "she hath told me so." Then as the other broke into a loud, sarcastic laugh, he continued earnestly:

"Listen, Cousin, for what I am about to tell you concerns the whole of your future. You are a penniless beggar now—nay, do not interrupt me—I have well weighed every word which I speak, and have an answer for each of your sneers—you are a penniless beggar—through no fault of your own, mayhap, but I was a beggar, too, through none of mine. My mother was left—almost to starve—alone in a God-forsaken village. For years I kept actual starvation from her by courting wounds in order to get blood-money. That has been your fault ever since the old uncle's death, Cousin, for you knew that your kinswoman starved, and did naught to help her. But that is over, let it pass! I was a wastrel, a reprobate, a dissolute blackguard an you will! Had I been a better man than I was, you had never dared to offer me money to dishonour a woman. Let that pass too. But this I swear before God that I never meant to dishonour the girl. I was ready to take her to my heart, to give her all that she asked and more, the moment you in your wantonness had cast her off. But she is too proud to take anything from me, and wants nothing but her rights. Nay, you must listen to me patiently, till I have told you all—She is loyal to you, with heart and soul and body, and hath come to England to beg of you to render her justice."

"Have I not told you, man," here broke in Rupert Kestyon, with a blasphemous oath which momentarily drowned the quieter tones of the other man, "have I not told you that were that accursed tailor and his miserable wench to go on their knees to me, I would not have her—no, a thousand times no—with the last penny left in my pocket I'll obtain the decree of nullity, and marry the woman whom I love—"

"If she'll have you, Cousin," quoth Michael drily, "now that you are a beggar."

In a moment Rupert was on his feet again, burning with rage, swearing mad oaths in his wrath, and clenching his fists with a wild desire to rush at Michael and grip him by the throat.

"Nay, Coz," said the latter with a smile, "let us not fight like two brawling villains. My fist is heavier than yours: and if you attack me, I should have in defending mine own throat to punish you severely. But why should you rage at me; I have come to you with good intent. Think you, I would have left you to shift for yourself in this inhospitable world? Great God, do I not know what it means to shift for oneself—the misery, the wretchedness, the slow but certain degradation of mind and of body? By all the saints, man, I would not condemn mine enemy to such a life as I have led these past ten years."

"You do the tailor's wench no good anyhow by preaching to me," growled Rupert sulkily, feeling somewhat shamed.

He sat down once more, in an attitude of dejection, resting his elbows on his knees and burying his head in his hands.

"I did not come to preach," rejoined Michael quietly. "A blackguard like me hath no right to preach, and a blackguard like you, Cousin, is not like to listen. Nay, man, we are quits; we have both of us a pretty black mark against us in the book of records up there. 'Tis nigh on a year ago now that you came to me with your proposals. They have had far wider reaching consequences than any of us had dreamed of at the time. When I made a proposal to you at the inn at St. Denis, you refused my terms peremptorily—they were not sufficiently munificent, it seems, to tempt you to right a great wrong. I felt my weakness, then. I had no more to offer than just the return of your own money. You were a rich man still and could afford to pay largely for the satisfaction of a wanton caprice. But now matters stand differently; the money which you so contemptuously flung away at St. Denis hath borne royal fruit. I made that money work; I forced it to toil and slave to gain my purpose. I have beggared you, Cousin, and made myself powerful and strong, not because I hated you, not because I any longer desire dignity and riches, but because I wanted to hold in my hand a bribe that would be regal enough to tempt you."

He paused awhile, with stern dark eyes fixed on the weak, somewhat feminine face before him. Rupert Kestyon's vacillating pupils searched his cousin's face, trying to divine his thoughts. He raised his head, and rubbed his eyes, like a man wakened from sleep, and stared at Michael as on a man bereft of his senses.

"I do not understand," he stammered in his bewilderment.

"Yet, 'tis simple enough," resumed Michael calmly. "The good tailor whom you despise hath come over from France because he had heard rumours that a charge of conspiracy against the king was being brought against you by false informers."

"Great God!" murmured Rupert, who at these words had suddenly become pale, whilst great beads of perspiration rose upon his forehead.

"Ay," said the other, "we know what that means, Cousin. Your name amongst those implicated in this so-called Popish plot—think you you'll escape the block? Hath any one escaped it hitherto who hath come within the compass of the lies told by that scoundrel Oates?"

"It's not true," murmured Rupert Kestyon.

"What is not true? That the information hath been laid against you? That, alas, is only too true. A man named Daniel Pye is the informant. It seems that his former mistress—your own liege lady, Coz—had him flogged for theft awhile ago. This has been his idea of revenge on her—to bring you to disgrace or death, he cares not which, so long as the desires of her life—which, it seems, are that she be wedded to you—are frustrated. I have all this from the Attorney-General whom I saw a quarter of an hour ago. Nay, there is no doubt that the blackguard hath informed against you, and in a vastly circumstantial manner. Come, you are a man, Coz," added Michael not unkindly, seeing that Rupert was on the point of losing his wits in the face of the awful prospect of this accusation, knowing full well its probable terrible consequences, "and men in these troublous times must know how to look on death in whatever grim guise it may appear."

"But not that," murmured the younger man involuntarily, "surely not that—"

"I trust not," rejoined the other. "Have I not told you that I was the bearer of good news?"

"Good news!"

"I own it sounds like irony, but, nevertheless, Coz, you'll presently see that it is better than it seems. Let me resume, and tell you all I know. Daniel Pye hath lodged his information against you. I have it directly from Sir William Jones, who in his turn had it from Sir Edmund Berry Godfrey. The villainous rogue says that on a certain day in April he was at the hostelry of the 'Rat Mort' in Paris, in the company of one Legros—tailor of Paris—and that there he overheard you talking over with one of the ministers of the King of France, a plan whereby Charles Rex is to be murdered, the Duke of York to be placed on the English throne, and the whole of England sold to France and to Rome. It is one of those impudent and dastardly lies which, alas, find ready credence in our poor country just now. You remember Stailey's trial on the information of that scoundrel Oates, who in spite of his own obvious blunderings and contradictions was absolutely believed."

"I know, I know," said Rupert Kestyon with a groan, "I am undone, I know. Cousin, I must fly the country at once—I can reach Dover to-night."

"Nay, that you cannot, Cousin; your arrest is imminent. The warrant is out and would take effect the moment you attempted to leave your house."

"But in the name of God, is there no way out?" came in tones of tragic despair from the unfortunate man.

"Ay, that there is and a right simple one. The regal bribe, Cousin," said Michael with a grim smile, "which I promised to offer you."

"My life—do you mean my life? You have not the power to save my head from the block. If I am arrested and brought to trial on one of these infamous charges, the king himself could not save me."

"No; the king could not—but I can."

"How?"

"On one condition."

"I can guess it."

"The same I put before you at St. Denis."

209

Rupert Kestyon broke out into a laugh, a harsh, disagreeable laugh of irony and of despair.

"Man, the wench would not have me now. Am I not beggared and a fugitive from justice? Her father would now be the first to take her from me. She married the Earl of Stowmaries and Rivaulx—"

But Michael interrupted him, saying:

"And after a brief sojourn with her in her old home in Paris you, as Earl of Stowmaries and Rivaulx, will bring your wife back as chatelaine of Maries Castle, even before the last leaf has fallen from the oak."

"But you—'tis you who—"

"I stay here to meet the charge of high treason and conspiracy preferred against the Earl of Stowmaries," said Michael very quietly.

Like one in a dream, Rupert Kestyon passed a trembling hand over his damp forehead.

"You—you would—" he stammered.

"Am I not the Earl of Stowmaries?" queried the other simply. "Was I not actually in Paris on that memorable day in April? True, I am not a Romanist by religion, but the travesty of justice which, alas, now goes on under the guidance of Chief Justice Scroggs, will not ask too many questions and will be satisfied as long as it has one more prey to throw to the hungering intolerance of the mob. When I am gone, Cousin, you are the rightful heir to the title and estates which the king's mandate hath just conferred on me. You see how simple it is. It but rests with you to accept or refuse."

"But why—why should you do this?" murmured the other, whose brain seemed almost reeling with this sudden transition from tragic despair to the first glimmer of hope. "Why should you give your life— and—and mayhap die such an awful death?"

"Not for love of you, Coz; you may take an oath on that," said Michael with a humorous twinkle in his eye and a quick smile which softened the former stern expression of his face.

"No, I know that," retorted the other, "'tis because you love her— my wife."

"My head will no longer grace my shoulders when you return with your bride to England, Cousin; you have therefore no cause for jealousy."

There was silence between the two men now. Rupert was of a truth too dazed to understand fully all that his cousin's proposal would mean to him.

"But, by the Mass, man!" he said, "I cannot accept such a sacrifice."

"'Twill not be the first act of cowardice that you'll have committed, Cousin. This one will atone for the graver sin of a year ago. Take what I offer you. Now that we are both face to face with the problem of life or death, we can look back more soberly on the past. We

210

have both done an innocent woman an infinite wrong. Fate hath so shuffled the cards that we can both atone; after all, methinks that mine is the easier rôle. It is ofttimes so much simpler to die than to live. Nay, Cousin, your part will not be altogether that of a coward, not even though your path in life will henceforth be strewn with roses. She loves you purely, loyally, good Coz. 'Tis your duty as a man to render her happy. Above all, think not of me. Odd's fish, man, death and I have looked at one another very straight many a time before—we are friends, he and I."

"But not such a death, Cousin—and the disgrace—"

"Bah, even disgrace and I have held one another by the hand ere this. And now before I leave you, Coz, your solemn word of honour that you will make her happy, for by God!" he added more lightly, "methinks my ghost would haunt you, if ever it saw her in tears."

"Will you take my hand, Cousin?" asked Rupert in simple response, as he somewhat timidly held his hand out to the other man.

Michael took it without a word and thus at last were the hands of these two men clasped for the first time in friendship. Kinsmen by blood, Fate and human passions had estranged them from one another; yet it was blood that told, else Rupert could not even for a moment—and despite his love of life and joy in living—have accepted the sacrifice.

Even now he hesitated. This taking of his cousin's hand, this tacit acceptance of another man's life to save his own, wore an ugly look of cowardice and of dishonour. Yet the young man was no coward. In open fight in a good cause, his valour would have been equal to that of any man, and he would on the field of honour have met death, no doubt, with fortitude. But what loomed ahead was far different to the glamour, the enthusiasm of courting death for honour. It meant disgrace and shame, the trial, the ignominy: death dealt by the hand of the executioner in sight of a jeering mob. It meant the torture of long imprisonment in a gloomy, filthy prison; it meant the ill-usage of warders and menials, insults from the judge, rough handling by the crowd. It meant, above all, the supreme disgrace of desecration after death, the traitor's head on Tyburn gates, the body thrown to the carrion, an ignominy from which even the least superstitious shrank in overwhelming horror. Ay, and there was worse shame, more supreme degradation still—for a traitor's death was rendered hideous by every means that the cruelty of man could invent.

This picture stood on one side of Rupert Kestyon's vision, on the other was only a hated marriage and the somewhat cowardly acceptance of another man's sacrifice.

Rupert Kestyon did hesitate, the while the insidious voice of Luxury and of Ease whispered sophistries in his ear:

"He does not do this for thee, man, but for the woman whom he

211

loves. Why shouldst thou stand in the way of thine own future comfort and peace?"

The battle was a trying one and whilst it lasted Rupert Kestyon felt unwilling to meet his cousin's eyes. Yet had he done so, he would have seen nothing in them save expectancy, and from time to time that same humorous twinkle, as if the man derived amusement from the conflict which was raging within the other's heart.

As usual under these circumstances, Fate put her lean, sharp-pointed finger into this grim pie, and it was the small incident which settled the big issue in the end, for even as Rupert stood there, shamed, hesitating, fighting the inward battle, there came a timid rap at the door, and a serving-man entered, bearing a missive which was tied down with green cord but otherwise left unsealed.

"What is this?" asked Rupert Kestyon, who seemed to be descending from the stars, in so dazed a manner did he gaze at the man who was handing him the letter.

"A man hath just brought it, my lord; he said that the message was urgent but would not say from whence he came—he went away down the street very quickly as soon as I had taken the letter from him."

"Good; you may go."

With hands still trembling from recent emotion, Rupert Kestyon, as soon as the servant had gone, tore open the missive, on the outside cover of which he had at once recognised the ill-formed scrawls which emanated from the untutored pen of Mistress Peyton. It was addressed in that same illiterate but deeply loved hand to Mister Rupert Kestyon, erstwhile my lord of Stowmaries, and began:

"Honord Sir.

"This is to warn you that the villan Daniel Pye hath informed against you, he did make brag of it befor my servants to-day saying that you will be arrested for treson and he be thus revenged upon me. i think it were best you did not com to my house until this clowd has clered away. But i am yr frend always."

The lady had signed the missive with her name in full. The hot blood rushed to Rupert Kestyon's face, for despite his own natural vanity he could not help but see the callous indifference as to his own fate which pierced through the fair Julia's carefully-worded warning.

Without a word, however, he folded the letter and slipped it into the inner pocket of his coat. Then he turned once more to his cousin.

"Is there no other way?" he asked, whilst the weakness of his nature, the vacillation peculiar to his character, was very apparent now, in the ever-shifting expression of his face, the pains he took to avoid looking Michael quite square in the face.

"I see none now," rejoined the other. "Methinks, Coz, that you have received confirmation of what I told you."

"Yes. I have. Unless I leave the country to-day I shall be a prisoner ere nightfall."

"And Rose Marie, beyond all that we have made her suffer already, will be left to mourn for you. To torture a woman then leave her desolate! Nay, man, the shame of that were worse than a traitor's death."

"When shall I see her?"

"Anon, I think. Master Legros is on his way to you."

"Then I'll to France to-day, taking my wife with me," said Rupert resolutely, "and may God guard you, Cousin."

"Nay, we'll not ask Him to do that just now," rejoined the other with the same quaint smile; "rather may He protect her, and give her happiness. We both owe her that, methinks."

Thus was the compact sealed. It had of course been a foregone conclusion all along, and Michael had never for a moment anticipated that his cousin would refuse the sacrifice.

The great game begun a year ago across the supper table of a tavern and in the midst of a drunken orgy, ended here and now. Both the gamblers lost all that they had staked. One was losing his self-respect, the woman he loved with a capricious passion, the freedom which he had coveted; the other was throwing away his all so that a fair-haired girl, the cold ice-maid who had no love for him, should still be the only winner in the end.

CHAPTER XXXIX

Are the skies wet because we weep,
Or fair because of any mirth?
Cry out; they are gods; perchance they sleep!

—*Swinburne*

Rupert Kestyon—erstwhile styled my lord of Stowmaries and Rivaulx—turned away from his house in Piccadilly with a comparatively light heart.

Comparatively only, because strive as he might he could not altogether banish from his mind the last picture he had of his cousin, standing all alone in the gloomy withdrawing room, tall, erect, perfectly cheerful and placid, just as if he were awaiting a summons to some festivity rather than to disgrace and to death.

"It is best that I should remain here pending the execution of the

213

magistrate's warrant," Michael had explained simply. "It will then be done without confusion of identity or difficulties of any kind. The informer will probably not see me until I am on my trial, and, in any case, I imagine that he will be just as content to tell his lies against me as he would against you."

Rupert, of a truth, did marvel not a little at his cousin's coolness at such a moment; he himself felt a tingling of all his nerves and his faculties seemed all numb in face of this terrible crisis through which he was passing. He could not really imagine that any man could thus calmly discuss the details of his own coming dishonour, of the awful public disgrace, the physical and mental agony of a coming trial and of ignominious death. Yet Michael was quite serene, even cheerful, and ever and anon a whimsical smile played round the corners of his lips when he caught the look of shame, of perturbation and renewed hesitancy in the younger man's face.

He himself was ever wont to decide quickly for good or ill, to map his course of action and never to deviate from it. Many there were who knew Michael Kestyon well, and who declared that he had no conscience, no real sense of what was right or wrong. That may be so. Certain it is that whatever part in life he chose to play, he never paused to think whether morally it was right or wrong that he should play it.

Even now he did not pause to think whether what he was doing was sublime or infamous. He gave his honour, his name and his life not in order to right a wrong, not in order to atone for a sin which he himself had committed, but because his love for Rose Marie transcended every other feeling within him, overshadowed every thought. She had told him that her happiness lay there where duty and loyalty called. He—poor fool!—imagined that she loved Rupert, her husband, from a sense of duty mayhap, but loved him nevertheless.

With an accusation of conspiracy threatening that man, an accusation which could only find its complement in a traitor's death, Rose Marie could not be aught but unhappy. So thought Michael to himself, whereupon the giving of name, of honour and of life to the man whom Rose Marie loved, was as natural to Michael as to draw his breath.

The fact that this sacrifice meant dishonour and shame was no pang. Michael cared less than naught for public opinion. To himself he would not stand disgraced. He had weighed his action, looked at it from every point; had in his mind's eye seen the public trial, the ignominious condemnation, all the disgrace which pertains to such a death. He had seen it, and decided without the slightest hesitation.

All this Rupert could not of course understand. In this he was different to Michael, that he felt poignant remorse for his own action, the while he had really not the moral power to reverse his decision. Had the acceptance of another man's heroic sacrifice to be done again, he again would have accepted it, and again have bitterly repented, hesitated, repented and accepted again. He would have understood Michael's attitude better if there were any prospect of an admiring world knowing subsequently the truth of the sacrifice, of there being a chance of the public recognition of the heroism, even after death. But here there was no such prospect. For Michael it would be humiliation, and nothing but humiliation, shame and disgrace even beyond the grave.

Therefore, the young man was over-glad when—the preparations for his journey being all complete—he at last turned his back on the old house in Piccadilly. All the servants had been enjoined that if any one came thither and asked for my lord of Stowmaries the new and only real lord of Stowmaries would receive the visitor, whatever his errand might be. Then Rupert took his leave of his cousin; not a word more was said on the subject of the future, nor did the young man attempt to express any gratitude. I do not think that he felt any in the true sense of the word, and Michael's attitude was not one that called forth any outward show of sentiment. An hour later Rupert Kestyon had finally turned his steps in the direction of Fleet Street; soon he found himself inside the yard of the Bell Inn, asking if he might have speech with Master Legros of Paris, lately come to the hostelry.

There was something almost comical in good Papa Legros' expression of surprise when he realised who his visitor was. Rupert's face was of course unfamiliar to him, and it took him quite a little time to collect his thoughts, in view of the happy prospect which this unexpected visit had called forth before him.

His kindly heart, ever prone to see good, even where none existed, quickly attributed to this erring sinner the saving clause of loyal repentance. Knowing nothing of what had occurred between the cousins, Papa Legros naturally sprang to the conclusion that the young man, tardily smitten with remorse, had come of his own accord to make reparation, and the worthy tailor was only too ready to smooth the path of atonement for him as much as lay in his power.

"Milor," he began, as soon as he understood who Rupert was, and stretching out a cordial hand to him.

"Nay! I am no longer milor now," broke in Rupert Kestyon with a slight show of petulance. "My Cousin Michael is Lord of Stowmaries now. I am only a poor suppliant of high birth and low fortunes who would humbly ask if your daughter—my wife before God—is still prepared to link her fate to mine."

"My daughter, milor—sir—will answer herself," rejoined the tailor with at least as much dignity as a high-born gentleman would have displayed under the like circumstances; then he went to the door, and opening it called to Rose Marie.

Rupert Kestyon, despite the deep-rooted antagonism which he felt against this woman to whom now his future was irrevocably bound,

215

was forced to own to himself that Fate tempered her stern decrees with a goodly amount of compensation.

Rose Marie's beauty was one which sorrow doth not mar; in her case it had even enhanced it, by etherealising the childlike contour of the face, and giving the liquid blue eyes an expression such as the mediæval artists of old lent to the saints whom they portrayed. She came forward with quiet self-possession, through which shone an air of simple confidence and of sublime forgiveness. Though she had not expected Rupert's coming, yet she showed no surprise, only pleasure that he had so nobly forestalled her, and saved her the humiliation of coming to him as a suppliant.

Rupert Kestyon was young, and his senses were quickly enflamed at sight of so much loveliness, and though inwardly he railed at chance, that had not made of this exquisite woman a great lady, yet when she so graciously extended her hand to him, he kissed it as deferentially as he would that of a duchess.

"Madam," he said, as soon as she was seated, and he standing before her, "we are told in the Scriptures that there is more joy in Heaven for the conversion of one sinner than for the continued goodness of one hundred holy men. It had always struck me ere this that this dictum was somewhat unfair on the holy men, but now I have come to be thankful for this disposition of Heaven's rejoicings, since you—who no doubt have come straight from there—will mayhap show some consideration to the repentant sinner who hath so miserably wronged you, and who now craves humbly for pardon at your feet."

He was very much pleased with himself for this speech, accompanied as it was with pretence of bending the knee. He felt sure that Michael would be pleased with him for it, nor did it cost him much to make it, for of a truth Rose Marie was exquisitely beautiful.

"By Gad," he murmured to himself, "meseems that I am ready to fall in love with the wench."

"My lord," she said quietly, meeting with perfect impassiveness the sudden gleam of admiration which lit up his eyes, "'tis not for me—your wife—to judge you or your conduct. The wrong which you did to me, I do readily forgive, so be it that my father and mother, whom you have wronged as deeply as you did mine own self, are equally ready to forget all that is past."

"An my lord is willing to make amends," said Papa Legros with an involuntary sigh. He thought of Michael and how different he had looked when first he had wooed Rose Marie; Michael with the handsome proud head, the merry smile, the twinkling dark eyes so full of fun at times, at others so earnest and so infinitely tender. Papa Legros sighed, even as he felt that rectitude was a hard taskmistress, and that 'twas a vast pity Rose Marie was quite such an angel of goodness. But Rupert's impatient voice broke in on these thoughts.

"I pray you," he said, "do not persist in calling me my lord. My

216

Cousin Michael is and has always been, it seems, the rightful Lord of Stowmaries. I am a poor man, now—"

"And my father, sir, is rich enough that your poverty need not fret you," said Rose Marie quietly. "An you'll have me as your wife—"

"It is my duty as well as my pleasure, Madam," he broke in decisively, "to ask you if you'll permit me to lay my submission at your feet."

"You have but to command me, sir," she rejoined coldly.

"An unfortunate incident, of which I understand you have some inkling, will force me to leave England for a time."

"We know that a false charge has been preferred against you, sir, and we came to England—I trust not too late—to warn you of your danger."

"Nay, not too late, Madam; as you see I am still free. I had warnings from other quarters yet am equally grateful for your pains."

"The cloud will blow over," she said stiffly. "When do you propose to go to France?"

"To-night an it please you, Madam," he replied. "Will you journey in my company?"

"If you so desire it, sir."

She rose, and with the same calm dignity prepared to go. Rupert's glowing eyes followed her graceful movements and dwelt with unconcealed pleasure on every line of her young figure, which the somewhat stiff mode of the day could not altogether disguise. A warm tinge of colour flew to her cheeks when, raising her eyes to his for a moment, she encountered his bold look; then when the colour flew as swiftly as it came she looked pale and frail as the snowdrops to which Michael had ever loved to compare her.

But beyond that quick blush, she showed no sign of emotion. Her almost mediæval sense of duty to her husband caused her to accept his every word, his every look, without a thought of censure or even of rebellion. She had so schooled her sensibilities that they were her slaves, she their absolute mistress—the rigid and mechanical being come into existence from out the ashes of her past happy self in order to right the great wrong committed by another.

Obedient to her lord's mute but peremptory request, she gave him her hand, and accepted his kiss as she would have done his scorn, coldly and humbly, for her father stood there and watched her, and she would not let him see what this interview was costing her in agony of mind, in humiliation of her entire soul. For, look you, when she left Paris in order to offer herself a willing sacrifice on the altar of filial love, she had steeled her pride against her husband's scorn, but not against his capricious passion, and now that his boldly admiring glance swept over her face and form, she felt a wild, mad longing to flee—to hide her sorrow which had suddenly turned to shame, and to put the whole world between herself and the pollution of her husband's kiss.

217

Her father's voice recalled her to herself, and even Rupert Kestyon had not noted the swiftly-flying look of agony which had momentarily darkened her eyes.

"Sir," said Papa Legros now, with firmer decision than he had hitherto displayed, "you see that both my daughter and myself are over-ready to forget the past. You are young, sir, and methinks sinned more from thoughtlessness than from any love of evil. Rose Marie is ready to follow you, withersoever you may command. She is your wife before God, and directly we are in Paris we will ask His blessing in confirmation of your union. Monseigneur will not refuse to perform the ceremony—the other, alas, whereat a miscreant held my daughter's hand, was but a mockery—Monseigneur will pass it over. 'Twas he advised me to make a final appeal to your honour, and I thank God on my knees, sir, that with you rests the glory of having made such noble amends entirely of your own accord. I pray you only—and herein you must forgive a father's anxiety—I pray you to place in my hands the final pledge of your good faith towards my daughter."

"What may that be, sirrah?" quoth Rupert, whilst the first show of arrogance suddenly pierced through his borrowed armour of outward deference.

"The decree of His Holiness the Pope," rejoined the tailor quietly, "annulling your marriage with my daughter. An you mean loyally by her you will place the mandate in my hands."

For a second or two only Rupert seemed to hesitate. This simple giving over of a paper meant the final surrender of his will, the giving up of all for which he had planned and intrigued; the acknowledgment that Fate was stronger than his desire, God's decree greater than the schemes of men. That mandate once out of his hands, he could never get it back again, nor ever obtain another. It was real, tangible finality; therefore did he hesitate, but the next moment he had looked once more on Rose Marie, and the natural primitive man in him, the shallow nature, the masterful senses, caused him to shrug his shoulders in indifference. Bah, one woman after all was as good as another; this one loved him in her curious, cold way, and—-by Gad!—she was d—d pretty. So Rupert Kestyon delved in the deep pocket of his surcoat and drew out therefrom a parchment to which was appended an enormous seal that bore the arms and triple crown of His Holiness the Pope.

This he handed to Papa Legros.

The latter took it and glanced at its contents; one phrase therein caused a dark frown to appear on his brow, and a flash of anger to rush to his cheeks. It related to the misconduct of Rose Marie, the daughter of one Armand Legros, master tailor of Paris, in consequence of which His Holiness did grant dispensation to Rupert Kestyon, Earl of Stowmaries and Rivaulx, to contract a marriage with another woman, his former marriage being null and void.

For a brief moment good Papa Legros hated the young reprobate

218

before him with all the strength of which his kind heart was capable; for a moment he longed to throw that lying parchment back into the teeth of the miscreant who had dared to put an insult on record against the purest saint that had ever adorned her sex. The good man's hands shook as they held the paper, and during that brief moment Rupert experienced a hideous sensation of fear. If Rose Marie rejected him now, would Michael withdraw from the sacrifice which he was prepared to make?

But that anxiety was short-lived. With a deep sigh of resignation, and a firm compression of the lips, Master Legros looked the young man straight in the face.

"What is past, is past," he said, as if in answer to the other's thought, "and I am satisfied."

But he did not tear the parchment up, as Rupert had at first thought that he meant to do. He folded it up with hands still slightly shaking from the inward struggle which had just taken place within his simple soul, and then slipped it into the breast pocket of his coat.

CHAPTER XL

So many worlds, so much to do,
So little done, such things to be,
How know I what had need of thee,
For thou wert strong as thou wert true?

—*Tennyson*

It was later in the afternoon and Master Legros and his daughter had finished their preparations for the return journey. Strangely enough, papa's heart was not as glad as it should have been, considering that the object of his visit to England had been attained, and that he had reached the pinnacle of his desire much more easily than he had ever dared to contemplate, for he had reached it without the cost of humiliation to his child or rebuff to himself.

Nevertheless, the kindly heart was like a dead weight in the good man's breast, even though Rose Marie did her best to seem cheerful, talking ever of the joy of seeing maman again, and at times quite serenely of her own future.

"Thy husband looks kind, Rose Marie," said papa tentatively, whilst his eyes, rendered keen through the intensity of his affection, strove to pierce through the mask of impassiveness wherewith his child tried to hide her thoughts.

"He also seems greatly to admire thee," he added with an involuntary display of paternal pride.

But has any man—has even the most devoted of fathers—ever succeeded in reading a woman's thoughts on the subject of another man.

All that Papa Legros thought at this moment was that Rose Marie looked very pale and that a shiver seemed to go through her as if she had the ague. Mayhap she was over-tired, certainly she was unstrung. He himself felt uncommonly as if he would like to cry.

In the early part of the afternoon he persuaded Rose Marie to lie awhile on her bed and rest. "Milor"—for so he still persisted in calling Rupert Kestyon in his mind—would be here at six o'clock; his coach would then be ready for the journey to Dover. It was now little more than three.

Rose Marie obeyed willingly. She was very tired and she longed to be all alone. Papa declared his intention of going out for a walk and of returning within an hour.

A great longing had seized him to see Michael once again. The worthy man cursed himself for his folly and for his weakness but he felt that he could not go away from England without grasping once more that slender, kindly hand, which he once used to look on as that of a dearly-loved son.

Papa Legros did not see the reason why—now that all difficulties had been duly planed—he and Michael should not remain friends. He had more than a vague suspicion, too, that "milor's" repentant attitude was due to Michael's persuasion.

Asking his way from the passers-by as he went, he soon found himself once again before the house in Soho. But his disappointment was bitter when he heard that my lord was from home, and no one knew when he would return.

Sadder of heart then, Master Legros retraced his steps towards the Bell Inn. On the way he had wiped many a tear which had fallen down his cheeks, blaming himself severely the while for this display of weakness. But—strange though it may seem—this failure in seeing Michael and in hearing his cheery voice speak the "God-speed" had weighed the good tailor's spirits down with an oppressive weight which seemed almost like a foreboding.

In the yard of the inn, Master Legros encountered quite a crowd of gaffers. Some great excitement seemed to be in the air; they talked volubly to one another, with that stolid absence of gesture, that burying of hands in breeches pockets which always makes an Englishman's excitement seem so unconvincing to the foreign observer. In the centre of the yard, a heavy coach—a note of bright canary yellow in the midst of all the sober greys and drabs around—stood ready, with ostlers at the leaders' heads, the horses champing their bits and impatiently pawing the cobblestones. The driver, with thick coat unbuttoned displaying an expanse of grey woolen shirt, was quenching his thirst inside the vehicle; obviously it was not his intention to join actively in the babel of voices which went on all round him, although the coach itself and the horses seemed special objects of curiosity, since a crowd of gaffers surrounded it as closely as the impatient horses themselves would allow.

Master Legros made his way through the crowd, trying to catch a chance phrase or so, which might give him the keynote to all this unwonted bustle. The words "Papist" and "arrest," which he understood, caught his ear repeatedly, also the name "Stowmaries," invariably accompanied with a loud imprecation.

Feeling naturally diffident through his want of knowledge of the language, he was somewhat timorous of asking questions, but hurried up to his room, having bidden the barman downstairs take a bottle of wine and two glasses up to his room.

He found Rose Marie sitting quietly in the armchair, pensive but otherwise serene. To the father's anxious eyes it seemed as if she had been crying, but she returned his kiss of greeting with clinging fondness, and assured him that she felt quite rested and ready for the journey.

"My lord" had arranged that his coach should take them by night journey to Dover, and thence immediately to Calais if the packet-boat was plying; for "my lord" seemed in a vast hurry to get across to France as soon as may be, and Rose Marie herself was conscious of a great longing to put the sea between herself and this land which called forth so many bitter memories.

When the serving-man brought the wine, Legros asked his daughter to question him as to the excitement which reigned in the yard.

"Oh!" explained the man, who was eager enough to talk, "'tis only the news of the arrest of another of these d—d Papists. They do conspire, you know, to murder the king, and it seems that this time they've arrested another noble lord, no less a person than my lord of Stowmaries."

"My lord of Stowmaries!" ejaculated Legros in utter dismay, for he had partly guessed, partly understood, what the man was saying; "surely it cannot be—"

"When and where did this occur?" queried Rose Marie peremptorily.

"About an hour ago, at his lordship's house in Piccadilly," replied the man. "They do say that the miscreant hath confessed, directly he saw the musketeers. He was scared, no doubt, and blurted out the truth. By the Lord! If the people of England had their way, a man like

221

that should be broken on the wheel and the fires of Smithfield should be revived to rid the country of such pestilential vermin."

Fortunately Master Legros did not understand all that the man said, else his wrath had known no bounds. As it was he had only a vague idea that the man was being insolent, and he shouted an angry command of:

"Enough of this! Get out, sirrah!" which the man readily obeyed, being over-satisfied that he had annoyed and even frightened these foreign Papists, who, no doubt, had come to England only to brew mischief.

Directly the door had closed behind the serving-man, Rose Marie said decisively:

"Father dear, we must to my husband's house at once, and find out what has happened."

"He seemed to make so light of the danger which threatened him, when he was here just now, that I had begun to think that blackguard Daniel Pye was naught but a clumsy blackmailer. And yet, milor—I—I mean our milor—he thought the matter grave, and went forth very hurriedly to warn his kinsman."

"Father dear, I would give anything to have further news," said Rose Marie, who was trembling with agitation. "Do, I pray you, let us go forth and try and find out something more."

But even as with feverish movements, she began putting on a cloak and hood, the door opened and Rupert Kestyon entered. Rose Marie stared at him as if she had seen a ghost, and Master Legros murmured in complete bewilderment:

"You—you, my lord—then, thank God!—it is not true."

"What is not true?" queried the young man, who also seemed labouring under grave agitation, for his cheeks were almost grey in colour, and his lips twitched painfully as he tried to control the tremor of his voice.

"That you have been arrested, my lord!" said Legros. "They told us that you had been arrested for treason and—"

"They told you lies, no doubt," broke in Rupert roughly, "as you see I am safe and sound. The horses are put to," he added with obvious want of control over his own impatience. "I pray you, Madam, to descend as soon as you are ready, and you, too, good Master, and to enter the coach without parleying with the crowd. You need have no fear; they will not molest you."

"We are ready, milor—I mean sir," said Papa Legros, who was taken with an exceptionally severe attack of his usual fussiness. "I pray you give your arm to my daughter—I will follow close on your heels."

"My lord," it seems, was so agitated that he even forgot his good manners, and curtly bidding the others not to linger, he darted out of the room, and had even disappeared down the corridor before Rose Marie had had time to collect her little bits of hand luggage.

She went back to the window which gave on the covered balcony that on this floor ran all round the house, overlooking the yard. The excitement down below was evidently reaching fever pitch; every one was rushing toward the gate and the yard itself was for the moment left deserted. Only one ostler remained at the horses' heads, and his head, too, was turned in the direction of the gates. The driver had emerged from the depths of the vehicle and together with his mate was hoisting the Legros' luggage into the boot. He, too, however, craned his neck from time to time, trying to see beyond the dense knot of human heads which totally obstructed both the view and the passage out into Fleet Street.

Rose Marie, feeling still strangely perturbed, her heart beating with a nameless fear, which she could not herself understand, threw open the window and stepped out onto the balcony. Rupert Kestyon was standing just below, giving impatient directions to his men anent the disposition of the luggage. The sound of the opening window and of Rose Marie's footsteps above, caused him to look up and at sight of her he uttered a loud oath. It was evident that he had completely lost all control over himself.

"You have run it too late, d—n you!" he shouted roughly. "Now we cannot get through Fleet Street till after that accursed mob hath dispersed."

Rose Marie with lips compressed and brows closely puckered withdrew out of his sight, blushing with shame at the thought that a group of serving-girls who stood also on the balcony not far from her, giggling and chattering, should have heard her husband's rough words.

But the wenches were evidently too much engrossed with their desire to see something of what was going on beyond the hostelry gates to pay much heed to the pale, foreign miss and to her doings, and even as Rose Marie prepared once more to join her father, she heard one girl say excitedly:

"He won't be passing by for another few minutes—we'll have time to run to the gates—"

"No! no! Cannot you hear the shouts? They are bringing him along now," cried another, holding with both hands to the iron railing, the while her companion tried to drag her away.

"I can just see over the heads of the crowd," said another. "Here they come! Here they come! Can you hear them all hooting?"

And she herself indulged in a vicious "Boo! Down with the traitor! Down with the Papists!"

Beyond the gates, the crowd, invisible to Rose Marie, was evidently giving vent to its excitement. As the wench had said, they were hooting lustily. Shouts of "Death to the traitors!" mingled with obvious cries of terror and of pain following immediately on the clatter of horses' hoofs on the mud-covered street.

223

"It's a closed vehicle!" said one of the girls on the balcony in obvious disappointment.

"And you can't see even that with all that pack of soldiery."

"Boo! Boo! Death to the Papist!" screamed the other girls in unison.

Just for a moment then in the small space between the top of the archway, and above the heads of the crowd, Rose Marie caught sight of a closed hackney coach, being driven at slow pace and surrounded by an escort of musketeers. The hooting, hissing, and other expressions of hatred and opprobrium became almost deafening for the moment, and through the shouts of "The rope, the rack, the stake for the Papists!" could distinctly be heard the name, "Stowmaries!" accompanied by loud imprecations, whilst a shower of evil-smelling refuse was hurled at the vehicle by the enthusiastic staff of the Bell Inn, congregated at its gates.

Rose Marie felt sick with horror. Gradually that fear which had hitherto been nameless, gained more tangible shape. She peeped down again and saw that her husband had taken refuge inside his coach.

Then she understood.

It was Michael who had been arrested—the only Lord of Stowmaries, as he himself had proudly said awhile ago.

Did some inkling of the real truth of the case rise in her heart then and there, it were difficult to say. There is a strange telepathy which exists in nature and which warns the sensitive mind of the danger, the misfortune of another being. It was only a purely natural, human instinct which prompted her to ask the serving-wenches a final question, the answer to which she knew already.

"What is all the excitement about?" she asked, turning to the group of girls and steadying her voice as much as she could. "Who is it they are taking past in that closed carriage?"

"My lord of Stowmaries, Mistress," said one of the girls. "He is one of the Papists that do conspire against the king. He'll hang for sure—I wish they'd burn the lot as they did in the olden days."

"But 'tis my lord Stowmaries' coach that is standing here below," said Rose Marie; "he is safe and sound within."

"Nay! I know naught about that," quoth the girl decisively; "'tis my lord Stowmaries they are taking to prison sure enough, and 'twill be my lord of Stowmaries' head that'll be on Tyburn gate before many days are over, and I for one'll go to see him beheaded, if I can get a holiday on that day."

CHAPTER XLI

In the silence of the night,
How we shiver with affright
At the melancholy menace of their tone!
For every sound that floats
From the rust within their throats
Is a groan.

—Edgar Allan Poe

Rose Marie had told her father all that she feared, all that she, alas, knew to be true.

"We cannot go now, Father dear," she said with quivering voice, whilst her eyes burning with hot tears, looked down appealingly at her father, "we must surely hear what becomes of him."

"Nay, my child," said Papa Legros with a heavy sigh, "what can we do by remaining here? Your duty is to your husband. No doubt he, too, fears for his life, and would wish to leave this country ere suspicion fall upon him."

"But Father, methinks you do not understand. I know not if there hath been conspiracy or not, but this I do know, that the charge was preferred against my husband. Then why is my lord arrested?"

"I know not, my jewel," replied Papa Legros, deeply perplexed and miserable. "England seems to be a queer country just now. Mayhap all these gentlemen do conspire. God knows there always have been many conspiracies against our own most high and most Catholic King Louis, the ever victorious."

And Master Legros doffed his felt hat in token of deep respect.

"Thy husband waits, child," added the worthy man resignedly; "'tis him thou must obey."

Even as he spoke, Rupert's steps were heard once more along the corridor. He entered, still looking miserably anxious, but at sight of Rose Marie a blush of shame-facedness overspread his pale cheeks.

"Your pardon, Mistress," he said, striving to speak quietly, "methinks the coast is clear now. Will you deign to descend?"

He offered Rose Marie his arm. She felt like some wild creature trapped, looking round her with wild, terrified eyes as if for a means of escape. Her father gave her an appealing look, and Rupert reiterated his request with more distinct command in his tone. His eyes, wherein wrath, fear, and a certain look of shame were obviously fighting for mastery, seemed to dare her to disobey. He was her master after all, and a master of her own choosing. The bars of that cage against which she would henceforth for ever bruise her heart were fashioned by her own hands.

225

"Come, Mistress, I wait," said Rupert, and with a gesture which was almost rough in its peremptoriness, he took her hand and slipped it under his arm.

Papa Legros gathered the sundry small bags and parcels which formed his own and his daughter's hand luggage, and then he followed the young couple out of the room.

But Rose Marie once across the threshold and in the corridor soon disengaged her arm. This masterful appropriation of her person and of her will caused her an instinctive pang of fear. Good God! Was she going to hate this man whom through an impulse of loyalty and righteousness she had openly acknowledged as her lord, and to whom she almost wilfully had surrendered her whole young life, her hopes of happiness, her every thought and wish? Now with every look of unfettered admiration, with every word of command, he roused her numbed spirits into rebellion. Even now she could not bear to take his arm, she could not bear the touch of his hand on hers as he began to lead her along the corridor, as if already she were part of his goods and chattels, the obedient servant of his caprice.

When she withdrew her hand from his, he looked inquiringly on her face, then realising her motive, guessing her repugnance, he laughed a forced, ironical laugh and said with obvious intent to wound:

"Nay, Madam! I'm vastly sorry that even in this dark passage you cannot fancy that I am my cousin Michael. But you made your choice yourself 'twixt him and me, and therefore pray understand that 'tis too late to repent."

He walked, however, on ahead, keeping a little in front of her, and soon reached the door which gave on the yard.

His coach stood there all in readiness, the driver on the box holding the ribbons, the groom standing by the carriage holding open the door. But between the coach and the door through which Rupert with Rose Marie and Papa Legros had just stepped forth into the yard, there stood a group composed of three musketeers, one of whom was a little in advance of the others, and apparently in command.

Master Savage, landlord of the Bell Inn, was in close and voluble converse with the soldier, as Rupert with a peremptory voice called to his own driver to pull up a little closer.

At the sound, Master Savage turned, and the musketeer now came up to the little party in the door.

"Which of you two gentlemen," he said, looking from Rupert Kestyon to Master Legros, "is Master Legros, tailor-in-chief to His Majesty the King of France?"

Papa Legros, hearing his name thus mentioned, instinctively stepped forward, more fussy than ever, poor man, wondering indeed if some fresh misfortune was not coming his way. Rupert, pale to the lips, stood mutely staring at the musketeer.

"By order of His Majesty the King!" resumed the soldier now

226

addressing Legros, and presenting a paper to him, which the worthy tailor, hopelessly bewildered and not a little frightened, now took from him.

"My orders are to intimate to Master Legros, tailor-in-chief to His Majesty the King of France, that he is not to leave his present place of abode without express permission from the Lord Chief Justice of England."

"Qu'est ce qu'il dit?" queried Papa Legros, turning helplessly toward his daughter.

"That we may not leave England just now," she said, feeling not a little bewildered, too, for this was so unexpected. "Let me see that paper, Father dear."

Rupert, whom this incident had thrown into a well-nigh unbearable state of fear, had kept silent all this while, longing yet not daring to question the officer closer. But the latter seemed in no way concerned with him, his errand was apparently solely confined to these peremptory orders to Master Legros.

Rose Marie read the paper through, then she looked inquiringly on Rupert.

"What are we to do, sir," she asked coldly.

"You have no option," he said, as he took hold of her wrist and quietly drew her back under the shadow of the doorway.

"There is no doubt," he continued in an agitated whisper, "that if your father attempts to disobey the order, he would be stopped more forcibly, and his situation would then become more uncomfortable. Does this paper state on what grounds your father is thus forbidden to go away?"

"Yes," she replied calmly; "it says that by order of the king, Master Legros, tailor of Paris, is required to give evidence on behalf of the Crown in the forthcoming trial of the Earl of Stowmaries and Rivaulx, for conspiracy and treason."

"He is summoned as a witness. He has no option—he must stay— they would stop him if he attempted to go," reiterated Rupert Kestyon, whose trembling voice scarce contrived to pass from his dry throat through his parched lips.

"Then with your permission," she rejoined, "I will stay with my father."

"As you please," he said hurriedly.

Rose Marie bent her head in token of farewell. She felt more like a puppet moving and acting mechanically than like a sentient woman. She suffered such an agony of mind and heart at thought of what had occurred, what she visualized and what she guessed, that the mere act of speaking and of moving seemed no part of her present existence. She was called upon to act and to decide for herself and for her father—but as Rupert Kestyon very properly said, there was no option. Nor had Rose Marie anything to fear for her father; it was difficult for her to

227

imagine how the present situation had come about, and why the King of England should desire Master Legros to be a witness for the Crown against the Earl of Stowmaries and Rivaulx, accused of conspiracy and treason, nor did she quite understand what being a witness for the Crown really meant, but for her own part she was conscious of an intense sense of relief when she saw Rupert Kestyon—her husband—turning on his heel, and without looking either to right or left, making his way somewhat hurriedly to his coach.

She went back to her father's side, and taking his arm in order to assure him that all was well, she turned to the musketeer.

"Sir," she said to him, "are there any further orders which you have to transmit to my father?"

"No, Mistress, none," replied the soldier. "Your father must understand that he is free to come and go as he pleases, so long as he remains in the city. Strong measures would only be taken if he attempted to go."

"My father understands all that, sir," she said with a haughty little toss of the head; "though we are strangers, we respect the laws of your country just as we in France would expect you to respect ours. My father understands the order as set forth in this paper, and he will not leave this city until His Majesty the King of England hath no longer any need of his services. Come, Father dear," she whispered, in her own mother tongue and with gentle pressure trying to lead the good man away, "I will explain everything to you when we are alone."

"But thy husband, child!" urged Papa Legros, whose bewilderment had reached its veriest climax. "Thy husband!"

Without giving direct reply, Rose Marie pointed to the coach, just ahead of them both, in the middle of the yard. Papa Legros, following his daughter's glance, saw Rupert Kestyon in the act of stepping into the carriage, and the groom closing the door in after him.

"He goes to France without us, Father dear," she said simply.

And for the first time for many days now, a real smile lit up the girl's eyes, and chased away the miserable, haggard look from her young face.

She bowed graciously to the musketeer officer, who saluted her with utmost deference. Then she led her father away. The soldier's eyes followed her graceful form with undisguised admiration. At the door she turned back and gave him a final little bow of farewell.

For Rose Marie in the midst of her great sorrow and of her agonizing fear, looked on that young musketeer as a deliverer and was grateful to him, too, for the good news which he had brought.

CHAPTER XLII

This year knows nothing of last year
To-morrow has no more to say
To yesterday.

—Swinburne

That same afternoon, and at about the same time as Rupert Kestyon's coach swung out of the gates of the Bell yard, Sir John Ayloffe presented himself at his kinswoman's house in Holborn Row.

He had come in answer to an urgent and peremptory summons, and had made all haste, seeing that he had just heard the news that it was Michael Kestyon who had been arrested for treason, and not the fair Julia's erstwhile faithful adorer, Rupert. Visions of that exceedingly pleasant £12,000 which he had thought were lost to him for ever when Michael obtained the peerage of Stowmaries, once more rose before his mind's eye, surrounded with the golden halo of anticipatory hope.

Of a truth, if Michael was condemned and executed for treason—and there was but little doubt of that, taking the temper of Parliament and people on the subject of the hellish Popish plots—then young Rupert would come into his own again very quickly and there was no reason why the pleasing scheme of the fair Julia's marriage with her faithful admirer should not reach success after all.

To Cousin John's supreme astonishment, however, instead of finding his beautiful cousin in gleeful excitement at the good news, he saw her lying on a sofa in her tiny boudoir with her fair head buried in billows of lace cushions, and on the verge of hysterics.

She was clutching a letter in her hand, and when Cousin John approached her, with that diffidence peculiar to the male creature in face of feminine tears, she held out the paper mutely towards him.

It was a letter signed Rupert Kestyon. Cousin John quickly ran his eye over its contents. In flowery and elegant language and with many reproaches directed at the cruel beauty who that very morning had struck him to the heart at a moment when she believed him to be in the most dire distress, the writer explained that Fate would now part him from his beautiful Julia for ever:

"I go to France this night," he added, "with the wife whom God gave me eighteen years ago, and to whom I now see that 'tis my duty to cleave. You, I feel, did never love me, else you had not sent me that cruel message this morning."

He was his Julia's adoring and ever-faithful servant, but there was no mistaking the tone of the letter: he was leaving her for good and all.

Silently Cousin John folded up the letter and handed it back to his cousin. There was nothing more to be said. He could only console and even in this he was unsuccessful, for his own heart was heavy at thought of that £12,000 which now could never be his.

Mistress Peyton had by the selfishness of her own ambition allowed the trump card in the great gamble of life to slip through her dainty fingers. The incident was closed; the tailor's wench had won the stakes in the end.

No wonder that Julia fell into hysterics; indeed, indeed, Fate's irony had been over-cruel. It seemed as if every one of her schemes turned wantonly to a weapon against her most cherished desires.

Cousin John was vastly puzzled. He could not understand what had induced Rupert to make amends to the wife in order to repudiate whom he had spent a fortune, and lost his all. But when, anon, he heard through public news-criers that Michael had confessed to the charge preferred against him, and when his keen mind began to think over in detail the various events in connection with the arrest, he arrived at a pretty shrewd guess as to what had occurred between the cousins. Remembering the incidents of that memorable evening at St. Denis and Michael's offer to Stowmaries then, he bethought himself that men who are great blackguards are capable of strange things when they love a woman. Whereupon good Sir John shook his head and ceased his wanderings in the realms of conjecture, for he had come across a psychological problem which passed his understanding.

CHAPTER XLIII

Certes his mouth is wried and black
Full little pence be in his sack,
This devil hath him by the back
It is no boot to lie.

—Swinburne

Daniel Pye on that selfsame memorable day was literally floating in a blissful atmosphere of delight.

My lord of Stowmaries had not only been arrested but he had confessed to his guilt; a matter which at first had greatly surprised Master Pye, who had been at great pains to concoct an elaborate lie, only to find through some mysterious accident of Fortune, he must have hit upon the truth.

Of course he did not realise as yet that the man who had been arrested and who had confessed was not the former suitor for Mistress

230

Peyton's hand. He had only heard some pleasant rumours anent the reward which he would get as soon as conviction was obtained against the accused. Many spoke of fifty pounds, others that his reward would be as great as that given to Master Oates: a substantial pension and comfortable lodgings in one of the king's houses.

But the thought of Mistress Peyton's miserable condition of vain regrets and bitter disappointment the while her lover lingered in the Tower, pleased Master Pye as much as that of his own good fortune, nor could he resist the desire to brag of his prowess to those very menials who had witnessed his downfall. There would be no great pleasure in the discomfiture of Mistress Peyton, unless she knew whose was the hand that had dealt the death blow to all her cherished schemes.

Of a truth the lady was staggered when she heard of Daniel Pye's boasts. He had been sitting in the kitchen for the past hour surrounded by a crowd of gaping listeners, and enjoying one of the many fruits of notoriety. The cook had placed a large venison pasty before him, together with a tankard of ale, and lacqueys and wenches were hearing open-mouthed the account of how Master Pye had brought my lord of Stowmaries to disgrace, and that the life of more than one great nobleman lay in the palm of that same Pye's very grimy hand.

Mistress Peyton, when she heard of the man's boasts and of his popularity among her servants, had him incontinently kicked out of the house again, but not before he had told her with insolent spite that she was now paying for the injustice she had perpetrated on a faithful servant close on half a year ago.

To Daniel Pye the awakening from these pleasing dreams came all too soon. That same evening at the tavern in Whitefriars, he gathered the truth from out the conflicting rumours which he heard. It was the new Earl of Stowmaries who had taken upon himself the charge of conspiracy preferred by Master Pye, and 'twas he who had confessed his guilt. What could this mean, and what would be the consequences which would accrue to the informant, to his future reward and future safety through this unexpected turn of affairs?

Master Oates, consulted on the point, was for sticking to the lie on every point. The actual personality of the man could not matter in the least, and since this Earl of Stowmaries actually pleaded guilty to the charge, why then, all was for the best and it was not for Daniel Pye to worry about it all.

Master Tongue—more wary—feared a trap, but his objections were overruled, and on the whole the infamous fraternity decided that confrère Pye must uphold his perjuries to the end, since he would obtain the reward whoever was condemned on his information.

"You need have no fear, good Master," concluded Oates reassuringly; "you'll be believed in any event. Master Bedloe and myself never had any difficulty hitherto, even though at the Stayley trial we got

231

in vast confusion, seeing that we made several slips which could easily have been proved against us, had the judge and jury been so minded. Nay! nay! Do you stick to your story. Since one Lord Stowmaries desires to hang instead of the other, why, let him, so say I."

This cynical speech was, alas, an only too true exposé of the situation. Daniel Pye was almost reassured, and fell to applying himself to making his story more circumstantial. On consultation with his friends it was decided that the recent murder of Sir Edmund Berry Godfrey would be dragged into the indictment. That mysterious crime was indeed a trump card in the hands of the informants. It seemed a pity not to play it when the stakes were as high as they were just now.

Pye therefore prepared himself to state on oath that the murder was freely projected by my lord Stowmaries with the minister of the King of France, in the course of the treasonable interview in Paris.

But even then did the course of this true liar not run altogether smooth, for anon it became generally known that Master Legros, tailor of Paris, and his daughter who was none other than the wife of the dispossessed Lord of Stowmaries, had been compelled to give evidence for the Crown in corroboration of Master Pye's story.

Whereupon the latter fell into a state of agitation worse than before. He stared dry-lipped and wide-eyed at the man who had come in with this news. This was the first intimation which he had that one of his lies at least would find him out. When he had vowed that Master Legros had overheard the treasonable conversation between the Earl of Stowmaries and the minister of the King of France, he had no thought that the tailor would actually be compelled to give testimony, whether he would or no.

Pye turned well-nigh sick at the thought. Dotard though he was, he had no hopes that Master Legros would endorse his lies. Once more he turned to his friends for counsel, and briefly explained to them the terrible plight in which he now found himself.

"Mayhap I'd better disappear," he suggested timorously, "before I am caught for perjury. It means the loss of my right hand and years of imprisonment; mayhap in this case the rope."

"Bah, man, be not such a coward," admonished Oates boldly. He had gone through all the anxieties himself and knew how to make light of them. "'Twas a pity you did drag an alien's name into the case, of course, but—"

"'Twas the magistrate suggested it to me," broke in Pye, who was on the verge of tears; "he said that it would be better if another witness were forthcoming, who also had heard the conversation at the hostelry in Paris. It would strengthen my evidence, so he said."

"But why this French papist?" queried Bedloe with an oath.

"Because the tailor was in deadly enmity with my lord of Stowmaries—with the other one, I mean—and I thought he would help me and gladly too."

232

"And think you he'll turn against you?"

"I fear me that he will," quoth Pye, who truly was in a pitiable condition.

"Then, man, you must change your tactics," now said Oates decisively. "Nay! I repeat, do not be afraid. 'Tis you they will believe, and not the papist tailor or his daughter. What can they say? That they did not hear the treasonable conversation between the accused and the minister of the King of France. Well, what of that? 'Tis but a negation, and no evidence. The Attorney-General will soon upset such feeble testimony. But do you swear that on thinking the matter over you now remember that the tailor and his daughter had already left the hostelry of the 'Rat Mort' when that treasonable consult took place and that you were in my company and not in theirs. Then with one fell swoop do you destroy the whole value of the Legros' evidence, and place yourself once more in an unassailable position, for I too can swear then that I was with you at the time, and heard the whole conversation—so be that you are prepared to share the reward which you will get with me," concluded the scoundrel with earnest emphasis.

Daniel Pye had no option. Of a truth he was not quite such a hardened sinner as these professional liars who had thriven and prospered under their organized perjuries for close on half a year.

The whole of the information against Lord Stowmaries was therefore gone through all over again, nor was there any fear that this change of front would in any way prejudice the noble jury against the informant. In Coleman's case and in that of Stailey, and alas, in that of many others, the infamous witnesses contradicted themselves and one another to an extent which makes the modern historian gasp, when he has to put it on record that men in England were condemned to death wholesale, on evidence that was as flimsy as it was false.

Master Pye, once more at peace, therefore, with his prospects and with himself, learned his new lesson with diligence. But Master Oates was firm on one point, and that was on his share in the coming reward. Pye demurred for a long time. Emboldened by the encouragement of his friends, he now thought that he could carry the whole business through alone.

Ultimately it was decided that Master Oates was to receive £5 of the reward, provided he swore that on a certain day in April he too was present at the tavern of the "Rat Mort" in Paris when my lord of Stowmaries discussed with the minister of the King of France the terms of the shameful treaty whereby King Charles was to be murdered, the Duke of York be placed on the throne of England and the latter country sold to the French and to the Pope of Rome.

233

CHAPTER XLIV

For Death is of an hour, and after death
Peace!

—Swinburne

The news that Michael Kestyon—the hero of one of the most exciting adventures in the history of gallantry, the man who less than twenty-four hours ago had by the king's mandate obtained the titles and estates for which he had fought for over ten years—the news that he had been arrested for treason connected with the hellish Popish plot, horrified and astonished all London.

It seemed incredible that a man whose romantic personality had charmed all the women and even fascinated the king, could lend himself to such base treachery as to sell his country to the foreigners, and to incite others to poison the merry monarch who even at that moment had with one stroke of the pen seen that justice was done to the miserable reprobate.

Such is popularity! Michael, who a couple of days ago was the idol of society, the cynosure of all eyes at assemblies or in the playhouse, on whom the women smiled, and whom the men were proud to know, Michael now was naught but an abominable traitor, for whom hanging and the rack were more suitable than the block to which he was entitled by virtue of his newly acquired dignities.

And there was no doubt as to his villainies: the infamous blackguard had confessed, even at the time of his arrest, which no doubt had taken him wholly by surprise, and thus forced on an avowal which would expedite the trial and give every one a chance of seeing the traitor's head on Tyburn gate before many days were over.

Excitement and terror had by this time so taken hold of the people of England that all sense of justice had gone hopelessly astray, and there was but little chance of any man—however high placed he might be, however upright and loyal had been his conduct throughout his life—escaping condemnation and death, once the army of false informers and perjurers had singled him out for attack.

As for Michael, everything was against him from the first. His former dissolute life, his long wanderings abroad, where he was supposed to have imbibed all the imaginary desires of the foreigners to turn England into an obedient vassal of France and Rome, also his sudden accession to wealth and the rumours anent that certain adventure, the details of which grew both in confusion, in mystery and even in horror as they were passed from mouth to mouth.

When the fact that the young girl-wife of the dispossessed Earl of Stowmaries would be one of the witnesses for the Crown became known, gossip became still more wild. Interest in that former adventure increased an hundred fold, and the news did of a truth give verisimilitude to the most weird conjecture. The words black magic and witchcraft were soon freely bandied about. Michael Kestyon was no longer an ordinary plotter, but the veriest anti-Christ himself, who was in league with the Pope of Rome to ruin England and to bring forth her submission by such means even as the Lord employed against the Egyptians in favour of the Israelites. Only in this case, the devil was to be the instrument whereby the ten plagues were to be hurled on this defenceless isle.

There was to be a plague of locusts and one of rats, the waters of the Thames would turn to corroding acid and the miscreant Earl of Stowmaries had promised to give the devil the blood of every noble virgin in England as payment for his satanic help.

Had we not the testimony of sane-minded men and women who lived at the time, and who witnessed every phase of that amazing frenzy which swept over England during these awful years, we could not believe that the people of this country, usually so gifted with sound minds and above all with a sense of justice and of tolerance, could thus have rushed headlong into an abyss of maniacal fanaticism which hath for ever remained a blot upon the history of the seventeenth century.

There is a curious letter extant written by Mistress Julia Peyton in her usual almost illegible scrawl and embellished by her more than quaint spelling; it was addressed to her cousin, Sir John Ayloffe, a week or so before the trial, and in it she says:

"I wod Like to know the truth about this Story wich sayth that my lord Stowmaries wil be acused of witchcraft. They do sa he praktised Black Magic, and tried to kil the talor's daughter, so to use her blood for his Arts and his Inkantations. She being a Virgin. They do sa also that her Evidens against Him wil vastly startle Every one. As for me I tak vast Interest in the reprobate and do wish him well at his Trial. The husband of the talor's wench is naut to me. I do not desire to see him become Earl of Stowmaries, but rather that Michael be suksesful."

What other schemes the fair lady now nurtured in her heart we know from the fact that she made several attempts to have access to the prisoner, all of which were unsuccessful, despite the fact that she used the influence of her other admirers to effect her ends, whilst on one occasion she wrote to Cousin John:

"An Michael doth sukseed in getting an acquittal, I pra you bring him to my house forthwith afterwards. Remember good coz that I promisd you twelve thousand pounds if I do marry the Earl of Stowmaries."

But beyond these secret wishes of the fair beauty, and mayhap a sigh of regret or so from pretty lips for the handsome adventurer, popular feeling was raging highly against the accused, and many chroniclers aver that among the many conspirators who were brought to these shameful trials during this time, against none was there so much venomous hatred as there was against Michael Kestyon.

There is this to be remembered—though truly 'tis but weak palliation for the disgraceful antagonism displayed against the accused—that this was the first instance where a man so highly placed as was the Earl of Stowmaries was directly implicated in the plot; he was a sop thrown to the rampant radicalism of the anti-Church party as well as to its intolerant fanaticism.

Public sympathy on the other hand had at once gone out to the dispossessed Earl of Stowmaries, whom the traitor had tried to rob of his wife and had effectually succeeded in robbing of his inheritance.

But retribution for the guilty and compensation for the innocent had come together hand in hand. Michael Kestyon would hang, of course, whereupon the only rightful Lord of Stowmaries would once more come back into his own. The latter with commendable delicacy had left London directly his cousin's arrest became known; he would not stay to gloat over his enemy's downfall.

In fact, for the moment everything that Rupert did was right and proper and worthy of sympathy, and everything that Michael had ever said and done and all that he had never said or done was held up against him by all those who awhile ago were ready to acclaim him as a friend.

Of all these rumours Michael himself knew nothing. On his arrest he had at once pleaded guilty, hoping thereby to expedite his trial, and to curtail the time during which he would have to linger in prison. Echoes of the turmoil which was raging in the capital did reach him from time to time. The murder of Sir Edmund Berry Godfrey had sent raging fanaticism to boiling point. Needless to say that here was another crime to fasten on the already overburdened shoulders of the accused.

All these fresh outbursts of hatred and injustice, however, left Michael cold and indifferent, even when through a subordinate he heard the amazing story of how he was supposed to have tried to murder his cousin's wife by means of black magic, he had nothing but an almost humorous smile for the quaint monstrosity of the suggestion.

He quickly tired of prison life and though there was no pang of suspense connected with it, for the issue was of course a foregone conclusion, yet he fretted at the delay which the importance of his case had brought about in the otherwise simple machinery of summary justice.

CHAPTER XLV

Her game in thy tongue is called Life
As ebbs thy daily breath;
When she shall speak, thou'lt learn her tongue
And know she calls it death.

—*Dante Gabriel Rossetti*

For the rest, 'tis in the domain of history. Michael could have been tried by his peers had he so desired it. The few friends who rallied round him urged him to demand the right, but when we remember that in pledging his life to his cousin, his one wish was speedy condemnation and summary death, we cannot be astonished that he refused to be tried by those who might have been lenient toward one of themselves.

Among his peers, too, the fact would of a surety have come to light that he did not belong to the Catholic branch of the Kestyons, that he himself was a member of the Established Church, which—as all these trials, alas, really amounted to religious persecution—would almost certainly have obtained an acquittal.

Parliament—still suffering severely of its no-Popery fit—demanded that the traitor be tried as a common criminal before the King's Bench and required the king to issue a special commission that the day might be fixed as soon as may be.

The accused was of course allowed no counsel, and no defence save what he could say on his own behalf. Nor did he know the precise words of the indictment, or what special form the informant's lies had taken.

He did not know exactly what he was supposed to have said or done, he could only vaguely guess from what he knew of similar trials that had gone before.

The trial of Michael Kestyon, Earl of Stowmaries and Rivaulx, did, we know, take place before the King's Bench on the twenty-first day of November, 1678. Lord Chief Justice Scroggs presided, and the Attorney-General, Sir William Jones, once the friend of Michael, addressed the jury for the Crown.

We also know that the court sat in Westminster Hall for the occasion, as it was expected that a very large concourse of ladies and gentlemen would desire to be present. As a matter of fact, the élite of London society did forego on that occasion the pleasures of The Mall, and of the playhouse in order to witness a spectacle which would rouse the jaded senses of these votaries of fashion and whip up their blasé emotions more than any comedy of Mr. Dryden or the late Master Shakespeare could do.

This would be a tragedy far more moving, far more emotional than that of Hamlet or of Romeo and Juliet, for the element of romance mingled agreeably with that of crime, and the personality of the accused was one that aroused the most eager interest.

Outside, a gloomy November drizzle enveloped London with its clammy shroud. Ladies and gentlemen arrived in their chairs or their glass coaches, wrapped to the eyes in mantles and hoods of fur. There was a goodly array of musketeers guarding the approach to the Hall, and a small company of the trained bands of London lined the way from Whitehall to Westminster, for it was pretty well known that His Majesty would come—in strict incognito—to see the last of his nine days' favourite, who during the last few months had made Mistress Gwynne sigh very significantly, and caused Lady Castlemaine to make invidious comparisons between the gallant bearing of the romantic adventurer and the mincing manners of the gentlemen of the Court.

The less exalted spectators of to-day's pageant were being kept outside and pushed well out of the way by the soldiery; nevertheless, they stood about patiently—ankle deep in the mud of the roadway, their sad-coloured doublets getting soaked beneath the persistent drizzle and exhaling a fetid odour which made the street and the open place seem more dismal and humid than usual.

The men pressed to the front, leaving the women to shift for themselves, to see as best they could. It was pre-eminently a spectacle for men, since it carried with it its own element of danger. For, look you, the Papists would be mightily rampant on this occasion, and who knows but that a gigantic conspiracy was afoot to blow up the Lord's House of Parliament, which would sit this day to try the arch-conspirator.

Recollections of the Gunpowder Plot caused men to curse loudly, and to grasp with firm hand the useful flail safely hid inside the doublet: a good protection against personal attack, but alas, useless if the whole of Westminster was really undermined with powder.

The 'prentices, ever to the fore, had taken French leave to-day. At certain risk of castigation to-morrow they deserted work with one accord and were at the best posts of observation, long before the more sober folk had thought to leave their beds. They wriggled their meagre bodies between the very legs of the soldiery, like so many lizards in search of sunshine, until they had conquered their places of vantage in the foreground whence they would presently see the prisoner when he stepped out of the vehicle which would bring him from the Tower.

In the meanwhile the crowd wiled away the time by watching the arrival of the grand folk, and noting their names and quality as they descended from coach and chaise.

"That's my lord of Rochester."

"And this my lady Evelyn."

"I vow 'tis Master Pepys himself."

"And his lady, too."

"'Tis His Grace of Norfolk!"

Whereupon since the duke was a well-known Papist, there were hoots and hisses and cries of "The stake for heretics!" in which even the musketeers joined.

The informers came together and were vigorously cheered and loudly acclaimed.

"An Oates! An Oates! A Bedloe! Hurrah for the saviours of the nation!"

Daniel Pye, a little anxious, was being upheld by his friend Tongue, who kept up a running flow of encouraging words which he poured forth into the other man's ear. He not being known to the mob remained unnoticed. As the time drew nigh for making his lying statements more public, the East Anglian peasant felt his courage oozing down into his boots. Bedloe and Oates, who had gone through similar experiences several times now, added their own encouragement to that expressed by Tongue.

"No one will worry you," said Bedloe loftily; "they'll believe every word you say. Only stick to your story, man, and never hesitate. They can't contradict you: no one else was there to see."

Although the gloom outside had almost changed day into evening, yet on entering the great hall wherein a very few lamps flickered near the centre dais, Daniel Pye could see nothing of his surroundings. He was glad that Oates himself took him by the arm, and piloted him through the great hall toward a side door immediately behind the bench and which gave on the room that had been assigned to the witnesses.

A goodly number of ladies and gentlemen wore masks when they arrived, and among these was a man obviously young and of assured position, for his step was firm and his movements like those of one accustomed to have his own way in the world. He was dressed in rough clothes of sad-coloured material, but there was nothing of the menial about his person as he presented his paper of admission to the most exclusive corner of the hall.

Here he sat himself down in a dark recess beneath the sill of the great mullioned window, nor did he remove his mask as almost every one else had done. Had not the crowd all round him been deeply engrossed in its own excitement no doubt that some one would have challenged and mayhap recognised the solitary figure.

But as it was, no one took notice of him. Rupert Kestyon—like the criminal who cannot resist the impulse of once more revisiting the scene of his crime—had returned to London to see the final act of the great tragedy, wherein he himself was playing such a sorry part.

Not that Rupert had any fear that matters would not turn out just as Michael had mapped them out. He knew his kinsman far too well to

239

imagine for a moment that he would lift a finger to save the life which he had bartered for his cousin's loyalty to the tailor's daughter.

But in Paris, whilst waiting in seclusion and inactivity, the moment when—the tragedy being over—he could once more resume the more pleasing comedy of life, he felt an irresistible longing to see the fall of that curtain, to be present when Fate dealt him his last trump-card, the final sacrifice of the man who stood in the way of his own advancement.

Therefore he sat there in the corner, solitary and watchful, noting the arrival of the spectators, the appearance of the men of law, the whole paraphernalia of justice which was about to crush an innocent man.

The hall by now was packed to overflowing; to right and left temporary seats had been erected and covered with crimson cloth, forming an amphitheatre which accommodated over a thousand people, amongst whom were many that bore historic names, as well as the gayer crowd that formed the Court set.

Vast as was the room, it had already become insufferably hot; ladies plied their fans vigorously, whilst the men, worried with their heavy perruques, became restless and morose. On the right hand side, and somewhat in advance of the rest of the seats, a few more comfortable chairs had been disposed. Here sat a man dressed in sober black, with dark perruque pushed impatiently off his high forehead, and shifty, mistrustful-looking eyes wandering over the sea of faces all around him. To right and left of him ladies whispered and chatted, trying to bring a smile to the pinched lips, and not succeeding, for the man in the black surcoat was moody to-day, anxious, too, and vastly dissatisfied with himself, which is ever an uncomfortable state of mind. He had entered the Hall almost unobserved by the crowd outside, stepping out of a closed coach in no ways different to others that had driven up before. He had worn a mask when he arrived and only removed it when he was already seated. Several people recognised him then, but what cheering there came from the more brilliant members of this promiscuous throng was quickly repressed.

Despite the many supposed attempts on the life of the king, he was far from popular just now. Conscious of this, he frowned when he realised that—though he was recognised by many—yet he was acclaimed only by a very few.

Already the jury were seated and Sir Cresswell Levins was sorting his papers, and incidentally chatting with the Attorney-General. And now from outside came a muffled sound, like unto great breakers rolling into shore; distant at first, it gradually drew nearer, drawing strength as it approached. Soon through it there came, striking sharply on the ear, the stamping of horses' hoofs on the cobblestones of the road, and the creaking of heavy wheels through the mud. The sound of rolling waves turned to one which came from hundreds of human lips—

240

hisses and groans were distinctly heard; shouts of execration, with here and there a blasphemous oath loudly uttered against the cursed Papists.

The prisoner had arrived.

Inside the Hall all necks were craned to catch the first glimpse of the man who was destined mayhap not to leave this place save with the axe suspended over his head.

The romantic tales which had clustered around the personality of Michael Kestyon, the horrible suggestions of unavowable deeds, of black magic and devilish incantations, had borne fruit. Though eyes were fixed with eager curiosity on the man as he entered, though many a pleasing shudder ran along white plump shoulders as this confederate of Satan passed so closely by, there was not a single demonstration of sympathy on his behalf.

The women whispered:

"He is goodly to look on!" and took stock of the prisoner's bearing, the upright carriage of his handsome head, the quiet look of splendid aloofness with which he regarded his surroundings.

Whereupon the men retorted gruffly:

"The emissaries of the devil are always made handsome in the eyes of others. Satan arranges it so, else they would have no power."

Following on the prisoner's entrance, the great doors of the Hall had been closed, whereupon the noise outside became quite deafening. The hoots and hisses, the shouts of execration, were still apparent but they mingled now with the clash of arms, the tramping of many feet, and loudly repeated groans of agony. The mob, robbed of its spectacle, had turned restive, the men broke through the lines of the soldiery and made an effort to rush the gates of the Hall. From the officers came quick words of command, rallying their lines from where they stretched toward White Hall.

A few heavy blows, well aimed and vigorously dealt, with the butt end of the muskets, a few bodies trampled beneath horses' hoofs, some broken heads and shattered limbs, and the mob sobered down, withdrew grumbling and cursing, but understanding that the great pageant within was for their betters and not for them.

During the turmoil the Lord Chief Justice had entered and the prisoner had been led to the bar; he had been made to hold up his right hand whilst he was told why he had been brought here, and why he was made to stand his trial. Being a peer, the Chamberlain of the Tower stood beside him holding the axe.

Michael silently did all that he was bidden to do. The proceedings had no interest for him. Of a truth he had been more than satisfied if the more barbarous justice of two centuries ago had been meted out to him. An accusation, a brief interrogation, mayhap an unpleasant quarter of an hour in the torture chamber, then the block! How much more simple, how much more easy to endure than this sea of curious

241

faces, this paraphernalia of gorgeously-clad judge and of lawyers assembled there with the pre-conceived and firm determination to condemn the accused whatever might betide.

The while Sir Cresswell Levins opened the case, admonishing the jury to do their duty by the prisoner at the bar, Michael with indifferent eyes scanned the faces all around him. He saw Mistress Julia Peyton in the front rank of the spectators clad in exquisite pearl grey silk, her beautiful shoulders but thinly veiled beneath filmy folds of delicate lace. He saw the piquant face of Mistress Gwynne, the haughty figure of Lady Castlemaine. Most of the women as they encountered his look blushed to meet those dark eyes, which looked almost unnaturally large in the face rendered thin and pale through the nerve-racking experiences of the past few weeks.

Anon Michael's eyes met the restless ones of the king. He bent his head with deep respect, for he had not yet learned to despise the man to whom he owed all that he had, all that he was now sacrificing in order that his snowdrop might find happiness again.

Charles Stuart turned his head away with a sigh. All that was good and noble and kind in him went out to that man, in whose innocence he firmly believed but whom he found was well-nigh intolerable.

But Michael now was obliged to pull his senses back to the exigencies of the moment and he pleaded "Guilty!" in a calm and steady voice. He had not even grasped the full meaning of the indictment read out at full length by the Attorney-General. All he knew was that he was accused of having plotted to murder the king, whom he revered, and of having sold his country to the head of a Church to which he did not happen to belong.

Michael desired his own condemnation. He was here solely for that, in order that the man whom his ice maiden loved with that cold, passionless heart of hers might give her all that she wanted, all that was her due. But the inactivity of the moment was so terrible to bear. To a man accustomed to rule his own destiny, to choose his own path, and to say to Fate: "This will I do, and thou art my slave!" to a man of that stamp the present situation was well-nigh intolerable.

The long-drawn-out speech of the Attorney-General, the platitudes addressed to the accused by the Lord Chief Justice, his own answers mechanically given soon left him wandering into the realms of unreality.

The heat in the room pressed upon his temples like a monster weight of lead. Michael, gazing with eyes that saw not on the solemn scene in which he was the chief personage, soon fell into a kind of torpor akin to a trance. Ghost-like forms clad in crimson robes, grinning faces with perruques awry, began to dance before his fevered fancy. They twirled and turned, round and round the flickering flames of the lamps, until these were magnified an hundredfold and multiplied innumerably. Now faces and forms disappeared: there were only a thousand millions of eyes that blinked and blinked, the while the lamps were will-o'-the-wisps, glowworms with monstrous shining horns that stood upright on iron tails and joined in the wild saraband which had transformed the solemn Hall of Westminster into the precincts of Hell.

Then gradually all the grinning faces, all the glowing monstrosities and witch-like forms became a gigantic circle of ruddy light wherein flames flickered at intervals like unto a burning halo which seared the eyes of the beholder. And right in the very centre of that transcendent glow two faces appeared, white and ghost-like, spirits surely from a world beyond.

Michael knew that he was dreaming, his temples and pulses were throbbing. He had lost count of space and of time. He just breathed and held himself upright and no more; living had become an unknown thing to him. But the faces were there still, in the centre of the glowing halo, and they were those of his beautiful snowdrop and of Master Legros, tailor to the King of France.

CHAPTER XLVI

And now she spoke as when
The stars sang in their spheres.
—*Dante Gabriel Rossetti*

His snowdrop was gazing straight at him from out great, wide eyes, her lips were parted as if she meant to speak, and her hand lay on the arm of her father, good Papa Legros, dressed all in black, and above whose sombre surcoat shone a kindly face almost distorted by its expression of anxiety and from which ran streams of perspiration which the poor man wiped off ever and anon with a bright-coloured handkerchief.

With a mechanical movement Michael passed his hand across his eyes. His brain returned from its long wandering in the realm of dreamland; the light ceased to flicker, the sea of grinning faces receded into the darkness. Michael now only saw Rose Marie. The devilish visions had been transformed into peaceful dreams of Heaven.

Though his mind—still feverish and numb—refused to believe that she was really there, yet his eyes took in every tiny detail of the golden picture which they saw.

There were the tiny curls that, ever rebellious, would break through the confines of the lace cap and flutter tantalisingly round her ear; there was the little mole just above the lip, which gave the perfect mouth, that otherwise had been accounted too serious, an exquisite air of piquancy; there was the delicate rise of the throat, peeping above the lace kerchief, a god-like snare wherein he had once dared to hope that his lips would be entrapped.

And all the while that Michael looked on his beloved, Daniel Pye was busy with his perjuries, and Master Oates stood up to corroborate these. Once or twice the Lord Chief Justice had turned to the accused, expecting a contradiction of such obvious lies. But the only word that ever escaped the latter's lips came mechanically as from one who had learned a lesson by heart.

"I am guilty—what these men say is true."

Once the Attorney-General had spoken quite irritably:

"The prisoner's attitude, my lord," he said, "is one of contempt for this Court. He must be made to answer more fully the charges that are preferred against him."

"Then 'tis for you to question him," retorted the Lord Chief Justice drily.

Emboldened by Michael's attitude of passive acquiescence, Pye and Oates surpassed themselves. Their story gained in detail, in circumstantial broiderings under cross-examination. Once or twice their imagination and impudence carrying them too far, they palpably contradicted one another. A man's voice then rose from the midst of the spectators: "These men are accursed liars!"

The voice was authoritative and loud, as of a man accustomed to be obeyed. And no one cried "Hush!" to the remark, since it came from royal lips.

After an examination which we know lasted nearly an hour, the two witnesses were dismissed. They left the great hall together and walked with an assured air of satisfaction across to the small room beyond the bench, where they were bidden to wait in case they were required again. To a sanely judicial mind the only point which would present itself in the evidence of these miscreants as being uncontradicted and unquestionably established by them, was that the treasonable converse between the accused and a minister of the King of France did take place at the tavern of the "Rat Mort" in Paris in the evening of the nineteenth day of April of this same year.

Beyond that it was a tangle which Michael, had he chosen, could easily have unravelled in his own favour. But this he did not mean to do; he was only anxious for the end.

While the lying informer spoke of that same nineteenth day of April his thoughts flew back on the sable wings of a dead past to all the memories that clung to that day.

The religious ceremony at St. Gervais, the dance on the dusty floor of the tailor's back shop, the ride through the darkness along the lonely road with his beloved clinging to him, the while his arm ached with an exquisite sense of numbness under the delicious burden which it bore.

These men spoke of the evening of that nineteenth day of April! Oh, the remembrance of every hour, every minute which the date recalled!

The darkened room in the old inn, the streaks of moonbeam which kissed the gold of her hair, the April breeze which caused her curls to flutter, and the sighing of the reeds and young acacia boughs like spirit whisperings that presaged impending doom!

Her voice, her eyes, so tender, for that one brief day! Would not the remembrance of it be graven on his heart when after so much joy, such hopeless abnegation, it would cease to beat at last.

Of a truth can you wonder that Michael was impatient for the end? He had seen his snowdrop through the gossamer veil of a day-dream across the crowded court and the vision had caused him to realise more fully than he had ever done before how impossible life would be without her.

Thank God, that he had pledged his life to his cousin! Thank God, that Rupert had accepted the pledge, and gave in exchange for the worthless trifle, his own loyalty to Rose Marie.

Then why so many parleyings, such long, empty talk, such tortuous questionings? Michael had pleaded guilty and almost asked for death.

Even as with an impatient sigh of intense weariness he had for the twentieth time that day spoken his mechanical "Guilty!" there was general movement amongst the spectators. Imagine a hive of bees swarming round their queen: the women leaned forward clutching their fans, forgetting the heat and the discomfort of those long hours. The men put up spy-glasses the better to see what went on in the centre of the stage, the while a murmur of excitement ran right through the assembly.

Papa Legros was being led by a gorgeously-clad usher in the direction of the bar, opposite to the prisoner, whilst his daughter walked by his side.

Dormant attention had indeed been roused, necks were craned to get a better view of the interesting witnesses.

"She is the wife of my lord of Stowmaries," came in whispers all round the hall, like the swish of the wind through poplar trees.

"What—of the prisoner?"

"No! No! Of the man whom he dispossessed and who will be Lord of Stowmaries again, once this man is hanged."

"She is very young."

"Ay—a girl-wife. 'Tis her whom the accused tried to murder, so that he might offer her blood in sacrifice to the devil."

But this statement obtained little credence now.

"The accused does not look like a wizard, or an emissary of the devil," commented the ladies.

"Yet the girl is there to testify against him."

"That is because she must hate him so. She is the wife of the man whom the accused hath dispossessed. They say she dearly loves her husband, yet did the accused try and steal her from him."

"She will make a handsome Countess of Stowmaries anon," quoth Lord Rochester with his wonted cynicism, and speaking in the ear of his royal master, "What think you, sire?"

"Odd's fish!" retorted Charles Stuart. "If she proved as big a liar as these damnable informers then is there no virtue writ plainly on any woman's face."

There certainly was something infinitely pathetic in the appearance of father and daughter: he in his clothes of deep black, and with the tears of anxiety and perturbation rolling slowly down his cheeks. She fragile and slender, with pale, delicate face and eyes wherein girlish timidity still fought against a woman's resolve.

No wonder that for the moment every unkind comment was hushed. The Countess of Stowmaries—as she was already universally called—seemed to command respect as well as sympathy. With a great show of kindness, the Lord Chief Justice himself spoke directly to the two witnesses, asking their names and quality, as was required for form's sake.

Rose Marie now no longer looked at the accused. She stood beside her father, tall and stately as the water-lilies to which the man who loved her so ardently had once compared her. The mud of the world had left her unsmirched; she carried her head high, for the slimy tendrils of men's unavowable passions, of trickery, of lies and deceit had not reached the high altitude whereon her purity sat enthroned.

Her father was the witness called on behalf of the Crown; he had made his statement on oath, and stood here now to repeat it before all the world. His daughter was his interpreter, since he was unacquainted with the English language.

Her voice was clear and firm as in answer to the questions put to her by the Lord Chief Justice she gave her father's humble name and quality and then her own as Mistress Kestyon, wife of Rupert Kestyon, erstwhile known as my Lord of Stowmaries and Rivaulx.

246

CHAPTER XLVII

Love that is root and fruit of terrene things,
Love that the whole world's waters shall not drown
The whole world's fiery forces not burn down.

—Swinburne

Michael could scarce believe his own eyes. The reality had brought him back with irresistible force from his day-dream to the tangible situation of the moment.

Papa Legros was here with Rose Marie. So much was true; that was no longer in the domain of dreams. They had been brought here to add their testimony to the lies spoken by the informers.

Torturing devils, whispering in Michael's ears, made this hellish suggestion. With it came an intensity of bitterness. He had thought that the old man loved him, yet his appearance here and now seemed like petty vengeance wreaked on a fallen enemy.

Michael ground his teeth, trying to drive these whispering devils away. He would not—even at a moment such as this—lose if only for an instant his perfect faith in the purity of the woman he loved. If she stood here, it was for a noble purpose. What that purpose could be, not even the mad conjectures of his own fevered fancy could contrive to imagine; his veins were throbbing and he could not think. Only the puzzle confronted him now, mocking his own obtuseness; the laggard brain, that had suffered so long, and was now dormant, unable to guess the riddle which could not be aught save one of life or death.

All he did know was that Rose Marie was standing there before all these people, she the very essence of purity and of truth, and that she was being made to swear that she would speak the truth. Was this not a vile mockery, masters, seeing that naught but what was true could ever fall from her lips?

Now the Attorney-General was questioning her father, with thin, sarcastic lips curled in a smile. Rose Marie replied calmly and firmly, interpreting her father's answers, not looking once on the accused, but almost always straight before her, save when she threw a look of encouragement on good Papa Legros, who then would pat her hand with unaffected tenderness.

"And you were present, so the other witness swore in his original information, on the 19th day of April, with him at the tavern of the 'Rat Mort' in Paris, and you did on that same evening hear the accused hold converse with one who was minister to His Majesty the King of France?"

The Attorney-General's voice was metallic, trenchant, like a knife; it reached the furthermost distance of the great hall and grated unpleasantly on Michael's ear. He hated to see his beloved standing there before that gaping crowd. He cursed the enforced inactivity which made of him a helpless log when with every fibre within him he longed to take her in his arms and carry her away to a secluded spot where impious eyes were not raised to her snow-white robes.

"My lord," he interposed loudly, "I have confessed to my guilt. What this witness may have to say can have naught to do with the plain fact. I am guilty. I have confessed. Cannot your lordship have mercy and pass sentence as soon as may be?"

"Prisoner at the bar," rejoined the Lord Chief Justice, "'tis not for you to dictate the procedure of justice. 'Tis my duty to hear every witness who hath testimony to lay before this court. You have confessed your guilt, 'tis true, but on such confession the law will not hold you guilty, until you have so been proved; and for the sake of the witnesses who have testified against you, as well as for the sake of justice, we must obtain corroboration of their statements."

Then he turned once more to Papa Legros and graciously bade him to make answer to the questions put by the Attorney-General.

Rose Marie, before she spoke, turned and looked on Michael. Their eyes met across that vast assembly and as in one great vivid flash, each read in those of the other the sublime desire for complete sacrifice.

In a moment Michael understood; in that one brief flash and through the unexplainable telepathy which flew from her soul to his, the truth had burst upon him with the appalling force of absolute conviction.

She, the woman whom he adored, who was a saint exalted in his mind above every other woman on earth, she was about to throw her fair fame, her honour, her purity as a plaything to this crowd of hyena-like creatures, who would fall on the tattered remnants of her reputation and tear its last fragments to shreds.

This she meant to do. This was the grim and sublime answer to the riddle which had so puzzled Michael when first he saw his Rose Marie in this court. She meant to give her honour for his life. She loved him and came here to offer her all—her own, her father's good name, so that he—Michael—should be saved.

The terrible, awful agony of this thought, the mad, tumultuous joy! Here was the moment at last—the one second in the illimitable cycle of time—when if there be mercy in Heaven or on earth, the kiss of Death should bring peace to the miserable wastrel who had in this brief flash of understanding tasted an eternity of happiness.

She loved him and was here to save him! But Heavens above, at what a cost!

He looked round him like some caged beast, determined at all hazards to make a mad dash for liberty.

It could not be! No, no; it should not be! Surely God in Heaven could not allow this monstrous sacrifice; surely the thunderbolts from above would come down crashing in the midst of this mocking, jeering assembly before his exquisite snowdrop dragged her immaculate white skirts in the mire.

What he did or how he fought, Michael himself scarcely knew. What was he but one small, helpless atom in this avalanche of callous lawmakers? All that he did know was that with all the strength at his command he protested his guilt again and again, imploring judgment, uttering wild words of treason that might secure his own immediate condemnation.

"My lord, my lord," he cried loudly, "in the name of Heaven as you yourself hope for justice hereafter, listen not to these witnesses. I swear to you that they will only confirm what the others have said. I am guilty—thrice guilty, I say—yes, I plotted to murder the king. I plotted to sell England to France and to Rome. I admit the truth of every word the informers have uttered. I am guilty, my lord—guilty—judgment, in Heaven's name—I ask for judgment."

"Prisoner at the bar, I command you to be silent."

Silent, silent when so monstrous a thing was about to happen! As well command the giant waves lashed into madness by the fury of the wind to be silent when they break upon the rocks. The Lord Chief Justice commanded the musketeers to restrain this madman, to force him to hold his tongue, to drown his voice with the clatter of their arms.

The spectators stared aghast, women gasped with fear, the men were awed despite themselves in the presence of this raging torrent of a man's unbridled passion.

The general impression which this scene had created was of course that the prisoner was dreading some awful revelation which these two witnesses might make. He was avowing his guilt, therefore he did not hope to escape death; once more the superstitious dread of witchcraft rose in the minds of all. Was the accused—already practically condemned for treason—in fear that his death would mean the stake rather than the block?

A close phalanx gathered round the person of the king, who with a cynical smile was watching the confusion which occurred round the august majesty of this court. But he waved aside those who would have stood between him and Michael.

"He'll quieten down anon," he said simply, "and if I mistake not, gentlemen, we shall then learn a lesson which throughout our lives we are not like to forget."

Was it accident or design? Had Michael fought like a madman, or had his brain merely given way under an agonizing moral blow. Certain it is that suddenly he felt a terrible pain in his head, his senses were reeling, his tongue, parched and dry, refused to obey the dictates of his

249

will that bade it protest again and again, until his heart could no longer beat, until his last breath had left his body.

He tottered and would have fallen but for strong arms that held him up. He felt that irons were being placed on his wrists, that four pairs of hands gripped his arms and shoulders so that he could no longer move. The pain in his head was well-nigh intolerable; he closed his eyes in the vain effort not to swoon.

It was the butt end of a musket that had rendered him helpless. From the lips of many spectators came loud invectives against the miscreant who had dared to strike a peer; vaguely reaching the half-unconscious brain came the sound of voices, also the cry from a woman's throat, heard above all the others, uttered with an intensity of agony even as he fell.

With Michael's half-swoon the turmoil had somewhat subsided. The musketeers round him, terrified at their comrade's act, were bathing the prisoner's head with water hastily obtained. The spectators, deeply moved—unable to understand the inner meaning of the strange scene which they had just witnessed—were talking excitedly to one another.

Conjectures, wild guesses, flew from mouth to mouth.

And in the midst of all this noise, and of all the confusion, Rose Marie had remained calm, holding her father by the hand. Only when the dastardly blow felled the fighting lion down, then only did a cry of pain escape her trembling lips. Now when comparative stillness reigned around her, she once more faced the judges. Michael was now helpless, she could offer up her sacrifice in peace.

The Lord Chief Justice repeated his question and even as he began speaking complete silence fell upon all.

"Will you swear before this court that on the evening of the nineteenth day of April you were present with Master Pye and Doctor Oates at the hostelry of the 'Rat Mort' in Paris and there on that same evening did hear the accused holding converse with a minister of the King of France?"

"No, milor," replied Rose Marie firmly; "my father was not present on the evening of the nineteenth day of April in the tavern of the 'Rat Mort' in Paris, nor in any other tavern, nor did the accused hold converse on that same evening with a minister of the King of France. And this do I swear in my father's name and mine own."

"But," interposed the Attorney-General in his dry, sarcastic tone, "the former witnesses have sworn that you were there present together with them, when the converse did take place."

"Those witnesses have lied, my lord," spoke Rose Marie.

"Take care, Mistress," admonished the Lord Chief Justice, "you do bring a grave charge against those witnesses."

"A grave charge yet a true one, my lord. Yet what they have sworn to is both false and grave."

250

"Yet are you sworn in as a witness for the Crown."

"And as a witness for the Crown do I speak," rejoined Rose Marie simply, "for the Crown of England is the crown of truth, and my father and I are here for the truth."

"Which mayhap will bear fuller investigation," quoth Sir William Jones with a sneer.

"As full an one as you desire, my lords."

"Then pray, Mistress, since you and your father do swear that you were not at the hostelry of the 'Rat Mort' in Paris on the evening of the nineteenth of April, how comes it that you can state so positively that the accused did not then and at that place hold treasonable converse with the minister of the King of France, as the other witnesses have testified?"

Rose Marie paused before she answered; it almost seemed as if she wished to wait until all disturbing sounds had died down in the vast hall, so that her fresh and firm voice should ring clearly from end to end.

Then she spoke, looking straight at the judge:

"Because of the truth of the statement, my lord," she said, "to which my father hath already sworn before the magistrate, and to which he must, it seems, now swear openly before this court, according to the laws of your country. The accused, my lord, could not have been present at a hostelry in Paris, or held converse with a minister of the King of France on the evening of the nineteenth day of April, for on that day did I plight my troth to him at the Church of St. Gervais, and he did spend the full day in my father's house. At five o'clock in the afternoon he did journey with me to St. Denis and there remained with me at the hostelry of the 'Three Archangels,' when my father came and fetched me away."

"It is false," came faintly whispered from the lips of the prisoner, whose consciousness only seemed to return for this brief while, that he might register a last protest against the desecration of his saint.

Rose Marie's words had rung clearly and distinctly from end to end of the hall. After she spoke, after that protest from the accused, dead silence fell on all. Only the fluttering of the fans came as a strange moaning sound, hovering in the over-heated air.

Excitement like the embodiment of a thousand spirits flew across and across on wings widely outstretched—unseen yet tangible. Soon a half-audible curse spoken from beneath the mullioned windows broke the spell of awed silence.

Rupert Kestyon, with rage and shame surging in his heart, fear, too, at the possible consequences of this unexpected interference, muttered angry oaths beneath his breath. Then like the ripple of innumerable waves, an hundred exclamations rose from every corner of the court. Lord Rochester was seen to whisper animatedly to the king. Mistress Peyton turned and held hurried converse with Sir John

Ayloffe, who sat at her elbow. A few women tried to titter; the lowering cloud of scandal made vain endeavour to spread itself over the head of that slender girl who stood there before the judge, fearless and impassive beneath this gathering tempest of sneers and evil words.

She had heard the muttered oath, spoken by lips that she had already learned to dread, and her calm, blue eyes, serene as the skies of her native Provence, sought the lonely figure beneath the mullion, and rested on it with a look of challenge and of defiance. She had meant and desired to be loyal to him, she would have clung to him through sorrow and loneliness, humiliation and derision, if need be, but Fate had been too strong for her. The man she loved was in peril of his life and could only be saved at the sacrifice of her own loyalty and of her honour.

There had never been any conflict within her. The moment she knew how the accusation stood against her beloved, she mapped out her course and never swerved.

Come contumely and disgrace, public scandal and her own undoing, she was ready for it all. It had been over-easy to guess what had occurred: how Michael had come to be accused of that which was threatening his cousin. Rose Marie understood it, even as if she had been present at the interview between the two kinsmen, when one man sold his life for the other's loyalty and for her happiness.

All this and more her glance across the court told to Rupert Kestyon. It told him that ready as she had been to follow him even at the cost of her own misery, she was not ready to pay for his safety with the life of the man whom alone she loved.

Michael may have sinned. He did sin, no doubt, against God and against her, but God of a truth had made him suffer enough. It was Rupert's turn now to pay, and pay he must. Small coin it was, for his child-wife's disgrace, his own humiliation at the inevitable scandal and consequent gossip was but small money indeed beside the boundless wealth of self-sacrifice which Michael had been ready to throw in his cousin's lap.

Perhaps that something of the magnetism which emanated from her personality, perhaps the subtle and mysterious magic which Love exercises over all who think and who feel, affected these people who were present at this memorable scene. Certain it is that there were but very few men and women in this stately hall who did not feel an undefinable sense of sympathy for the three chief actors of the drama which they were witnessing.

The Lord Chief Justice—at best a hard and cynical man of the world, a man on whom history hath cast a mantle of opprobrium—was strangely impressed. He had watched the girl very closely whilst she spoke, had noted the looks which passed between father and daughter and thence across to the prisoner at the bar, and something of the truth of the soulful sacrifice which all three were prepared to make dawned upon his alert brain.

His words were the first clear tones that rose above the babel of whisperings and titters; he turned directly to Master Legros and addressed him personally, speaking in fluent French.

"Your daughter, Master," he said, "hath made a strange statement. Do you endorse its purport?"

"My daughter spoke the truth, milor," replied Papa Legros quietly, "and I endorse every word which she hath said."

"Upon your oath?"

"On mine oath."

"It is false, my lord," murmured Michael still feebly, but making frantic efforts to keep his wandering spirits in bondage. "It is false, on my soul—I was in Paris—not at St. Denis—the lady is unknown to me—I am guilty."

"You hear the prisoner's protest, Master?" queried the judge, once more speaking directly to Legros. "If your statement be true, he is your bitter enemy."

"He did my daughter a great wrong, my lord, but he is an innocent man, unjustly accused of a grave crime. I cannot let him die for that which he hath not done."

"Yet doth he protest his guilt."

"'Tis natural that he should thus protest, my lord. He hath taken on his own shoulders the burden of another. Yet I would have you believe that I would not stand by now, and see my daughter sacrificing her good name for any cause save that of truth."

Papa Legros spoke with so much simplicity, such perfect dignity, and withal had made so logical a statement, that it seems impossible to imagine that it should not carry at least as much conviction to the minds of judge and jury and of all the assembly as the obviously lying statements of the informers had done. Yet such was the temper of the times, such the wave of intolerant fanaticism which had passed over the country, that even whilst good Master Legros was stating so noble and simple a point of truth, the first murmurs of dissent against him and his daughter rose throughout the hall: whispered words of "foreign papist," of "prejudiced witnesses," of "a wench and her lover," flew from mouth to mouth.

Rose Marie, whose sensibilities were attuned to their highest pitch, felt this wave of antipathy, even before its first faint echo had actually reached her ears.

She was quite clever enough to know that the simple mention of an actual fact by herself and her father would not be sufficient to turn the tide of judicial sympathy back toward Michael, after the perjuries of men who had for some time now been exalted into popular heroes; she had, alas, known only too well that she had not yet reached the summit of that Calvary which she had set herself to climb for the loved one's sake.

There were yet many cups of bitter humiliation which she and her kind father would have to drain ere an innocent man was forbidden to give his life for another, and the first of these was being held to her lips even now by the Attorney-General, as he said, turning once more to her:

"You are aware, Mistress, of these statements to which your father hath sworn in open court. Do you on your own account and independently of your father, add your sworn testimony to his?"

"I do, sir," she replied; "I swear, quite independently of what my father hath said, that on the evening of the 19th day of April, when the false witnesses aver that my lord of Stowmaries was in Paris, he was at St. Denis with me."

"You are quite sure of the date?"

"Am I like to forget?"

"Odd's fish!" he retorted, with a sarcastic curl of the lips, "when a pretty wench is in love."

"I am the wife of Rupert Kestyon, formerly styled my lord of Stowmaries," she rejoined with calm emphasis. "Had my father kept silent, had he not endeavoured to clear an innocent man of an unjust charge by giving up that which he holds most dear—his daughter's honour and his own good name—had he remained silent, I say, then would the accused have suffered death, my husband would have succeeded to his title and estates, and I would have duly become the Countess of Stowmaries and Rivaulx, the richest, mayhap the most honoured lady in this beautiful land. Think you, then, that 'tis the caprice of wanton love that would make me swear what I did? Think you that—unless truth and honour itself compelled him—my father would lend a hand to the degradation of his own child?"

What Michael endured in agony of mind throughout this time, it were almost impossible to conceive. Imagine that type of man—the adventurer, the soldier of fortune, the carver of his own destiny, good or bad, the dictator of his own fate! Imagine that man for the first time in his life rendered absolutely helpless the while his fate, his life, was being decided on by others. After those first mad and useless protests, after that wild struggle for freedom of speech, for the right to refuse this whole-hearted sacrifice, this offering of the lily on the altar of love, he had remained silent, with his head buried in his hands, driving his finger nails into his own flesh, longing with a mad longing of pain to find a means of ending his own existence here and now, before his snowdrop had suffered the full consequences of her own heaven-born impulse.

Ye gods above! And he—Michael—had doubted her love for him! Fool, fool that he had been, even for a moment, even in thought to give her up to another. He who had ever been ready to account for his own actions, who with the arrogant pride of fallen angels had always looked his own sins in the face, grinning, hideous monsters though they may have been—how came it that when first she spoke cold words to him he did not then silence them with a kiss, how came it that he did not then and there take her in his arms, defying the laws of men, for the sake of the first, the greatest of God's laws which gives the woman to the man?

Fool that he had been to think of aught save love, and of love alone.

And all the while, Rose Marie, calm and still as the very statue of abnegation, was completing her work of self-immolation. When the Attorney-General-with sneering lips and mocking eyes threw discredit on those statements which she and her dear father were making at the cost of their own honour, she felt the first terrible pang of fear. Not for herself or her future, but for him whom she longed to save and lest her sacrifice be made and yet remain useless. Just for that moment, her serenity gave way. She looked all round her on that sea of jeering faces, longing to cry for help, just as with her whole attitude she had until this moment only called for justice.

Once more her eyes lighted on Rupert Kestyon, her husband, throwing him a challenge, which now had almost become a prayer. He could if he would help her even now. She had become naught to him, of course. Whatever he said could not add to her disgrace; but he could help to save Michael if he would.

She met his lowering glance, the look of hatred and wrath which embraced her and her father, and the obstinate set of jaw and lips which spoke of the determination to win his own safety, his own advancement and the furtherance of his own ambition now and at any cost.

But when the iron determination of a woman who loves, and who fights for the safety of the man she loves, comes in contact with the cold obstinacy of a man's ambition, then must the latter yield to the overwhelming strength of the other.

Rupert Kestyon could have saved Michael at cost of his own immediate exaltation, and thus saved Rose Marie a final and complete humiliation, but this, his every look told her that he would not do. Therefore after that quick glance, her eyes no longer challenged him; she feared that if she dragged him forcibly into this conflict with perjury, his own self-interest would make a stand against justice. Heaven alone knew to what evil promptings his ambition would listen at the moment, when the one life—already so splendidly jeopardised—stood between him and the title and wealth which he coveted.

She did not know that any one save her father and herself could speak with certainty as to that memorable evening of April nineteenth when she went forth—cruel, cold and resentful—leaving Michael alone and desolate at the inn of St. Denis.

255

Even now the Attorney-General, fresh to the charge, pressed her with his sarcastic comments.

"You speak well, fair Mistress," he said blandly, "but you know no doubt that your story needs corroboration. Two witnesses who are Englishmen and members of our National Church have sworn that the prisoner spent the evening of April the nineteenth in treasonable converse with an enemy of this country and in their presence; mark you that the accused himself hath confessed to his guilt. Yet do you swear that he spent that day and evening in your company, until so late that a cruel father came and dragged you away from the delectable privacy. But with all due acknowledgment to the charm of your presence, Mistress," added Sir William Jones, suddenly dropping his bland manner and speaking with almost studied insolence, "you must see for yourself that if a wench desires that she be credited, she must above all bear a spotless reputation, and this on your own acknowledgment you flung to the winds, the day that you—avowedly married to Mr. Rupert Kestyon, formerly styled Earl of Stowmaries—did publicly flout your marriage vows by leaving your father's house in company with the accused. Now justice, though blind, my wench, doth wish to see farther than a minx's tale which mayhap hath been concocted to save her gallant from the block."

The girl had not winced at the insults. Happily her father had not understood them, and the issue at stake was far too great to leave room for vain indignation or even for outraged pride. What bitter resentment she felt was for Michael's sake. She knew how every insolent word uttered by that bland cynic in the name of the law and of justice, would strike against the already-overburdened heart of the man who loved her with such passionate adoration. The impotence that weighed on Michael now was of a truth the most bitter wrong to bear in the midst of all this misery. Samson bound and fettered was helpless in the hands of the Philistines. Prometheus chained to the rock saw the vultures hovering over him and the eagles pecking at his heart.

"As to that, sir," replied Rose Marie quietly, after a brief pause, "these honourable gentlemen here whom you call the jury will have to judge for themselves as to who hath lied: those other witnesses or I— they who have everything to gain, or I and my father, who have everything to lose. But you say that the justice of this land will need corroboration of our statements ere she turns to right an innocent man. This corroboration, sir, you shall have, an you will tell me what form it shall take."

"Some other witness of the prisoner's presence in your company at the inn of St. Denis during the day and evening of April nineteenth," retorted Sir William Jones brusquely.

"I know only of the innkeeper himself and his wife," she rejoined. "Simple folk to whose testimony—seeing the temper of the people of England just now—you would scarce give credence, mayhap."

256

"Mayhap not," quoth the Attorney-General mockingly.

"Yet think again, Mistress," interposed the Lord Chief Justice not unkindly, "corroboration the law must have—if not to right the innocent then to punish the guilty."

The young girl's eyes closed for a moment. She clung to her father in pathetic abandonment; beads of perspiration stood on her forehead; her eyes were dry and hot and her throat parched. But for Papa Legros' presence mayhap her magnificent calm would have deserted her then. She drew herself together, however, and a look of understanding passed between father and daughter. Then the tailor drew a paper from his pocket.

It was a large and heavy document and it bore two huge seals engraved with the arms of the Holy See. This Papa Legros gave into an usher's hand, who in his turn handed it up to the Lord Chief Justice.

"What is this paper?" queried His Lordship.

"It is a dispensation, my lord," replied Rose Marie firmly, "signed by His Holiness the Pope, as you will see. It was granted to my husband, Rupert Kestyon, then styled my Lord of Stowmaries and Rivaulx, giving him leave to avail himself of the laws of England, which would, on his request, annul his marriage with one Rose Marie Legros, who did on the nineteenth day of April, 1678, break her sworn marriage vows by contracting with Michael Kestyon a—"

But even as the awful words trembled on the girl's lips, Michael's restraint completely gave way. Despite the soldiers around him—who of a truth were taken by surprise—despite the hopeless futility of his former attempt—he broke through the rank of musketeers who were surrounding him, and with a cry as that of a wild animal wounded unto death, he bounded forward to where his snowdrop stood, and with one arm round her, pressing her to him with all the strength of passion held in check so long, he, with the other hand placed upon her mouth, smothered the word which would have escaped her lips.

"My lord, my lord," he cried, "is this justice? Sire, you are here present! Where is your kingly power? Will you not stop this desecration of the purest, holiest thing on earth? Are we in the torture chambers of our forefathers that men in England will listen unmoved to this?"

He had taken the guard so completely by surprise that the men were still standing mute and irresolute, the while the prisoner with defiant head erect challenged the king himself to intervene. He had sunk on one knee, his arm still round the form of his beloved. No one would have dared to touch him then, for he was like a wild beast defending its mate.

Rose Marie's strength had indeed failed her at last; when she felt herself falling against the breast of the man whom she so ardently loved, all her calm, all her resolution suddenly gave way. Once more she was the woman, the pure, tender-hearted, gentle-nurtured child, content to rest in the protecting arms of her lord, content to live for his happiness, or to share his disgrace.

"If I feared you before, my lord—meseems that I could love you now," her cold lips seemed to murmur the echo of the very first words of love which they had ever uttered.

And a groan of agony escaped the poor blackguard's overburdened heart. No longer splendid now, no longer defiant or proud—but humbled from his self-exalted state of arrogant manhood. And she, the slender water-lily, had of her own free will allowed the mud of a polluted world to soil the exquisite whiteness of her gown. She had descended from her lofty pedestal of saint-like aloofness, in order to link her fate to his—her sins to his—her life and love to his own. Fate and the overwhelming love of a woman had conquered his will.

"I am a man and what I do, I do!"

"No!" love triumphant had retorted, "for what I command that must thou do. I am the ruler, thou my slave! Whoever thou art, I am thy master and the arbiter of thy destiny!"

CHAPTER XLVIII

And not ever
The justice and the truth o' the question carries
The due o' the verdict with it.

—Henry VIII. V. 1

At Michael's call, at his sudden rush for the protection of his beloved, general confusion prevailed such as had never before been witnessed in the sober halls of Westminster.

Gorgeously-clad gentlemen of high degree, ladies in silks and brocades, elbowed and pushed one another, climbing on their chairs, in order to have a clear view of the small group on the floor of the hall at the foot of the judge's bench—Michael kneeling on one knee, Rose Marie half prostrate on the ground, Papa Legros with large coloured handkerchief mopping his streaming forehead.

These were times when men gave freer rein to their emotions than they do now; they were not ashamed of them, and modern civilisation had not yet begun to propagate its false doctrine that only what is ugly and sordid is real, and what is fine and noble—and therefore mayhap a trifle unbridled and primitive—is false and must be suppressed.

That public feeling had—with characteristic irresponsibility—veered round to the accused and to these two witnesses was undoubted. The poignancy of the situation had told on every one's nerves. It had been a moving and palpitating drama, vivid, real and pulsating with love, the noble passion that makes the whole world kin.

The same men and women who awhile ago had clamoured for the traitor's head, who had heaped opprobrium, invectives and curses upon him, were now quite prepared to demand his acquittal, with as little logic in their sympathy as they had shown in their unreasoning vituperations. The same primeval vices of bigotry and intolerance that had presided at the trials of Stailey and Coleman and sent them to the gallows, sat here in judgment, too, equally intolerant of contradiction, equally bigoted and peremptory.

In the midst of this unprecedented turmoil which had turned stately Westminster Hall into an arena filled with wildly-excited spectators, the ushers' loud calls for silence were absolutely drowned. Nor could the Attorney-General and the Lord Chief Justice make themselves heard by the jury, even though his lordship did his best to admonish these twelve honourable gentlemen not to allow their sentiment to run away with their conscience.

"Justice, good Masters, justice above all! Remember these people are all Papists. They will help one another through thick and thin. What is a papal dispensation, good Masters? It can be bought and bartered. 'Tis a true witness we want, an honourable witness to prove the truth of what may be but a fabulous concoction, devised to cheat the gallows of a traitor."

"Nay, then odd's fish!" here interposed a loud voice from out the crowd; "since it must be, it shall be, and here, my Lord Justice, is a witness to your hand whose honourability I'll challenge you to doubt."

The tones rang clear and loud; they were those of a man accustomed to be heard in large or small assemblies, of a man who knew how to make his presence felt and his word obeyed.

Instantly the waves of murmurs, of cries, of excited whispers were stilled. Eyes so long fixed on the moving spectacle at the foot of the bench were turned in the direction of the speaker.

It was my Lord of Rochester, standing beside the king. He waited a moment, then taking the judge's silence for assent, and obviously encouraged by a nod from His Majesty himself, he made his way to the witness bar.

"My Lord of Rochester," protested the Attorney-General sternly, "by what right do you come forward at this hour?"

"By the right that every man hath in England, to bear testimony for or against a man or woman accused of crime," replied my Lord of Rochester. "I stand here as a witness on behalf of the prisoner, and

259

called by the other witness—Rose Marie Legros—to corroborate what she already hath said."

"Do you swear?"

"I'll swear to tell all the truth and nothing but the truth, so help me God."

"All on behalf of the accused?" sneered Sir William Jones.

"Every word which I must utter will be in his favour, sir, seeing that on the nineteenth day of April, I too, in company with Mister Rupert Kestyon, then styled my Lord of Stowmaries and Rivaulx, and with Sir John Ayloffe, were present at the Church of St. Gervais where Mistress Rose Marie Legros did plight her troth to the accused. We witnessed their departure from the church to the house of Master Legros, tailor-in-chief to His Majesty the King of France, where great festivities were then the order of the day. The accused and Mistress Rose Marie Legros did start for St. Denis on that selfsame afternoon in the presence of a vast number of spectators, from whom I had detailed account of the event. We—that is Mister Rupert Kestyon, Sir John Ayloffe and myself—did make for St. Denis less than an hour after the accused and the lady had left the tailor's house. We arrived at the inn of the 'Three Archangels' at ten of the clock and there found the accused all alone, and we did stay with him, and supped with him until far into the night. This do I swear on my most solemn oath, and, therefore, any one who says that the accused was in Paris on the evening of that nineteenth day of April is a liar and a perjurer—so help me God!"

My Lord of Rochester's lengthy speech was listened to in silent attention. Michael, kneeling beside Rose Marie, scarcely heeded it. What happened to him now or hereafter mattered so little, now that he knew that she loved him with that strength which moveth mountains.

But to the vast company assembled here, all that my Lord of Rochester said mattered a great deal, for it was a confirmation of inward convictions. It gave sympathy free rein, having crowned it with justification.

Even Sir William Jones felt that the prosecution had completely broken down beneath the weight of my Lord of Rochester's evidence. He meant to demand further corroboration, seeing that Sir John Ayloffe was in court; but it would be an uphill fight now, against what was too obvious justice to be wilfully set aside.

But he did ask my Lord of Rochester why he had delayed in coming forward until well-nigh it had been too late.

"I was ready to come forward at any time," was Rochester's simple reply; "had the prisoner called me, I would have told the truth at once. But among gentlemen, sir, there is an unspoken compact, guessed at by those who understand one another as gentlemen should. That the accused did not desire mine evidence I readily saw. Only when a noble lady came forward in sublime sacrifice and I feared that this— great as it was—might prove purposeless, then did I feel in honour

260

bound to corroborate her testimony and to prove her true, whilst placing at her feet the expression of my most humble respect."

To have doubted my Lord of Rochester's testimony had been madness in the face of public feeling as well as of justice. No one would ever attempt to suggest that his lordship was either a Papist or biassed in favour of Roman Catholicism. Moreover, Sir John Ayloffe, also an unimpeachably honourable gentleman, was there to add his word to that of his friend. Sir William Jones having called him, asked him but a few questions.

What could Cousin John do, but swear to the truth? Believe me that had he found the slightest loophole whereby he could even now arrange a happy marriage between his fair cousin and any earl of Stowmaries who happened to be bearing the title at the time, he would have done it, and earned that £12,000 which now certainly seemed hopelessly beyond his grasp.

But he could find no loophole, nor could he attempt to deny the truth of what Lord Rochester had said.

By the time Sir John Ayloffe had given what evidence was asked of him, the spectators were loudly clamouring for the verdict.

"Not guilty! Not guilty!" came in excited shouts from the furthermost corners of the great hall.

Of a truth had the informers been recalled they could not have escaped with their lives, and as a measure of precaution the Lord Chief Justice, before he began his summing up, did, we know, order the removal of Pye and Oates through a back door and unbeknown to the crowd. Oates' villainies did, unfortunately, rise triumphant from out the ashes of this his first signal defeat in his campaign of perjuries. As for Pye, he passed through that back door out of ken. I believe that his name doth occur on several of the lists of witnesses brought up against the unfortunate Papists during the whole feverish period of the Popish plots, so we may assume that he continued his career of informer with some benefit to himself.

But in Westminster Hall to-day the verdict was a foregone conclusion. Even whilst the Lord Chief Justice summed up—as he did, we are told, most eloquently and entirely in favour of the accused—he was frequently interrupted by cries of: "Not guilty! Not guilty! The verdict!"

When the verdict was pronounced, with absolute unanimity by the jury in whose hands lay the life that had been so nobly fought for, it was received with acclamation.

Men and women cheered to the echoes, whilst many voices shouted: "God save Your Majesty!" There was a general rush for the centre of the Hall, there where that small group of three still stood isolated. The musketeers had grave difficulty in keeping any order.

In the midst of all this turmoil no one noticed that from the dark corner beneath the mullioned window there rose the figure of a young man dressed in rough clothes of sad-coloured cloth, whose pale face was almost distorted by lines of passionate anger.

He drew a mask over his face and made his way through the excited crowd. Under cover of the confusion, the rushing to and fro, the cheering for the acquitted and the king, he quietly passed out of sight.

CHAPTER XLIX

Time hath, my lord, a wallet at his back,
Wherein he puts alms for oblivion,
A great-sized monster of ingratitudes.

—*Troilus & Cressida III. 3*

That same evening in the small house in the parish of Soho, Michael sat beside an old woman whose wrinkled, toil-worn hand he held tenderly in his own.

Life had dealt hardly with her, unaccustomed toil and a rough life had done their work. Her sensibilities were blunted, almost extinct save one—her love for her son.

Obediently she had left her Kentish village, her miserable cottage, and ungrateful garden, to come to London when first he bade her so to do. She had exchanged her rough worsted kirtle for a gown of black silk, soft and pliable to the touch. This she had done to please Michael, not because she cared. It was many, many years since last she had cared.

Humbly acceding to his wish she had lived in the house in Soho Square, allowing herself to be tended by servants, she who awhile ago had been scrubbing her own floors. To please him she had accepted all the comforts, all the luxuries which he gave her. As for herself she had no need of them.

Then when he went away and she was all alone in the big house, save for the army of mute and obedient servants round her, she had wept not a little because she did not see her son. She knew not whither he had gone, and when she asked any of the servants they gave no definite answer, only seemed more mute, more obedient than before.

But she did not complain. Michael was oft wont to go away like this, to the wars mayhap; soon he would return all in good time and she would see him again. Not the faintest echo from the great world outside reached the lonely house in Soho Square; but then it had not reached the Kentish village either, so old Mistress Kestyon was quite satisfied.

To-night Michael had returned. She was over-glad to see him. It seems he had not been wounded in the wars, for which she was over-glad. He would not let her out of his sight, even when a visitor came desiring speech with him.

The visitor was Rupert Kestyon; the name hardly reached the feeble intelligence, and the face conveyed no meaning. The old dame was quite happy, however, for Michael sat beside her, holding her hand in his. She did not understand much of what went on between the two men. They were cousins, so Michael had said when first the young man entered and he himself went forward to greet him and warmly took his hand.

"You see me shamed before you, Coz," he said gravely. "You know that had I had the control of my fate, I should be watching you now from the height or depth of another world—"

"You sent for me," said Rupert, in no way responding to the other's cordiality. "I presume 'tis because you have something to say to me of more importance than excuses for your happening to be alive."

"Nay! There is nothing more important than that just now, Coz," retorted the other quietly. "I sent for you because a chance of word from your servant to mine revealed to me the fact that you were in London. You came, no doubt, to see me hanged. A beautiful woman of whom you, Coz, were never worthy, hath decided that I shall live."

The word that Rupert uttered in response brought an ugly frown on Michael's brow.

"Cousin," he said sternly, "in your own interest I pray you cease this wanton talk. I would have you know that I mean well by you."

He drew from out his pocket the paper that had the seal of His Holiness the Pope attached to it and handed it to Rupert, who with a savage oath took it from him.

"Here, Coz," he said, "is the papal dispensation which good M. Legros gave into my hands when I parted from him at Westminster Hall. The civil law of England will not take long in setting you free. What money can accomplish, that it shall do to expedite your case. My word on it! The lady will not defend it and the nullity of your marriage shall be pronounced ere the first bud appears on the chestnut trees."

"A free man and yet a beggar," murmured Rupert moodily.

"Nay, nay, Cousin, why should you look on me as your enemy? Have I ever acted as such? My mother, alas, is here as a proof that you and yours were enemies to me, but I, not to you, 'pon my honour. I have no need of great riches. The hundred and twenty thousand pounds with which you gambled a year ago are yours, Cousin. Let us call them a loan which you made me, and wherewith Fate hath worked its will for us. I give them to you freely and with all my heart. You are not a beggar, you see, and are free to marry whom you choose. You are still the cousin of, if not the actual Earl of Stowmaries; many a pretty

263

woman with taste and ambition will—an I mistake not—smile on you. Life is full of joys yet for you, Cousin, and Mistress Peyton will relent."

While he thus spoke lightly, almost gaily, the frown of moodiness fled from Rupert Kestyon's brow. He could not help but be gratified at his cousin's generosity, even though his heart no longer turned toward the faithless beauty whose callousness had killed in him all love for her. But there were plenty of pretty women yet in England, thank God, and a man well-born and well-connected could cut a very fine figure in London society these days on one hundred and twenty thousand pounds. In the far-off days in old Virginia he had been quite glad of as many pence.

He was quite manly enough to thank his cousin warmly. But before he went, he told Michael the news that had been all over London for some day before the trial, namely, that beautiful Mistress Peyton had finally decided to bestow her hand and fortune and her heart—on John Ayloffe.

Good Cousin John! Confronted with beggary and the irretrievable loss of that £12,000, he had bethought himself of the only plan whereby the latter goodly sum could, after all, find its way into his own pocket.

The money with the lady was his only chance, and we are told that he took it boldly, even contriving not to make too wry a face when the capricious beauty—realising that Cousin John was her only hope of matrimony now that her name had been so plentifully bespattered with ridicule—decided to bestow her £20,000, her house and her person, on the one man who would accept.

Cousin John became exceedingly fat after his marriage, for he led a life of ease and comfort even though his former merry haunts knew him no more.

CHAPTER L

And o'er the hills and far away,
Beyond their utmost purple rim,
Beyond the night, across the day,
Thro' all the world she followed him.

—*Tennyson*

Michael did not see Rose Marie in England, for her father had taken her away that same evening, after the acquittal, and journeyed with her forthwith to Paris.

And it was in the little room of the Rue de l'Ancienne Comédie that Michael once more beheld his snowdrop. It was December now and the room was filled with Christmas roses. Outside, the snow lay heavy on the ground. Maman Legros, with sleeves well rolled up over her sturdy arms, was stirring the contents of her stock-pot. Papa—a little more grey, a little more bent, mayhap, than he had been a year ago—was staring silently into the fire.

Rose Marie sat at her harpsichord in the window embrasure, and sang to her own accompaniment. Through the panes of the leaded window the pale rays of a December sun lit up the golden radiance of her hair, and rested on her hands as they wandered over the ivory keys.

Thus Michael saw her again after all these months of suffering. He stood for a moment in the doorway, for happiness at times is more difficult to bear than grief. But Love was triumphant at last. The splendid blackguard, the reckless adventurer, was only an humble lover now. He gazed on his snowdrop with eyes wherein ardent passion mingled with deep reverence.

Let the veil of oblivion be drawn across those leaded windows; let it shut out all light which comes from the outer world. Michael at Rose Marie's feet forgot all save that he had won her—the pure, stainless girl—even through the infinity of her pity which had first called into being her infinite love.

Papa and Maman Legros, looking on their child's exquisite face, suffused now with the glow of perfect love and perfect trust, exchanged a knowing look.

Then they very softly tiptoed out of the room.

THE END

www.ingramcontent.com/pod-product-compliance
Lightning Source LLC
Chambersburg PA
CBHW010832250626
47157CB00010B/3256